To Ian

Regards

Walter E Beaney

Tales from the Liars Club

Stories for Naughty Boys (& Girls) from 19 to 90

by
Walter E Beaney

Bloomington, IN Milton Keynes, UK

authorHOUSE

AuthorHouse™
1663 Liberty Drive, Suite 200
Bloomington, IN 47403
www.authorhouse.com
Phone: 1-800-839-8640

AuthorHouse™ UK Ltd.
500 Avebury Boulevard
Central Milton Keynes, MK9 2BE
www.authorhouse.co.uk
Phone: 08001974150

First published by AuthorHouse 5/9/2006

ISBN: 1-4259-3245-2 (sc)

Printed in the United States of America
Bloomington, Indiana

This book is printed on acid-free paper.

Illustrations by Richard Duszczak at Cartoon Studio Ltd.

THE MEMBERS STORIES

In fact he has lots of guns, but this one has such a long range that it can reach Battalion HQ. Who has to sort it out? Well, not the General, that's for sure.

Tales From The Liars Club
A book by Walter E Beaney

Grey, weathered and somewhat seedy in appearance, the Lyre Club had stood for more than ninety years. Its musical connections had long since faded into history as had many of its elderly members.

It had not taken long for some wag to re-christen the place the Liars Club, a name which fitted nicely with the club's tradition of telling stories every Friday night after dinner. Most of these stories were based in fact, but over the years they had tended to become increasingly outrageous as members vied with each other to get away with the tallest or funniest anecdotes.

FRIDAY NIGHT AT THE CLUB

1

ONE
All That Glitters

The snow had lingered long and cold, and the oldest member was having a good old moan.

"The worst winter in human memory," he grumbled.

"Nonsense," said Harry Cummings, "this is midsummer compared to my time in the frozen north where the nights are six months long."

"Tell us about it, Harry," a couple of the members said in unison.

"I thought you'd never ask," said Harry, voice dripping with irony, as he prepared to launch into his story.

It was up in British Columbia, where I was working as a lumberjack, chopping down the giant redwoods so they could be cut up to make useful things like little boxes. A rough tough place it was, where men were men, and so were the women, come to think about it.

Every Friday was payday, and after having our weekly bath in the freezing river, we made our way in to the wild town of Elkhorn to drink, gamble, and have a good fight -there's nothing better for the soul than having one's head rammed through the walls of a saloon!

On the Friday I am thinking of, we whooped our way in to town, had a fight with some silver miners, then made our way to the Bull Moose saloon, where the losers (us this time) had to buy the drinks, and after a couple of bottles of rotgut whiskey we sat down to play cards.

As usual the game was pontoon - most of the guys couldn't count much above twenty-one anyway. There were six of us playing; me, young and wild; on my left sat Pierre LeClerk, a Canadian lumberjack; next to him was a stranger who had come into town, an old guy with a bushy white beard, called Gabby Hunter. Opposite me sat Dangerous Dan Magruder, leader of the silver miners, six foot six tall, with red beard and hair. Seated beside Dan was his henchman, Black Jack Johansen - a lean moustachioed villain. Completing the six, and seated on my right, was my mate Paddy O'Halloran, a charming but dim Irishman.

For a change my luck was in, and my pile of chips grew steadily in size, matched only by Dangerous Dan's. The cards were kind so I decided to up the stakes a bit. I was dealt a six and a five, making eleven - an excellent hand. One of the bar room floozies had come and draped herself over my shoulders as she looked at my hand.

"Buy a card for a hundred dollars," she said.

"Is that OK?" I asked the white-bearded stranger who had the bank.

Looking at his cards, he smirked and replied "You bet it is."

I was dealt another five, sixteen - not so good. The floozy took a look and whispered,

"Buy another card for a hundred dollars."

I did so and was dealt a three - nineteen - that was better. Once again she looked and whispered,

"Buy a card for a hundred dollars."

Now this was decidedly risky, but hey, she knew what she was doing. She must have watched a thousand games, so I bought another card - a two that gave me twenty one; a five card trick.

"You jammy bastard!" she shrieked.

The old stranger turned over his cards - twenty, he couldn't win.

"Three hundred dollars," he whined, "I can't pay."

I leapt up and my hand flashed down for my pistol. Then I remembered that this was BC, and we didn't carry pistols up there.

"Slow down pardner," he said as I picked up an empty bottle. "I've got no cash, but I have here the map to the richest gold mine in Alaska. It's up on the Klondike. It's worth millions. You can have it."

"A gold mine," I said putting the bottle back down. "Do you own it?"

"No, but all you have to do is go up there, put a fence around it and a notice up with your name on it, then you just go to the local land registry office, pay $100 and the claim is yours."

"So how come you didn't do that yourself?" I asked him suspiciously.

"I didn't have $100, and I always thought that I could go back and sort it out later."

I looked at Paddy, "Well Paddy old chap," I said, "do you fancy a bit of gold mining?"

Dangerous Dan and Black Jack were exchanging meaningful glances with each other as I took the map off the old guy; and then as a gesture of goodwill, I split my winnings into two piles and pushed half of them over towards the old timer.

"Well thanks friend," he said. "You are a gentleman, and the owner of a gold mine."

There didn't seem much point in playing cards any more, so I cashed in my chips, and together with Paddy set forth in search of fun. There wasn't too much happening as we sauntered down the main street. My bootlace was trailing so I bent down to tie it up. There was a noise that sounded like 'THWUNK'.

"What was that?" I asked.

"I don't know," said Paddy, "but look at this nice knife stuck in the post just above your head."

"I never noticed that."

"Well it's my knife now," Paddy told me, putting it in to his pocket.

I began to think that my luck had changed, as a series of bizarre incidents followed Paddy and me all around the town; like the iron safe that fell out of the third floor window of the Hotel, missing us by inches. And the runaway horse team that almost trampled us down as we passed the stables. We went into the 'Yankee Diner, home-made food a speciality', ducking as something flew past my head and shattered one of the windows.

We ordered steaks, and sat having a beer while they were being cooked. Fifteen minutes later the waitress brought in our 20-ounce steaks. I cut the fat off mine and threw it to a dog which was sat waiting for tit bits; the little blighter swallowed it whole and then played dead, laying on its back with all four legs sticking up in the air. Paddy and I laughed and laughed, until the waitress rushed out, grabbed our plates and ran back in to the kitchen with them.

"Hey, what's going on?" roared Paddy as the waitress ran out again and said

"Sorry, steaks off. Would you like beans on toast?"

Someone came in from the back and dragged out the dog, which was still playing dead, to our great amusement.

We finished our meal and went back outside, carefully stepping over the trip wire which could have sent us hurtling down a dozen concrete steps and onto the busy road.

"They really shouldn't leave things like that around," complained Paddy.

"Definitely not," I said, slipping on some grease. "Mind you, how come we never noticed it when we came in?"

Paddy never answered, because he had just fallen down a hole in the sidewalk, which some inconsiderate person had made and covered with a piece of cardboard.

4

I helped him out of the hole.

"Are you all right old chap?" I asked with some concern.

"I suppose so, apart from this thirty-inch spike, which went straight up my trouser leg," he told me.

"Ouch, that could have been nasty," I replied.

"Yes, it's lucky I've got a thirty-one inch inside leg," he finished.

"I've had enough of this place. A chap could get hurt around here. Obviously they have no idea about health and safety," I told him. "Let's get back to Dead Mans Creek and plan our trip north to Alaska."

Paddy waved at Dangerous Dan and Black Jack Johansen, who chose this moment to gallop past us.

"Will you look at those idiots," said Paddy. "They're heading in the wrong direction. The Lumber camp's up that way, not the silver mine."

We hitched a lift from a passing lumber wagon, and started the trip back to the camp. The bizarre accidents just seemed to continue following us: first a huge tree crashed across the trail just after we had passed by, then an avalanche of large boulders rained down on us as we passed through Dry Gulch.

"Lucky someone wasn't hurt there," I remarked, but Paddy was fast asleep.

We arrived back at our cabin in Dead Mans Creek, and went inside, immediately after deactivating the bear trap which some ignorant person had left on the porch in our absence. It was a rough place; just a table, two chairs and the bunk beds filled most of the single room, but this was necessary to maintain our macho image. One of the lumberjacks, who had put curtains up in his cabin, had been tarred, feathered, and run out of camp on a rail.

Once inside I took out the map.

"Right Paddy old friend," I told him, "first of all we are going to make a copy of this map. We can't risk losing the only copy we have," so I made a very accurate copy and gave it to Paddy. Then, after the normal fight for who was going to have the top bunk, we retired for the night.

Several hours later I woke up. By Jove it was warm. I lay there with my eyes closed enjoying the warmth. It had never been this warm before, and what was that crackling sound? I opened my eyes, and the cabin was a mass of flames, a raging inferno.

"Paddy, get out!" I shouted, and stood up on the top bunk and punched a hole through the roof. After ripping off a couple of planks I scrambled out through the hole and up on to the roof which was getting very hot indeed: sliding down the shingles I fell to the ground, then got up and stood looking at the burning cabin.

Poor Paddy, but at least I have saved the map, I thought to myself.

CRASH -, a Paddy shaped hole appeared in the side of the cabin, and Paddy lurched through it, beating out the flames in his hair.

"What took you so long?" I demanded.

"I was looking for my map, but it had vanished from the table where I left it," he said, extinguishing the last few sparks on his clothes.

"Never mind about that," I told him, "we have my copy and the die is cast. The cabin has gone, so we leave in the morning and go north to Alaska."

As if to prove my point, the cabin's roof collapsed in a great burst of flames and sparks, and we sat and warmed our hands on the fire.

"I should have brought the bread out, we could have made some toast," said Paddy.

Dawn's early light found us hitching a lift back in to the town of Elkhorn. We had counted up our money, and had over $500 thanks to my winnings from the night before.

"OK Paddy old mate," I said. "First a bath at the hotel, then breakfast, then we buy some warm clothes, and then we take the train up to the Alaskan border."

As we entered the town we stopped to let the early train through the crossing.

"Well, what a coincidence," laughed Paddy. "A fellah on that train was the spitting image of Black Jack Johansen."

"What was he doing?"

"Well it looked as if he was giving us the finger," said Paddy.

Two hours later, washed shaved and fed, we went into the 'General Store - Best prices in the State', where I bought two rather smart fur coats, mittens, thick socks and warm scarves. Then, suitably attired for the frozen north, we made our way down to the railway station.

Dawson Creek, just over the border, seemed the place to head for. Then it was just a short walk up to the mine, about six inches on the map. I took a look at the map scale - one hundred miles to the inch. Hmmmmmm.

The train was running only an hour late as it pulled in to the station, and we climbed aboard arguing furiously about why my fur coat was a nice shade of grey, whilst his was black with a white stripe up the back.

"Look Paddy, it's definitely not made of skunk skins," I told him.

"So what is it then?" he demanded.

"Um, probably black bear," I said.

"Going a bit grey on top then wasn't it," he snorted. The train pulled out of town and Paddy sat and sulked.

"Look when we find the gold, you will be able to buy a really nice fur coat," I told him.

"What, one like yours?" he replied.

"OK then, enough is enough, lets swap our coats over," I told him, and the ungrateful swine actually took his coat off and held it out.

"Did you see the attractive redheaded girl who got on the train at the station?" I asked him, taking the coat.

"No," he answered.

"Well, I overheard her saying how much she fancied the guy in the black and white coat," I fibbed. "She will probably be going up and down the train looking for this coat," I said, as convincingly as I could.

Paddy snatched the coat back and put it on again. He was so gullible. He spent the next quarter of an hour looking anxiously up and down the carriage, until his attention wandered. That man had all the attention span of a drunken grasshopper. We sat counting the passing houses, and after three hours we had counted two.

The train wound its way through forests and mountains, while we sat and made plans, most of which revolved around spending the gold. Paddy was the first to notice that the train had stopped moving, and after waiting for fifteen minutes we climbed down onto the tracks to find out what the delay was.

The conductor was trying to get everyone back on to the train.

"What's happening here?" I demanded.

"Well sir, this here's Snake Pass, and some rotten swine on the last train through dropped a stick of dynamite out of the caboose and it has destroyed the track. We will have to go back to Elkhorn. It will take at least a week to repair the rails all the way up here."

"Oh no," I told him. "It's only twenty miles to the border. We can walk it. Who's coming with Paddy and me?"

Thirty seconds later Paddy and I stood there alone, as the last of the passengers climbed back onto the train. Two minutes after that, the train puffed its way back to the southeast, whilst Paddy and I marched off towards the northwest.

"Harry, have you thought this through?" asked Paddy. "We've got no maps and no compass. We don't even know where Dawson Creek is, and we will be lost in the wilderness."

"Well I suppose that we could follow this railway track," I told him. "I have a strange feeling that Dawson Creek might be next to it up that way."

"Ahhh, but of course," he said. "You're so clever Harry."

"Now just hold on a minute," interrupted the oldest member. "This story had better not be leading up to where you find a beautiful girl frozen to death in the snow."

"Absolutely not," said Harry indignantly, and continued.

The next two hours saw us cover a brisk ten miles, and as we descended through the forest we decided to take a ten-minute break. It had been snowing, but there was a mere ten-inch deep scattering.

"Very mild for the time of year," as I remarked to Paddy.

I wandered into a clearing and looked for a place to drop my trousers. A nice inviting mound stood at the edge of the trees. Just right for a little sit down, I thought to myself. I felt at the mound and brushed some snow off it. Strangely, it felt almost like fur. I kicked at it, and an outraged Grizzly Bear reared up to its full nine feet height.

"Down boy," I said in a somewhat squeaky voice, and it responded by grabbing me in a bear hug and waltzing me around the clearing.

Now, being squeezed to death by a grizzly bear is bad enough, but this particular bear had the worst breath on the planet. Whatever it had been eating, he must have laced it well with garlic, and I gagged and retched under the smell of its bad breath.

My eyes were going dim and my life began to flash before me, when a voice said,

"Stop playing with that bear," and Paddy stumbled his way into the clearing. The bear turned round and looked. It did a double take on the black and white coat, dropped me down, put a paw over its nose and fled into the forest.

"I'm hungry," complained Paddy. "Are you ready to move yet?"

"Just give me two minutes Paddy," I said. "There's something in the seat of my trousers I need to get rid of."

We started off again, and two hours later, at 10pm, we reached the border crossing, wearily staggering in to the Border Post, where a young sprog sat shuffling papers.

"Where have you come from?" he asked, and we launched into our tale of burnt cabins, dynamited railways, attacks by Grizzly Bears and all of our other adventures.

"I see," he said. "Do you have anything to declare?"

"Only my genius," I replied. He looked at me stony faced as he stamped our passports and waved us through.

"How far is it to Dawson Creek?" I asked him.

"Just around the next bend," he told me.

"Do you mean that bend around that mountain over there?" asked Paddy, peering out across the moonlit snowdrifts.

"Yup that's it, about twenty miles," the customs officer replied.

Paddy set off, and the customs man looked at his disappearing back.

"Why is he dressed up as a skunk?" he asked. I glared at him and hurried after Paddy.

"What was he saying?" Paddy asked me.

"Oh he was just admiring your coat," I told him. "Look, it's starting to snow again," I said, desperately trying to change the subject.

Well I can tell you that that next twenty miles was really tough going. Most of the way we were wading through waist deep snow drifts. Several times one of us stepped off the rails and disappeared completely, but we were tough in those days, and 7am saw us arriving at the tough border town of Dawson Creek.

We headed for the saloon and went inside. Avoiding the broken furniture we made our way to the bar and had a whiskey breakfast.

"Right, Paddy me lad," I told him, "lets get a couple of hours rest, then we must go and get equipped for the run up to our gold mine."

High noon saw us in the general store, buying in our supplies; some food, tobacco, snowshoes, blankets, a rifle and ammo, some picks and shovels, lots of sacks to put the gold in and various other useful items.

Paddy looked at the mountain of equipment and said, "How on earth are we going to carry all this stuff?"

"Well you need a dog sledge and team," the store keeper replied, "and I happen to have one for sale. I did have two, but I sold the number one team to a couple of guys who passed through here yesterday; a great six foot six red bearded fellow, and a lean hombre with a dark moustache."

"That's a shame," I said. "I suppose that we will have to have the second team."

"It's out the back," I was told as I paid up. I counted my remaining money - $100 and 10 cents - just enough to pay the land registration once we had staked our claim.

We then went out the back to inspect our new dog team; a rather dilapidated old sledge was hooked up to ten mean, vicious looking dogs.

"Watch out for the pack leader," said the storekeeper.

"Which one is that?" I asked him.

"That one - he's called One Eye," he replied, pointing at the big black one with a white patch on its back, which was glaring at me with its one yellow eye.

"Good dog," I said, holding out my hand.

The storekeeper's "Noooo!" was drowned out as the beast woofed, took a flying leap at me, and bit into my throat. It had the worst breath I had ever smelt; worse even than a certain bear. My eyes were going dim, and my life began to flash before them, when Paddy's voice said,

"Will you stop playing with that dog?"

The dog took one look at Paddy, released my throat, and rushed over to him furiously wagging its tail.

"Good dog," said Paddy, and the blighter lay on its back for its tummy to be tickled.

We loaded up the sledge, with me receiving several nips and bites, while Paddy received ecstatic licking and tail wagging from the entire team, huh.

At last we were ready to go.

"MUSH, MUSH" I shouted, and received ten frosty stares from nineteen yellow eyes.

"Mush," said Paddy, and the team leapt joyously forward, forcing me and Paddy to run beside the sledge to keep up.

We made a furious pace along the trail towards the town of Broken Jaw, which was ninety miles to the north, and by late afternoon we had covered thirty miles.

"Lets stop and camp up here," I said to Paddy as we entered a sheltered clearing. "I need some food and rest." Paddy clicked his tongue and the team obediently stopped.

As Paddy began to unload some pots and pans I wandered around the clearing, picking up sticks and logs to build a fire.

I approached a snow covered mound and remembered my last experience with such a mound. I gently prodded it and it didn't feel furry, more soft and silky. I gently removed some snow, and there laying cold and frozen to death was the most beautiful girl I had ever seen.

"Right, that's it," said the oldest member. "Get out."
"No, no," said Harry.

As I held her in my arms her eyes fluttered open; the biggest bluest eyes you have ever seen, incidentally, and she whispered,
"Please help me."

THEY RESCUED A FAIRHAIRED MAIDEN

I cleared away the rest of the snow and found that she was tied hand and foot, and was dressed only in a silk slip, and very fetching she looked too.

We quickly unbound her and wrapped her up in our blankets. There was soon a roaring fire blazing away, and we fed her hot soup.

My goodness that girl was a corker, about twenty years old, five foot three tall, slim, shoulder length blonde hair, cherry lips, and so pretty it gave you a pain in your chest just to look at her.

There was a bit of a silence in the club as the members imagined what the beautiful girl must have looked like. The oldest member demanding that Harry get on with the story broke this pleasant interlude.

As movement returned to the poor girls body, she told us her story.

"My name is Sally Hunter," she told us, "and my only living relative was my grandfather, Gabby Hunter. A couple of days ago I had a telegram saying that he was in the town of Elkhorn, and had been playing cards with a gang of ruffians."

Paddy and I looked at each other a bit uncomfortably.

"And straight after the game he left the saloon, and apparently accidentally drowned in a water butt," she continued. "Well, some time before that, he had sent me a map of a gold mine he had found, so I came north to claim my inheritance straight away."

"Do you have the map? I'd like to see it," I said.

She burst into tears. "No, I haven't got it anymore," she sobbed. "You see, I took the train to Dawson Creek and looked for a guide to take me up to the Klondike, where the mine is situated. As luck would have it, two men who had just purchased a dog team approached me, and they asked me if they could give me a lift as they were heading in that direction.

One of the men was really big with a bushy red beard, and the other one was lean with a dark moustache.

I was so grateful to them. We set off yesterday and then camped here last night, but this morning when we were about ready to go they jumped on me, stole my map and all my money, stripped my clothes off, tied me up and left me in the snow to die. And as they rode off on their sledge, Dangerous Dan said to Black Jack, 'Now we have two maps to the goldmine.'"

"Dangerous Dan and Black Jack," I said. As a flash of inspiration hit me like a thunderbolt, "Paddy you don't think that those two silver miners could be trying to steal our goldmine do you?"

12

"It beggars belief," said Paddy, "but stranger things have happened."

We fussed around little Sally, drying her tears and keeping her nice and warm, and as Paddy fed the dogs she whispered to me,

"Why is he dressed up as a skunk?"

"Actually I think that he might be wearing dog skins," I whispered back, "but don't say anything, he gets easily offended." She gave me a little kiss, snuggled down, and went to sleep, while I got the rifle and went to stand guard.

The next morning I was awakened by the smell of bacon, eggs and coffee. Sitting up I looked across the clearing and Sally was just finishing cooking our breakfasts, while contriving to look really cute; dressed up in some of our spare clothes which were far too large for her, and with the trouser legs and sleeves rolled up. One Eye the dog was frisking around her like a puppy.

We rushed across to get our food and were told to go away and get washed before we ate, or else. Sheepishly we obeyed and washed and shaved. Then we went back and presented our hands to her for inspection.

"I should hope so," she said, and served up the most amazing meal. How she could produce food like that over an open fire in the wilds of Alaska I just don't know.

Afterwards, Paddy took the pans across for the dogs to lick out. "Saves having to wash them," he explained.

Sally looked at him thoughtfully and said, "I can see that there is some training needed there."

"Yes they are really mean dogs," I told her.

"No, I meant Paddy," she replied.

"Oh, I knew you meant that," I lied, hoping for another kiss, but none was forthcoming.

Paddy came back and said, "Well, the dogs are ready to go." He turned to Sally, "I don't suppose that you'd like a lift?" he asked her.

"Oh, yes please, kind sir," she said and hopped on to the sledge.

"MUSH, MUSH" I shouted and received ten dirty looks from the dog team.

"Mush," said Sally in a gentle voice, and the team leapt off and tore down the track with Paddy and me in hot pursuit.

It was sixty miles to Broken Jaw, and by midday we had covered thirty of them.

"Time for a rest," gasped Paddy, so we pulled the sledge into a small clearing. Paddy made up a fire, while Sally got some food and coffee out. I was incautious enough to get to close to One Eye, and was pulled down and savaged by the dog pack.

"Will you stop teasing those dogs," Paddy shouted across, as I at last managed to crawl away from the pack.

Sally tut-tutted, and gently bandaged my cut hand after she had kissed it better for me.

As we dined on a nice meat pie and chips that Sally had conjured up, I told them that we had better make a plan, as we didn't want Dangerous Dan and Black Jack Johansen trying to get the drop on us.

"I've got a good plan," said Paddy.

"Yes?" we asked.

"I'll kill them."

"Well it's certainly simple," I told him, "so as soon as we reach Broken Jaw we get ourselves some pistols and go look them up."

"How are we going to buy pistols? We've only got 10 cents," Paddy reminded me.

"Yes, I don't suppose that we will be able to buy very good ones for that," I replied despondently.

"Not to worry guys," said Sally loosening her trouser belt, "I have something under here that I can sell to raise some money."

"SALLY NO!!!" we both shouted in unison.

"What ever is the matter?" she asked, as she fished a large gold signet ring out of her inside trouser pocket, "Surely we can sell this and buy some pistols."

"Where did that come from?" I asked her.

"Luckily I wasn't wearing it when I was robbed," she told us. "It was tied to a piece of ribbon inside my slip; it was my fathers, and far too big for me to wear."

Sally grabbed the pots and washed them in the snow, much to the disgust of the waiting dog team, and we got ready to move. Just as the sledge began to move off, the woods echoed to an eerie howling.

"Oh no," said Paddy. "The wolves are closing in. We could be in trouble now."

The sledge leapt forward, and we ran beside it on our snowshoes. Through the trees we could see grey shapes keeping pace with us.

"Lighten the sledge," I shouted, and Sally threw the rifle out. "Oh that's just great," I shouted as we rounded the next bend leaving our only weapon behind.

"Look," shouted Sally, "there's a cabin by the trail down there."

The sledge swooped down and skidded to a halt by the small cabin; there was a great jam in the doorway as Paddy, Sally, me and ten dogs pushed and scuffled to get inside.

I slammed and barred the door.

"Will you just look at the state of this place," said Sally, producing a duster from somewhere and starting to clean up.

"SIT," said Paddy, and the ten dogs obediently formed a line and sat, all the while staring at me and licking their lips.

The wolves sat outside howling while we sat in front of the nice log fire that Paddy had made, and while Sally produced some sandwiches and tea. Eventually the wolf pack drifted off in search of easier prey.

There was no bed in the cabin, and we all cuddled up on the hard-packed earthen floor for a good night's sleep.

I woke up in the early hours, and found that I was cuddling little Sally, so soft and warm. I leaned forward and planted a kiss on her lips, which were strangely cold.

"Grrrrrrrrrr!!!" rumbled One Eye, who had crawled in between us, and had received my kiss.

"Quiet," ordered Sally from the other side of the beast, and both One Eye and I settled into an uncomfortable silence.

The next morning we were up at dawn, and after a quick full English breakfast, we were ready to complete our trip up to the town of Broken Jaw. The trail was now mostly downhill, so Paddy and I were able to ride for considerable distances on the sledge runners while the dogs made top speed, and 2pm saw us driving into Broken Jaw.

A tough and lawless place it was in those days, renowned for its gunfights and hangings. A bit different now mind you; I heard that they recently won an award for the best-kept town flowerbeds.

We drove the sledge down the main street and pulled up outside the 'Gunsmiths Shop, We Aim to Please'.

All three of us trooped inside and looked at the display of guns under the glass counter.

There were big ones and small ones, some as big as your head, and I pointed out two sleek black 'Colt' revolvers and asked to see them.

They felt absolutely right; comfortable, perfectly balanced, and they seemed to point themselves automatically at any target you wished.

"How much?" I asked.

"$200 for the pair," the gunsmith replied.

Sally produced her gold ring and asked "How much will you give us for this?" He took a look and then weighed it on some small scales. Gold was a common form of currency up in Alaska in those days.

"Seventy dollars," he told her.

"Ah well. What can we get for seventy dollars?" I asked. He put the Colts away and produced a pair of old Adams revolvers.

"For fifty dollars, I can do you these two beauties," he told me, "complete with two gun belts, ammo, and a cleaning kit."

I tried one for size; it was clumsy and heavy, and automatically pointed at the floor.

"Are there any strangers in town?" Paddy asked him.

"There sure are," said the gunsmith. "There's a great red-bearded guy, with a swarthy moustachioed side kick. They've spent twenty four hours in the Silver Dollar saloon, creating merry hell. Killed three men already, including the sheriff."

"Do you have any idea who they are?" I asked him.

"Yes, it's Dangerous Dan Magruder and Black Jack Johansen," said the gunsmith, "the Terrors of the Frozen North."

"We'll take the guns," I said, and Paddy and I put on the gun belts and got tooled up.

"Where's the saloon?" demanded Paddy.

"Straight across the road pardner," said the gunsmith, "but be careful. Those are two mean mothers."

We strode out of the shop and headed across the road, and what followed has passed into Alaskan legend.

In fact they made up an epic poem about it, which went something like

Harry Cummings and Paddy came up from Dead Mans Creek,
They'd been on the trail of Dangerous Dan for more than half a week.
Then rescued a fair haired maiden, little Sally Hunter, who
Loved them both, our heroes, with a love both strong and true.

They reached the town of Broken Jaw, a dangerous lawless town,
And at last caught up with Dangerous Dan, who'd shot the sheriff down.

And if you think that's really bad, then you'd better think again,
For he and Black Jack Johansen, had also killed two other men.

They'd blazed a trail from town to town, throughout the frozen north,
And whenever they entered a crowded bar, the gunplay soon came forth.
Tough lumberjacks and miners had fallen dead, or ran,
Before the deadly pistols of that terrible Dangerous Dan.

Our heroes went through the swinging doors, and into the smoky hell.
Look at the size of that skunk and rabbit, they heard Johansen yell.
Now the Silver Dollar was crowded, with hard men from near and far;
But every man in the room stepped back, as Paddy reached the bar.

Now look at this said Dangerous Dan, to those who had not fled,
A six-foot skunk and rabbit are about to wind up dead.
Paddy stepped out from the bar, Fill your hand, they heard him roar,
But a bottle of beer caught him round the ear, and Paddy bit the floor.

Black Jack from behind him said, I see you've brought your whore.
And Harry stepped up to the bar, as Sally came in through the door.
Through the swinging bar room doors, and into that smoky fog
Walked little Sally Hunter, with One Eye, her faithful dog.

You all stand still, young Sally cried. I'm going to make this fair;
And the sawn-off shotgun in her hand, held everybody's stare.
I'll kill the first man that I see reaching for his gun.
Now you can take them Harry, unless these cowards run.

Harry put his gun belt on the bar, and called to Dangerous Dan.
Now come and fight me with your fists, if you are half a man.
Dangerous raised his six foot six from out of his wooden chair,
And as he stepped up to the bar, his face was as red as his hair.

He said, get me a Gin and a whiskey in, for after I've killed this pair.
Then if she plays her cards right, I'll have me some yellow hair.
They chalked a line across the floor, and stood there toe to toe.
Look over there, said Dangerous, Harry looked and received the first blow.

For Dangerous was a good fighter, who'd won every brawl he'd been in,
And he wanted this over quickly, so he could finish his whiskey and gin.
A flurry of punches hit Harry, and a tear ran down Sally's sweet face.
As he went down alongside Paddy, it looked like he'd sink without trace.

17

Harry picked himself up and went back to the line, from where he'd hit the floor.
Dangerous sneered, from the depths of his beard, and said, Next I'll kill the whore.
But he'd spoken too soon, to the rest of the room, as a boot crashed into his crutch;
Now shut up and fight, if you want to see night, instead of talking so much.

Dan took a step in and smacked Harry's chin, his future was looking real bleak.
For Dan was a man with blood on his hands, and the tears ran down Sally's cheek;
But Harry was tough and he'd not had enough; he fought like an angry wildcat.
So the fight it did last, the blows coming fast as Dan fought like a cornered wild rat.

And the crowd placed their bets, the odds ten to one; poor Harry was on the rack.
The blows rained in straight on to his chin, Dan swore he would break Harry's back.
Dan took a huge swing at Harry's head, which our hero easily slipped aside,
He swung a punch in, to the point of Dan's chin, and wished that he'd never tried.

It was like punching iron, or concrete at least, and Dan began to chuckle;
Harry had given Dan his best punch, and received just a broken knuckle.
Then the room turned red, as a chair hit his head, and his knees began to go.
Blood filled his eyes; Dan doubled in size, as Harry reeled from the foul blow.

For Black Jack Johansen had joined the fight, from behind of course, the rat,
And Harry was in big trouble now as the blows rained down upon his back.
Go sic him boy, young Sally cried, setting her fierce dog One Eye free.
The black and white dog raced across the bar and joined in the melee.

One Eye sure enjoyed a fight; he needed no second invite.
Sinking his fangs into Harry's leg, he proved how hard he could bite.
And Harry now was fading fast, as the blows and bites rained in;
Three on to one was just a bit too much, even for a man like him.

Then everyone who was in the saloon, shouted out Hooray,
For Paddy had got back up to his feet, and entered the affray.
Smashing the head of Black Jack with a mighty left and right,
The dark haired villain hit the floor; Paddy had put out his light.

One Eye at last got the point; he was attacking the wrong man.
He turned about and sank his teeth in the groin of Dangerous Dan.
Now the thing about old One Eye was, his teeth were hard and bright,
And a crocodile fresh from the Nile couldn't match his bite.

Have you heard those great steam whistles on the mighty CPR?
They'll burst your ear if you stand too near;
Well you know what whistles are.
But the yell let out by Dangerous Dan, it beat them all by far.

18

Dan fell down, on to his knees, and hit out at the black and white dog.
Then he fell like dead, as the back of his head, was smashed in by the log,
Which was wielded by Harry Cummings, who was aiming it at One Eye.
It was just as well Dangerous caught it, because it was Harry's last try.

And now the fight was all over, as a US Marshall came in through the door.
He handcuffed the unconscious villains, who were laid out on the bar floor.
And now the story has ended, with a twin hanging that was long overdue.
It was attended by Harry and Paddy, and Sweet Sally came along too.

And after the swinging occasion, the judge had just one thing to do;
Sally had made her decision, as to who would share her life through.
He married young Sally to Paddy; she would love him till death they did part,
And the best man of course was old Harry, in spite of his broken heart.

So Sally and Paddy went north, in search of the old mans gold,
While Harry set off for England, he'd had enough of the cold.
And if he couldn't have Sally, then what use was it being so brave.
For he knew he could love no other; he'd be alone till the grave.

So Harry works now in a bank, sending the bank statements forth
And every now and again, he dreams, of his days in the frozen north."

"Is that it?" asked the oldest member.

"Yes," said Harry who was staring out of the window at the snow.

"So did they find any gold?" someone asked.

"No," said Harry, "there was no mine, and no gold, except for Sally's hair of course, and Paddy got that."

"So you finished up with nothing then," said the oldest member.

"Well, not exactly. You see, as soon as they headed north with the dog team, I went back to Dawson Creek and claimed the $10,000 reward which had been posted for Dangerous Dan and Black Jack," said Harry, cheering up considerably.

TWO
The Policeman's Ball.

Jack Robinson had arrived late at the club, still dressed in his dinner jacket and bow tie.

"Where have you been to, Jack?" demanded the oldest member.

"Tonight was the Annual Ball, of the Transvaal Mounted Police," replied Jack, settling down into a leather armchair, and loosening his tie.

"That's South Africa isn't it?" asked Jumbo Fowler, "there couldn't have been many of you there tonight."

"Just a couple of dozen of us of us, Sid Green was there, but he won't be coming in to the club tonight."

"Are you telling us that both you and Sid, served in the South African Mounted police at the same time?" asked the oldest member.

"The Transvaal Mounted Police," corrected Jack, "I was the inspector and he was one of my constables."

"That sounds interesting," said the oldest member signalling for a round of drinks, "did anything interesting actually ever happen?"

Jack settled back and began his story. I thought that it was going to be just another normal day at my police post in Kronje, up in the Transvaal. It was a rough place situated near the gold fields, they talk about California and Alaska, but they were kindergartens compared to South Africa.

"Did the Zulus give you trouble then?" asked Spencer Harris.

The Zulu, good heavens no, they were perfect gentlemen, compared to the roughnecks who inhabited that part of the world in those days. I can remember it was a Tuesday and I was sitting in my office doing some important paperwork.

When suddenly the door burst open and Constable Green rushed in.

"I take it you are talking about Sid Green, the member of this club," intervened the oldest member.

Yes, that's right, Sid rushed in, and he was as white as a sheet.

"Boss," he croaked." Guess what's happened?"

I put my pen down, and told him to calm down and tell me.

"Big Albert Deville has been let out of jail!" he said, looking as if he was about to burst into tears.

"The Law must take its course," I told him, "what has it to do with us?"

"Do with us," he squeaked. "Boss it was you that put him away."

"Yes I did, but he shouldn't have killed those gold prospectors, should he," I reminded him, flicking a speck of dust off my immaculate uniform.

"Don't you understand Boss?" he cried, "he is on his way here, with three of his old gang members."

I laughed, "Well if they dare to show their faces here in Kronje, they are in for a big surprise. If they cause any trouble, I'll have them locked up and doing time before you can say, 'Jack Robinson'. Anyway, who has he got with him?"

"Well Boss, according to the telegraph, he has Frankie Stein, and the brothers."

"The brothers," I queried with a frown, "who are they?"

"Dewulf Mann and his brother, Haard Mann," he told me.

"Hmmmm, I've heard of those gentlemen, they are all killers aren't they," I said, finishing off another report. "What do you suppose they would want here?"

"Its perfectly obvious Boss," Sid squealed, "they mean to kill you."

"They can't go around killing officers of the law," I told him, "who said that they are heading up here, anyway?"

"Deville did Boss, when his gang let him out of jail, they are on the train and heading up here at this very minute."

"And what time does the train arrive here?" I asked with a smile.

"Twelve o'clock Boss, High Noon!!!"

I looked at my watch, it was 10.15am, so I had one and three quarter hours before the train was due in, time to finish some work before I had to deal with Mr. Deville and his cronies.

"Come on Constable Green," I ordered, "I've had information that there is going to be an attack on Chief Betulatasi's Kraal, and I intend to stop a tribal war before it begins."

"But Boss, what about Deville?"

"Time to deal with him later," I told the quaking Constable.

We set off, walking down the Main Street, and I saw half a dozen local hard cases standing around outside the saloon, they were laughing and pointing at me.

I walked up to them.

"Would you like to share the joke, gentlemen?" I asked.

"The joke doesn't start until noon," said Karl Günter, the local bullyboy.

"Well move along, because if I see you hanging around here at noon, you are all going into the pokey." They disappeared in to the saloon

"Boss," said Sid, "I've got some holidays due, and I thought that I might take a trip down to Joburg."

"Fine," I told him, "when are you thinking of going?"

"Well now, is as good as time as any, I thought that I might borrow a horse and leave right away."

"Oh, this hasn't got anything to do with the noon train, has it Constable Green?" I asked.

"NO! of course not sir, absolutely not, I just fancied a spot of holiday," he assured me.

"OK, I believe you," I told him, thinking that thousands wouldn't. "But I'm afraid that I can't spare you until tomorrow; you see if I have to arrest Deville and his men, I will need you to look after the cells."

He followed me up the Main Street ashen faced.

It all seemed very quiet, the shopkeepers were nailing wooden boards over their windows, and women were dragging their children in off the streets.

"It looks as if the word has got around," I told constable Green, "I'll go on and sort out Chief Betulatasi's problem, while you go round town and see if you can round up half a dozen Special Constables, we might as well put on a show of strength before any trouble can start."

Sid ran off up the Main Street, while I got my horse and rode out to the Chiefs Village.

It was about seven miles, and twenty minutes later I rode into Chiefs Betulatasi's Kraal.

I glanced at my watch, it was ten 10.45am, H'm. I looked around and took in the two thousand warriors, formed up in their Impi. Every man was six foot tall and they all carried their hide shields, assegeie's, and knobkerries, men of the Uzula Regiment, unless I was very much mistaken.

I dismounted and pushed my way through the warriors, until I arrived in front of the Chief, who sat on a dais.

"Greetings, Great White Elephant, who commands the sun, destroyer of enemies, fountain of all wisdom," I said in Swahili.

"Morning Jack," he replied in English, "lovely day for it eh."

"A lovely day for what exactly?" I questioned.

"For sorting out those infernal Bantu," he told me, "I've had enough of their cattle stealing, last night we raided their Kraal, and took two hundred head back, my scouts have reported that they are on their way here now!"

"I'm not surprised, that they are on their way here," I told him, "but I'm not having a tribal war on my patch, it's not the old days anymore, we have to go to court to settle disputes now."

I heard a drumming sound, and walked to the gates of the Kraal, and there they came, around two thousand Bantu warriors in fighting formation, approaching at the trot and beating their spears on their shields.

The Uzula Regiment formed up in front of their Kraal, while the Bantu stopped a hundred yards away and began a war chant. This was answered by the Uzula beating their spears on their shields and shouting 'ZULU.'

I looked at my watch, 11am, H'm. I walked out into the open ground between the two armies and held up my hand, the chanting and shield banging died away.

"I'm only going to say this once," I shouted, "anybody who is still here in two minutes time will be arrested, and charged with violent disorder."

The warriors looked at each other, and then the Bantu Chief came forward to me.

"Greetings, Lion of the veldt, avenger of the forests, lord of all the birds and the beasts," I said, in Bantu.

"Good morning Sir," said the Bantu Chief in English, "what are you doing here?"

"Stopping a war," I told him, I'm not going to allow it on my patch!"

Chief Betulatasi, arrived and said. "You are right Mr. Robinson, the times they are changing, when the Boers ruled here they would send a whole troop of cavalry after a solitary Bantu chicken thief. But here you are, facing down four thousand warriors single handed."

"Give them the cattle back Chief," I said, "and I will not arrest your men."

He gave a signal and his men began to drift away, while the village boys drove the cattle out of the Kraal.

"Take your cattle, but leave ten of them here as a token of friendship." I told the Bantu chief.

He nodded his agreement, and two minutes later his army and one hundred and ninety cattle were disappearing to the north, I looked at my watch, eleven fifteen, H'm.

I galloped back into town, and cantered down the Main Street, where I heard shots coming from the Bank. I quickly dismounted and took up a position beside the Bank entrance, the door burst open and a masked man ran out, I stuck out a foot and tripped him. Over he went, falling down the steps and sprawling on to the road.

I jumped down and slipped the hand-cuffs on him. Dragging him upright I pulled off the mask, it was Karl Gunter.

"Damn! I thought that you had run away, leaving the town wide open," he said.

"So you decided to make a withdrawal then," I replied, "let's go."

I took him to the police station and locked him in the cell.

"You will not be alone in there for long," I told him, taking a look at my watch, H'm, eleven forty. Where was Sid with my Special Constables I wondered?

A minute later Sid ran in, "sorry Boss, he gasped, but no one will help you, they are all too scared to sign up."

I smiled grimly, "so it's just you and I then Sid," I told him.

"Sorry Boss, but I'm feeling a bit unwell," he replied. "I think that I should go and have a lie down," he finished lamely, disappearing back out of the door.

I sighed unlocked the gun cabinet, and took out my .38 Webley revolver, should I take it, I wondered, I certainly didn't like having to use guns, but it appeared that on this occasion there would be little choice. I buckled on my Sam Browne, and slipped the revolver into the holster. I looked again at my watch H'm eleven forty five, time to go to the station and meet the High Noon train.

Ten minutes later I walked on to the station platform and approached the stationmaster.

"Is the noon train on time?" I asked him.

He looked at me as if he was measuring me up for a coffin.

24

"Albert Deville is on that train isn't he?"

"Yes, I suppose he is," I replied.

"Where are your Special Constables then?" he wanted to know.

"There aren't any."

"Yes, the train is on time," he said walking rapidly down the platform and disappearing. In the distance I heard the train whistle blowing.

I left the station and walked back on to the Main Street, it was deserted, I looked at my watch it was eleven fifty nine, well the paperwork would have to wait, there was some unfinished business arriving.

Walking back up to the police station I went inside and sat down at my desk, from the cell Karl Gunter laughed and said, "I'll soon be out of this flea trap you lousy pig."

I ignored him and began to fill in his arrest report; it looked as if the paperwork couldn't wait after all. I looked at my watch it said twelve o'clock, I shook it, and yes the thing had stopped.

It was then that I heard Deville shouting from the street outside. "Come on out inspector, we know that you are in there!"

I stood up and walked to the door, then out onto the footpath. There they were in the middle of the road, four of them.

Albert Deville, stood well over six feet tall, lean and mean, his hand hovering near his pistol, which was sticking out of the top of his pants.

On either side of him stood the brothers, to his right Dewulf Mann, medium sized, and carrying a shotgun, he was so hairy that all you could see were his eyes, red, and glaring through the brown hair that covered his face.

On the other side stood Haard Mann, he was much bigger, a huge bully of an Afrikaner, he held a twelve-foot long bullwhip in his great hand.

Then last but not least, Frankie Stein, infamous for his brutality throughout South Africa.

"Shall I kill him now Boss?" he asked Albert, as he put his hands on to the pearl handles of his holstered pistols.

"No, I told you he was mine," snapped Deville, but Frankie Stein ignored him and went for the guns that he wore.

In less than a heartbeat his challenge was answered, as my pistol flashed into my hand as if by magic.

25

BANG BANG, my revolver roared out twice, and the Frankie Stein monster lay dead on the floor.

"Give it up Albert," I said, but 'CRAAAACKKK,' Haard's bullwhip snaked out and knocked the pistol out of my hand, so I was now unarmed.

Dewulf raised his shotgun; I leapt out into the road and punched him on the point of his hairy chin, dropping him like a sack of potatoes into the dust of the road.

The next instant I was flattened, as both Deville and Haard Mann leapt on me at the same time, and we rolled and fought into the middle of the Main Street. I was beginning to get the upper hand, when a revived Dewulf Mann joined the fight and it looked as if my number was up.

Every time I knocked one of them down, two more were there to fill his place, and then to make matters even worse, two of Karl Gunter's mates came across and joined in the attack on me, So it was now five on to one, I wouldn't have been surprised to have seen Frankie Stein coming back to life and joining in the assault.

I fell to my knees bloodied and exhausted, and they surrounded me.

"Give him a taste of the whip Haard Mann," said Deville through his cut and bloodied lips, as the rest of the gang pointed pistols and a shotgun at me.

Haard pulled back his whip hand, when suddenly everyone's attention was caught by a drumming noise; we looked up the Street and saw a thousand Zulu's advancing in formation, banging their assegeie's against their hide shields.

Deville and his men began to back away down the Street, when a great shout of 'Kwazulu', made them spin around, and there coming up the from other end of the Street were another thousand warriors.

The gang dropped their weapons, and crowded around me as I climbed to my feet.

"Do something Boss," they were all saying, trying to hide behind me.

I held up my hand and the Zulu Impi stopped. Chief Betulatasi walked forward.

"Hello again Jack," he said. "We heard that you might be having a spot of bother, and thought that we would return a favour, shall we kill them for you?"

"No its ok, the law must take its course," I told him, pointing at the police post, the five not so hard men fled inside and I heard the cell door slamming as they locked themselves in.

So that was that, they were all back on the next noon train, heading for the state prison and long terms of hard labour. While I got down to the serious business of completing all the paperwork.

The Policeman's other Ball.

The following Friday Sid Green turned up at the Club, although there was no sign of Jack Robinson.

"Good evening Sid," said the oldest member, "Jack Robinson was in last Friday, he told us quite a story of your days together in the Transvaal Mounted Police."

"I'll bet he did," replied Sid, "and what story would that have been?"

"All about Albert Deville and the high noon train," Spencer Harris told him.

"Ah, you mean Albert Debill, yes I remember that."

"Do you want to tell us about it?" interjected the oldest member, sensing another stirring tale.

Yes of course, began Sid, Jack and myself were both Corporals at the Kronje Police Post, a tiny settlement in the middle of nowhere, if it hadn't been for the rail stop it wouldn't have even existed, a population of around 205 I recall.

"So why did it require two policemen then?" asked the oldest member.

"Actually there were around twenty of us including the native constables," Sid replied, "you see we also had about twenty five thousand square miles of bush to police."

"Crikey, that's some gold field," said Jumbo Fowler.

"Gold Field, don't you mean maize and bean fields?" Sid told them.

Anyway it was a Thursday and I had just checked the mail, there was only one item of any interest so I went out into the office. Jack was sat there, his feet on the desk, dressed only in his tattered shorts, doing the crossword.

"Look at this Jack, Albert Debill has been let out of jail," I said.

27

"Who's Albert Debill?" he asked scratching his belly, and blowing off.

"Surely you remember Jack; he is the one guy you arrested last year. No visible means of support wasn't it? Hardly surprising though, he does have a wooden leg."

"So what's that got to do with us?" He asked, going back to his crossword.

"Nothing really," I told him, "except for the fact that he is on his way back here with three of his friends."

"Friends, what Friends?" he wanted to know.

I looked at the letter, "well there's Francis Finklestein, and the brothers"

"What brothers?" he demanded.

"Foxy Mann and his brother Herbert Mann, apparently they are coming back here to sort you out."

He leapt to his feet, sending his tea all over the floor.

"Bloody hell Sid," he croaked "what time does the next train arrive?"

"Ten past three, providing that it's on time for a change." I told him.

"We have to get out of town," he said.

"Yes, I've just had a report of some trouble brewing in the Kaffir village, we need to go and sort it out," I replied, "and put a shirt on while you are at it."

We left the Police post, with Jack looking around him all the time.

"I'm due some leave you know," he told me, "I was thinking about going down to Joburg, I could start walking now, couldn't I."

"Come on Jack," I told him, "we are far to busy to spare you at the moment, lets just get on with the job."

We paused outside the saloon and spoke to a couple of lads who were waiting for it to open.

"Hey! We hear that old Albert Debill is on his way back here," said Karl Gunter.

"That's enough of that sort of talk," said Jack, "anymore and we will run you in."

They disappeared into the saloon, "what's up with Robbo?" I heard Karl asking his mate, Sam Browne.

"Just being the usual Prat," came the reply from Sam.

"Shouldn't you be arming the native Constables, and swearing in some Specials?" asked Jack.

"No let's go and deal with this little problem before we consider what to do about Debill," I replied.

"Is this where he got on to his horse?" asked little Martin Fletcher.

"Horse, we never had any horses, the police had been mounted thirty years earlier, but we had bicycles. There was supposed to have been a car, but it never turned up during our time there."

It was about a mile outside town so it only took us twenty minutes to walk it. As we approached the village, a small huddle of breezeblock bungalows, we could see a group of half a dozen men arguing furiously.

"Half a dozen," interrupted the oldest member, "so how were they dressed?"

"Much like anyone else, I suppose," said Sid, "shirts and slacks, a couple of them wore shorts, Mr. Betulatasi was wearing a suit and collar and tie."

We walked up to them and stood between the antagonists.

"You're all under arrest," said Jack.

"No your not," I told them, "what exactly is the problem?"

Mr. Betulatasi, turned to me and said, "we bought a cow from these rogues and it is dry, so we are having to drink our tea black, we want a refund!"

I turned to the two cattle traders.

"We never said that the cow gave milk, caveat emptor," they told me.

"That cow is older than I am," complained Mr. Betulatasi.

I looked at it, it had certainly seen better days, "how much did you pay for it?" I asked him.

"Eight shillings," he replied indignantly.

"OK, then here is what we shall do," I told them, "slaughter the cow and have half each, the cattle traders will refund you four shillings; they will have meat for a week, and enough money to buy two calves. You Mr. Betulatasi will also have meat for a week, plus enough money to buy a calf, and also enough money left over to buy milk, until it is old enough to breed."

"The wisdom of Solomon," they agreed, and settled down to a cup of tea, while Jack and I walked back in to town.

"Alls well, that ends well," I told him.

"Lets get to the bank, I want to see if I have enough in my account to buy a horse," he said increasing his pace.

We stopped at the bank, and waited behind Karl Gunter who was making a withdrawal.

"Come on Jack," I said, "we can see off old Albert and his crew."

He made a sort of whimpering noise, which increased when he found out that he was overdrawn, and that no funds were forthcoming.

We arrived back at the police Post and went inside.

"Where are the native constables?" Jack wanted to know.

"They cycled north yesterday to investigate the reports of ivory poachers," I reminded him.

He unlocked the gun cabinet and took out a Thompson machine gun.

"What's that for?" I enquired.

"Albert Debill," he replied.

"Now look here," I told him, "you can't go shooting off a machine gun in town, someone could get hurt."

"Well that's OK as long as it isn't me," he informed me.

"Yes, but that thing takes .45 calibre bullets doesn't it?"

"So?"

"We haven't got any .45 bullets, nor any ammunition at all, the constables took everything that we had, yesterday," I reminded him.

"That's ridiculous, who ordered that?" he wanted to know.

"You did," was all I could tell him.

He slumped into his chair and buried his face in his hands.

"Sid, you wont leave me on my own will you," he said.

"Of course not," I assured him.

I put the kettle on for a nice cup of tea, and looked at the clock, it was two pm, and we had an hour to kill, an unfortunate simile I thought, as I poured boiling water into the pot.

Henry Hill came into the post and joined us in a cup of tea; he wanted to make a complaint about some graffiti that had been daubed on his wall, something about Jack apparently.

"OK Henry," I said," I'll come and have a look," and left the police post with him.

We made our way to his house which was at the edge of town. I looked at the graffiti, two-foot high letters whitewashed on the side of his house that said, 'ROBBO IS A PRAT'.

"I think that I will pay a visit to the saloon, and have a word with Sam Browne," I told Mr. Hill, and made my way back up to the saloon.

I entered the premises and froze, for there drinking with Karl and Sam was Francis Finklestein;

I grabbed his arm and said. "What the hell are you doing in here Finklestein?"

He turned and looked up at me through his thick spectacle lenses, "the train was cancelled so we came by car," he told me, "I'm with Albert Debill and the Mann brothers."

"And where are they?" I asked, desperately looking around the bar.

"Oh they had some business with Robbo; they went straight up to the police post."

I released him, he turned away and started drinking his beer, while I ran for the door and headed back to the police post.

I was just in time to observe the final moments of the confrontation, as I ran up the Street,

Robbo was on his hands and knees, kneeling in the road, there had obviously been a fight, Herbert Mann was raising a rolled up newspaper to hit Jack with, while Albert and Foxy held rolled up magazines in a threatening manner.

Herbert stepped forward, and then fell down into the road. A cast iron milk pail had flown across the Street and hit him on the back of the head knocking him out cold.

Albert and Foxy turned around and their jaws dropped, as Mr. Betulatasi and his three sons walked up to them. They quickly hid behind Jack who was climbing to his feet.

"It's lucky we hadn't bought the milk yet," said Jacks helper, as he picked his milk pail up.

I pulled up beside them puffing and panting from the run.

"It's about time you showed up." said Jack, "I've dealt with it now, take these three villains inside and lock them up, they are due for another stretch in the State prison."

"Well doesn't that just go to prove what I have always said, that there are two sides to every story," said the oldest member.

THREE
The Secret Society.

The author wishes to apologize in advance to all members of Clubs, Society's, Freemasons, and other noble pastimes, who are sure to be offended by the following story. (Ha ha).

Claude Cusworth was very upset, a friend whom he had put up for membership of the club, had been blackballed, and refused membership.

"This place is becoming just like a ruddy secret society," he grumbled, as he sulked by the fireplace.

The oldest member, who for once hadn't actually put the black ball into the velvet bag, asked, "What would you know of secret society's Claude?"

"Well I was a prominent member of one a few years back," said Claude, still feeling a bit resentful. "Would you like to hear about it?"

"I thought that it was secret," said Jumbo Fowler, but most of the other members called for Claude to continue.

"The secret society was called SODDEM, which of course stood for **S**ecret **O**rganization **D**edicated to **D**ominating **E**very **M**an." said Claude.

"Ah, to do with Dominos was it?" asked the oldest member.

"No, not at all, we were intent on taking over the world and creating a new order," Claude told him.

"Aha, you're talking about the Inland Revenue Department aren't you," said Harry Cummings.

"No I am not," said Claude, "now will you all shut up and listen."

Spotty Simpson, who worked in the post room, approached me one day at work.

"Claude, old bean," he said, "you're a good reliable sort of chap, how would you like to join a rather special club?"

Well the drama group had folded, following our disastrous production of 'Oh What A Lovely War'. Bert's idea of using real gunpowder to stage the battle scene hadn't worked to its best advantage, and we hadn't got a theatre anymore. Also, the Bird Watching Society had suspended me, following my report of a flock of Albatrosses nesting in the local park. So I was up for a new interest.

"What sort of club is it then Spotty? " I wanted to know.

"Sssshhhh, walls have ears," he told me in a whisper, "be in the back-room of the Fox and Hounds Public House at 8pm tonight, and all will be revealed."

So that night, dressed in my best pullover and plastic Mac, I turned up at the appointed time in the Fox and Hounds Public Bar.

Spotty was there, and he immediately dragged me through into the back room, which was also the headquarters of SODDEM.

The members were sat around in a semi circle, wearing blue anoraks, except the Imperial Wizard Eugene Egbhert, who was wearing a red anorak and a silver skullcap with a lightning bolt on the top. I noticed that all the members were wearing thick rimless spectacles and had rather prominent teeth. In all a rather smart and well turned out gathering, I remember thinking, as I adjusted my spectacles.

Spotty stepped forwards and introduced me; I already knew several of the society's members through my previous memberships of other society's, such as the Model Railway Enthusiasts Club, and the Birdwatchers.

"Are you aware of the initiation test, and the terrible blood oath that you must take?" asked the Imperial Wizard.

I pretended that I was.

"Then let the initiation test begin," intoned Eugene.

Up stands Brother Andrew Anderson.

"First of all you must recite all ten Doctor Who's from memory," he told me.

Well that was dead easy, everyone knows that, although there was some discussion when I reached Peter Cushing, some of the members thought that he shouldn't count. But I sailed through it and I could see that they were all very impressed.

Up stands Brother Brian Bryant.

"Now you must tell us what type of locomotive, usually pulls the 12.05pm London Express?" he demanded.

"Ah easy, that's one of the Star class. 4,6,2's," I told him, "mind you, on Saturday I noticed that the Duchess of Richmond had an unofficial modification to the front thrust splinkle pin mountings. I wonder if that constitutes a change in class. That started a frantic discussion, but eventually the members decided that it was probably just the Euston Heavy Loco Depot doing some unofficial modifications.

Now it was the turn of Brother Damien Dawson

"Name the entire cast of 'Happy Days'," he said.

"Er, Fonz, er um, er, er, did I say Fonz yet?" I replied.

"That's near enough," said the Imperial Wizard, "we need members like Claude. Let's move on to the terrible Blood Oath."

There was a murmur of assent, and I had to present my thumb, Spotty heated a needle over a candle and then pricked my thumb with it, drawing a drop of blood. Of course I immediately fainted, and that was it, I was a member of SODDEM. Quite a lowly member of course, I was a **Newly Enrolled Retro Declarent**, or a NERD for short.

Eugene looked at his watch, "Crikey!" he exclaimed, "it's ten past nine, I have to be off, my mother doesn't like me being out too late."

Everyone else jumped up and we quickly paid in our sixpences for the hire of the room, and then made for our bicycles, tucking our trouser bottoms into our socks.

"So how many members did this secret society have?" asked the oldest member.

"Nine, once I had joined," replied Claude.

"Not many to take over the world with," retorted the oldest member.

Unabashed, Claude continued with his story.

We were actually affiliated to a large number of organizations all over the world; known collectively as NGA, **No Girls Allowed**. There were the UFOlogists in Oklahoma City, the Train Spotters of Munchen Gladbach, the Bell Ringers of Little Finchley, the Alberta Model Helicopter Pilots Club, as well as Radio Hams all over the world.

Plus of course, the crème de la crème, the Minnesota Star Trekkies.

I also learned all about the structure of SODDEM. The Imperial Wizard, Eugene was a Poindexter, and the seven pens he had clipped into his breast pocket showed his rank. Most of the other members were Wurstsuckers, and wore five plastic pens.

While Steven Stevenson and myself were Nerds, and were only allowed to wear four pens in our breast pockets. Apparently, the Grand Puissant Master, Nyagi Kawasaki, of the 'Kyoto Unusual Car Registration Numbers Collectors Club', was a ten pen Wurlmonger.

We met every Tuesday night, at the Grand Dominator Lodge Chapter House, in the back room of the Fox and Hounds, to discuss the furtherance of our cause. Several grand designs were thought up, discussed, and rejected. Although I must admit that I rather liked Terence Tingles suggestion, that we got a book on hypnosis, and hypnotized everybody else into our way of thinking.

No, as usual it was Eugene who came up with the answer. We would take over Parliament, assume the government, then we could call a Summit Meeting of all the Heads of State in the world, convert them, and BINGO, we would be able to rule the World. I was to be promoted to Munchbucket, and appointed Supremo for finding out everybody's business. Eugene would be Super Grand Puissant Master of course.

Now you are all wondering how we were to complete the first step, the taking over of the government. Well as it happened, Eugene was a brilliant inventor; and he already had some major accomplishments under his belt, such as the anti cat cage.

First of all he had come up with the brilliant idea, of leaving the contents of his refrigerator on his back doorstep overnight, to save expensive electricity. Then a couple of days later he had invented the anti cat cage, to stop stray cats from eating the contents of refrigerators left outside on doorsteps overnight. Idea's which were just waiting to be snapped up by some enterprising company.

And now his greatest masterpiece was nearing completion, the SUBLIMINAL SUBVERTOR.

The secret machine that he had been assembling in his mum's garage for months, worked by sending out Radio Waves, which would allow Eugene to impose his will on anybody within a half a mile radius. The whole society began to meet at the garage every Saturday afternoon, as we hurried the fantastic machine onwards towards completion.

I was dispatched on my bicycle to the local scrap yard, to find some switches and controls. I had the good fortune to find a SKODA car, only three years old. Its floorpan completely rusted through of course, but absolutely full of useful bits and pieces. I filled my brown paper carrier bag, paid my one-shilling and sixpence and then cycled back to Eugene's mum's house.

The society members were very excited when they saw the parts, and left off comparing their slide rules.

"My word, haven't you done well," said Eugene, and I blushed at this high praise from the Imperial Wizard.

We set to work under Eugene's guidance and soon had the SUBLIMINAL SUBVERTOR taking shape. We had constructed a platform out of an upturned bath, which was full of old car batteries to provide the power.

The transmitter was built out of old radio receiver parts, and the 'SUBVERTOR' had been secretly built in Eugene's bedroom, I remember going up there to help him lift it down to the garage, and how impressed I had been, by his collection of model trams.

It took us twelve Saturday afternoons, to finish the building of our machine, and at last we were able to stand back and admire the results.

The mighty machine was mounted on a set of old pram wheels that Spotty Simpson, had recovered from the local rubbish tip; the upturned bath had been painted black and sported our emblem on its side, a picture of that American chap, Jimmy Carter.

On top of this were two boxes made out of old oil drums, which housed the 'SUBVERTOR' and the 'TRANSMITTER'. Coming out of the top of the transmitter box was the aerial, which Eugene had made out of an old fireguard; he had painted 'AERIAL' on it so no one could get confused. My instruments filled the control panel, most of them weren't connected to anything, but they looked really good.

Of course much of the Tuesday night meetings had been taken up in discussion about how we were to avoid being subverted ourselves, when the machine was switched on. But as usual Eugene rose to the occasion and invented protective caps for us to wear.

The caps were made out of vegetable colanders worn over the head; they had little boxes on top containing radios which would of course use up all the radio waves coming in our direction from the machine. Eugene would obviously have to wear the transmission headpiece, which he had made up out of a Wok, it had a TV type aerial mounted on top and was connected by wires to the Subvertor, ipso factso when he thought commands, everyone within half a mile radius would have to obey his every wish.

As soon as he had control of the government he would order the construction of a giant mobile transmitter, so that he would be able to

'Dominate' all men. He even had a name ready for it,' Super Kinetic Yellow Transmitting Vehicle. Or SKY TV'.

It actually took us several months to decide the date for our takeover of the country, there was always a problem. We almost went, on the August Bank holiday, but when we arrived at the gates of Parliament dragging the machine behind us, we were told by the duty policeman that the building was closed until November, when Parliament reconvened. And to remove our pile of rubbish from the pavement forthwith.

We toiled our way homewards, arguing furiously amongst ourselves, and by the time we arrived back at Eugene's Mum's Garage, blame had been placed squarely on the shoulders of myself and Steven Stevenson, the two NERD's. The next night at the weekly Lodge meeting we both had to pay a forfeit, and buy crisps for everybody as a punishment.

It was quite an acrimonious meeting, with the Wurstsuckers demanding to know just exactly when, were we going to take over the world. Eugene of course was master of the moment, once he had restored order, he told the meeting he had decided that the moment to strike would be on the day of the State Opening of Parliament, November 5th.

This would also celebrate the anniversary of Guido Fawkes, who had tried it before in 1605, but had turned out to be a bit of a sad loser, unlike us of course.

November 5th dawned damp and cold, I phoned in to work, and informed them that I wouldn't be in as I had a touch of Enteric fever. I was disappointed with the lack of sympathy forthcoming; but never mind for by tomorrow I would be part of the government of the country, then we would see who deserved any sympathy.

I dressed carefully, the grey trousers that rode four inches above the ankles, white socks, and sandals, check shirt and paisley tie, a nice pink and green hooped pullover, all set off by my Blue Anorak. I looked into the mirror, very smart indeed, I thought, as I set my thick rimless spectacles straight and examined my teeth in the bathroom mirror, perfectly clean and yellow, no point in cleaning them today.

I set off for Eugene's and met up with Harold Harrison on his way there, I gave him the secret recognition signal, picking my nose and attempting to flick the result into the road. He responded with the answer, scratching his backside, then licking his finger. We fell into step and marched on to Eugene's, swinging our colander helmets confidently in our hands.

At exactly ten am, we arrived and entered the secret garage, along with the other seven members of SODDEM. Quite a lot of nose picking and butt scratching went on as we gave recognition signals to each other.

The Imperial Wizard, Eugene, called the gathering to order, and launched into the Society's anthem 'Tie me Kangaroo down sport'. That had been the brainwave of Bruce Briscoe, our lone Australian member, although we had replaced Kangaroo with 'Tie me Ginger Cat down sport,' a bit more British you see, although we did consider ourselves an international society.

The singing was cut short by Eugene's mum shouting down to, "shut that noise up or else."

The singing died away, and Eugene shouted, "Sorry Mummsie, we'll be quiet." He continued in a whisper.

"We leave here at 13.00hours, and push the SUBLINIMAL SUB-VERTOR to the gates of the Palace of Westminster, arriving there at 14.59hours. At precisely the same time the Gentleman Usher of the Black Rod will hammer on the closed doors of the commons, and request the commons presence in the chamber of the Lords. Then at exactly 15.01 I shall switch on the machine transferring my thought command to the Black Rod, ordering him to come down to the front gate and let us in. Once inside I shall order the government to obey me in every command, and you men must be obeyed as well of course. Thus our takeover of the world will have begun, First Britain, then Poland and France, and then the world, ha ha ha ha."

We passed the next couple of hours drinking non-alcoholic beer, and discussing whether the speed of light was actually slowing down, the further it traveled from the centre of the universe. Until at last it was 13.00hours, and time for us to go. We pushed our machine along Broadway, and lost a bit of time when one of the wheels came off. Undeterred we borrowed one off a pram parked outside Rumbelows, effected repairs and continued on our way, arriving at Westminster's Gates at 15.30hours.

Eugene was in a bad mood, he couldn't stand being late, and he pushed the machine up against the wrought iron Gates.

"Put your helmets on," he barked, and we hurried to obey, not wanting to be 'Subverted.' Eugene put on his Wok helmet and we noticed that it was now adorned with the Imperial Wizard's thunderbolt.

Eugene started throwing switches and the machine began to hum, red blue and green lights began flashing on the control panel. Two police constables noticed it and began to walk towards us.

The Imperial Wizard pressed his hand to his forehead and shouted "Stand by, here we go," he then threw the main switch.

There was a crackling sound and a smell of ozone, then a great blue bolt of lightning flashed out of the machine and earthed out through Eugene's thought transference helmet.

Poor Eugene turned transparent, and we could see the electricity raging through his body, as he jerked and danced all over the pavement, like a string puppet.

Then 'FLASH BANG', the machine threw out a last bolt of lightning which turned Eugene upside down and dumped him on to the pavement, before subsiding into silence, and we were assailed by the smell of burnt out wiring.

Seven accusing pairs of eyes turned on me, "You and your bloody SKODA Controls," yelled Spotty Simpson, "you've ruined everything."

We scraped Eugene up off the pavement, and sat him on the top of the machine, His clothes were burnt to cinders as was his hair, his big white eyes stared at us from a blackened face, and he made some little croaking noises.

The two policemen arrived and one of them said, "No penny for the Guy allowed here, move along at once."

We pushed off and delivered Eugene home, where his mother grabbed him by what was left of his collar and dragged him inside, making loud remarks about him being forty two years old and acting like a big child. The rest of us slunk off with our metaphorical tails between our legs. Not even having the heart to give the farewell signal, where you cupped a hand under your armpit, then brought your arm down hard, expelling the air and making a trumping sound.

No we were well chastened, and that was really the end of SODDEM, no one turned up for the following Tuesday's meeting, and before long we had all found other interests, mine for instance was this club.

The members of the Lyre Club looked around at each other.

"The friend that you put up for membership tonight, it was Eugene wasn't it?" said the oldest member.

"Yes, it was" replied Claude, "why, are you going to reconsider him?"

"We certainly are," said the oldest member, "If he is proposed again in a years time, I want all the white balls removed from the Clubs premises

FOUR
The Rivals

"I say," said Spencer Harris, as he filled his glass with port, "did I ever tell you of the time when I took part in the greatest golf match of all time?" The members settled back into their leather armchairs, aware that Spencer could spin a decent yarn, just as long as it was about golf. All except the oldest member, of course, who querulously asked if this was about the time Spencer claimed to have won the British Open.

"Oh no," said Spencer, "that of course resulted in a great final game, but this was definitely the greatest game of golf of all time. You see, some years ago Ginger Morris and myself were the leading lights of the local Golf Club; both of us had a handicap of minus six."

"How can you have a minus handicap?" interrupted the oldest member.

"Local rules of course," said Spencer hurrying on with his story. "Anyway, we had played each other so many times, first me winning by the odd shot and then him, it seemed that we would never be able to decide who the best player was, when suddenly it was decided for us in the strangest way.

The club gained a new member. Not just any member, mind you, but the most beautiful girl any of us had ever seen. Her name was Amelia; five foot eight tall, good shoulders and muscular arms - the perfect golfing figure in fact."

"Was she pretty?" asked the oldest member.

"Oh, I suppose that you could call her pretty, but when Ginger and I first spotted her carrying her clubs out onto the links we both fell in love at first sight. The problem was, of course, who would stand down and let the other fellow pay court to the girl. The answer was obvious. We would play a 'winner takes all' round of golf for her.

We retired to the nineteenth hole to set out the rules for this important match; eighteen holes over a course that we knew like the backs of our hands would obviously be totally inadequate for a match as momentous as this.

"I know," said Ginger eventually, "we should play from the club's first 'tee off' to the first hole, via the whole town."

41

"I'm not quite sure how that fits in with the Royal and Ancient rules," I replied.

"Not afraid to decide it on a single hole, are you?" asked Ginger in his superior voice. That settled it; one hole around the town it would be.

The match was arranged for that coming Sunday, and at 10am Ginger and I met at the first tee. Old Angus McPhee was caddying for me, while Ginger had young Rennie Gribben as his caddy. As we walked out, I felt exactly as our ancestors must have felt as they walked out onto the duelling field, with pistols and swords at the ready.

I had honours, so I teed up and started off with a number one iron; a smooth drive took my ball just past the corner of the clubhouse, and dropped it gently into the entrance of the car park ready for the dogleg down to the main entrance.

"That's a butterfly, Meester Spencer," said Angus.

"Why a butterfly?" I asked.

"Because it landed like a butterfly with sore feet," he said with a smile.

Both Angus and I were somewhat surprised when Ginger took a one wood and made a ferocious drive straight into the car park; the surprise vanished as his ball ricocheted off the door of my new car and disappeared in the direction of the main gate. As we walked up to take our second shots I knew that the grin on Ginger's ugly face would soon be wiped off.

"Now where's my ball gone?" asked Ginger. Of course, nobody knew except me and old Bunny Woods, who, true to his word, had quickly parked his car with the wheel over Ginger's ball and darted out of sight. I made the main gate in three, and Ginger, losing a shot for a lost ball, joined me on three. Honours even again.

The hole continued along the grass verge of Bramley Road for about a mile and a half. Angus handed me a four iron and I made a corking 180-yard drive straight and true along the verge. I turned and smiled at Ginger; just in time to see him chip his ball onto the platform of a trolley bus, which had stopped by the club entrance. The blighter and his caddy hopped aboard and the bus disappeared up the road.

Angus and I toiled on up the road, and ten shots later caught up with Ginger and Rennie, sunning themselves on a garden wall.

"And about time too," smirked Ginger, lining himself up for a chip across the roundabout hazard. His ball landed with pin point precision outside the garden of number seven, and my niece, little Belinda Cunningham, released her Jack Russell dog, which picked up Ginger's ball in its mouth and raced off back in the direction of the club car park to drop it, exactly as we had been training it to do for several days. As Ginger and his caddy set off in hot pursuit, Angus and I had a few minutes to rest and plan tactics, not to mention having a snort of the Highland Malt which he always carried in his flask.

Forty-five minutes later a golf ball landed close by us, and Ginger followed it up the road with a dangerous glint in his eye. The caddies compared cards and I was one stroke in the lead.

We both safely negotiated the roundabout hazard, and I took a five iron and blasted my ball straight and true up the middle of Henniker Road. Ginger grinned and chipped his ball up the garden drive of number three. I instantly realised that the cunning devil planned to cut out the dogleg into Sproughton Road by playing through a couple of back gardens. We reached my ball, which was in a difficult lie in the gutter.

"What do you think Angus?" I asked.

"I'd say a wedge shot sir," he said. I agreed, took the wedge, and chipped my ball straight in through the open parlour window of number thirty seven, finding a lovely lie on the carpet, just in front of the fire. As the old lady who lived there opened the front door, I slipped a fiver into her hand and asked her if she minded opening the kitchen and back doors, so that I could play through her garden. Bemused, she did as I requested; a couple of delicate puts and a short pitch took me into the garden of that big white house in Inkerman Street, where I found Ginger glumly looking for his ball which appeared to have gone into the ornamental pond. The caddies compared cards, and it was all even."

Spencer broke off for a moment to glare in the direction of the oldest member, who was making loud snoring sounds.

"So this left us with a fairly easy run up to the police station. We matched each other stroke for stroke up Inkerman Street and into the high Street, where I was incautious enough to risk a brassie. Sure enough, my ball caught PC Jinkinson, who was just leaving the police station, right behind the ear, and he went down like a sack of potatoes.

I looked in dismay at Angus, who asked,

"What are ye goin Tae do noo?"

43

"I'm going to stick with the irons, Angus," I said. "I can't afford to keep dropping shots like that."

Well, after I had been cautioned, we drove off again down the pavement, landing just outside Curry's. By this time we had gathered quite a crowd of interested spectators, many of whom were busily placing bets. So from there it was a simple chip across the road, followed by a three iron into the park, ready to drive up to our next marker, the War Memorial.

Ginger kicked at, and missed, the little Jack Russell dog, which was having a sniff at his ball, so the trick wasn't going to work twice then. We played across the smooth grass of the park to the base of the War Memorial, where we stopped for a snort of scotch. I stood and looked up at the memorial - a statue of a really ugly soldier holding his rifle upside down. He looked a lot like Ginger.

"I say," said Ginger, "that fellow on the statue looks just like you, you know."

Well, the next leg was across the park to the 'Krazy Golf' course, where we had to play through the nine holes. Two easy drives took us to the entrance, where we paid our admission fee and then strolled out to the first hole, which went through the wooden windmill, out of the little back door, down the slope and into the cup, about a par three I'd say.

Ginger teed up and drove sweetly in through the front door; trouble was his ball didn't come out of the back.

"Never mind old bean," I sympathised as I took my shot. The sympathy vanished as my ball trundled back out of the front door and landed at my feet.

"Shared hole," suggested Ginger.

"How about shared Krazy Golf course," I whispered. "This could make us look a bit amateurish if we went over par here."

"Right," said Ginger, "let's play straight down to the park gates."

"Any chance of a refund?" I asked the Park Keeper who had taken our money.

"What's up then, course to hard for you?" he replied, keeping his hands firmly in his pockets.

Two brilliant drives with my number one wood took me back to the park gates, ready for the dogleg up London Road to the car park of the Dog and Duck public house. I was quickly joined by Ginger and the crowd, and we set off up the road with me one stroke in the lead.

Four strokes later I was in position to chip over the wall and into the beer garden of the Dog and Duck. No sooner than my ball had landed when a great bally crowd of red-headed people came out of the bar and walked right over my lie, and would you believe it when they had gone so had my ball.

"Oh dear," said Ginger, "not another lost ball!" I dropped my last remaining ball and once again we were honours even.

We had a quick pint of beer and discussed tactics with our caddies; the next leg was certainly a difficult one; up to the door of the parish church; not long you understand, but London Road does have a serious traffic hazard. I decided to risk a four iron, and shouldn't have been surprised when my ball bounced off the side of the passing number forty-nine omnibus and landed in the garden of number thirty one. Ginger waved cheerily as he walked past in pursuit of his long drive, which had gone almost as far as the churchyard wall. Angus and I searched for my ball in the front garden, eventually finding it nestled behind a garden gnome.

"Tha's a brae deefecult shot sir," said Angus. "I'd consider dropping a shot here."

"Nonsense," I replied, "I can drive through." I blasted the ball with a two iron straight up to the churchyard wall, and we hurried off leaving the headless gnome lying in the garden.

Ginger had waited for us by the wall, and after we arrived he executed an elegant chip into the churchyard. Angus and I couldn't help but smile, as his ball bounced off a headstone and dropped into a freshly dug grave.

"Now that's what I call a bunker," said young Rennie, his caddy.

"I think I'll have to drop a shot here," said Ginger.

"Oh no," I told him. "That ball is playable. You will just have to go in after it." With what I considered to be remarkably bad grace, Ginger climbed down into the open grave and asked for a wedge to be handed down to him. He took his shot and I had the immense satisfaction of seeing a large clod of earth, but no ball, emerge from the hole.

"Hey! There's a coffin down here," said Ginger. "I've just uncovered a bit of it. What should I do?"

"Try a sand wedge," I advised him.

Rennie lay down on a nearby comfy grave to keep score, while Angus and I moved back to the flowers and wreaths, where I was able to take a few practice grass cutter swings at the flower heads, while we chatted to the small crowd of spectators. Ding Dong, Ding Dong, the church bells suddenly went; the church doors opened and a bride and groom emerged. Five seconds later they were showered with an absolute deluge of mud and divots from the open grave, and two minutes after that, when Ginger had been dragged out of the grave by two burly ushers and roughed up, I grudgingly conceded that he could drop a shot. Just five minutes later, after the angry mob of wedding guests had moved to the other side of the churchyard for photographs, and the vicar had placed a five bob bet on me winning, we putted up to the Church door. The caddies compared cards and I was four strokes up. In the bag, I thought. Little did I know that the game was about to take a turn for the worse.

Well, the next leg went back over the churchyard wall, down London Road, over the canal, and then into the beer garden of the Bull and Butcher Public House. I took my shot and sliced badly; the bally ball hit a large statue of an angel in mourning, ricocheted back towards us, hit a Celtic Cross and rolled neatly into the same open grave.

"That's the first hole in one you've ever had!" smirked Ginger, as I gazed into the grave. The ball was in a really difficult lie, just below the freshly exposed brass plate, which read, 'R.I.P'.

"What should I do?" I asked Angus.

"Ye cud try praying, sir," he said.

Suffice to say, a nip of whiskey and six shots later and I was out of the grave and following Ginger down to the wall, two strokes behind.

We caught up with him by the said wall, and he was in a beautiful lie which would allow him to blast a three wood, long and straight down London Road towards the canal bridge. I wasn't as lucky as him and dropped another stroke trying to cut off the corner of the churchyard.

I drove down the road with my number three wood, and set off, followed by the crowd, with my odds increasing by the minute.

Ginger played down towards the canal bridge, and I decided to gamble by cutting off the bend in the road and playing through the fields on the right hand side, then straight over the canal; this could save about half a mile and four strokes.

I used a four iron to play over the hedge and into the centre of the field. Forcing my way through the obstacle, I discovered the concealed barbed wire, and left a large piece of my plus fours fastened thereto. Watched by Angus and the crowd, I walked to the centre of the field, where my ball sat squarely on a large cowpat, and studied the lay. Strangely, I could hear a noise like thunder, and the crowd began cheering. I looked around and saw the most enormous damned black bull charging down on me. I swear that it had flames and smoke snorting out of its nostrils, and that his horns were made of brass. Of course, my first instinct was to whip off my tweed jacket and play the beast like a matador but, on reflection, it occurred that my back up plan was probably better. I turned and sprinted for the hedge, accompanied by an enraged bellowing from the bull and the roaring of the disappointed crowd. I dived back through the hedge, losing more of my plus fours on the way, as the bull skidded to a halt and took up a guarding position on the other side of the hedge.

"Well sir," said Angus "ye can consider that one a lost ball and drop a stroke."

"But that was my last ball," I protested.

"Weel sir," he says, "I have a few spares here for sale, five poonds each ye ken."

I paid up and drove up the road towards a resting Ginger; five strokes behind and my odds now going to ten-to-one with no takers.

SPENCER PRESENTED A RATHER EASY TARGET

Now if you know London Road, you will know that the verge is somewhat rougher than an elephants graveyard, but by a combination of brilliant shots I was able to play through the rough and had pulled a stroke back as we came to the top of the hill overlooking the canal bridge; with me now just four strokes down. Ginger was faced with a difficult choice, whether to play a long three iron and attempt to clear the canal, or a short five iron, to drop the ball just short of the water, leaving a difficult two strokes up to the beer garden of the Bull and Butcher. Being four strokes up, Ginger opted for the easier short shot and landed neatly on the canal Towpath.

"Give me the putter Angus" I said. I then putted my ball hard on to the road, from where it rolled one hundred and fifty yards down the hill, coming to a rest at the edge of the bridge, and in a far better lie than Ginger's.

"Tha's quite a put sir," said Angus. Ginger just turned red in the face.

He addressed his ball and drove a good 180 yards up the road. Unfortunately for him, the road ran uphill for 185 yards; the ball landed and then ran all the way back down the hill, bounced over the bridge, and finished up within four feet of mine. The crowd roared its approval; a passing barge hand made rude gestures with his hand and asked Ginger if he could give him a lesson.

"Get stuffed," said Ginger, turning even redder.

"Who are you telling to get stuffed?" said the bargee fellow, leaping the four feet from the barge to the towpath and towering over Ginger.

"Him," said Ginger, pointing up at Angus.

"Well just you watch it mate," said the bargee, leaping the seven feet back onto his boat, which was now heading towards the opposite bank.

Ginger, whose face had now turned quite white, climbed wearily up the canal bank, back on to the road, and looked at his ball, which had miraculously moved another thirty five feet further back down the road, and into a really difficult lie in the gutter. I made a mental note to slip Angus an extra quid at the end of the game.

So it was an iron over the bridge and three quarters of the way up the hill, finding a safe lie in the grass verge on the left hand side. Ginger followed up by dropping a further stroke getting out of his gutter, and I was now only two strokes behind, while the crowd started placing bets again.

Now in theory the next shot was relatively simple; a four iron should clear the crest of the hill and drop into the beer garden of the Bull and

Butcher, the roof of which we could see peeping over the brow of the hill on the right hand side.

"FORE" yelled Ginger, striking out with a three iron. The ball sailed over the brow of the hill and we heard the distant tinkle of broken glass.

"Bally hard luck old chap," I said, addressing my ball with a five iron. I shouted "FORE", smoothly hitting the ball over the crest and well to the right, with not a sound of broken glass to be heard.

We walked up and over the brow of the hill, and into the beer garden, where I found my ball laying beside an ornamental flower tub. Meanwhile, Ginger looked at the golf-ball-sized hole in the lounge window. He went inside; money changed hands; the door opened and a long putt placed him back beside me, only one stroke up. The crowd moved into the bar, while Ginger and I had a pint of beer and a whiskey chaser out in the beer garden as we planned tactics for the next leg - out over the back wall of the pub's beer garden, down a long winding track to Bluebell Woods, through the woods past the glue factory, over the railway line, then through the allotments, before going back out on to Bramley Road beside the Presbyterian Chapel.

I addressed my ball, or rather the two balls which now appeared before me, with a six iron, in order to clear the back wall of the beer garden.

"I'm really going to have to slow down on the refreshments," I told Angus.

"Yesh shur," he said.

I swung and missed.

"Just a practice shot" I said, addressing the ball again. "Fore!" I called, and the ball sailed safely over the wall, landing some ninety yards down the track. Ginger smiled and went and opened the gate.

"Hey, you can't interfere with an obstacle," I protested.

"What, like you didn't open the back door of that house in Henniker Road," he smirked, selecting a number one wood. He smashed his ball through the open gate, narrowly missing a tough-looking farm hand who was about to enter the beer garden.

"You stupid useless swine," he yelled.

"What did he say?" asked Ginger, bellicosely.

"You should have used a nine," said young Rennie Gribbens, diplomatically.

Well, of course, that drive had taken Ginger a good eighty yards further down the track then me. A good brassie shot took me to the edge of the woods; then Ginger using his one wood again blasted his ball up in the direction of the tree line. I was extremely gratified to see his ball hit the very first tree, bounce on to a second, third, and then a fourth, before landing and rolling back to join mine.

"That sounds like a wee woodpecker in yon woods," said Angus. Ginger just glared at him, knowing better than to get into an argument with the club's chief caddy.

The crowd, which was now somewhat smaller, having left two thirds of their number ensconced in the bar of the Bull and Butcher, laughed and nudged each other. They were beginning to smell blood.

We stood and surveyed the tree line, and I was reminded somewhat of the great Amazon jungle; I wouldn't have been surprised to have seen a bally great bear lumbering through the trees. Grabbing our wedges we began to chip our way through the woods.

Ginger made an incautious shot into a small glade, which happened to be full of small button mushrooms; every one of them looking exactly like a golf ball.

So we had another tipple while he examined four or five hundred mushrooms looking for his ball. I didn't have the heart to tell him that I was sitting on it, so - lost ball.

Ginger, now also having run out of balls, passed a fiver to Angus and dropped his new ball behind him, honours even again.

Rather surprisingly, we negotiated the remainder of the woods without incident, except of course for a bit of a scuffle that Ginger had with a member of the crowd; he really had a bit of a temper did Ginger. So eventually we stood at the jungle's edge looking down on to the broad expanse of the glue factory. The caddies compared cards, and it was four hundred and seventy strokes each; what a match, and so close."

"I bet that it hadn't lasted as long as this story," said the oldest member. Spencer ignored him and carried on.

"Ginger hit a cracking drive across the open fields, landing just short of the factory gate. I followed with a bit of a grass cutter and my ball bounced a few times before rolling to a stop thirty yards behind him.

"That's what I would call a 'Mae West' sir," said Angus. "A bit too much top."

We walked down to my ball and I pitched it up to the factory gate; one stroke down again.

50

Desperately holding our breaths, due to the smell emanating from the factory, we continued to play along the boundary fence until we overlooked the railway line.

Now the shot was no problem; a simple four iron over the barbed wire fence, the six foot stream, a small embankment with the railway track on top, a hawthorn hedge on the other side, and then into the ploughed field. No, the problem was: do we climb after the ball, or walk the three quarters of a mile to the footbridge, and then back again on the other side?

Well, old Ginger was in no doubt. He made a nice shot well out into the middle of the ploughed field, and set off for the barbed wire fence.

"Oooh," went the crowd, as he lost a chunk out the seat of his smart chequered trousers on the barbed wire.

"Aaah," went the crowd, as he lost a shoe in the mud and sprawled into the swollen stream.

"Ha ha ha," the crowd laughed, as the four o'clock express roared past, sprinkling him with soot and cinders.

He clawed his way through the hawthorn hedge bottom, and emerged into the ploughed field with all the decorum of a drunken hobo. I played my shot, and as one man, Angus, Rennie, the crowd and I, all turned to our left and headed for the footbridge.

Half an hour later we came back down to the scarecrow, which actually turned out to be a rather morose looking Ginger, who had been standing around waiting, ankle deep in the mud. Certain rough elements in the crowd began singing 'Buddy can you spare a dime'.

It was two simple shots out of the field and into the allotments behind the chapel. We all followed the balls, keeping well up-wind of Ginger, who had apparently crawled through some manure while negotiating the hedgerow.

I played out of my lie in a small gully, and my ball carried to the allotment gates; perfect for a two iron down to the road. Ginger, meanwhile, had got himself into a row with the allotment plot holder where his ball had landed. Apparently the chap wasn't too taken with the idea of Ginger letting fly amongst his prize marrows. Much to the disappointment of the crowd, Ginger took a dropped ball and played up to join me; honours even again.

Angus passed me my niblik and I played a smooth stroke past the left hand side of the chapel, landing just by Bramley Road.

"Seven iron," said Ginger.

"Are you sure, sir?" asked young Rennie, his caddie.

"Yep, I'm going over the chapel roof and landing fifty yards up Bramley Road," said Ginger, as if it was the most obvious thing in the world.

"Pride commeth before a fall," said Angus, and sure enough his ball went straight through the stained glass window, stopping the organ and melodious rendition of 'Abide with me' in its tracks.

"No problem," said Ginger, heading for the chapel door. He went inside and we were treated to the sound of raised voices; the door opened and poor old Ginger hurtled out and landed upside down in the blackberry bush just near the road. Seconds later, the door opened again and his ball followed him.

"Nae problem there then, Meester Woods," old Angus said, as the triumphant sound of 'Onward Christian Soldiers' resounded from the chapel.

Well, the end was in sight; it was a simple couple of long woods up Bramley Road and back into the club car park, then back to the tee and a par five to the first hole. Ginger addressed his ball and delivered a beautiful three hundred yard drive up the verge.

"Beat that," he said, and his jaw dropped six inches as young Belinda, who just happened to be walking past, released her Jack Russell dog, who picked up my ball in his mouth and hared off in the direction of the car park. Five minutes later we all arrived back at the car park, with me two strokes up.

"Where's my ball?" I asked, and a guilty looking Jack Russell dog dropped the badly chewed up remnants of the ball at my feet.

"I've a good mind to make you play that," said Ginger, while Angus produced another five-poond ball from out of his bottomless pockets. We played up past the corner of the clubhouse and back to the tee, with me one stroke up.

Now, I'd played this hole a hundred times, and it was certain that I could play a birdie here; same for Ginger of course, so I was now odds on for the hole and the match.

I finished off the last few mouthfuls from old Angus's flask, and took my shot. Well, I put so much top on it that it rolled forward six inches and stopped.

"I know, Angus," I said, as he opened his mouth, "another Mae West."

"Noo sir," he said. "I was just going to say, what a bloody awful shot."

Ginger stepped up and played an absolute corker of a drive, straight and true up the middle of the fairway. I then did the same and it was all-square with the peg in sight.

A one iron took both of us to within chipping distance of the green, and Ginger played a beauty which trickled gently to within six inches of the hole, and my backers made ready to pay up on their losses. I addressed the ball for what was clearly going to be the most important shot of the match. As I let swing there was a great yell from Ginger, who pretended that he had been stung by a wasp. I wavered, and miss-hit the ball completely. It disappeared skywards and seconds later came down and hit the flag, before dropping into the cup.

Shouts of "You jammy bastard" filled the air, and my supporters claimed their winnings.

Ginger looked devastated, not just because of the girl, but because we all now knew who the best player was. We made our way back to the club bar to celebrate my famous victory, and whom should we see as we entered the bar, none other than the fair Amelia.

I made my way up to her to claim my 'prize'.

"Good evening my dear," I said. "Would you care to play a round of golf with me?"

"Certainly not!" she replied. "I just can't stand the silly game - grown men following a little ball around."

"But we saw you carrying your golf bag out onto the course," I croaked, holding on to the edge of the bar for support.

"Oh, those stick things," she said.

"S s s s sticks" stuttered Ginger, looking as if he was about to pass out.

"Yes, I was bringing those out for my boyfriend who was meeting me from work. Anyway, what girl in her right mind would want to go out with a tramp like you!" she finished, flouncing out of the bar.

Ginger and I looked at each other aghast.

"There's no doubt about it," he said, "the girl's quite insane. We had a real close escape there old chap."

"No doubt at all, she is as mad as a hatter," I replied. "It's lucky we had a drink as a side bet; get them in."

FIVE
The Hunters Tail

Friday night at the club. Dinner was over and the members savoured their port.

"I say," said Spencer, "did I ever tell you of the time that I took part in the greatest golf match of all time?"

"Is it about golf?" asked the oldest member from his chair by the fire.

"Well of course it bally is."

"Then we've heard it," said the oldest member.

"OK then, it's your loss," said Spencer, sounding anything but OK about it.

"Well, there was this time when I hunted the 'Great Man Eating Tiger of Mahatraphur'," said Foggy Winnard.

"Where's Mahatmawotsit?" asked the oldest member.

"Oh it's up in northern India of course," said Foggy. "I was the Northern District Inspector."

"Didn't you work on the railways?" asked the oldest member. "So you were a ticket inspector then," he added, delightedly.

Foggy appeared not to hear him and carried on with his story.

"It was the time of the monsoon, so the memsahib and I had gone up to the hill station for the rainy season."

"That'll be a railway station," came a whisper from the fireplace, which reached every corner of the room.

Now it didn't take long before I heard about the problem in the area; a giant man-eating tiger was on the loose, and it had taken over a hundred of the tastiest hill people.

"You must help us, Muntas Mun," they said.

"Muntas Mun?" queried the oldest member.

"Yes, it means mighty hunter," said Foggy.

"No it doesn't, it means fat belly," said the oldest member, who had served in India.

Well the local Maharajah was a friend of mine; Eton and Cambridge you know, a thoroughly good egg, and it wasn't long before I received a summons to the palace.

"Greetings Muntas Mun," he said.

Foggy tried to ignore the sniggers coming from the direction of the fireplace and gamely carried on.

"You absolutely have got to help us and kill this beast," said Raj, as I liked to call him.

"Yes of course," I told him modestly, "but I may need a little help."

"Of course my dear fellow," he said, "I was thinking of a company of the Twenty Ninth Regiment of Foot; two hundred heavily armed men should do it, especially under your command."

"No, no," I said modestly, "I was meaning someone to carry my suitcase."

"Ah ha, then you could have no finer assistant than my butler Ranjit Singh," he told me picking up a hammer and striking a silver gong. The room appeared to shrink in size as Ranjit Singh entered the audience chamber.

"You rang, your highness," he said, in the deepest voice that I had ever heard. The chap was enormous; about six foot four, built like a brick karsi, and with a beard that a Risalder of Sikh cavalry would have been proud of. Not only that, but he was absolutely immaculate; he wore a dark blue turban and a white uniform that dazzled the eye.

"Now look here," said Raj, "would you mind looking after Mun…. er Winnard here for a day or two while he tracks down and kills the Great Man Eater of Mahatraphur?"

"Your wish is my command," he boomed, looking down at me as if I was some form of loathsome reptile.

So, at dawn the next day Ranjit turned up at the bungalow, carrying an enormous Gladstone bag.

"Are you ready to begin sahib?" he asked me.

"Yes almost," I told him, yawning, and after I had had breakfast, a brief siesta, tiffin, and a few pegs of G & T, we were ready for the off; me in my largest shorts, bush jacket and pith helmet, him in his snow white uniform.

"Here, grab hold of these," I ordered, passing him my hunting rifle, kit bag, folding bed, and suitcase.

We set off with me in the lead, casting around for the tiger's spoor, and him following behind with a stately tread.

After four hours with not so much as a worm cast in sight, I decided that it was time to rest up for the night.

"We shall build bashers here, Ranjit Singh," I told him.

"Why should we do that, sahib?" he asked me, feigning surprise.

"Because I'm not spending the ruddy night in the open, that's why," I told him.

"Then why not spend the night in the bungalow?" he says.

"Spend the night in the bungalow?" I echoed blankly.

"Yes," he said, "it's just behind those bushes; we have come around the complete circle."

"Well I know that, Ranjit Singh," I told him, "I just thought that you might like to spend the night out here, while I go and see the memsahib."

"That's alright sahib, I'll make myself comfortable," he replied heading off towards the palace.

After I had had a scolding off the memsahib over the state of my shorts, which had fallen into a couple of monsoon ditches, we had a meal and I retired to bed early, ready to start again early next morning.

It was barely ten thirty am, when I was awoken by a great trumpeting noise; I looked out of the window and beheld Ranjit, with a ruddy great elephant.

"Be quick, sahib," he shouted, "for we have a report of the man eater dining in the village of Merhutt last night. It is ten miles away so I have borrowed one of the Maharajah's elephants for you to ride on."

Well, I needed no second bidding, and less than two hours later I was ready to mount up and go. Off we set, with Ranjit Singh leading, and me following on my elephant. We hadn't gone more than a mile when we passed two holy men squatting by the side of the road.

"Look at the asshole on that elephant," said one to the other.

Intrigued, I slid off and had a look under the beast's tail; it all looked perfectly normal to me though. Ranjit Singh just smiled.

Two hours later we entered the village, where I was immediately ushered into the presence of the village chief.

Foggy paused and glanced in the direction of the fireplace, where the oldest member appeared to have nodded off.

"Muntas mun," said the chief, "thank goodness you have come. The man eater was here last night. We had two armed guards in the village and this morning they had gone; only their boots were remaining."

"Two of them, eh!" I said, "so the greedy beggar had seconds."

Ranjit Singh came into the room.

"The tiger headed west, sahib," he boomed. "Do you want to go after him?"

"Of course I do," I said. "Unload the elephant and grab the luggage; we'll be on our way within the hour."

Two hours later we left the village behind and headed west, and after an hour I decided to make camp for the night.

"Righto, Ranjit Singh," I said, "we'll build bashers here for tonight by this stream."

"Shall I build one for the both of us, sahib?" he asked.

"Certainly not," I informed him. "Guides and hunters can't share bashers, and anyway I have very high standards of building you know."

I set about cutting down bamboo canes and palm fronds, and quickly constructed a neat little tepee. Nothing fancy, you understand, but big enough for me to curl up in during the night, as well as keeping some of the rain out. I went to find Ranjit Singh to show him how it should be done, and found him sitting on the veranda of the small bungalow that he had built for himself.

"All right then, Ranjit Singh," I said, "enough of this sitting around; I'll light up a fire while you see if you can rustle up some food."

I found two sticks and began to rub them together as I had learned in the Boy Scouts, and after an hour they were beginning to feel distinctly warmer.

My concentration was suddenly broken by the sound of a dinner gong. I turned around and saw Ranjit Singh holding a steaming soup tureen beside an impeccably laid table.

"Dinner is served sahib," he boomed.

I went across and sat down.

"Where did this table and chair come from?" I asked.

"I made them, sahib," he said. "Would you like a glass of wine with your soup?"

Well, after a three-course dinner it was time to retire to our bashers.

"Perhaps you would be safer if I slept in your bungalow, Ranjit Singh," I said.

"As you wish, sahib," he said. "I have taken the precaution of building you a separate bedroom, and have set up your folding camp bed for you.

Presumptuous beggar, I thought to myself.

As it happened, some infernal beast disturbed my sleep, roaring and coughing all night, so next morning I was feeling a little bit fragile, I can tell you.

After breakfast I waited until Ranjit Singh had finished packing and dismantling the bungalow - after all you can't leave the jungle untidy you know - then we set off, me in the lead, with Ranjit Singh following carrying the luggage.

I searched for spoor all day with never the trace of a track anywhere, until, just as I was about to call a halt for the night, I found tracks right beside a waterhole.

"My god, look at this, Ranjit Singh," I said. "These ruddy prints are as big as soup plates."

"Yes, sahib," he said, with exaggerated patience. "This is where I did the washing up last night, and those are the marks of soup plates."

"What? Are you trying to tell me that we've gone round in a circle all day?" I asked him.

"Well actually sahib, this is the third time we have been past here today," he said.

"I don't see how that could happen," I replied.

"Well sahib, the heel on your right boot is an eighth of an inch shorter than the heel on the left, so you are always walking in a clockwise direction," he explained.

I refrained from telling him where I thought my boot should go next.

"We should build a basher here," I told him settling down for a rest.

"No, that's alright sahib," he said. "I'll stand watch tonight. Didn't you hear the man-eater roaring all last night?"

"Is that what it was?" I said. "I thought it was a donkey."

I crawled into the little tepee that I had built the day before, and tried to sleep, and even though Ranjit Singh brought me toast and drinking chocolate, I had a rough night.

The next morning, I looked as if I had spent the night on a dung heap, but Ranjit Singh was still immaculate in a white uniform and grey turban.

"Would you like some breakfast, sahib?" he boomed.

"No, I'll just make do with some eggs and bacon," I said, "and you might as well rustle up some coffee and toast while you're at it," I finished, as he headed for the water hole, and an hour or two later I was ready for the off.

"Follow me, Ranjit Singh," I ordered as I set off, leaving him to pick up the baggage. I entered the jungle and began forcing my way through the dense vegetation. I had gone about two hundred yards when I pushed aside a palm frond and found myself looking straight into two enormous yellow eyes.

Now, as an experienced hunter I knew that in a situation like this one must hold the beasts gaze until the 'weaker will' gave way.

"Don't even think about it," Foggy said to the oldest member, who had opened his mouth to say something.

"So the beast and I tried to out stare each other for several minutes, until, sure enough, he looked away and turned to flee. Well, I was on him like a flash, riding on his back as he raced around the clearing, until eventually I managed to trip him and we both went down, rolling over and over until he began to visibly tire. Quick as a flash, I whipped my hankie out of my shorts pocket and tied his four paws together.

"Quick! Ranjit Singh," I hollered, "come and see." He appeared silently beside me and looked down at the trussed up tiger. "Well, what do you think I should do now?" I asked him.

He thought for a moment, and said, "Perhaps you should scarper sahib, before its mother turns up."

"What do you men its mother?" I said.

"Yes sahib," he says, "that's just a baby; we call them cubs."

"A baby! Well, just how big do these things grow?" I demanded.

"Oh anything up to sixteen feet including the tail," he told me.

"SIXTEEN FEET! Where are the Twenty Ninth Regiment of Foot stationed?" I asked.

"At the palace, but they marched off eastwards two days ago," he said.

"Right," I said, rapidly heading north towards the midday sun.

"Since when has Northern India been south of the equator?" interrupted the oldest member, but Foggy who obviously hadn't heard him carried on with his story.

"So after an hour's hard march, we had covered about eight miles."

"That sounds more like an hour's hard running, to me," commented the oldest member delightedly.

"We'll stop here for lunch," I told Ranjit Singh, and settled down for forty winks while he prepared some food, and a bit later I was woken by the sound of the dinner gong. He had set up a small table, with a rather sumptuous buffet laid out upon it, complete with a bowl of punch. I tucked in, and as I gnawed on a leg of chicken and eyed up the chocolate gateaux I asked the question that had been bothering me for some time.

"Ranjit Singh," I asked him, "where is all this fresh food coming from?"

"From the grocer's shop in the village of Merhutt," he replied.

"But that's miles away," I told him.

"No sahib," he said, "we have never been more than a mile or two away from the village. You are running up quite an account at the shop, you know. I also took the liberty of charging last night's hotel bill to you."

"Hotel bill?" I spluttered. "Do you mean to tell me that while I was shivering in that damn basher you were in a hotel?"

"But of course, sahib. Where better for listening out for the man-eater? Also, while you were sleeping I received a message from the Maharaja; the beast has been spotted near the ruined temple of Turkut, eight miles to the south. We should set off at once."

"Look, it's about time you took a turn at leading," I told him. "I'll follow up with the elephant gun." It took us about four hours to cover the eight miles back, though I would swear that it was more like twenty eight miles.

"Ah ha, there's a cave," I finally called to Ranjit Singh. "The perfect place to rest up for the night."

We entered the cave, and the first thing that struck me was the large amount of well-gnawed bones strewn all over the cave floor.

"It looks as if the dirty beggars who stopped here last couldn't be bothered to clear up before they left," I told Ranjit Singh, who was looking around with a worried expression.

"I do not think that it is a good idea to stop here sahib," he said.

"Why on earth not?" I replied. "It's warm and dry."

"Yes, and that is precisely why the tiger has made his lair here. Don't you know that these are all human bones?"

"Alas, poor Yorrick, I knew him well," I said picking up a skull, but Ranjit had already left the cave.

I didn't want the fellow getting lost, so I hurried out after him.

At last we reached the temple ruins of Turkut, and Ranjit Singh started constructing a smart little hut in the corner of an overgrown courtyard, while I walked around examining the remains of the wall carvings. Well you wouldn't believe the graphic content of them; naked men and women doing all sorts of impossible things; the memsahib would have been absolutely horrified. I found myself wishing that I had brought my brownie camera to record them, so that I could make a formal complaint to the Maharaja of course, when the dinner gong went and I sat down to a rather nice three course meal. There was even an ice statue centre piece, and

THERE WAS OBVIOUSLY ONLY ONE MAN FOR THE JOB!

candles in a silver candelabra. I didn't even bother asking where it had all come from. Ranjit Singh served the meal, dressed as usual in his immaculate white uniform.

I'm going to bring that chap down a peg or two, I thought to myself. When he takes the dishes down to the water hole to wash them, I'll take the slops down there and accidentally throw them over his nice white uniform.

So after I had had a glass of port, he disappears in the direction of the river and I shortly followed up with the bucket of leftovers and other slops. It didn't take long before I spotted the back of his grey turban peeping over a bush. I cheerfully chucked the bucket over the bush saying,

"Where are you Ranjit Singh?"

The water buffalo which had been settling down for the night on the other side of the bush jumped to its feet and looked at me with red rimmed eyes, and I could see its slops-encrusted nostrils flaring. I needed no second warning and sprinted for the river.

"Yes sahib, nothing like a cold bath after looking at those cheeky wall carvings," said Ranjit Singh as I dived past him into the river.

"Watch out for the crocodile sahib," he said rather pointlessly as I came out even quicker then I had dived in, minus a large piece of my shorts.

"I'm surprised that you missed the water buffalo," he said.

"Oh, I didn't miss it," I replied wearily.

I circled my way back to the temple ruins, investigating several water holes, dung heaps and thorn bushes on the way, and an hour or so later I wandered back into the camp where Ranjit Singh had already made cocoa and had turned my bed down for me.

Exhausted, I slumped into bed and drifted off to sleep, listening to the roars of the tiger somewhere out in the jungle.

The next morning, bright and early, I was up and having a wash and shave.

"Did you hear the tiger last night, Ranjit Singh?" I asked.

"No sahib," he said, "all I could hear was the croaking of a bullfrog down by the waterhole."

After a spot of breakfast and several cups of coffee I was ready for the off.

"Where's the gun, Ranjit Singh?" I asked.

"I don't know sahib," he said, "You were carrying it yesterday."

"I can't recall that," I lied. "Be a good chap and go and find it."

I was treated to one of his reptile looks, and he strode off to the north.

He was gone for around six hours, and while he was gone I passed the time studying the erotic wall carvings.

I almost jumped out of my skin as he boomed over my shoulder.

"I have returned with the gun, sahib." I stopped the sketch I was making of three very athletic people doing something that was clearly quite impossible.

"Where was it?" I enquired.

"You must have dropped it when you fell into that cess pit about half a mile back," he replied.

"Half a mile," I echoed. "You've been gone an awful long time for half a mile.

"Yes, sahib," he says. "I called in at the village shop; we were running low on nutmeg and garlic cloves."

"Never mind that," I replied, checking over the gun. It wasn't loaded. "Better pass me a couple of bullets, I've a feeling that we may soon need them."

"Bullets, sahib? I have no bullets," he said.

"Now look here, Ranjit Singh," I told him, "bearers are always responsible for the bullets."

"That is true, sahib, but I am not a bearer, I am a butler," he replied.

"So all we have, to tackle this man-eater which has eaten over a hundred people, is my folding pocket knife with two blades and a spike for getting stones out of horses' hooves then," I said.

"Surely the perfect implement for building a trap with," he told me.

"You really must try to stop anticipating what I was about to say, Ranjit Singh," I replied.

"Righto then," I said, "we'll head for the cave, and each of us will build a trap for the beast, somewhere between here and there. We'll soon see who can kill tigers."

Little did he know about my highly refined Boy Scout training; I'd have the last laugh yet.

A couple of hours later I stood back and admired my handiwork; several saplings had been bent over and tied down, and an elaborate series of trip ropes and nooses would snare and trap the beast. Ranjit Singh appeared silently beside me resplendent in his white uniform.

"Have you completed it, sahib?" he boomed.

"Yes, Ranjit Singh," I replied. "Look and learn. The tiger comes down the path here, moves to his left to avoid this protruding bush, puts his foot here and …" PTWANG!! I found myself suspended by one leg, twelve feet above the ground.

"Stop standing there like a flaming butler and get me down," I bawled. He kicked at a peg that I had hammered into the ground and I hurtled down, landing on my head, and completely crushing my best pith helmet in the process.

"Wipe that supercilious smile of your face and let's have a look at your effort," I said, heading up the track.

"Wait, sahib," he called as I rounded the corner.

It will be a cold day in hell before I wait for a butler, I thought as I walked even faster.

WHOOOSH!! The perfectly level path suddenly disappeared, and I plunged down into a twenty foot deep pit; the sides were as smooth as glass and the top was ringed with barbed wire. Ranjit Singh's face appeared above me.

"I see that you have discovered my trap," he called down. "Never mind, I have a ladder here for you to climb out." Wearily I climbed up the ladder and exited the pit.

"How could you have dug out that hole and got rid of all the soil in two hours?" I demanded. "That would need fifty men."

"Sixty-Five actually, sahib. I hired them from the village on your account," he said.

"Well I don't like it, so you can jolly well get them back to fill it in. The tiger would have to be a ruddy idiot to fall in there," I told him, while I tried to brush the mud from my shorts.

"You are absolutely right, of course," he said, with that knowing smile covering his face.

Well at this point the monsoon decided to give us a bit of rain, and three seconds later I was soaked to the skin.

"I'm going to shelter in the cave," I said. "You go back and collect our luggage."

I headed north while Ranjit Singh made off in the opposite direction, sheltering under a large umbrella which had appeared as if by magic from nowhere.

I soon reached the cave and gratefully hurried inside, where I found myself staring into two enormous yellow eyes; they were as big as saucers and the fires of hell burnt in their depths. I held the gaze, but something must have broken my concentration for I briefly looked away, and quick as a flash a mighty clawed paw grabbed the front of my bush jacket and pulled me further into the cave."

Foggy paused to allow the laughter from the area of the fireplace to die down.

"Gentlemen, I swear to you that I looked death in the face, and death was wearing a rather smart black and yellow fur dinner jacket. The man-eater, for it was he, licked his lips and tried to make up his mind as to where to start lunch, when suddenly a flaming firebrand was thrust over my shoulder and the giant shape of Ranjit Singh filled the entrance to the cave. The tiger backed off to the back of the cave, and Ranjit Singh dragged me outside to where the rain had just finished.

"Quick, sahib, take the firebrand and keep the man-eater in the cave, while I build a large bonfire across the entrance," he said.

And within minutes a most enormous bonfire, giving the beast no chance of getting out, covered the entire cave entrance.

"Did you notice, sahib?" he asked me, "those rocks in the cliff face above the cave entrance are quite loose. I bet that we could start a landslide and seal off the cave with the tiger inside."

"I was wondering how long it would be before you spotted that," I said.

Quick as a flash he shinned up the vertical cliff face, while I warmed my hands at the bonfire and wished that I had some bread, so that I could make some toast.

Then, two minutes later, there was a great booming shout:

"Watch out below, rocks coming down!" and I leapt aside as a thousand tons of rocks and boulders crashed down, completely burying the cave entrance, and incidentally extinguishing my fire.

Well, that was the end of the man-eaters reign of terror, and I returned to the palace in triumph. I was the hero of the hour, I can tell you. Raj laid on a triumphal procession, with me leading the way, followed by bands playing and maidens strewing flower petals, then Ranjit Singh was following some way behind riding on a damn great white elephant, and holding a golden umbrella. A contingent of the 24th Rifles followed up the rear. The crowd politely waited until I had gone past before they started cheering, and Ranjit Singh was waving at them, as if he had had something to do with killing the tiger.

Raj gave me a new title; it was, Manet Tuk Berhenti Muckrat, which means Him who speaks with great wisdom.

"No, it doesn't," said the oldest member. "It means 'He who speaks from the great orifice between his legs'."

SIX
The Steel Soldier

Several of the members had been telling war stories, tales of daring, of heroic acts and skulduggery.

"Wars aren't just about fighting you know," said the Professor, "wars are actually won by the boffins and backroom boys."

The oldest member wasn't having that.

"Nonsense," he growled," wars are won by soldiers!"

"There is a lot of truth in that statement as well," continued the Professor, "let me explain."

During the last conflict, there was a spell from September 1939 until May 1940 which was known as the 'Phoney War'. We and the French sat in the great fortifications of the Maginot Line, while the Germans sat in their Siegfred Line and thumbed their noses at us.

Being a scientist I had been drafted into a special unit, whose purpose in life was to invent and develop 'War Winning Weapons'. We were a mixed bunch, scientists inventors, engineers, plus of course loads of civil servants; but we all had just one aim in life, to invent the weapon that would win the war for us.

There was 'Blind Pew', actually his real name was Algy Pew, and very early on he had come up with the 'Lightning Light', a sort of searchlight that worked by magnifying the light beam through a series of lenses and mirrors. It gave out a light so bright that anyone looking into the beam would be blinded. The potential was enormous, we would be able to take it to the Maginot Line, shine it along the German Lines and blind all the Germans; and then while they were arranging for guide dogs and white sticks, we would just walk in and win the war.

It could be fitted to our aircraft and tanks, and any German looking at them would be blinded, thus giving our boys an incredible advantage. It was soon built and we transported it to the Maginot Line for testing. Lets face it, what better guinea pigs could there be than Nazi Soldiers?

'B Day' arrived and Algy was all set up to start his machine, it hissed and clicked as the light intensity built up, then Algy threw the switch. A brilliant beam of light flashed across no mans land into the German fortifications.

The dastardly Germans immediately deployed their counter weapon, a giant mirror went up opposite and the beam was reflected straight back. Straight at poor old 'Blind Pew'.

The next potential 'War Winner' was the 'Unsinkable Ship', Bertram Smith was the brains and instigator behind that one. All we needed to combat the U boat menace, was a ship that they couldn't sink. The answer seemed obvious, ships were being sunk by having torpedoes fired into their hulls, making a big hole. They then filled up with water and sunk.

Bertie proposed that we built a ship with three hulls, they call them trimarans now, but our version was to be three hundred feet long, with three hulls welded together side by side.

Trials were conducted with a model, in a great water tank behind Whitehall. We floated the three foot long model 'Unsinkable Ship'; then Bertie punctured the right hand hull. Within three minutes the model boat had turned on to its side, and then it plunged down to the bottom of the test tank. Back to the drawing board we all went.

"It's just a matter of stability," said Bertie, "all we have to do is allow water into the left hand hull at the same rate as it goes into the right hand one."

The model was recovered and patched up, Bertie developed a series of float switches and pumps in the two outer hulls, so if one of them allowed water ingress, it was immediately balanced out in the other hull. Back to the water test tank we went for further trials. Bertie punctured the right hand hull, and we watched as the unsinkable model ship settled lower and lower into the water, until it disappeared smoothly beneath the surface, all the while maintaining perfect stability.

"I see what the problem is," said Bertie, "it just needs more hulls, probably six.

The trials went on, continually refining Bertie's design, until at last the twelve hulled 'Unsinkable Ship' was ready to go into production.

It was built in the greatest secrecy, Bertie and his crew made the ship ready and set off on their maiden voyage to America. Unfortunately the

'Unsinkable Ship was so slow that the war was over by the time it arrived back in this country. Not only that, but the crew had eaten all the cargo.

Next Arnold Ackerman designed the 'Rocket Powered Fighter Plane'; it only needed a twenty foot square to take off from. We weren't so sure about the landing area, because no one had ever flown one before. The rocket theory was well known; we just had to leave out the multi coloured star effects, from the gunpowder that propelled it. The design team hurried into production and it was quickly built, not surprising considering all the talents we had at our disposal. Although in my opinion, I was the only one there with the vision to see what was really needed.

We tested the 'Rocket Fighter' on Salisbury Plain. It was about thirty foot long and four foot wide. At front end there was a little glass bubble though which the pilot could see; and it was fitted with a forward facing single cannon in the middle of the nose cone.

The rear twenty feet were filled with the propellant which acted as the en-gine. The whole rocket was fixed to a long wooden pole which supported the aircraft before take off, and provided stability during flight.

   Direction was given by the pilot, to climb he would shift his weight to the rear, to dive he had to move forwards. He could move left or right by transferring his weight to either side of the rocket. For landing, Arnold had decided that the pilot would be better off jumping out and parachuting down, after first of all having shot down lots of German planes of course.

The call went out through the RAF for a volunteer test pilot, but once the volunteers found out what the job involved, they quickly changed their minds. At last enough was enough, if we wanted to win this war Arnold would just have to test fly the rocket himself.

   We picked a fine day and took out the giant rocket and set it up. The firing base resembled a large milk bottle. We quickly assembled the fuselage to the pole and set up the rocket facing skywards. Arnold came out of his truck dressed in a flying suit and wearing his parachute. The ground crew fastened him into the rocket, and then ran like mad for cover.

   Now it was down to me, I stepped forward, lit a match and applied the flame to the rockets blue touch paper. As it smouldered away I turned and walked slowly and calmly back to the sandbagged firing point, exactly as Arnold had instructed me. He should have instructed me to walk a bit faster, because there was a loud roar, and then a great flash of smoke and flames washed over me, blackening my white technicians overalls, and singeing my hair.

I turned around and watched in awe as the big rocket shuddered, then shot into the air at an incredibly fast speed. Up it sped faster than a speeding bullet and disappeared from sight. There was a distant muffled boom, which I now know was the sonic boom of the rocket passing through the sound barrier.

Everyone was cheering and waving, telling each other what they were going to do once we had won the war. Until someone said that Arnold had been gone for three minutes now, what time is he coming back down?

A dozen pairs of binoculars looked up into the sky, then we saw it, the most fantastic firework display of all time, great cascades of coloured stars falling earthwards.

Oooh, Ahhh, we all went, then quickly shut up as we remembered that this wasn't actually supposed to be a firework display.

The next 'War Winner' was a bit of a joint effort, we would completely demoralise the German Army, so they would run across no mans land and surrender in their thousands.

It was a well known fact that none of them really wanted to fight anyway, and this little idea should do the trick alright. We would set up a giant Cinema Screen above our lines and show the Germans opposite, war films. That demonstrated just how good fighters our boys were, and how hopeless it would be trying to fight us.

The screen was enormous about one hundred feet square, and we had to build a special high powered projector to show the films on it, that's where some of Algy Pews work finally came in to its own. We set up some enormous speakers so that we could broadcast the sound to the Germans opposite, all re-dubbed in German of course.

That night we prepared to show the Germans a film demonstrating British invincibility. Henry the Fifth was the film, stirring speeches, gallant English Longbow-men defeating an arrogant bullying foe. The film finished and we could hear a lot of applause coming from the direction of the German Line, and quite a bit of booing and jeering coming from the French Troops to our right.

Undeterred we set up and went again the following night, this time the Film was Waterloo. The Germans had obviously packed thousands of troops into their Siegfred Line tonight, and we could hear them clapping and cheering as the screen lit up. We didn't mind, they would soon change their tune when they saw British Troops really hammering an arrogant bullying enemy.

The Germans applauded from the very beginning, but when Blucher and his German Army arrived on Napoleon's flank, it brought the house down; the soundtrack was literally drowned out by the cheers coming from the German Lines. At the end of the film as the French ran, and the Germans mopped them up, the applause from our front was unremitting, and so were the bricks and stones being thrown into our positions by the French Troops off on our right.

The next day we had a conference, even though the French had a sulk on and refused to take part, we decided to have one more try, something a bit further in the past perhaps.

That night we set up and showed Joan of Arc, valiant British troops fighting an evil arrogant foe, and having to deal with a Witch as well. The Germans appeared to be enjoying the show immensely, and cheered and whistled every scene. Then we came to the scene where the English tortured, and then put little Joan of Arc to the fire.

That was it, hundreds of French Troops stormed in from the right, and the biggest Anglo French battle since Waterloo developed along our Lines, as British and French fought each other again. All the while being applauded by the Germans sat opposite. Finally the fighting was broken up and the French withdrew back to their own fortifications, but not before they had burnt down our screen and destroyed the projector.

We held a meeting to try and find out what had gone wrong, and the answer was obvious, we had been fighting the French for nine hundred years, of course all of our war films were about fighting them, the next one scheduled was Trafalgar. We returned to England to think of something else.

We thought of the 'Sticky Bomb', a sort of grenade that would stick to German tanks or vehicles. The problem was of course that the 'Super Glue' we developed really did like sticking to soldiers hands.

The troops didn't think much of our 'Super Pogo Sticks', designed to allow the men to pogo over barbed wire and minefields. The fatal flaw was when they where in full bounce, army braces were just not strong enough to withstand the forces involved, and the troops invariably arrived at the objective with their trousers around their ankles.

They didn't even like the mobility skates, a whole company of two hundred men being towed along the road on roller-skates by a single truck. It worked fine until the first man fell over at 20mph. The resultant pile-up of soldiers was forty foot deep.

Undeterred we turned our skills to aircraft defences, and developed an 'Anti Aircraft Net'. The idea was to have a series of captive barrage balloons, and then between them we could suspend large nets, so any enemy aircraft flying along would be caught up in the net, allowing us to shoot it down.

Why we could deploy a complete circle of nets around any of our cities, making them completely bombproof. Even if it was extremely unlikely that the Germans would ever have a plane with a long enough range to reach Britain.

The next 'War Winner', was called the 'Dog Destructor', it was Fergie Ferguson's idea so he took charge of all its development. It was quite simple really, we recruited German Dogs, there were 'German Shepherds', 'Rotweillers', 'Dobermans', 'Wiemarers', have you noticed how many different German Breeds there are?

Fergie designed a bomb coat that fitted onto the dogs back. The coat was covered in dog fur and fitted with dozens of detonators. The plan was that the dogs would be fed on nothing but sausages; they would then be fitted into their 'Bomb Coats'. And released into no mans land. Their keen noses would smell the sausages cooking in the Siegfred Line, and across they would race. Hearing them whining outside the bunkers, the Germans would open their steel doors and look out. Upon seeing the rather fat German dogs they would invite them inside and start to pat them, As soon as they touched the dog's back, 'KABOOOOOM!' No more German bunker. Yes it was definitely foolproof.

We constructed the bomb coat and covered the top with faux Alsatian fur. Out on to Salisbury Plain we went with Rex, the volunteer German Shepherd Dog. Fergie led the gallant guinea pig out on to the test range and proceeded to fit him with his bomb coat.

There was a clockwork motor which would bring a dummy hand down to pat Rex on the back, as soon as Fergie was safely inside the Firing Bunker. Eventually the coat was fitted,.

"There's a Good Boy," said Fergie.

Rex immediately lay on his back to have his belly tickled, "KA-BOOOOOM!"

The next day two policemen arrived, and served the Commanding General a summons for cruelty to animals. He was fined £200, and the dogs left for new homes.

The next brainwave came from Oswald Marks, and as usual it was simple and foolproof. Every member of the British Army must grow a moustache.

Then on the command, they would all trim their moustaches into little Hitler toothbrush moustaches. They would comb their hair forward over their foreheads, and change into grey jackets.

The whole Army was then to advance. All the Germans would immediately start Hitler Saluting our men, and while their right hand was up in the air, our boys could shoot them. Not only that, but once word got out what our men looked like, we wouldn't have wanted to be in the Fuhrer's shoes.

Oswald excitedly took his idea to the Commanding General. The General sat and listened, stroking his large handlebar moustache; he then reached for paper and pen and started writing orders. The next day two Military Policemen came, collected Oswald and put him on a plane bound for the North Pole Weather Station, and that's where he spent the next six years.

Then the 'Brass' decided that we needed a weapon to breech the Siegfred Line, so we could achieve the vital breakthrough and march on Berlin. We got our heads together and put our inventiveness into overdrive. There were three ways that we could proceed, over it, through it, or under it.

We built a scale model of the weakest part of the Siegfred Line, and studied it. It didn't look very weak to us, a mile deep, hundreds of concrete pill boxes and bunkers, minefields, barbed wire, thirty foot deep ditches, thousands of machine guns, hundreds of artillery pieces and tanks, it would take an army to crack it. Someone reminded us that we did actually have an army. We just needed to open the door for it to get in.

73

Harry Embree came up with a solution, we could go over it. We didn't have the resources to equip and train a parachute army, which would mean designing and building transport aircraft. Plus the training of a complete Division as paratroopers, a troop type that the Brass were convinced could never work in practice. New equipment, parachutes, the list was endless. No it needed something a lot simpler if we were to succeed.

Harry's idea was to design and build a one man balloon harness; each soldier would have his own helium filled balloon attached to his shoulders. He would wear lightweight clothing and carry just a sub machine gun, ammunition and grenades. He would climb up into the sky, by emptying ballast weights from his trouser pockets, and descend again by pulling a cord and releasing helium from his balloon.

All we would need was for a wind to be blowing in an easterly direction, and it would waft our 'Balloon Troops' over the Siegfred Line. Once over, the troops would descend, go into the bunkers through their back doors, capture them and allow our army across and through, then next stop Berlin.

Out we went to the proving grounds on Salisbury Plain, and Harry fitted on his harness while the engineers inflated the one man balloon. As the balloon began to fill it unfolded and began to rise. Bigger and bigger it grew, and we held on to Harry's legs to prevent him from flying away. The balloon was about fifteen feet across and shaped like a ball.

At last it was fully inflated and we let him go, he rose an inch from the ground and then settled back down again. Harry began taking the stones, which were acting as ballast, from his pockets and dropping them. The one inch hops gradually increased to three foot hops, a wind blew up and he was off in great fifty foot long hops, but never more than three foot from the ground.

"Watch out Harry," we all yelled as he headed for the barbed wire entanglements three hundred yards downwind. But Harry hopped gracefully into the middle of the wire and became entangled. We saw him struggling and that did the trick, he floated back up into the air minus his trousers. Levelling off he floated on at a height of around thirty feet, holding his hands in front of his groin.

We ran behind, excitedly keeping our balloonist in view as the wind got stronger and Harry's rate of drift increased, soon we couldn't keep up and he was heading for a small wood.

"Let some gas out," we were all shouting, but there was no way that he was going to raise his hands and expose himself to the female members of the pursuing group.

At last he reached the trees smashing through branches, hitting tree trunks, until finally his balloon was pierced and he hurtled the thirty feet down to the ground, landing trouserless in the middle of a blackberry bush.

We walked back to the trucks congratulating ourselves on the success of the test, while an ambulance took Harry to the Military Hospital.

Things moved swiftly from there, guided by Harry from his hospital bed, we increased the balloon size to twenty three feet, and had them made up in a sky blue material, so the Germans wouldn't see them going over.

It was decided that the Balloon Troopers would number a thousand men in the first unit and would begin their training immediately. They were divided into sub units of one hundred men, called 'Rubbers', and each Rubber was subdivided into ten, ten man units called 'Johnnies'. The training proceeded brilliantly, and a week later we boffins were called into a meeting with the General Commanding.

"Are the troops ready for action yet?" He wanted to know.

"No," we told him, "we need another three weeks."

"Now look here," he said, "you have been training for one week and three hundred of your men are in hospital, in three weeks time you will not have any men left"

He certainly had a point; we had been losing around forty men a day, due mainly to broken legs, or cuts and bruises.

"How about another week?" asked Harry who had rejoined the team and was still on his crutches.

"Certainly not, you men have injured more of our troops than the Germans have," he informed us, "I need some results now,"

There was no point in arguing; besides we wanted to see our Balloon Troops in action; so the unit packed the balloons into their containers and entrained for France and the Maginot Line.

Four days later we were in position opposite the Germans weakest point, getting ready to penetrate.

Sickness and further accidents had reduced our headcount to six hundred, so we had six Rubbers in two packets of three.

We weren't too bothered; we still had plenty of Johnnies for the job, deployed all along our front.

A Division of infantry was moved up to the front line, and stood by, ready to advance, into the welcoming captured emplacements and bunkers of the Siegfred Line.

At last the weather forecast was perfect, a four mile an hour wind would be blowing to the east, perfect for wafting our rubbers over the Fortified Line. 'F' hour (Flight hour) was set for 10pm; we would 'F' the enemy under the cover of darkness.

At 9.45pm all the Johnnies were standing up, and inflating their balloons. At exactly 10pm the rubbers were released and rose silently into the air.

"Hands up all those who think that the wind suddenly changed direction," said the Professor, every member of the Club raised their hand.

Well you are quite wrong, the wind continued to blow gently to the east and the Johnnies all silently rose fifty feet into the air. They drifted silently towards the dark German front line, while we watched until they disappeared from sight.

Then slapping each others backs, and making plans for meeting up, after the war finished in a couple of weeks, we headed for the Officers Club and a celebratory drink.

What happened next was related to us by one of the few survivors of that night. The Balloon Troops take off and approach to the Siegfred Line was fine, text book stuff in fact. But as they passed over the line of gun positions, large barrage balloons rose rapidly into the air in front of them, and those balloons had big nets strung between them.

Our balloon Troops sailed straight into the nets, and the Germans lit them up with spotlights. Air rifles and shotguns began to pop away, and into the bag went all of our Johnnies. One or two managed to descend into no mans land and escape back to our lines, to tell their tale.

Back we went to Salisbury Plain and studied our scale model; we obviously weren't going over, so how about going under?

The answer was staring us in the face; we would tunnel under the Germans, come up in their rear, march one hundred thousand men through the tunnel and head for Berlin.

We called in mining engineers and explained the problem. How long would it take a team of tunnellers to dig a roadway for five miles under the Maginot and Siegfred Lines we asked?

They pursed their lips and estimated around ten years. How far in four months we wanted to know? Around this area, they said pointing out a spot fractions of an inch from the start point on our model, leaving around four foot to be completed. I did an estimate, that would take twenty years, I said. Or thirty they replied cheerfully.

That was no good at all, "We need a Tunnelling Machine," said Nick Tomaci, and so the Giant Mole was developed. It took several weeks to design and even longer to build, the main problem was automotive power. It didn't take me long to come up with the answer however.

If we took plutonium atoms and split them, then contained the resultant explosion, the atoms would continue to split other atoms, it would in effect become a self contained continuous explosion producing great heat. The heat could boil water, producing steam which would drive turbines.

The turbines would drive generators producing unlimited electricity. The steam would then go through condensers, return to water to be boiled again, giving us a very powerful self regenerating engine. The Tomaci Engine, as I called it, was quickly built and worked perfectly.

The Giant Mole was indeed impressive, it was fifty feet long and it had a great rotary cutting device on the front. We took it out onto the Salisbury Plain proving ground for its trials.

The mighty machine was set on a 45 degree ramp pointing towards the ground, while Nick climbed aboard and prepared to dig a tunnel.

The hatches closed and he engaged the digging disc, round it spun with thousands of smaller blades whirling and spinning all over it. He pressed the release lever and the machine slid down the ramp and hit the earth, the blades gripped and the Giant Mole slid into the ground like a knife into butter.

We all cheered, and began talking about what we were going to do after the war, until someone said.

"So where has Nick actually gone?"

We all rushed to the tunnel entrance, and watched as it collapsed in on itself and disappeared from view. We scratched our heads until someone shouted.

"Over there!"

Sure enough a gigantic mole hill had appeared half a mile down the field. We jumped into our cars and trucks and drove down to the mole-hill.

"Over there!" shouted someone else, and we all headed for the next mole-hill, that had appeared another half a mile ahead.

So it went on, for mile after mile; we would rush to the next mole-hill, and then another would appear half a mile ahead. Ten miles on and the Giant Mole passed underneath that Stonehenge place, all the nicely balanced stones buckled and leaned as the tunnel caused subsidence under them, and down half of them crashed. Leaving the Neolithic temple lying around in ruins.

Shortly after that the trail ran cold. The Mole must have dived and disappeared into the earth.

Sadly we returned to base, and began an inquest into what had gone wrong.

"Who designed the steering?" I wanted to know.

Everyone looked at everyone else.

"Was it Nick?" I demanded.

"No, Nick designed the cutting blade," seemed to be the general consensus.

"So there is no steering system then, we will have to sort that out." I said.

The next day as we sat discussing steering systems, who should walk into the laboratory but Nick. We crowded around him asking what had happened.

It appeared that the Mole had just kept on going, rising close to the surface every now and again, and then diving. Eventually the machine had come up on the sea bed, promptly flooded and stopped.

He had bailed out and floated to the surface, where after a few hours he had been picked up by an Air Sea Rescue Launch and brought ashore.

He was only sure of one thing now; never again would he get involved in another Giant Mole.

So it was back to the drawing board again, and we studied the scale model. We had tried going over it, tried going under it, that just left going through it.

We wracked our brains and thought and thought, we were the finest scientific minds in the country, even the world; surely we could come up with something.

Then I had a flash of divine inspiration, I rushed over to the blackboard and began to sketch out my idea, the team gathered around and everyone got very excited. People were putting their own ideas into the pot, and the project quickly began to take shape.

I drew up hundreds of sheets of plans, and the engineering teams rushed things in to production. The weapon began to take shape, and this was definitely going to win the war for us. We started discussing plans about what we were going to do after it was all over.

Within a matter of weeks it was ready and we transported the component parts down to Salisbury Plain and assembled the weapon. The generals turned out in force to watch as we unveiled the 'Steel Soldier'.

He stood fifty feet high, and was built of iron and steel. He was dressed in an iron British Army uniform, and had a gigantic steel helmet on his iron head. Great iron boots and a steel sledge-hammer completed the awesome figure. The commanding general came over and asked me to explain how it worked.

I told him that it was fully articulated, was driven by the new Tomaci Engine which gave it tremendous power.

It was bomb, and bullet proof, but best of all we had built an electronic brain inside its great head, which made it think exactly like a British Soldier.

The General was impressed and asked us for a demonstration, we hurried to put our giant through his paces. I pulled the switch in his heel the engine engaged, electricity flowed into his brain and the motors that controlled his limbs bust into life. The giant looked around and then stood waiting.

I spoke into the radio transmitter, walk forwards, I commanded. The giant took a step forward and then another, the assembled boffins and brass hats applauded as he walked down to the end of the field turned around and walked back, fully under my command.

He came to a halt in front of us.

"What else can he do?" asked the General.

I ordered the Steel Soldier to turn to his right, he did so. Now to his front was a row of pill-boxes, concrete bunkers, and barbed wire entanglements with some obsolete tanks dotted around.

"Attack!" I ordered him; he raised his great thirty foot long tungsten steel sledge-hammer and strode towards the defences, his enormous feet set off mine after mine, to no effect at all.

He paused in front of the first concrete bunker, his mighty hammer went into the air then crashed down, the bunker split into half and he stamped up and down on it pulverising it to dust, seconds later he was on his way to the next one, it suffered the same fate. He picked up a tank and hurled it straight into the front of another pill-box, destroying both the pill-box and the tank. .Next he picked up a great mass of barbed wire, and tore it into shreds.

Within minutes the whole area had been demolished, and he was looking for something else to attack. Stand still, I ordered into the transmitter, and the Steel Soldier stood still. The audience burst into rapturous applause, and everyone agreed that here was the decisive, 'War Winning Weapon.'

The giant robotic soldier was dismantled and taken over to France in the greatest secrecy. A week later we reassembled him behind one of the great concrete block houses in the Maginot Line, well concealed from prying German eyes.

At last we were ready to go, and win the war at a stroke. All the top brass turned up and took up seats overlooking the German positions. I set up my transmitter and spoke into it.

"Go forwards," there was a few seconds delay then the gigantic Steel Soldier strode out from behind the Blockhouse.

"Turn left," I ordered.

He turned left and continued to walk towards the German Siegfred Line. As he reached our edge of no mans land I ordered him to stop. He did so and stood looking across at the German bunkers and pill-boxes.

"Show Hitler what you think of him," I ordered. He raised a mighty steel arm and gave an enormous two fingered gesture towards the German Lines.

The watching Dignitaries broke into loud applause. I was enjoying this.

"Attack!" I ordered and the Steel soldier hefted his huge hammer and began to stride purposefully towards the Siegfred Line.

He was about a third of the way across no mans land, when disaster struck. A gigantic fifty foot tall figure stood up from behind a German blockhouse and began to stride out into no mans land from the German side.

We all grabbed our binoculars and took a look. Our Steel Soldier stood watching and its steel mouth dropped open, as a fifty foot tall Iron Maiden wiggled its way across no mans land towards us.

It stopped in front of the Steel Soldier and a great hand reached down and inched up an iron petticoat. It waved a shapely twenty five foot long steel leg, and then continued towards us. The Steel Soldier turned around and began following the Iron Maiden.

"Stop!" I ordered into the transmitter.

His great arm came up and I was given an enormous steel two fingered gesture. 'Dammit' we had given the metal monster a 'Soldier's Brain,' and forgotten what soldiers liked most of all, 'GIRLS'.

The spectators ran for cover as the two metal giants, stopped in the car park and trampled the Dignitaries' staff cars' into scrap.

They then walked off in the direction of Paris together, holding iron hands.

"Back to the drawing board then guys," I sighed, "it's the 9th of May, and we really must find a way of breaking through the Siegfred Line."

"So what did you do next," asked the oldest member.

"That night the Germans invaded Belgium and Holland, and a couple of days later we were heading for Dunkirk," finished the professor.

SEVEN
The King of the Cannibal Isles

The wind howled around the weathered stonework of the Lyre Club, and the rain hurled itself against the windows and doors; thunder and lightning filled the sky. Captain Jonah turned away from the window and said,

"This reminds me of the great South Seas Typhoon, when my ship went down and I became a king."

He had our attention, so he continued.

"It was on the good ship Venus, by gad you should have seen us; the figurehead was a woman in bed..."

"All right, that's enough of that. Just get on with the story," interrupted the oldest member.

"Well," said the Captain, "we were sailing out of Singapore, laden with a cargo of baked beans and Scotch whisky; cargo for the windward Isles. The old lugger had seen better days and this was my first voyage in her. We cast off and immediately ran down a couple of sampans. I was leaning over the aft rail, apologising to the boat people floundering in the water, when we struck an American battleship which was moored in the Roads; I just hadn't noticed it.

We bounced off, leaving a long brown skid mark on their immaculate paintwork.

"God-damn stupid limeys," shouted down the officer of the watch.

"Get lost, you Yankee pimp," I bawled back, speeding up as I heard the call to action stations sound through the battleship.

With no more than a couple of scrapes, and a row with the skipper of the Jahore ferry, we cleared the harbour and sailed west.

"You mean east," said the oldest member. Captain Jonah appeared not to have heard him and carried on regardless.

After a couple of hours I had the hands piped to dinner; it was baked beans of course.

"Do we have anything to wash this down with?" I asked the cook, with a sigh.

"We have some scotch whisky sir," he answered.

Later we set the night watch and retired to our beds for the night. The next morning I got up and ate my baked beans before going up on deck; the sun was shining and I could see nothing but water all around.

"Where are we?" I asked the helmsman.

"I don't know; you're the Captain," he said.

I looked around for inspiration. No land anywhere to be seen; it was a deuced tricky situation.

"Keep steering on this course," I told him. "I'll go and see if there is a map aboard."

Well, if there was one I couldn't find it. So I went back up on deck.

"There's a Chinese junk off on the port quarter," said the first mate, Gordon. I took a piece of paper out of my coat pocket and studied it. It said, 'port is left, starboard is right'.

I walked to the left hand side, took a look, and sure enough there was a Chinese junk sailing towards us.

The boat bore down on us until it was in hailing distance.

"Ship!" corrected the oldest member.

"No, it's perfectly true. There it was, a boat right out there in the middle of nowhere," Captain Jonah informed him.

"Halloo!" I shouted. The Chinese captain waved. "Which way to the windward Isles?" I called.

"About a thousand miles that way," shouted the other skipper, pointing in the direction we had just sailed from.

"Right. Change course by 360 degrees," I ordered the helmsman.

"No sir, you meant to say 180 degrees," said young Jimmy the cabin boy, who was on deck; skiving no doubt.

"Did I?" I asked him, frowning.

"Yes sir. It's on my map here; the Windward Isles are almost due west," he told me.

"Where did you get that map from?" I asked him suspiciously.

"It's one of the set I bought back in London, sir," he said.

"Well it's confiscated," I told him, "now go and do some cabin boy things." He disappeared below decks.

"What are cabin boys supposed to do?" I asked Gordon.

"I don't know;" said Gordon, "make things for cabins I suppose."

I looked at the map. The damn thing seemed to consist mainly of water. How on earth was one supposed to find one's way from that sort of nonsense? Hadn't anybody ever thought of putting out buoys, every mile or so, with signposts on them? An idea well worth patenting, I remember thinking.

So as the sun set, we sailed back through the Singapore Roads, giving the American Battleship a wide berth, but running over and sinking a row of moored private yachts. The damn things shouldn't have been there anyway.

"Keep steering west," I told the night watch, before going down below to eat my baked beans and to sleep.

The next morning I was up bright and early, and went up on deck. Young Jimmy was steering the boat.

"And where are the crew?" I asked him.

"They were up all night, drinking Scotch whisky," he reported. "They decided that they didn't like this ship, they couldn't stand the smell in the fo'castle, so they took the lifeboat and headed back to Singapore."

"So we are lost then," I said.

"Not at all, sir. We are at latitude 1 degree 18 minutes north, longitude 104 degrees 10 minutes west; seven hundred and twelve miles east of the Windward Isles, steering eighty-six degrees, speed twelve knots."

"Oh really," I said. "Better make that eighty-seven degrees."

"Aye, aye, sir," he said, not moving the wheel an inch; the insufferable little monster.

"The cook is still aboard, Captain," he told me.

"What's he doing?" I asked.

"Making breakfast," he reported, "Baked beans."

The cook brought breakfast up on deck, and yes, it was baked beans.

"Haven't we got anything else?" I asked him.

"No, Captain," he said. "You haven't paid the chandlers bill, and you said that there was plenty of food aboard anyway."

"And so there is," I said, doggedly chewing some beans.

Two days later we were still heading west, and I wandered into the galley to see what cook was preparing. Surprise, surprise; it was beans. I studied him as he stirred the pot; a small fat man. My mind went over the rhyme of the Ancient Mariner:

I loved that cook like a brother I did
And the cook he worshipped me

84

But I upped with his heels and
Smothered his squeals
In the scum of the boiling broth.

No, better not, I thought, at least not yet anyway. I took my beans and moved up-wind of the cook to eat them.

"Why don't we catch some fish, Captain?" suggested young Jimmy from his position at the ship's wheel.

"Are there fish this far out to sea, then?" I asked him.

"Yes of course, sir," he said. "There is some fishing tackle in my cabin."

"Where did that come from, London?" I asked sarcastically.

"No sir. I bought it in Singapore when I noticed that we only had baked beans aboard sir," he told me, the little monster.

So, cook quickly fetched the fishing tackle, and set the line and hooks trailing out astern. For bait we used a piece of silver foil which young Jimmy had made up to resemble a fish. I had to admit it looked damned realistic; I could have eaten it.

Five minutes later, cook got a bite and slowly hauled the line in. The fish got closer and closer to the surface.

"I reckon that this is a big 'un Cap'n," grunted the cook, as he leaned over the aft rail.

This was the truth, for the great white shark he had hooked broke surface, grabbed his arm, pulled him in to the water and swallowed him whole.

As the shark sank back below the surface, I gloomily considered the fact that we had no meat on board at all now.

"Here, captain, take the wheel," said young Jimmy, and he quickly re-set the hooks and cast out, while I spun the wheel from side to side. In next to no time he had four small fish grilling over the little barbecue that he had set up, and we were soon enjoying our first proper meal in days; one for him and three for me - well, I was the Captain, after all.

I retired to bed early, leaving the boy to do the night watch. Well, he hadn't done much except stand holding the ship's wheel all day, and I'd just found out how easy that was.

The next morning I got up and went on deck; the sky was a curious metallic grey in colour, and there was a brisk wind blowing from the North West, or the South East. I was never really quite sure of how to work it out.

"The glass is falling, Captain," called young Jimmy, who was looking a bit blurry-eyed.

"Well pick it up then, you stupid boy," I told him in my best Captain's voice.

"No sir, I mean the barometer is falling, sir," he said. "There's a storm coming."

"Well hadn't you better batten the hatches or something?" I told him. "Am I expected to think of everything on this boat?"

"It's alright, Captain," he replied, "I've been round and fastened everything down."

"Oh, so who was steering the ship then?" I asked him.

"I tied the wheel so that it maintained its course, Captain," he said.

"Hmmm, have you been sleeping?" I asked.

"No sir," he lied.

"I'm a bit worried though, Captain," he told me. "This old ship Venus is rotten and falling apart. If the storm is very violent, the crew have already made off with the lifeboat, and we could be in trouble."

"Nonsense," I told him, trying to replace the section of railing which had just come off in my hand. "The Greek chap who sold it to me said it was a gift at the price."

Well, during the course of the day the wind got stronger and stronger, and it was all we could do to hold the ship on its course, especially as we always seemed to be pushing the wheel in opposite directions, until it finally came off in our hands. By six thirty pm it was dark and the waves resembled mountains and valleys.

"It's no good sir, we must shelter below," said Jimmy.

"No, I think that you should tie yourself to the fore mast and keep a lookout, while I repair the wheel," I told him.

There was a crash as the foremast was ripped out of the deck like a rotten tooth, and it disappeared over the side.

"On second thoughts..." I said, as we hurried below.

We made it safely in to my cabin and I lit the hurricane lamp.

"It's alright, Captain," said young Jimmy, beating out the small fire which developed from the spilt oil. "You sit down, and I'll get together a survival kit, in case we have to abandon ship."

The cabin floor was under a foot of water, and I passed the time trying to count the number of baked bean cans floating around. He disappeared into the corridor so I tried to get some sleep.

It seemed like minutes, but it must have been hours later when I woke with a start. There was no sound or movement, and sunlight streamed through the cabin porthole.

I staggered up on deck and looked around. The sea was calm, and the ship had neither masts nor wheel remaining; the deck was bare, and everything seemed unnaturally still. I looked over the side, and sure enough we were stranded high and dry on a reef.

Hmmm, that's going to slow us down a bit, I thought, and looked around for young Jimmy, but he was nowhere to be seen, so it looked as if the little blighter had been washed overboard. I looked around the horizon and was quite surprised to see land a hundred yards off the port, that's the right hand bow.

The oldest member made a "humph" sound.

The land was a typical tropical island; you know, palm trees edging a beautiful beach of white sand. I looked to see if there were any sun beds out, but it seemed quite deserted.

There was only one thing to do; I had to get ashore and find a hotel, so I dived over the side and belly flopped into eighteen inches of water.

Minutes later I was on the beach, having a look around. I wandered up the beach and back down again, when I suddenly came upon some footprints in the sand. Aha, I thought, I'm saved. I followed them back until I arrived at the spot where I had floundered ashore. Yes, they were my own footprints.

Now, I had read a book about a chap in this situation; Robert Caruso I think it was called, and I knew that I had to recover stuff from the wreck to build a house and things, so I waded back out to the ship to recover what I would need.

I quickly gathered together all manner of useful things; there was an accordion, and some gramophone records, a golf club and a picture of some Morris dancers. Not bad for a first load, I thought, as I carried them ashore.

The next trip I looked into young Jimmy's cabin. There was a box on the bunk, and I tipped it up; matches, a mirror, a book on catching and cooking tropical island animals, some fishing tackle, a jack knife, some pots and pans, an oil lamp and a ball of string. I might have known that there would be nothing of any use in that little blighter's cabin.

I sauntered up on deck and stood watching as the proud ship Venus, making loud groaning noises, disintegrated around me.

"Time to go," I said to myself, and waded ashore with the ship's wheel in my arms. Well, it would make a start on building a new boat. Once ashore it was clear that there was some urgency if I was to survive this adventure, and so, after a couple of hours nap, I surveyed what was available to make my life easier. Well, for starters there were several thousand tins of baked beans that now littered the shoreline, not to mention dozens of cases of Scotch whisky. Pity it wasn't my brand. Never mind, I thought to myself, I could always set up a little bar on the edge of the beach, and make a few pounds there.

So, several thousand trips along the beach later, I had built a large silver pyramid of cans, neatly circled with whisky bottles. All I needed was just a few customers.

It was definitely time for a snack, so I had a look around for some food - nothing, and I wasn't about to disturb my beautiful pyramid. Was this to be my fate - starving to death on a mountain of baked beans? Surely not, so I had to start exploring my island; it was time to move inland.

The food problem was quickly resolved as I found bananas, mangoes and all manner of tropical fruits, and washed them down with sparkling spring water; they ought to bottle this, I remember thinking to myself. Once past the coconut fringe, the island seemed to consist of patches of jungle interspersed with clear grassland, and I could see a volcano smoking away a couple of miles further inland. Very nice, but it could have done with a few shops and bars. After an hour or two I made my way back to the beach and pushed through the palm fronds onto the sand, which was completely deserted.

"My god," I said, "somebody's stolen my beans!" and even the reef with its few timbers had gone. Even the trees looked different. A complete mystery. It could almost have been a different side of the island, but my sense of direction is quite infallible.

I checked my pockets to see what little luxuries I had on me; some small change, an old diary with one entry on the first of January saying, 'This year I am going to keep a diary', a dog licence, and a comb with most of the teeth missing. Well at least I was OK for toilet paper and tooth picks. It was time to make a shelter for the night; I could build a bungalow tomorrow, and in the meantime a tent made of palm fronds should do the trick.

The next morning I woke up, crawled out of my tent, and was a bit disappointed not to see a cruise liner moored close to the beach. I meandered down to the water's edge and stood looking at the line of footprints moving along the sand.

"I'm not getting caught like that again," I said to myself. Strange though, these footprints were of bare feet, and I couldn't remember taking my shoes off, but I must have.

I had a lot to do today; a bungalow to be built, not to mention a new ship, and not even a useless cabin boy to lend a hand. But first, breakfast. I moved back into the palm groves and had a strange feeling that I was being watched. I spun around and could only see the bushes shaking all about me.

"I know you're in there. Come out at once," I shouted, and my jaw dropped as a dozen burly natives stood up and moved into a circle around me.

We sized each other up. They were all six-footers dressed in grass skirts; they had bright feathers in their hair and some had bones through their noses. One or two of them wore necklaces with small ornaments which looked just like shrunken heads, and they all carried sharp looking spears and clubs.

"Me great white chief from the sea," I said, and they scratched their heads and looked at each other. The one who seemed to be in charge said something like:

"Mugga mugga mugga," and indicated which way he wanted me to go by prodding me with his spear.

Well, I didn't have much else to do so I decided to play along with them, and an hour later I followed them into a small village which consisted of a couple of dozen bamboo huts. The native people came running out to meet me, giving me the island greeting of rubbing their stomachs and saying 'yum yum'.

The chief pointed at the great black pot of water which was heating up over the fire, so at least they were civilised enough to have hot baths. Gratefully I took off my tattered rags and climbed into the hot tub.

They were obviously into herbal and natural skin care, as a couple of women diced vegetables and added them to the pot. I laid back and relaxed as the women gave the bath an occasional stir, frowning whenever I passed wind.

A crowd had gathered around the tub, which by now was getting quite hot, and I could see the chief making his way towards me carrying a big ceremonial mace. The whole crowd started clapping, and I assumed that this was some sort of formal welcome, when suddenly a familiar sounding voice shouted,

"Migga magga wagga mugga!" The crowd fell back, and who should come sprinting up but young Jimmy, the cabin boy.

"Captain, get out of that pot at once," he said, as impudent as ever. Luckily it was getting a bit too hot, so I stood up and climbed out while he held up a towel to shield me from the crowd. I quickly dressed and was soon ready to continue the adventure.

"Have you eaten, sir?" he asked. "You sit over here and I'll go fetch you some eggs and bacon." He rushed off and soon reappeared with a tray of good food, which I tucked into.

CAPTAIN JONAH ENJOYED A REFRESHING HOT TUB.....

As I ate, he had a heated conversation with the chief, and finally said,

"It's OK, Captain. They are not going to eat you now; you are my guest."

The stupid boy actually thought that they were going to eat me.

"How come you speak their language?" I asked, wiping my plate clean.

"I bought a book in London, sir," he told me, "and I have been studying it every night. I thought that speaking the island languages might come in useful."

"Surely it's easier for them to learn English," I told him, even though I was stating the obvious.

"Yes, of course sir," he replied.

"So, tell me about this place, and how you came to be here," I commanded.

"Well, Captain," he told me, "at the height of the storm I thought that I had better take a look on deck. I clawed my way to the bow and saw that we were headed for the reef. I managed to loosen the anchor and drop it so the ship was pulled up a few yards short of the reef, and as it jerked at its anchor a giant wave swept over the deck; I lost my hold and was swept over the side."

"You useless boy," I said.

"Yes Captain," he said, "sorry about that. Anyway, I was wearing my life jacket and I was swept over the reef and around the island, landing near this village."

"Stop right there," I said. "Where did you find a life jacket?"

"I bought it in Singapore, Captain," he answered, "immediately after I had conducted a survey of the hull. To cut a long story short, I found the village, made contact with the islanders, saved the life of the chief's youngest son, and was made an honorary member of the tribe"

"OK, I've heard enough," I told him. "I can see that you have been very lucky."

"Yes Captain," he said.

Our conversation was cut short by two warriors running into the village. They went up to the chief and said "jabber jabber jabber." All the villagers gathered around them and they all turned and looked at me.

The chief said, "jabber jabber jabber," and as one they all knelt in a semicircle before me and touched the ground with their foreheads.

I found this all very puzzling, and scratched my belly and watched as young Jimmy had a frantic conversation with the chief.

At last Jimmy came up to me and said,

"This is very strange Captain, but those two warriors have been following your tracks back to the other side of the island, where they found a giant silver pyramid on the beach."

"Aha," I said, "so that's where the tins of beans are."

"Must be, Captain," he continued. "The strange thing is though, that there is a legend on this island; it say's that a great king will come from the sea, and his sign will be a great silver pyramid. They think that you are the great king."

"A natural enough mistake," I told him, sitting up six inches taller.

He had another conversation with the chief and said,

"The chief says your coronation must be tonight. It might be better to play along with him. These guys are easily offended."

"Well, why not," I told him. "I've nothing else to do, and I think that I will make a very good king."

So that was it; a great feast was prepared and a giant bonfire lit. The crowning was performed by the Archbishop, a little old islander wearing a grotesque mask. He shuffled around me mumbling and splashing me with yellow water that tasted distinctly salty.

At last a golden crown was placed on my head, and a necklace, consisting of a thousand pearls, was hung around my neck. The ensemble was completed by a golden club studded with diamonds, and I was the king.

I tucked into the food. Most of it was unfamiliar, and I chewed on some meatballs.

"What are these, Jimmy?" I asked.

"Monkey's testicles sir," he joked, keeping a deadpan expression, the young rascal. There were objects floating in a clear soup that you could have sworn were goat's eyeballs, rice that looked like fried maggots, and all manner of other exotic foods.

Jimmy was having a bit of a row with the chief, who eventually stalked away.

"What was that all about?" I asked him.

"You'd never believe it, Captain," he said, "but he wanted his youngest daughter to be your bride."

"Oh really," I said. "Which one is she?"

"The very pretty one over there," he replied," but its OK, Captain, I told him that you would never ever consider it."

"Now look here," I began, but he was already disappearing into the crowd.

The feasting, dancing and singing went on for hours, and I sampled all manner of exotic dishes, washed down with the yellow salty liquid. At long last it was time for bed, and I retired to my royal palace, which was a bamboo hut that stood slightly taller than the others, and had a couple of hefty native guards posted outside of it.

I took off my royal regalia and retired to bed, thinking of all the things I had to do in the morning; write a new constitution, create a High Court and legislative body, set up a Royal Court and have a chat with the chief's daughter, send ambassadors to Britain and America to arrange a few subsidies, and exchange diplomatic visits. Yes, all in all it was going to be a busy day, I thought as I drifted off to sleep and dreamed of the chief's youngest daughter.

A few seconds later, or so it seemed, I was woken by young Jimmy who had brought my breakfast in for me; eggs, bacon, baked beans and toast.

"What, no meat balls?" I asked.

"No Captain, the monkeys are all hiding," he said, with that deadpan expression, the little scamp.

A short while later I made my way to the stream for a wash and brush up, accompanied by Jimmy and the chief, who were conversing furiously.

I sat back, while Jimmy shaved me with a very sharp knife and then trimmed my hair, all the while wearing a very worried expression.

"What's up, you scamp?" I asked.

"Captain, I think that we have a little problem," he whispered.

"Nonsense," I told him. "I'm the king, don't you know."

"Yes indeed you are, Captain," he said. "The trouble is that the king really only has one duty."

"And what's that?" I asked, admiring my reflection in the mirror Jimmy had found from somewhere.

"Well sir," he said, "on the night of the full moon he has to sacrifice himself by jumping into the active volcano to appease the Island God who is supposed to live inside it."

"WHAT!" I squawked. "So when's the bally full moon?"

"Tonight, Captain," he told me frowning, "but never mind sir, I'll think of something."

"Huh, as if," I retorted.

I stood up and four burly tattooed warriors closed around me and shepherded me back to my hut.

Once inside I sat and gloomily weighed up my chances, which appeared to be something less than zero. The hours passed and I still hadn't thought of a plan - except perhaps to construct some sort of helicopter and then fly out - and then the sun began to set.

The doorway darkened as the Archbishop entered the hut, followed by young Jimmy.

"It's alright, Captain," said young Jimmy. "The witch doctor here has come to begin the purification ceremony."

I looked at the witch doctor, a scrawny little native guy, wearing a hideous mask. He knelt down and began casting a handful of bones onto the floor.

"Now look here, old chap," I told him, "I'm hardly in the mood for games," and then almost jumped out of my skin as Jimmy smashed him over the head with a club, knocking him out cold.

"Quick, Captain," he said, "get out of your clothes and into the grass skirt that's hanging on the ridgepole."

"I've got some burnt cork here to black you up with, and if you wear the mask you will be able to pass off as the witch doctor."

"But what about the guards?" I asked. "They will check me as I go out, won't they?"

"Oh I don't think so, sir," he said. "You see, I've replaced their monkey urine wine with Scotch whisky. They will be out for the count."

"So that's where the cork came from," I said.

"Yes sir," he replied. "In fact, the whole village will be a bit worse for wear in the morning."

I put on the mask and took a look out of the door, and sure enough the guards were snoring away like giant tattooed babies.

"Look, Jimmy," I said, "no one will mistake me for that ugly scrawny witch doctor."

"Oh I think that they might," said Jimmy, unsuccessfully trying to hide a smile.

We sauntered through the village, and the few natives that seemed to be out and about staggered past and gave us drunken waves. We reached the dock area and Jimmy led me onto a large canoe fitted with a mast and sail.

94

"Whose boat is this Jimmy?" I asked.

"Yours now, Captain," he replied, and I settled onto the stern seat while he raised the sail and headed for the open sea.

Half an hour later the island disappeared below the horizon and Jimmy had set a course for the Windward Isles.

"Would you like a spot of supper now, Captain?" he asked me. "I've packed plenty of provisions."

"Huh! Ham sandwiches are all very well," I said, "but I'm completely broke. I've lost my ship, my cargo, and all I have in the world is this grass skirt."

"Here you are, Captain," he said. I've brought your uniform, and you needn't worry about money either; you see, I've also brought your crown jewels with us. I loaded them earlier."

"My crown jewels?" I said. "Do you mean that crown thing?"

"Yes of course, Captain," he replied. "It's solid gold. Then there's the 1000-pearl necklace, and the diamond studded gold war club, plus a big chest of gold coins. I'd say that you were very wealthy."

And do you know, the little perisher was right. When we arrived back in Singapore I sold them for an absolute fortune. I bought several new boats, but they all sank for one reason or another, and so eventually I retired and bought my present house and a little yacht, which unfortunately sank.

And the strangest thing is that little Jimmy Haughton joined the Royal Navy and is now a ruddy Admiral.

"Now just hold on," interrupted the oldest member, "are you talking about Admiral of the Fleet, Sir James Haughton?"

"Yes, that will be him," said Captain Jonah.

"The man who won the war almost single-handed," said the oldest member.

"Apparently so," agreed the Captain. "Mind you, I must say that I never saw anything remarkable about him when he was my cabin boy."

"Which just goes to show, you never can tell about people."

EIGHT
The Legion's Lost Patrol

Friday night at the club and all was very quiet.

"Surely someone has a story that doesn't involve golf," said the oldest member.

"Well, as it happens," said the major, "it was only this morning that I was looking at my diary of the days when I served in the Legion Etranger."

"What? You served in the French Foreign Legion?" queried the oldest member.

"Yes, but of course," said the major. "I commanded the first battalion of the first assault regiment."

"I thought you had to be French to hold field rank," said the oldest member.

"Yes. I was given honorary citizenship when I saved the life of the President," said the major. The oldest member retired, temporarily defeated.

"Now the first battalion consisted of the toughest soldiers, of the toughest regiment, of the toughest army in the world, and I was the toughest man in that battalion," said the major, drawing himself up to his full five foot six inches.

"In fact they called me 'L'enforcer'."

The major appeared not to hear the sniggering coming from the direction of the fireplace.

"Now on the occasion I am thinking of, the colonel had called me into his office. The poor chap looked quite distraught.

"Major L'enforcer," he began, "we have a disaster on our hands. The general's daughter, sweet little Clementine, was visiting Fort Diablo out in the desert, and it appears that she has been kidnapped by the Riff Tribesmen. A regiment stumbling around in that desert will just keep them on the move, so I am relying on you to take out a small patrol and rescue the poor sweet little girl".

96

"Consider it done, mon Colonel," I answered. "I know the very four men for this little job," and so I made my way down to the Kasbah, where I knew that I would find my men having a drink in Black Mike's saloon.

I pushed my way through the swinging doors, ducking as a chair flew over my head, followed by what looked like a military policeman, and there in the corner sat my four volunteers.

Sergeant Schultz was a lean mean fighting machine, with cropped iron-grey hair, a duelling scar and monocle. He was a Dutchman.

"What? Dutch Schultz?" asked the oldest member.

"Yes, of course," said the major, "and on his forearm he had a tattoo, which said 'SS'."

"SS?" queried the oldest member

"Yes, it stood for Sergeant Schultz," explained the major patiently.

Next to him sat Corporal Crowell, the six foot four American cowboy, as blonde as a Viking berserker, but unfortunately lacking half the sense of one. Very useful with his guns and fists though; they called him Texas Rouge.

"Texas Red," echoed the oldest member in disbelief. "What on earth was he doing in the Foreign Legion?"

"Well, rumour had it that he had fallen off his horse, and had joined to hide his shame.

Opposite him sat Legionnaire Carlos, a small Spaniard, as mean as a cobra and an expert with his stiletto knife. They called him 'Le mercer.' The last member of the group was a crazy Australian called Legionnaire Chunderer, a man without fear, or any sort of brain at all, come to that.

"Bonjour, mes amis," I said, as I sat down at their table, smiling as they all pretended to ignore me. "Garçon," I called to the barman, "a bottle of your finest brandy please."

The bottle arrived; Sergeant Schultz gave me a cold Dutch stare.

"Vell, vot do you vant, shortenhausen?" he asked, while Corporal Crowell began to swig the brandy straight from the bottle.

"I've come to ask you to undertake a dangerous mission with me, down in the Riff desert", I told him, and sat waiting until the laughter subsided. These guys certainly enjoyed a good joke.

"What's the job, pom?" asked Legionnaire Chunderer.

"Well, mes enfants, the general's daughter, sweet little Clementine, has been kidnapped and we have to rescue her."

"Now, hold on pardners," interrupted Corporal Crowell. "I think that I'd like to meet this little lady. I say we go." The men held a whispered conversation.

"Ja, ok den", said the Sergeant. "Ve go, but you vill owe us, shorten-hausen, OK?"

"Right lads," I said, "we meet outside the main gate at 0700 hours in full marching order," but they were already dealing out cards and playing for who would be escorting sweet Clementine.

Seven am the next morning, and I stood waiting outside the deserted main gate. Twenty minutes later my patrol turned up, looking distinctly the worse for wear.

"Ach, so dis iz der gate you meant," said Sergeant Schultz, giving me a sour look. I refrained from reminding him that this was the only gate.

"Vite, mes enfants," I said. "Fort Diablo is fifty kilometres due south. Follow moi."

And so we set off into the scorching desert, five desperate men on an impossible mission. Hour after hour I pushed relentlessly on, under the pitiless desert sun. Sweat soaked my uniform, and I could feel exhaustion overtaking me.

Time to give the men a rest, I thought to myself, pausing and taking a look behind me.

Sergeant Schultz was practicing the goose step; Corporal Crowell was reapplying factor thirty sun cream to his arms and face, and Carlos and Chunderer were having a mock bull fight - with Carlos twirling his poncho and Legionnaire Chunderer racing up and down pretending to be a bull.

"OK men," I ordered, "take a half-hour break." They sat down around me and produced bottles of brandy, which they began to drink. At least they had the manners not to offer me any.

"Bloody hell, pom," said Legionnaire Chunderer, "this is bloody hot work. Why didn't we go on the bus?"

"Le bus?" I said in disgust. "We are the men of the Legion Etranger; we march or die, not go on the bus."

"There, I told you," he said to the others, "I told you he was a bloody stupid idiot, didn't I."

I was disappointed to see that they were all nodding in agreement.

"Alright then, if that's the way you feel, I am going to set an even faster pace," I told them. "You'd better keep up or you may not survive," and five minutes later I was breaking into a run as they disappeared over the horizon, half a mile in front of me.

A few hours later I came up to them, just half a mile short of Fort Diablo.

They were sat in a circle dealing out cards, and Corporal Crowell was looking distinctly self-satisfied.

"What are you smiling about?" I asked.

"Oh, I've won sweet little Clementine," he told me, adjusting his Raybans.

"Won her?" I said. "What do you mean?"

"Er, I'm just going to look after her," he said. "Gee, look over there; I can see the fort."

I looked, and sure enough there was the fort, looking ominously still.

My soldier's instincts told me at once that something was wrong, and as I looked through my binoculars, I could see the sentries propped up against the walls in unnatural positions, and there was not a movement anywhere.

"I do not like the look of this, mes amis," I told them. "Spread out and skirmish towards the gate."

Cautiously we moved forward, well spread out, creeping closer and closer to the walls.

Eventually we reached the wall, and could see the guard leaning over the parapet, his eyes closed, and his rifle propped up beside him.

"You lazy schwines," bawled Sergeant Schultz, making me jump a foot into the air.

"Vake up before I put ein bullet in you."

The guard jumped up as if he had been shot.

"Sorry Sergeant Schultz," he called down, "please enter Fort Diablo."

And so we entered the fort, a truly grim place, and the legion's last outpost in the great Riff desert. The patrol broke into a run as they headed for the soldiers' bar, while I made my way down to the commandant's office.

I knocked on the door and entered the office; the commandant sat slumped in his chair nursing a glass of brandy. I clicked my heels and saluted.

"Greetings, mon Colonel," I said. "So what is this little mess we have gotten in over the General's daughter?"

He invited me to sit down and poured out another two large glasses of brandy, one of which he pushed in my direction.

"Well, it is like this, L'enforcer," he began. "The general's daughter Clementine paid a visit to the fort."

"What ever for?" I asked. He looked embarrassed. "Well I think that she was looking for a husband," he said.

"Huh, she shouldn't have had any trouble finding one in this god forsaken place," I told him.

"Yes, that's what she thought too. Anyway, she decided to take a walk outside the walls, and a raiding party of Riff tribesmen swooped down and carried her off."

"So why didn't you send out a rescue patrol?" I asked puzzled.

"Well Major, we were all rather busy," he said, taking some papers out of a drawer and spreading them over his empty desk.

"Never mind, mon Colonel," I said. "The men of the first Battalion are now here, and we will rescue her."

"Oh," he said, "then will you be taking her straight back to HQ?"

"Undoubtedly," I said, and he looked strangely relieved.

"Then I wish you well then, Major," he told me. "The Riffs headed south in the direction of the Wadi Wallah oasis. I'd advise you to get a good night's sleep and start off early in the morning."

I retired to bed in the officer's quarters, ignoring the sounds of breaking glass and fighting coming from the direction of the soldier's canteen, and drifted off to sleep, dreaming of the General's beautiful daughter, sweet Clementine; young, blonde, delicate, and looking for a husband zzz zzz zzz zzz zzz zzz zzz.

'Ta ra, ta ra,' went the bugle outside my window, almost making me fall out of bed, and my dream of sweet little Clementine vanished as if in a puff of smoke. I got up and dressed in a fresh uniform before going out to round up my men. First stop was the soldiers' canteen, and sure enough there they were, surrounded by empty bottles and broken furniture.

"Ach so," said Sergeant Schultz, giving me one of his cold stares. "You iz up at last," he joked.

"Mes enfants," I told them, "we must make immediately for the oasis Wadi Wallah, for that is where we shall find the general's daughter."

"What the hell are we waiting for," shouted Corporal Crowell, leaping to his feet and sending the table flying over.

The others got up, donned their equipment, and followed him outside.

And so we set off again, out into the unmapped interior of the great desert, where even the Legion did not go. Hour after hour we marched under the burning sun, my feet were raw and blistered, and even the hard sergeant put his sunglasses on. Corporal Crowell had taken his shirt off and was wearing a reflective collar to get an even tan under his chin.

Carlos and Chunderer were having a discussion, I think about origami, though I couldn't understand why Japanese paper folding would make women scream.

Sergeant Schultz quickened his pace and caught up to me.

"Vere exactly iz you heading for, shortenhausen?" he asked.

"The oasis Wadi Wallah," I told him.

"Dats ubber dere," he said in his Dutch accent, pointing off to the right.

"No, it's another 10 miles in this direction," I told him. He shrugged and said

"Vell it's up to you, but Texas rouge vill not be pleased."

"Trust me," I said. "I am your leader," and we continued on, accompanied by the sound of happy laughter.

For hour after hour we marched, drawing ever closer to the oasis, until at last, just before the sun sank below the horizon, I decided that we must camp up for the night, allowing us to approach the oasis in the half light of dawn. Sergeant Schultz posted Carlos on guard, while Chunderer brewed up some coffee, and Corporal Crowell toasted some frogs legs over an open fire. After a brief meal, we settled down for the night - even Carlos, I noticed - well never mind, not much chance of being surprised out here.

I was woken next morning by the sun streaming into my eyes; I sat up and looked at my watch. 10.30am, and I was all alone. I climbed out of my sleeping bag and packed my haversack. So, they had deserted. I'd make them swing for this, I thought to myself. No-one escapes from the Legion Etranger and lives.

Ten minutes later I climbed to the top of the next sand dune, and there they were, lying in firing positions observing the oasis.

"So, I was heading in the wrong direction was I, Sergeant?" I gloated.

"Vill you get down," hissed the sergeant, kicking my feet out from under me, and I crashed down beside him.

101

"Dat iz not ze oasis Wadi Wallah," he said.

"Well of course it is," I told him.

"Nein, it iz far smaller," he said, "and vot iz dat building beside it?"

I took a look through my binoculars, and he was right. There was a building there.

"So vere, I mean where are we then?" I asked him.

"Haf you not heard about the lost temple of Tut?" he asked me. "Vell dat could be it."

And he was right. The building did indeed look like an Egyptian temple.

He clicked his fingers, and Corporal Crowell and Carlos crawled forward through the sand and skirmished up to the oasis. Ten minutes later they had reached the water with its fringe of palm trees, and signalled us forwards. Sergeant Schultz led us up to them.

"No sign of life Sergeant," said Carlos, ignoring me and going through the chain of command, and quite right too, I thought to myself.

I AM QUITE SURE THAT THE OASIS IS IN
THIS DIRECTION.

Sergeant Schultz clicked his fingers again, and Corporal Crowell ran up to the temple doorway, looked around and then darted inside.

Five minutes later he reappeared and waved us over. We walked up to him and he reported the building clear to Sergeant Schultz.

We crowded inside, and stood looking in wonder at the great stone idol that took up most of the inside of the place. A great statue of the Egyptian god Horus, a man with the head of a hawk, but what we were all looking at was its single eye, which appeared to be made out of a giant ruby.

The sergeant clicked his fingers, and legionnaire Carlos climbed up the statue and used his stiletto to prise out the jewel. He tossed the ruby to the sergeant, who caught it and put it in his pocket.

"Now you just give that to me," I said, holding out my hand.

"Vot for?" he asked.

"Because it is the property of the Republic," I told him. "Do you want to be hunted down by the Legion?"

I was treated to one of his long cold stares, and then he handed it over. I studied it; a ruby sure enough, and very valuable too, if I wasn't mistaken.

The sergeant and the others were whispering together under the statue, so I took the precaution of swallowing the ruby; I could always recover it later. I walked to the doorway, and as the others came up behind me I threw a small pebble out over the water. As it splashed into the oasis, I called out,

"Just a piece of useless glass, Sergeant." They put their knives away and went back into the temple.

Alors, I thought, I will have to watch this bunch.

"Le mercer, get on watch," ordered the Sergeant, and Carlos slid outside. Corporal Crowell got some coffee going, while legionnaire Chunderer cooked up a pottage of snails.

I walked back and took a look out of the door, and sure enough Legionnaire Carlos was out in the middle of the oasis, diving and exploring the bottom. Well, he's got a long search, I thought with some satisfaction.

We had our meal and were joined by a bedraggled Carlos. He looked at Sergeant Schultz and shook his head, and the sergeant gave me another cold Dutch stare.

"So vat now?" he asked.

"Where has the oasis Wadi Wallah gone?" I asked him.

"It iz twenty miles vest, vere it vas yesterday," he said.

103

"Surely not," I told him.

"Ja, ve go dere every payday to play cards," he informed me.

"And to dance with the women," said Corporal Crowell, "and when are we going to meet my lil sweetheart Clementine?"

"Quiet, Texas rouge," said the sergeant, avoiding my glare.

We stayed in the temple until dusk, and the sergeant set a compass course for the oasis Wadi Wallah.

"Better ve march in the cool of the night, and arrive at der oasis at dawn," he said.

That's a damn good idea, I thought, making a mental note to do it more often in the future.

So, at twilight's last gleaming we set off, and it was actually quite pleasant following the sergeant through the cool of the night. Corporal Crowell was singing a song about little doggies going to Texas, and Carlos and Chunderer were discussing women's reproductive organs.

"I tell you its spelt W- H- O- O- M - 'whoom'," said Chunderer,

Rubbish its spelt "W- O- O- M- B - 'woomb'," said Carlos, and they bickered backwards and forwards for ages.

At last I'd had enough.

"Look, mes enfants," I said, "I think you will find it's spelt W- O- M-B - 'womb'."

"Womb," they echoed. "That doesn't sound anything like an elephant passing wind."

And so dawn's early light found us overlooking the oasis Wadi Wallah.

With typical Dutch military precision, Sergeant Schultz led us to the perfect hide overlooking the oasis, and sure enough, there were a dozen Riff tents encamped beside it.

"Okay, settle down and rest," said the sergeant. "Ve vill creep in and effect the rescue at midnight tonight."

Lucky that was my plan too, I thought. This sergeant is getting a little bit presumptive.

So we rested. Corporal Crowell was licking his lips in anticipation; Carlos sharpened his knife; Legionnaire Chunderer picked his nose. Sergeant Schultz and I just passed the day giving each other dirty looks.

The sun continued its circuit of the heavens, and it was mid afternoon when we were alarmed by the sound of loud angry voices coming from the direction of the Riff encampment.

Sergeant Schultz and I slid up to the rim of the dune we were hiding behind, and took a look.

A group of Riffs were arguing furiously - one big one against three smaller ones.

"What are they saying?" I asked the sergeant.

"Vell, shortenhausen," he said, "it sounds like ze little ones are saying to the big one, 'Get out!', 'Stay out!', 'Don't come back, not ever!!!', unt sum very rude insults on top of zis."

"Watch out, Sergeant," I said, "the big one is heading in this direction," and we slid back down the dune. All in vain I'm afraid, as five minutes later a giant figure strode over the top of the dune and marched down towards us. Sergeant Schultz leapt up and levelled his rifle, but the giant snatched it from his hands and smashed it over his shaven head. The hard Dutchman went down like a sack of potatoes.

Up jumped Texas Rouge, fists swinging, only to be knocked out cold by a mighty right uppercut. Carlos's knife flashed out and flew towards the giant; it was plucked out of the air and it hurtled back, the handle hitting Carlos between the eyes. Down he went like yet another sack of potatoes. Legionnaire Chunderer fainted, and I was left alone to face the giant, who was wrapped in a burnous, his face covered.

"And who might you be?" he asked me, in a surprisingly feminine voice.

"We are men of the Legion Etranger," I replied, getting ready to die for the honour of the Legion.

"Oh, you must be some of daddy's men then," he said.

"What?" I said. "What do you mean?"

"I'm Clementine," the giant said, unwrapping the headscarf to reveal quite the ugliest women it had ever been my misfortune to look upon.

Well, she must have stood six foot one, and even made corporal Crowell, who was staggering to his feet, look diminutive.

"And who are these wimps?" she asked, giving the comatose sergeant a vicious kick in the ribs. He groaned and tried to get up.

"Mein gott," he said, "vot hit me?"

"Oh no, not a ruddy kraut," she said, taking another kick at his ribs. The sergeant crawled away to safety.

"Not me. I'm Spanish not German," whimpered Carlos as her eye fell upon him.

She ignored the sleeping Chunderer, and stood in front of Corporal Crowell.

"Aha!" she said, looking him up and down. "Now you I like the look of. Are you married?"

"Uh, uh, y y y y yes," he stammered,

"No he's not," shouted the sergeant and Carlos in unison.

"Look here, I was cheating at that game of cards, I didn't really win her," said Corporal Crowell, desperately looking around for an escape route.

"An American, eh?" the harridan exclaimed. "I just love Americans, and you won me did you? Well you must claim your winnings."

A muscular arm shot out. A great fist gripped the unfortunate Corporal's collar and off she marched, taking the whimpering Texan with her.

They disappeared round the next dune and the resourceful sergeant leapt to his feet.

"Quick, mein mensch," he said, "let us get away quick, tut suite!" He kicked Legionnaire Chunderer to his feet, and they raced around gathering up their kit and weapons.

"Non, non, mes amis," I said, "we cannot leave a comrade in such danger. He must come with us."

"Not mit zat dragon, he doesn't," snarled the sergeant. "He von her fair unt square, she iz his problem not mine."

"Too bloody true," agreed Legionnaire Chunderer. Carlos was already half way out of the dune.

"OK, OK I have a plan," I told them.

"You, ein plan?" said the sergeant. "I don't believe you."

"Well the first bit involves me going to the toilet," I said, grabbing a shovel and heading for the next dune. Ten minutes later I was back with the freshly polished ruby.

"Vy are you walking zo funny," demanded Sergeant Schultz, "mit your legs so far apart."

"Never mind that," I told him. "Everyone gather round me." They did so and as I explained my plan I was pleased to see that even Sergeant Schultz was looking impressed.

The sun was setting when Clementine marched back into our small encampment, Corporal Crowell following behind her with tears in his eyes. She sat down and looked at us. "Texas Red, huh! Texas Dead more like," she said, as her gaze rested on me.

"Are you married?" she asked me.

"Yes, to the Legion," I replied hastily.

"Get me some food, shorthouse," she said, and I hurried to obey.

Ten minutes later she was working her way through a tray of frogs legs and recounting her adventures to us.

"So after I had decided that there wasn't a proper man in Fort Diablo," she said, "I saw a group of Riff Tribesmen approaching the fort's walls. I rushed down to take a look and was quite taken with their chief - a tiny little man only six feet tall. He pretended not to be interested, but I pulled him out of his saddle gave him a thump, climbed onto his camel and put him across my knees. The rest of the party turned and raced off into the desert, so I trotted after them and followed them to their encampment at the oasis Wadi Wallah. That's where I've been ever since, waiting for the chief to pop the question."

The patrol exchanged frightened glances with each other.

"So what are you going to do now?" asked Corporal Crowell, in a small voice.

"Well if the chief doesn't want me, I'll have to choose one of you lot," she said.

My god, I thought, I hope that my plan works.

Clementine fell asleep an hour later, and the desert trembled to a hideous snoring.

It was time. Sergeant Schultz and I crept out from the shelter of the dune, and headed for the Riff encampment. Minutes later we entered the camp, and a couple of guards escorted us to the chief's tent, all the while looking nervously out into the desert, as if a frightful beast lurked out there.

We entered the tent, and the chief rose to greet us; a tall hawk nosed Arab, a true son of the desert.

"Welcome effendi," he said. "My home is your home."

"Yes I know it is, I won it at cards last week," snarled the sergeant.

We sat cross legged on the carpet; the chief clapped his hands, and a heavily veiled woman came in, with a tray holding three small cups of coffee.

"So, what is it, effendi?" asked the chief. "Have you come to play cards?" The Sergeant looked interested, but I said,

"No, we have come to ask a favour."

He appeared to notice me for the first time.

"And how can a poor Riff be of any sort of service to an officer of the Legion?" he asked.

"Well, it's like this," I told him. "You have a beautiful French girl stopping here, who is madly in love with you, and wants to get married," I finished lamely.

He leapt to his feet and rushed to the door and looked out. Reassured by the empty camp, he came in and sat back down.

"For the love of Allah, tell me that that's a joke," he said.

"Not at all," I told him. "You would be a very good match, and receive the protection of the Legion Etranger. She also has a very good dowry."

"Dowry!" he said. "There is not enough money in Casa Blanca to make me do this."

"Perhaps not," I told him, "but what about this?" and produced the enormous ruby eye of the god. I laid it on the coffee table in front of him and we gazed in awe upon it.

And so we got down to some serious haggling. Eventually, in return for the ruby, my gold watch, and the cancellation of the chief's gambling debts, the match was agreed, and we returned to our camp to fetch the ashen-faced chief's bride.

The next morning, the marriage ceremony was performed by the camp cleric, and the joyful Clementine picked up her new husband and carried him into his tent.

"Well, mes amis, I think that we can call this a successful outcome," I told the patrol. "Time to go home."

"Oui, L'enforcer," they answered in unison; you see, I had won their respect.

"We march north," I told them.

"Bloody hell, pom," complained Legionnaire Chunderer, "there's a bus in half an hour. Can't we catch that?"

"Alors, we are the French Foreign Legion!" I said." March or die!"

108

NINE
The Great Escapade

It was a week before Christmas, and the snow lay all around, deep and crisp and even.

Jumbo Fowler looked out of the window and said, "That's a bomber's moon. Reminds me of Christmas 1943, when I was serving in Bomber Command."

"Tell us more," invited the oldest member, and Jumbo began the most extraordinary tale.

"Well," said Jumbo, "it was Christmas Eve and there wasn't much happening in the war, so me and the rest of the squadron were trying to think of a way to liven things up.

"Let's go and blow up the Mohne dam," said Lofty.

"What about destroying Gestapo HQ in Copenhagen," suggested Archibald.

"No, no, lets fire-bomb Hamburg," insisted Chalky.

"Hold on lads," I said, "it is Christmas, so how about dropping a bomb down the Fuhrer's chimney." My idea was instantly seized upon, and the chaps debagged me and bumped me off the ceiling in delighted approval.

So it was decided that it would be just Tommy Gunn and I flying the Mosquito, with just the one 1000-pound bomb. We moved over to the mess piano and sang about rolling out barrels, and run rabbits running.

At 4.30pm, Tommy and I walked out to the Mossy, dressed in our flying suits. The plane stood alone on the runway, looking black and sinister. I had personally honed and tuned the twin engines and polished the fuselage. This was the fastest plane in the RAF, without a doubt. We climbed in and started the engines; they sounded like a pair of racing cars as they warmed up.

"Chocks away," I shouted, and as Santa's Special rolled towards the main runway the entire base waved us goodbye.

The plane roared up into the evening sky and we headed east, towards Berlin and the Fuhrer's Christmas party. We crossed the English Channel, and roared over occupied France. I felt just like Santa as I looked down over the snowy towns and villages lit up by the bright moonlight, until at 7pm we crossed the German frontier, and all feelings of peace and goodwill vanished as we had to duck and dive to escape the searchlight beams and anti-aircraft fire.

"Warm work, what, squadron leader Gunn," I remarked.

"Yes sir, it certainly is," he said, keeping his finger on the map and looking out of the window for Essen. We followed the autobahn northeast, all the while keeping a sharp lookout for the Hanover exit, where we had to turn right and head east for Berlin. 9.30pm saw us flying over Templehof aerodrome, looking to pick up the Unter der Linden Strasse and the Reich Chancellery.

Coming down to rooftop level, we flew onwards through a virtual storm of flak, and I noticed that there were no chimneys on the chancellery.

"Never mind, Tommy," I said, "let's put it through that window, the one with the Christmas tree in it."

"Bombs away, skipper," he chortled, and our present flew through the window, bursting into the Fuhrer's study.

'KABOOM!' went the 1000-pound bomb, and the plane was pushed a hundred feet up into the air by the blast. Berlin had snow again, this time from the charred remains of Christmas wrapping paper, which fell gently over a half-mile radius. We headed northwest.

"We might as well go back by the scenic route," I told Tommy.

"Righto, skipper," he said, "lets give Hamburg a wake up call."

But suddenly we were surrounded by the entire Luftwaffe, all six of them. I dived and evaded the first two.

"God, Tommy," I said, "I wish I hadn't removed all the guns to give us more speed. We could have taken these blighters out."

The very next moment a Fokker got onto our tail and put a burst of canon fire through the rudder.

"Ah, that would be a Fokker 190D night fighter," said the oldest member.

"No, it was a Messerschmitt," said Jumbo. "Anyway, all control disappeared and we began to fly round in a large circle, quite in danger of disappearing up our own ailerons."

"It's no good, Tommy," I shouted. "We have to bale out."

"What, over bally Germany?" he groaned.

"No choice, old boy," I said. "Santa's special is about to go down." I pulled the release handle and the canopy flew off.

"Undo your seat belt, old chap," I shouted, flipping the plane upside down, and we fell out. My parachute opened and I drifted down towards the sleeping town below. Meanwhile, my plane disappeared westwards, followed by a virtual flock of the enemy.

All was now quiet and peaceful, as the parachute dropped me gently, lower and lower, towards the town square. I narrowly missed the roof of the town hall and landed bang on top of the 40ft Christmas tree, with my harness well and truly tangled, and the chute spread out behind me like ruddy angel's wings.

I hung there for an hour, hoping that Tommy would turn up and chop down the tree.

I felt like scrooge wishing to spoil everybody's Christmas. It must have been midnight when the doors of the little church fronting the other side of the square opened, and the congregation of fat German burghers and plump little hausfraus came out, circled the tree, and began to sing carols while I hung there like the Christmas Fairy. Someone eventually spotted me, and as the crowd began pointing and nudging each other, I had the feeling that my number was up.

They fell silent, and an elderly policeman shouted,

"What are you doing up that tree? Come down at once."

"Sorry old chap, afraid I'm stuck up here," I shouted down, and at the sound of my English voice the crowd began to scream and run away, the women as well as the men.

"MEIN GOTT an Englander!" said the policeman, pulling out his pistol and dropping it onto the pavement. A couple of nasty little boys came up and practiced taking pot shots at me with wooden guns.

Someone must have been busy on the phone, because ten minutes later a truck roared into the square and a dozen German soldiers piled out of the back.

"Do you surrender schweinhund?" shouted up the officer.

I took a look at the dozen machine guns pointing at me, and agreed.

"Yes, I surrender."

Someone produced a ladder and a soldier climbed up and cut the harness. I slid down and landed on the ground, my fall broken by the fir tree's branches. Now why hadn't I thought of doing that an hour ago?

I was prodded towards the back of the truck and climbed aboard.

"Hello skipper," said Tommy Gunn, who was already sat in the back of the vehicle.

"They caught me as soon as I landed in the back yard of the police station; a fair cop, you might say."

We drove off towards the south. Tommy and I tried to pass the time playing 'I spy'.

"Something beginning with N," I said.

"Nazi," said Tommy.

"Yes, that's correct," I told him.

"I spy something beginning with M," said Tommy.

"Machine gun?" I asked.

"Not much fun this game," said Tommy, so we lapsed into silence and looked at the passing snow covered countryside.

Half an hour later, the truck pulled into the courtyard of a military building, and we were pushed down off the back, and into the building. As you might have expected for 2am on Christmas morning, the place was deserted, and we were marched down the stairs to the basement and locked in a cell.

We sat on the single bed and looked uncomfortably at each other.

"You take the head and I'll take the foot," I told him, "and keep your trousers on."

As we lay there I said, "The first thing to do is set up an escape committee. I'll be chairman and you can be head of ideas and plans."

"Righto, skipper," he said. "So what escape plans have you got?" I asked.

"Working on it, skipper," he said, and we drifted off to sleep.

I awoke with a start. Sure enough I was cuddling Tommy's sweaty feet, and I could hear the tramp of jackboots in the corridor. The door swung open; a tray containing two small pieces of dumpling and a glass of water was thrust into the cell, and the door crashed shut again.

"Well, they could at least have put a sprig of holly on it," said Tommy, as we gloomily surveyed our breakfast.

An hour later and once again the tramp of nailed jackboots sounded in the corridor.

The door swung open, and a Nazi officer shouted, "Aus schnell Englander schweinhunds." We went out and were surrounded by four heavily armed guards.

"Links rechts, links rechts!" shouted the officer, and we marched into the interrogation room. "Setzen!" shouted the officer, and we sat down gratefully on the two chairs, and stared at the lamp pointing into our eyes.

The guards looked at us, and we looked at the guards, for ten minutes.

"Merry Christmas," I ventured.

"SILENCE!" roared the officer. "It is not such a merry Christmas for you schweinhunds."

The door opened and two more Jerries entered the room. These two were not in uniform, unless you considered the black leather overcoats and black homburgs a uniform.

"So, these are the terror flyers," the taller one said.

"Ja, Herr Uberstantertsturmbahnfuhrer," said the officer, turning a whiter shade of pale.

"Und I understand that they resisted arrest and killed several innocent civilians."

"Nein, they came very quietly," said the officer. The Uberstantertsturmbahnfuhrer looked disappointed.

He turned to me, "Good morning," he said. "I am Herr Wiesel of the Gestapo," and my associate is Herr Gerfreiter Heinkle."

"Merry Christmas," said Heinkle. We looked at the Nazi officer who gazed into space.

"Now is the time for some answers," said Herr Wiesel. "You will tell me everything you know. What are you doing here?"

"Well," I said, "dropped the egg, then mixing it with Jerry, the kite copped a packet and pranged, finished up here toot sweet."

"Yes," said Tommy, "ducked the archie, made for Blighty, rudder went for a burton, copped one, inevitable pancake."

"MEIN GOTT," interrupted the Gestapo man, "they don't speak English."

"Damn cheek," I said, "of course we do, and better than you blighters do too."

"OK then," said Wiesel, "Now tell me everything you know."

"Well, that won't take long because I don't know anything," I answered.

He turned impatiently to Tommy, "You will tell me everything," he told him, "or we will torture the stupid one here."

"Well you just torture away, because I am not saying anything," replied Tommy.

"Now hold on a minute," I said, "couldn't you tell them just a little bit."

"No skipper," he said, "I won't say anything even if they shoot you."

"Now that's a good idea," said Herr Wiesel.

I reached over and gave Tommy a dead leg.

"Hey, that's my job," said Heinkle, looking up from unrolling a set of dentist's instruments.

The door opened again and yet another German officer came into the room, this one a senior officer of the Luftwaffe.

"What's going on here?" he asked. The German soldiers jumped to attention and saluted, while the Gestapo men looked a little uncomfortable.

"We are questioning the terror flyers," said Herr Wiesel; Heinkle nodded his agreement.

"Well, all air force prisoners of war are the responsibility of the Luftwaffe, and as I am the senior Luftwaffe officer for this region, I am taking them with me," said our hero.

Some papers were signed, and we climbed into a Mercedes staff car to be driven away leaving an angry looking Herr Wiesel at the doorway of the Komandanture.

"How do you do," said the German. "I am Hauptman Joachim Rimmel of the Luftwaffe. I'm afraid that you will be my guests for a few days."

"Pleased to meet you old boy," we said.

"Tell me," he said, "are you the pilots who ruined the Fuhrer's Christmas party last night?"

We admitted that we were.

"Oh bloody top hole!" Joachim said. "What a brilliant wheeze!" and we all rolled around the car roaring with laughter.

"How I wish I had thought of that, and had paid a visit to number ten Downing Street!" said Joachim. "Never mind though, there's always New Years Eve."

Tommy and I exchanged uncomfortable glances and changed the subject.

"So what happens to us now?" I asked.

"Well, I had the honour of shooting you down." he said, "so you are my prisoners until it is decided where you shall go. We have a Christmas party in the pilots club tonight, and I hope that you will join us."

"What? Fraternizing with the enemy?" said Tommy.

"Not at all," said Joachim, "just flyers enjoying Christmas."

"Shut up, Tommy," I said. "Of course we will come."

And so we enjoyed one of the best Christmas parties that I have ever been to. Champagne flowed, with fun, games and singing, and the little German nurses weren't bad either.

Tommy and I did our Flanagan and Allen impression, singing, 'We'll hang out the washing on the Siegfred Line' which absolutely brought the house down, and afterwards we retired to bed and slept like babies.

The next morning, Joachim took us for a tour around the airfield, and showed us everything, except inside a hanger which was locked and guarded. It was just like being back home. We had some lunch and a glass of wine.

As we drank our coffee, Joachim said,

"I've had a message from Berlin. The Gestapo have made them aware of your presence here, and the Fuhrer isn't too happy about your little joke on Christmas Eve. I'm sorry, but this afternoon I must send you to Castle Coldbitz, the most feared prisoner of war camp in all Germany. It's the place where they send all the troublemakers, and it is, of course, escape proof."

So straight after lunch we shook hands and exchanged addresses with Joachim, promising to meet up after the war, and set off in his staff car for the dreaded Castle Coldbitz.

Dusk was falling as our car wound its way up the mountain road, and we looked for the first time upon the Castle, a sinister gaunt building, not unlike this club.

We stopped outside the great gate and surly guards examined our paperwork, while equally surly Alsatian guard dogs had a sniff at us.

"All is in order. You may enter," said the sergeant of the guard. The gates opened and we entered the castle courtyard and got out of the car. The Luftwaffe driver and guard said 'best of luck old chaps' and drove away.

"Follow me," said the sergeant, and we followed him through the main entrance.

Everywhere was cold and gloomy, and we were led into the commandant's office.

"Aha, the terror flyers from Berlin," he said, getting up from behind his desk, a middle aged officer wearing rimless spectacles. "I am Hauptman

Freyer," he told us. "Before the war I was Governor of the toughest prison in the Reich, and I can assure you, gentlemen, that escape from here is impossible. Do I make myself clear?"

We assured him that he was making himself very clear, and after handing over our RAF escape kits, maps and compasses, we were escorted to the British prisoners' wing of the castle.

We entered the British Officers dorm and were surrounded by a veritable horde of prisoners - 'where have you come from?' they wanted to know. We told them of the Fuhrer's Christmas party raid and the whole building erupted into 'Roll out the barrel', and rabbits were running everywhere. We were introduced to the Senior British Officer, a Brigadier General, who told us about Coldbitz Castle; all the troublesome prisoners from all the allied nations were kept there in escape-proof conditions; there were Brits, Yanks, Poles, Dutch, and of course the enemy, the French.

"Report to Big B," said the SBO. "He's chairman of the escape committee, sure to have a job for a couple of aces like yourselves."

And so we reported to Big B, a diminutive Scottish officer, and asked if there was anything we could do to affect an escape.

"Well, we are not actually into escaping," he said.

"So what does the escape committee do then?" I asked him.

"Well, actually it's more about stopping the French escaping," he said. Every night we dig down and fill in all their tunnels."

"So where do they put all of the soil?" I asked.

"Into our tunnels, of course," said Big B.

"Anyway, I must rush, in a minute some of the Froggies are going out over the wire, and I have to nip down and turn on the outside lights. That will foil them." He rushed out and Tommy and I looked at each other.

"Looks like it's just me and you then, old bean," I said.

"Too true skipper," he answered. "We'll be home for Easter."

Day after day we wracked our brains, and could think of nothing, until one day, while we were looking out of the window, I finally had it.

"Have you noticed, Tommy old chap," I said, "that every Friday night the guards have a dance, and a lot of girls come up from the town to dance?"

"Yes, I suppose so," he answered. "What about it?"

"Perfectly obvious," I said, "we climb out of that fourth floor window in the American dorm, and swing across the courtyard on that telephone wire over there, drop down onto that windowsill there, which is the guards

116

barracks, climb through the window and escape out of the guards entrance."

"Blimey skipper, have you flipped?" said Tommy. "The place will be absolutely full of Jerries, we'll be shot for sure."

"No not at all," I remarked smugly, "we'll do it on a Friday night, dressed as women, mingle with the town girls, leave with them and escape."

Tommy whistled in admiration. "You're a ruddy genius, skipper," he said, and I had to agree with him.

Now I happened to know of a polish tailor who would be able to make us up some women's clothes, so we sought him out and explained exactly what we wanted; a couple of nice party frocks, two stylish coats with padded shoulders, two pairs of high heels, and some makeup. He gave us a rather strange look, but agreed to do the job for two hundred cigarettes.

"Well if you think I'm escaping in this weather wearing a skirt," said Tommy, "you're mistaken. Let's wait until spring." I agreed that this was a good idea.

A few weeks later our women's clothes arrived and were hidden away. Next we had to acquire wigs, easily made by unravelling Red Cross parcel string, ironing it flat and sticking it to papier mache skull caps. Tommy's was a rather fetching shoulder length blonde with a nice little flick at the bottom, while mine was a brunette piled up and held with a little bow.

Life in the camp continued its monotonous cycle of camp concerts and football matches. Tommy and I performed our Flanagan and Alan number, 'We'll Hang Out The Washing On The Siegfred Line', and were pelted with rubbish until we abandoned the stage. And all the time we fought and squabbled with the French.

March turned into April and we decided that it was time to go; the great escapade was on for that Friday night.

Thursday night we paraded in front of the SBO and Big B, dressed in our women's clothes. I was wearing a rather fetching little check number that resembled the missing canteen curtains, while Tommy had on a little purple dress that bore no resemblance to the tablecloth that it used to be.

The SBO cast a critical eye over us as we teetered on our high heel shoes and showed a bit of leg.

"Not bad," he said, "but aren't you going to shave off the moustaches?"

"That's a good point," I said. "We'll do that just before we leave."

"Better shave the legs as well then," said Big B.

I looked down at our hairy legs, and agreed that yes, we would have to shave our legs as well.

"Well, I wish you the very best of luck," said the SBO. "What papers do you have?"

"Oh, we won't need papers," I told him. "After all, who's going to bother two pretty maidens?"

The SBO appeared to be choking over something as we left his room.

Friday night, 10pm arrived, and it was time to put the escape plan into action. Tommy and I dressed up in our costumes, shaved and carefully applied our makeup.

"Absolute perfection," said Big B. "You look exactly like two German women."

"I'm not sure that's so good," I said. "We are supposed to look attractive."

We made our way across the block and climbed the stairs to the Americans' quarters.

"Won't they be surprised," said Tommy, "when two pretty girls walk into their dorm."

As we entered the crowded American quarters a silence fell across the room as thirty Americans stared at us. I smiled at Tommy and inched my skirt up a fraction.

"Oh my God," said the Senior American Officer, "it's two bloody Brits in drag."

We quickly explained our plan of climbing across the telephone wire and escaping with the German girls.

"But you're over six feet tall in those heels," said the SAO.

"Yes," I said. "I just hope that the Germans don't fancy us too much."

10.30pm saw Tommy and I prepared to swing across the abyss of the castle courtyard; Tommy went first.

"Keep your legs together, old bean," I told him. "Someone might look up."

Tommy completed the hazardous journey, dropped on to the barracks windowsill, forced the window and slipped inside. Now it was my turn; hand over hand I swung until I was over the middle of the courtyard, then suddenly I was illuminated in a beam of torchlight shining from the window of the French quarters.

"Hey Jerry, looken sie hier," came a chorus of shouts as I dropped onto the windowsill.

A German officer came out of the barracks and pointed his pistol at the torchbearer, it quickly blinked out.

I slid in through the window, and there was Tommy waiting for me.

"I've had a shufti, skipper," he said. "The dance is this way, along the corridor and down some stairs. Shall we go?"

I led off and we cautiously descended the stone staircase and made our way into the large hall where the dance was taking place. The place was filled with a hundred German guards and around forty town girls.

TOMMY AND JUMBO PROUDLY SHOWED OFF THEIR
ESCAPE OUTFITS!!!

"My word," said Tommy, "look at that little blonde girl. I'm going to ask her for a dance."

I pulled him back as he made for the dance floor.

"Come back, you idiot," I hissed at him. "We are here to escape." He nodded and we sidled around the edge of the floor towards the entrance doorway.

We were almost there when a familiar voice said,

"Ach so, what have we here then?"

I turned and found myself looking at Herr Wiesel and Herr Heinkle of the Gestapo.

My heart sank into my size eleven stiletto shoes as his hand reached across and grabbed my arm. I looked at Tommy, who was being held by Herr Heinkle.

"My sweet little dumpling," said Herr Wiesel, "I must have this dance," and without further ado I was dragged out onto the crowded dance floor.

The band oompahed away, and we waltzed our way through the throng.

"Very nice steps," said Herr Wiesel, "but do you mind if I lead for a bit?" I quickly changed hands and allowed him to lead.

I must confess that he was a fair dancer, and before long we were whirling away before an admiring crowd, who applauded as we went into the rumba, and I was bent over backwards and just managed to avoid being kissed. I saw Tommy pinned in the corner by Herr Heinkle, who had just accidentally received a knee in the region of his German groin.

Midnight struck and I was still in the possession of an increasingly ardent Herr Wiesel. Well, at least Tommy had fared no better and was resisting Herr Heinkle with great gallantry.

"Liebling," Wiesel whispered into my ear as he nuzzled it, "we have rooms in the Gaststadt; you must come back and have a look at my gold party badge."

That's it, I thought, what better way to get out of Castle Coldbitz, than being escorted by the Gestapo! So, simpering in agreement, I went with him to collect Herr Heinkle and Tommy, who was looking slightly the worse for wear.

"Aus schnell," said Herr Wiesel, and we went out of the door, down the stone steps and climbed into the little Opel staff car that the cringing guards had fetched for us. We swept out of the castle gates to an absolute flurry of salutes, and it was all I could do to stop myself from returning them. Herr Heinkle was driving and a reluctant Tommy sat beside him, while I sat in the back with Herr Wiesel and desperately defended my honour.

Fifteen minutes (which actually seemed like fifteen hours) later we pulled up outside the hotel, and Tommy and I were dragged out of the car and up the wooden staircase to Herr Wiesel's room.

Tommy and I sat on the bed while Wiesel produced a large bottle of schnapps and four glasses; Heinkle meanwhile was looking at a selection of whips, and smirked at Tommy.

"Beautiful maidens," said Herr Wiesel, "I give you a toast, 'Der Fuhrer'." We drank our schnapps and I said,

"Time for a kiss, boys. Close your eyes and pucker up." The two Gestapo men dutifully closed their eyes and puckered up. WHAM! BANG! The schnapps bottle exploded over the head of Uberstantertsturmbahnfuhrer Wiesel, and Tommy smashed the silver plated whip handle down onto the head of Gerfreiter Heinkle. They hit the floor with a most satisfying pair of thumps, and at last Tommy and I were able to adjust our bras.

Fifteen minutes later Tommy and I were dressed in smart black suits, leather overcoats and Homburgs, while the still unconscious nazis were well and truly trussed up, wearing just their underwear.

"Just one last thing, skipper," said Tommy, and he knelt down and shaved their smart Errol Flynn type Gestapo moustaches down into little Hitler toothbrush moustaches. Then, taking our women's escape outfits with us, we made our way down to the Opel staff car, climbed aboard and headed north out of the sleeping town.

The very sight of our Gestapo plates took us through a couple of military roadblocks, and the car clock now said 4am.

"We haven't got too long Tommy," I said. "As soon as those two goons are found, they will be looking for this car and two bogus Gestapo men."

"So it's back to the women's clothes then, is it, skipper?" he asked.

"No, they will have a good description of those little outfits as well," I told him. "We must think of something else." We had been driving for another hour when Tommy said

"Do you know what, skipper? I recognise this road, and Joachim's airfield is about a mile over that way."

"It's worth a try," I said, and swung the staff car up the approach road to the airfield. "If we can steal a plane we could be home for lunch."

Just the sight of our Gestapo Plates made the guards on the gate raise the barrier pole and we drove unmolested onto the airfield, avoiding the Headquarter buildings.

"Bother," I said. There are no ruddy planes here."

"What about the locked hanger, skipper?" asked Tommy.

"What - the one that says 'EINGANG VERBOTTEN'?" I said. "True, there could be a plane in there." We drove across the grass and pulled up outside the locked hanger; as soon as we climbed out of the car we were approached by a machine gun wielding guard.

"Gestapo," I said importantly.

"Bugger off," he replied.

"I want to inspect this hanger," I told him, and he flicked off the safety catch on his machine gun. We quickly climbed back into the staff car and drove off.

"OK, I've got it Tommy," I said. "Get into your skirt, and then you distract him while I break into the hanger." Tommy quickly changed back into his escape outfit, put on a bit of slap and minced his way back to the hanger, where I saw him chatting to the guard. I watched as they disappeared around the corner of the building.

I rushed across and quickly forced the padlock with the car's jack handle. Opening the door a tad, I slid inside and found myself looking at a sleek silver plane; it was beautiful and I stood taking in every aspect of it. I heard Tommy come in, wig awry and dress torn.

"Well, that jerry won't be waking up for a long time," he told me.

He looked up at the plane. "Well isn't that just our bally luck," he said. "The damn plane has got no propellers on it."

"No, no, old bean," I said. "It's one of those new jets that we've been hearing about. Get the hanger door open while I hot wire it.

I climbed into the cockpit, and looked at the instrument panel; it all seemed straightforward enough, and jerry had obligingly left the starter batteries connected up. Ignition on, spin one, fire one, spin two, fire two. Tommy sprinted back, disconnected the start leads and climbed into the cockpit behind me, sliding the canopy shut. I throttled up and the jet rolled smoothly out of the open hanger door and across the grass. Germans were running from the buildings as I opened her up and we screamed down the runway and into the air as fast as a speeding bullet.

Within minutes we were at twenty thousand feet and the world was our oyster.

"My word, skipper," said Tommy, "there's not a plane in the world that can catch us. We'll be home for breakfast, and with this little beauty in the hands of our boffins, we'll win the war as well."

"Too true, old bean," I said. "By the way, did you notice the 500kg bomb slung underneath?"

"Yes, skipper," he answered. "What of it?"

"What's the date?" I asked him.

"April 20th," he said.

"I thought so," I told him. "Today is the Fuhrer's birthday. How about we call over Berlin and deliver a little birthday present to him?"

"Yoicks, tally ho, skipper!" roared Tommy, as we sped towards Berlin and the Fuhrer's birthday party.

"And did you get back home safely?" asked the oldest member.

"Of course we did," said Jumbo, "but that's another story."

TEN
Be careful what you wish for

The members looked up as the sound of breaking glass and muffled curses came from the next room.

"It sounds as if Lucky Lawson is in tonight," said the oldest member.

Several members nodded in agreement as the door burst open and Lucky stumbled into the room, barking his shin on a coffee table.

"Be careful, Lucky," grumbled the oldest member, grabbing for his port.

"Sorry old chap," said Lucky, who was in fact the unluckiest man any member had ever met - the sort of man who gave you that warm feeling that no matter what was going wrong, here was someone who was having an even worse time of it.

"Are you betting on the cup final tomorrow, Lucky?" asked Spencer.

"Oh yes," said Lucky, "I've got ten bob on United to win." Every member of the club made a mental note to have a bet on City winning, because there was no way that Lucky Lawson would be winning anything.

Lucky sat down, and immediately leapt up again as the chair broke under him, narrowly avoiding depositing him on the floor.

"It looked as if you were half expecting that to happen," said the oldest member, as Lucky lit up a cigarette and hot ash fell down, spoiling his smart jacket.

"Yes, one does get used to it," replied Lucky, spilling some port down his trousers.

"Have you always been, erm, so accident-prone?" asked the oldest member.

"No, not at all," said Lucky. "It really is the strangest tale."

"Then you must tell us," said the oldest member.

"Yes, please do," said several other members, as they edged away from Lucky while he sat down.

"Well," began Lucky, "there are some things between heaven and earth that just can't be explained easily, and my story is one of them.

You see it was about ten years ago, and I was visiting a small seaside town on the East Coast. As usual, it was raining, and I was mooching around the shops looking for antiques; you never know what you might find in those little places. I was walking along a side street in the rougher part of the town, when I spotted a junk shop; you know the sort of place, broken furniture piled up outside, and the inside a veritable warren of old junk. 'Norske Antiques' it was called. That's a strange way to spell Not Antiques, I remember thinking.

I entered the premises and introduced myself to the owner, a large overweight moustachioed Viking.

"Do you do trade?" I asked him.

"We do anybody we can, mate," he replied.

"I'll have a browse around," I told him, and he went back to his Swedish magazine. The inside of the shop was even more miserable than the weather outside, and I was preparing to face the rain again when the small glass cabinet on the counter caught my roving eye. I took a look. Not much of interest, except perhaps a small brass figure of a monkey.

"Can I see that monkey, please?" I asked, and the proprietor took it out and handed it over to me.

"I see that you have a discerning eye," he said. "That's the most valuable thing in the shop."

"What, this brass monkey?" I quipped. "It's certainly cold enough for it."

"Actually it's not a monkey," he told me, "it's the old Norse god, Loki." I put on my glasses and took a closer look, and sure enough, it was a small statue of an ugly little Viking wearing furs.

It was certainly unusual, and extremely well modelled.

"How much is it?" I asked him, and he took a long look at me.

"That came over from Norway," he said. "It's hundreds of years old."

"That's OK, I don't mind buying second hand things," I told him, and strangely I could hardly bring myself to put the little figurine down.

"How about a fiver," he said, and again strangely my hand was racing for my wallet and passing over a crisp five-pound note.

He took the money, and I thought that he was looking a bit guilty.

"We have a no returns policy," he told me, "and once you have left the premises the item is yours."

"No problem," I answered, and he looked even more uncomfortable. I placed the figure in my coat pocket and prepared to leave.

"Wait a moment," said the junk dealer. "There is something that I must tell you about it."

"Oh yes, what's that?" I asked.

"Well, you are now the owner of a magic talisman," he told me with a perfectly straight face. I laughed out loud.

"No," he said, "if you rub the top of his head and make a wish it will come true."

"That's wonderful news," I told him. "There are plenty of things that I can wish for."

"Yes sir," he said. "That's the trouble; just be careful what you wish for."

I left the shop and stood in the rain, fingering the talisman in my pocket, ignoring the sound of the shop door being closed and locked behind me.

I took it out and looked at it. It certainly had a nasty scowl on its face, evil almost.

"I wish that it would stop raining," I said aloud, and as if by magic the rain stopped. Within seconds the sun was shining, and that was the beginning of the long drought that they still talk about now.

I got home and prepared a small meal. Then, while I ate it I looked at Loki. who I had put at the centre of the table. He was about four inches tall and wore a skullcap, a fur jacket and tights. He had pointy ears, a sharp nose and an unpleasant smirk. The kettle boiled and I got up to make a cup of tea. When I sat back down and looked at Loki, he was now on my side of the table and very close to my plate. I put him back at the centre of the table and continued eating my meal.

What a wheeze, I thought as I finished eating and picked up the talisman. I rubbed his head and said,

"I wish that I had loads of money." Well, of course nothing happened, and I actually found myself feeling slightly disappointed. "Come on, grow up," I told myself and prepared for bed. I slept quite well, except that I think there was a mouse somewhere in the house, which I could hear pattering about every now and again.

The next morning I woke up to a beautiful bright day, and got out of bed to make myself some breakfast. The first thing I noticed in the kitchen was that Loki wasn't on the table any more. He was on the mantle piece over the fireplace. My short term memory was playing up as I couldn't remember putting him there.

I went to the front door to fetch in the milk and tripped over the large mailbag that someone had left there.

I pulled it into the house with some difficulty, and opened it. I could hardly believe my eyes; it was stuffed to the top with bank notes.

I slammed and bolted the door, and looked out of the front room window; the street was deserted. And I was rich. Rich! I swept the breakfast cutlery off the table, and poured the money all over it, watching it cascading down to the floor.

I picked up a handful of banknotes and looked at them in stunned disbelief. They were Roubles on the Czarist Bank of Moscow. I grabbed another handful, the Nationalist Bank of Peking, and then Hitler's Reich marks, and what was this, thousands of dollars of the Confederate States of America!!! The whole ruddy sack was full of money alright, and every single piece of it worthless.

I spent the rest of the day burning worthless banknotes, and glaring at Loki who seemed to have a bit of a sneer on his lips. As I burnt the useless paper, I mulled over the events of the last twenty-four hours; it had stopped raining when I wished it, and I had wished for lots of money. Perhaps there was something to this after all.

I looked at Loki, and then got him down and had a closer look. The detail on the figure was extraordinary, and what was this writing, surely runes of some kind. Perhaps I wasn't being specific enough in my wishes.

I rubbed his head and said, "I wish I had a million pounds sterling, in modern English current banknotes." Nothing happened, and I listened to the radio before turning in for the night, and once again I could hear that mouse scampering around the house.

The next morning I was up bright and early, and it was even brighter outside. I went to the door to fetch the milk, and once again nearly tripped over the mailbag on the doorstep.

I dragged it in and opened it. WOW! It was full to the top with crisp clean banknotes, and all English and current legal tender. Excitedly, I began to pile it up on the kitchen table, and as much as I took out of the sack, the money hardly seemed to go down. Why, there must have been a million pounds! Hours later I had finished piling it up and the table was groaning under the weight.

As I made a cup of tea, and sat gazing at my treasure, I switched the radio on and a voice said,

"We interrupt this programme to bring you a news flash about a major bank robbery; thieves have shot their way in to the City Bank and made off with one million pounds in crisp new banknotes. However, every note was marked and is quite worthless. Even at this very moment armed police are closing in on the villain's hideout."

"Eeeeek!" I yelped, as I began to shovel piles of banknotes onto the fire, almost weeping as they burned up in front of me. As the last note went on the fire, the radio said,

"We interrupt this programme to inform you that the City Bank robbers have been captured, and the entire million pounds has been recovered."

I looked up at Loki who was standing on the mantle shelf looking down on me, and do you know what, the statuette was smiling at me.

I took it down, put on my glasses, and yes it was definitely smiling.

Well, smiling or not, there was definitely something to this. It just had to be the way I was making wishes, so tonight I would rub his head and make a secret wish. Later I retired to bed full of anticipation. The next morning I was up early and into the shower, and was feeling quite disappointed, a common feeling over the last couple of days. I shaved, then dressed and went downstairs and put the kettle on. That's when I heard a monstrous crowing noise coming from out the back. I rushed to the back door and looked out. I couldn't believe my eyes. There, strutting around in the garden, was the biggest chicken I had ever seen. It was gigantic; it must have stood three feet tall. Charlie, my neighbour, was looking over his fence at it in awe.

"Tell you what mate," he said, "I reckon that you might have the biggest cock in the world there."

I returned indoors and looked at Loki, who was wearing a large grin on his ugly little face. Turning the radio on I wasn't at all surprised to hear the announcer say,

"We interrupt this programme to bring you news of the theft of the world's biggest chicken, from Ringaling Circus and Carnival. Even at this moment armed police are closing in on the suspect's hideout."

"Eeeeek!" I yelped, as I rushed outside and chased the giant bird inside the house, and yes, as you have probably guessed, I was eating chicken for the next two weeks.

I avoided the figurine for the rest of the day, but as bedtime came I took the figure off the mantle piece and rubbed his head.

"I wish that I was the most handsome person in the world," I said aloud, then retired to bed.

The next morning I got up and rushed to look in the mirror. Huh! No change and no surprise. I had some breakfast and then went out to do some shopping. The street was strangely deserted. I walked to the bus stop; no one there, and not only no bus but no traffic of any kind. I started to walk into town and met no one; the shops were locked and silent. The school closed, not a single person anywhere. The realisation struck me that I was the only person in the town. I ran home and switched on the radio – nothing. The lights - nothing. Yes, I was the most handsome person in the world; I was the only person in the world. I grabbed Loki, who was wearing a broad smile, and unwished my last wish. I dropped the figurine onto the table, as a great bolt of pain like an electric shock smashed up my arm, and I heard the clink of milk bottles outside as the milkman made his delivery.

Tricky, I thought. I really did have to be careful what I wished for, but this talisman was too valuable to give up on; I would master it. That night I took it down again and stared at it. It looked as if it was laughing at me. What an imagination, I thought to myself. Now, what to wish for? I rubbed his head and said,

"I wish I was irresistible to women." Loki smiled up at me.

The next morning I woke up to yet another glorious day, with not a cloud anywhere in sight, and had a quick breakfast before putting on my smartest clothes and setting out for the town. As I reached the street corner a charabanc screeched to a stop a few yards in front of me, and thirty screaming women piled out of it and raced towards me. It was the local Women's Institute coach trip and they had spotted me. I took to my heels and was chased up the high street by an ever-increasing horde of screaming women.

I passed the 'Young Ladies Finishing School', and another fifty females joined the horde as the playground emptied. I was beginning to tire, and some of the younger girls began to catch up with me. Rip…. a large piece of my jacket was pulled off my back, and my best shirt was ripped to shreds; a policewoman dived for my legs and succeeded in ripping one of the legs off my trousers. The girls of the school hockey team were closing in fast as I reached the river and dived in. The current swept me away and I disappeared downstream leaving a great crowd of frustrated women on the riverbank.

A mile downstream I managed to crawl out, and hid in the bushes as small parties of girls searched up and down the riverbanks. Around 11pm I felt safe enough to creep back into town, and making my way from cover to cover, at last I reached the safety of my house. I rushed in and locked and bolted all the doors. Picking up Loki, I unwished my wish and the bolt of electricity from him knocked me across the room.

I didn't make any more wishes for several days, but then the temptation was just too much, so just before retiring for the night I took him down and thought very carefully. Obviously I was wishing for too much - the most handsome man, and irresistible - far too strong terms, so I wished that I was famous, that should do the trick, and then retired for the night.

I was woken up the next morning by the sunlight pouring in through the bars.

"BARS!" I yelped, sitting up in bed, and sure enough I had been lying on a prison cot in a small cell. I jumped out of bed and tried the door. It was locked tight.

LUCKY WAS DETERMINED TO MASTER THIS
WISH THING...

I sat on the cot with my head in my hands, until I heard the rattle of keys in the lock.

"Stand up, Lawson," roared a large prison warder as he marched into the cell. I stood up, and a dapper little chap followed him in and looked at me with some interest.

"So you're the famous axe murderer," he said. "Hmmmm, about five foot nine I'd say, and eleven stone," he said to the warder.

"Yes sir," said the warder, "that's exactly right." He turned to me, "Turn around," he said. "The hangman wants to have a look at your neck."

"Eeeeeeeeeeek" I managed to gasp as they left the cell. I sat down and looked around me, and there on the window ledge stood Loki, positively laughing at me. I jumped up and grabbed him, and desperately unwished my wish. 'FLASH BANG', it felt as if a train had run over me, and when I managed to reopen my eyes I was back home in my own bed and still holding Loki. I dropped him as if he was red hot, and weakly made my way downstairs. I made a cup of tea, laced it with whisky, and as I sat at the kitchen table drinking it I glanced at the fireplace; there stood the cursed little statuette, his face absolutely full of glee.

Well that was it, he had to go. I got dressed, pushed him into my coat pocket then quickly set off for the town. As I walked down the high street I took it out of my pocket and dropped it onto the pavement and hurriedly walked away.

"Hoi you!" bawled a loud voice. I looked around and saw PC Jinkinson beckoning me towards him. I went back to him.

"I saw that," he said, "chucking your rubbish onto our nice clean pavements. Now just go and pick it up."

Sheepishly I picked it up.

"Try that again and I'll be giving you a summons," the policeman told me, and I set off again with Loki back in my pocket.

Next the park; it was deserted. I took out the little fiend and looked at him; he glared back at me. I pulled back my arm and threw him as far as I could. A grey streak shot past me, and a dog that looked like a wolf ran down and fetched the statuette back to me.

"Its not mine," I said, trying to walk away, but a vicious growl stopped me in my tracks. I took one look at the great fangs and decided that discretion was the better part of valour, so Loki went back into my pocket.

I walked out of town and down to the boating lake. A few shillings changed hands and I rowed a rowing boat out into the middle of the lake.

Then, taking a look around, no dogs or policemen to be seen, I took the statuette out of my pocket.

"Goodbye you little monster," I said, and threw him over the side. Well, I would have done if he hadn't been clamped onto my finger. I shook my hand and he came off, along with a chunk of my finger, and sank down into the depths of the lake.

I rowed ashore, ignoring my bleeding finger, and then ran back into town and on towards home.

Once safely inside I examined my wound; a perfect little circle of flesh was missing, almost like a bite mark. I put on a plaster and breathed a sigh of relief. Now life could get back to normal. I looked out of the window at the blazing sunlight, then went out and sat in the garden with a nice cup of tea. Charlie, my neighbour, poked his head over the fence and said,

"When are we going to get some rain? All my plants are dying." We discussed the weather for a bit and then I went in to listen to the radio. There was a news item about a rowing boat sinking on some boating lake.

That night I went to bed and slept like a baby, except that in the early hours I was awoken by the scratching and pattering noises from downstairs; obviously the mice were back. I must get some traps, I thought as I snuggled back down and drifted off to sleep.

The next morning I got up and went downstairs, making plans of how to spend my day. I entered the lounge and almost collapsed as I saw Loki standing in his place on the mantelpiece, looking at me with hatred in his eyes. I sat at the table and wracked my brains.

What if I wished him away? No, he was to clever for that, and any unwishing was becoming increasingly violent, so, what to do? Only one thing for it, I thought, I'll take him back to the junk shop, today.

Six hours later the train deposited me in the seaside town, and I hurried to the shop. I entered the street where it was located, and looked aghast at the café which was just being fitted out where Norske Antiques had been. I went in and almost grabbed hold of the guy who was hanging up a menu board.

"Where is the antique man?" I asked.

"Not sure mate," he told me, "but I think he may have packed up and gone to Norway."

Norway, that was it. I had to take the little blighter home.

I had to be very careful not to think wishes as I headed north to the terminal where I could get the ferry directly to Norway, and purchased my ticket. We sailed all night, and the next morning found us approaching Norwegian waters. I stood at the stern rail, looking at the ship's wake and worrying about how I could get rid of the infernal thing when I got there.

At last I made my decision. I was going to throw it over the stern. It was in my trouser pocket and I tried to take it out, but it seemed to be caught on the material. I pulled and pulled but it still wouldn't come out.

That's it, I thought, and dropped my trousers and stepped out of them.

I picked them up and threw them overboard, and had the satisfaction of seeing them slowly sink in the ship's wake.

Seconds later, the clear blue sky had turned dark and threatening, and the great storm broke. Rain sheeted down and the wind rose to hurricane level. I managed to get into the ships restaurant, and the air was full of screams as everybody noticed that I had no trousers on. And that was the start of my bad luck. Everything that I touched seemed to go wrong. I was arrested for indecency, and fined. I had to make my way back by land as I was banned from the ferries. Train crashes, road accidents, riots and floods - I suffered them all. I lost all my money and had to downsize my house, girls won't look at me and no one will employ me. I also have this great worry.

"What's that?" asked the oldest member.

"How long would it take two-inch legs to walk back to England under the North Sea?" asked Lucky. "About ten years, I'd say."

ELEVEN
The Defective Detective

Sam Slade sprawled in his chair, and said, "Let me tell you of the time when I was a private detective, and handled a very strange case." No one objected, not even the oldest member, so Sam continued.

It was a Monday morning, and I was feeling flatter than the front tyres on an abandoned Morris Minor. My mouth had all the taste of a Turkish wrestler's jock strap, and I was depressed.

I'd only been at work for ten minutes in my small office, and already felt like calling it a day and going down to Irish Mick's for a bottle of whiskey.

I sat at my desk and looked at the glass panel in the door; it was frosted glass, but I could make out the sign writing on the other side. It said:

EDALS MAS
EVITCETED ETAVIRP

What awful spelling, I thought gloomily to myself. So much for professional sign writers.

The phone suddenly rang, and I picked it up.

"Can I interest you in double-glazing?" said the girl on the other end. "We are doing a special offer in your area, and you have been chosen from millions of people to take part."

"I'm really glad you rang," I told her.

"Oh, that's wonderful," she replied.

"Yes, I have a superb offer on time share apartments I'd like you to take advantage of." There was a long silence, and then she slammed the phone down.

I sat for another half hour, nothing. With nothing happening, I dialled a random wrong number and sat listening to the telephone girl with a very sexy voice saying that I have to put a 2 after the area code. It was so much cheaper than the 0909 numbers. In fact, it was free.

My hangover was playing tunes on the inside of my skull. It sounded like seventy-six trombones with a full percussion section. I took out my wallet and took a look inside, empty. Would Irish Mick extend my credit, I wondered? Then I heard a gentle tapping on the door.

"Come in," I croaked. The door opened and this girl came in. Wow!!!!!

I pointed to the chair in front of the desk, and she sat down crossing her shapely legs.

I did a quick inventory; long black waist length hair, an elfin face with big blue green eyes, lips like cherries, lovely shoulders and long slim arms, two really big....

"Excuse me," said the girl, "but are you awake?"

I jumped up with a start, "Of course I'm awake," I said, "I was just working out who you are and what you want."

"Oh, then who am I, and what do I want then?" she asked.

"Well, I deduce that your name is Samantha Smith," I told her. "You live in a small village about twenty miles away, and this visit has something to do with a death."

Her jaw almost hit the floor.

"Oh my, that's wonderful," she said. "How on earth could you have worked all that out?"

"Well, your name and address are written on that envelope I can see in your bag, and the envelope has a solicitor's address on it, and you are wearing black," I finished triumphantly.

"I see that I have come to the right place," she said. "You're a private dick, aren't you?"

"Well I've heard it put a bit more politely than that," I replied, "but how can Sam Slade, Private Detective help you?"

"Well, Mr Slade," she said, "my name is Samantha Smith, and last Thursday I received news that my dear little old grandmother, Lady Toadmore, had passed away."

"It happens," I said. "So, did she leave you the family jewels then?"

"That's why I'm here," she replied. "Not only did she die in the most suspicious circumstances, but her Ducal jewels have disappeared - the jewels she was going to leave to me."

"So how can I help?" I asked her.

"The reading of the will is on Wednesday, down at Toadmore Hall. I'd like you to come down and see if you can discover anything. You can pretend to be my fiancé," she finished.

"That's fine," I told her. "My fee is £20 a day, plus expenses."

"No problem at all," she told me.

"Is there any chance of a small advance?" I asked her, and she passed me £20.

"I'll pick you up here tomorrow at 10am," she said, and I studied her as she walked out of the door. Wow!!!!!!!

I got up and left the office. Locking the door, I made my way out onto the street. The pavement was wet, reflecting the run down buildings; the sky was cold and as grey as iron. Typical August weather, I thought as I made my way down to Irish Mick's Bar. I hadn't gone more than a few feet before I realised that I was being followed.

I'd developed this sixth sense, and the hairs on the back of my neck were standing on end, while little icy fingers were running up and down my spine. I span around and Miss Smith pulled her cold little fingers away from my back.

SAMANTHA TOLD ME THAT HER GRANDMOTHERS
JEWELS HAD DISSAPPEARED.

"Sorry about the cold hands, Mr Slade," she said. "I just wanted to tell you that you will need a dinner jacket if you want to stay on Tuesday night."

"No problem," I told her, making a mental note to add the hire cost to the bill, "and you had better call me Sam."

"OK Sam," she said, and climbed into the little red MG sports car parked by the kerb, showing me a fair bit of leg. I couldn't help whistling, and thinking WOW nice car!!!

I made my way to the newsagents, and asked Mr Chandra if he had a copy of last Friday's local paper. He quickly produced one, and I headed towards Irish Mick's bar for dinner and a read.

"Morning Mick," I called as I entered the bar, "I've come for dinner with Johnny Walker and Jack Daniels." I took my whiskey to a table while Irish Mick roared with laughter, as if I hadn't said the same thing every day for the last year or so.

I looked at the paper, and sure enough there was an article concerning the untimely death of Lady Toadmore. It seemed that she had been climbing a horse chestnut tree, and had fallen and broken her neck. That certainly was suspicious. After all, conkers weren't in season yet. There was more about her early career in the theatre, and subsequent marriage into the aristocracy. Some early photos showed her to have been a great beauty, and I could see where Samantha got her looks from.

So, I wondered, did she fall or was she pushed, where have the jewels gone, and why was a seventy-year-old aristocrat climbing trees when she probably had servants to do it for her? All mysteries to be solved tomorrow. I turned my attention to the crossword.

1 Across - Sherlock Holmes, nine letters. Are there any words with that many letters I wondered, and wrote in ANDWATSON. Yes, that fitted, trouble was none of the other clues made any sense now. I turned the page and looked at my horoscope. It seemed that I was going to come into a piece of good fortune; that was better. Then I realised that it was Friday's paper and any good fortune had already been and gone on its miserable way. I'd better get down to the men's outfitters and rent a dinner jacket.

I stopped outside the shop and looked at the sign. It said 'Men's suits 10/6d, dinner jackets 5/6d, trousers 5/-'. I went in and said,

"Let me see some 5/6d dinner jackets." The shop keeper looked at me and said,

"You're a private detective, aren't you."

"How did you know that?" I asked him.

"Because we are a Dry Cleaners," he replied.

An hour later, armed with my hired dinner jacket, I arrived back at my small flat, which I shared with Alicia - sleek, black haired and beautiful.

"I'm home," I called out as I let myself in. Alicia came through and rubbed herself up against me. "OK honey," I said, "I'll get your dinner." She sure was one spoilt cat. I poured myself a large scotch and sat and listened to the radio. 'Its time for Dick Barton, Special Agent' it said. I switched the radio off, and sat and thought about the new case that I would solve tomorrow, and later, as I drifted off to sleep, Samantha filled my thoughts. Oh yes, she was rubbing her long silky hair against my face. So soft, so sweet, and, "HEY, will you get off my bed Alicia. Damn cat!!!"

The next morning I crawled out of bed and took a cold shower. I really must put some money in that gas meter. I examined my eyes in the bathroom mirror; they were red and bloodshot. Now why is that? I wondered, as I poured some whiskey over my cornflakes. Then half an hour later, shaved, showered, and shampooed, I made my way to the office, arriving on the dot of 10am. Five minutes later a little red MG swerved around a cyclist, and hit the kerb. Samantha opened her door and the unfortunate cyclist ran into it and fell off.

"Oh, you poor man," she said. "Are you ok?"

"Yes Miss," he said.

"Can I have your address?" she asked him, the man gave it to her.

"Its ok miss," he said, "I'm not badly hurt."

"No, I just want to know where to send the paint shop bill to," she told him.

I put my overnight bag into the back, beside her four suitcases, and climbed in. We roared off, causing the 39 bus to brake and leave a thirty-foot skid mark down the road.

"Just bloody typical," she said "Look at that empty bus taking up the entire road."

"I think it's full of passengers, actually," I said, "but they are all lying on the floor."

"Huh!" she answered me, putting her foot down and going through a red traffic light at 90mph.

Now I've seen some bad drivers in my time, but this girl gave a new definition to bad driving. I put my fingers into the grip impressions that previous passengers had made in the dash top, and hung on for dear life. Why, there were even teeth marks embedded in the black leather trim.

"Hold tight," said Samantha as she mounted the pavement to avoid hitting a steamroller which was sat innocently in the road, and she waved cheerily at the furious pedestrians who were waving at her.

"I just love driving," she said. "All the people are so friendly, always waving."

"Yes I'm sure," I replied, hoping that she might look at the road soon.

The twenty mile ride took us just twelve minutes, and resembled a twenty mile roller coaster ride, swooping up and down and playing chicken with all the other cars, until at long long last we screeched to a stop on the gravel drive of Toadmore Hall, showering gravel in all directions.

"My goodness, I didn't realise how pale you are, Sam," she said. "You should get out into the sun more often."

An elderly butler appeared and looked at me as if I was something he had just spotted on the sole of his shoe.

"Good morning, madam," he said to Samantha. "You are in the blue room in the west wing. Your friend here is in the brown room in the east wing."

"That will be fine Jinx," Samantha said. "Where are the others?"

"On the rear sun terrace, madam," came the answer. "I'll arrange for your bags to be sent up to your rooms."

We went into the house and I took a look around me. It was large and Victorian in age; a tiled hall led to various doors, and a large ornate staircase curved its way to the first and second floors.

"Through here," said Samantha, "but before we go we must change your name. You see, they all call me Sam, and we can't both be Sam, can we." She led me through a lounge and out through some tall glass doors and onto the sun terrace.

As we went out I saw the Toadmore family for the first time. Eight of them, my detective's eye told me instantly. They lounged around in deck chairs, drinking gin and tonics, pretending to listen to a gramophone, but watching each other like hawks.

"Good morning, everyone," Samantha trilled. "Can I introduce my fiancée, Marmaduke Everard?" I glared at her, and made a mental note to add another five pounds to the bill.

"Hello, Sam," said a fat elderly man with a walrus moustache. Easing himself up, he took my hand. "I'm Lord Toadmore, and this is my wife, Lady Hilda."

"My aunt and uncle," explained Sam.

"Hi, Sam," said a slim, elegant young man in an effeminate voice. Then to me, "I'm Oscar, Samantha's cousin. Can I call you Marmy?"

"Not if you like the use of your legs," I told him.

"Ooooh my," he said. "Where did you get this troglodyte from, Sammi?" and he flounced away.

'Troglodyte' I thought, what's that? I'd have to find a dictionary and make a decision as to what further action I may need to take against young Oscar.

A svelte-looking redhead came up and took my hand.

"Hello Marmaduke, I'm Clarissa, Oscar's sister," she told me. "I like big men as well."

"Now look here everybody," I announced to the terrace, "you can call me Duke." A titter ran through the ensemble. I was starting to dislike this family.

Samantha continued the introductions. "This is my cousin Cedric and his wife Polly." I shook the hand of a sharp-looking character, complete with pencil line moustache and striped suit. I considered asking him if he had any petrol coupons for sale, and felt the hand of his tarty-looking peroxide wife.

"Hi, Duke," she giggled. I turned to the last couple.

"Uncle Harold and Aunt Mabel," Samantha said, and I looked at a nasty stuck-up couple who didn't even bother to shake hands. They were middle aged and overweight, with greedy faces.

"Good morning, Sam," they said, then turned away and resumed their seats.

Oscar was putting a new record on the gramophone, and 'Where did you get that hat' warbled across the terrace; self-consciously I took off my trilby and held it behind my back.

"So you're going to marry young Sam, then," said his Lordship, who was obviously head of the family group. "Cracking girl, what?"

I agreed, "Yes, she certainly is a cracking girl."

"When is the wedding?" asked Hilda, a thin elegant woman of about sixty.

"Oh, not this year, aunty," said Samantha.

"No, probably not next year either," I said.

"Good," said aunty. "Are you from the Gloucestershire Everard's?" she asked me.

"No, the Bethnal Green ones," I said.

"What time is the will going to be read tomorrow?" Samantha asked her uncle.

"Mr Scroat is coming down for midday, my dear," he told her.

"And about bloody time too," said uncle Harold, while cousin Cedric winked at his blonde wife, who giggled, and Oscar and Clarissa waltzed around the terrace.

"I'm going to show Marmaduke around," said Samantha, and guided me away from the terrace and out into the grounds.

We walked across the lawn to the shade of a large horse chestnut tree, and gazed up at it.

"Well, here's where grandmother fell," Samantha told me, poking her toe at a vaguely grandmother-shaped indentation in the ground.

"Did anybody see her fall?" I asked.

"No," she said. "Jinx the butler found her lying there with a broken neck."

"OK then, let's have a look at the house," I said, "and explain to me who stands to inherit what in the will."

"Now let me see," she said. "My daddy was the eldest son of the old Lord Toadmore, but he and mummy died years ago, before the Duke, so the title passed to Uncle Horace. Oscar and Clarissa are his children. The next son was Uncle Harold and his son is cousin Cedric, plus of course there was the old Duke's younger brother, great uncle Leonard, but he was a bit of a black sheep, got into some trouble and was packed off to the colonies and was never seen again."

"I see," I said. "Are they rich?"

"My goodness, no," she laughed. "There wasn't any money, just this house which was in grandmother's name, some old family jewels which should have passed to me as the only daughter of the eldest son, and some pictures and furniture and stuff. With the value of the house I suppose we stand to inherit about £100,000 between us."

"I thought you said you weren't rich," I remarked.

"Well two hundred years ago we owned most of Lancashire," she said, "but great grandfather was a lousy gambler and lost nearly everything, just as grandmother seems to have lost her jewels."

We went into the house and upstairs to her grandmother's room.

"Where would the jewels have been kept?" I enquired.

"In her jewellery box, here," she said, pulling out a brass bound oak chest from under the bed. She retrieved a key from a secret compartment in the bureau, and unlocked it. It was as empty as yesterday's bottle of Jack Daniels.

"So who knew where to find that key?" I asked her.

"Only family members, I suppose," she said.

I looked around. There was a large scrapbook. I looked inside it and read the newspaper cuttings from fifty years ago, when a beautiful dancer called Betty Adams had become a Lady. Then there were pictures of children and the family. Nothing at all about who the murderer could be, if indeed she was murdered.

"What did the police make of it?" I asked.

"They said it was accidental death; she shouldn't have been climbing trees at her age."

"And the missing jewels?"

"They weren't insured, so they doubted that there were any jewels. They said that they had probably been sold off years ago to pay for the upkeep of the house."

"So how do you know that's not true?" I asked.

"Because grandmother told me as recently as six months ago that she had held on to them just for me," Samantha said. "So what do you think, Mr Slade?"

"Well, it's perfectly straightforward, toots. Once we eliminate the impossible we are left with the probable, so who couldn't have killed her? Obviously you, or you wouldn't have hired the services of the best detective in the country. That leaves burglars, or people who stand to gain from her death, and that's the family. There are no signs of forced entry, and how could an intruder have known about the secret compartment with the hidden key, and nothing else was taken. So that just leaves the family."

"Oooh, you are clever, Mr Slade," she said, and secretly I had to agree with her.

"I'll show you your room," she told me, and we set off for the east wing, a particularly run down part of the house, I noticed.

"Watch out for the sixth step," she advised me as we climbed the staircase, and sure enough most of the tread was missing. We traversed the dusty corridor and entered the brown room. I could see why it was called the brown room, it was absolutely disgusting and every thing was brown, including the objects floating in the bath. Obviously Mr Jinx wasn't much of a butler.

"I'll see you at dinner, seven o'clock sharp," she said, and skipped out of the room. I couldn't help thinking WOW!!! Nice ass....pidistra.

I unpacked my overnight bag; just the dinner jacket, shirt and dickie, shaving kit and a couple of bottles of Jack Daniels. I threw the dinner suit onto a clean bit of the bed and sat and checked out a bottle of whiskey. I then noticed that somebody had slipped a note under the door. I moved across, picked it up and read it. It said, 'Please meet me in the summerhouse at 6pm'. Oh boy, good for Samantha I thought, and was startled by a knock on the door. I opened it, making Clarissa jump with surprise.

"Oh my goodness, Duke," she said, "do you always move that fast?"

"I sure do," I drawled in my toughest voice. "Did you just shove this note under my door?"

"Oh no," she said, "I wondered what Oscar was doing here, but he's gone now."

I crumpled the note up and threw it into the fireplace.

Clarissa came into the room and closed the door behind her, then seated herself in my chair.

"So you're Sammy's bit of rough," she said. "You're a very handsome man, Duke. I just love the way the scars run across your cheeks."

She eyed the whiskey bottles and said, "Are you a private detective?"

"No, I'm a writer," I told her.

"Oh my, what do you write?" she asked me.

"Mostly reports for insurance companies," I told her. "Anyway, how can I help you?"

"It was more a case of me wondering if I can help you," she replied.

"So what's happening tomorrow?" I asked her. She looked a bit disappointed and said,

"It's grandmama's will reading."

"So who gets what?" I asked her.

"I don't really care," she told me, "there's only the house and a few personal effects, and daddy is already wealthy enough; he wouldn't be caught dead living in this old ruin."

"Don't you get anything?" I asked.

"No, shouldn't think so," she said, looking as if she really didn't care.

Two hours later, Clarissa staggered out of the room, and I considered the new facts that I'd learnt. Clarissa and Oscar stood to gain nothing by the old girl's death, and the list of suspects was dwindling. I finished off the bottle of whiskey, then washed and changed for dinner.

I admired myself in the dressing table mirror. The hired suit wasn't a bad fit, although I wasn't sure about the four inches of shirt cuff showing. And I was still trying to get the jacket buttons done up over my chest when I heard the dinner gong.

I made my way downstairs, carefully missing the seventh step, and putting my foot through the hole in the sixth, and limped through the hall and into the dining room where the family were gathered. Samantha rushed across and grabbed my hand while both Clarissa and Oscar both winked at me.

"Well, young Everard, what do you do for a living?" asked Uncle Harold. I looked around to see who he was talking to, and Samantha nudged me.

"Oh, I'm a traveller," I said.

"What in - ladies underwear?" Uncle Harold smirked, and a titter ran around the room.

Clarissa said, "Not at all uncle. He is a writer. Better watch out or he might write about you."

"Dinner is served," announced Jinx the butler. I looked at him; he was old and a bit decrepit, and he did remind me of someone. We moved to the table and I held Samantha's chair for her as she sat down, resisting the impulse to pull it away at the last moment. I then sat down beside her. From the other side of the table a foot reached across and stroked my leg; I looked across and Clarissa and Oscar smiled at me.

A plate of soup was dumped ungraciously in front of me, and I waited until everyone had been served. I tasted a spoonful and it was stone cold. Well they weren't going to catch me out; I'd heard about this cold soup, consume I thought they called it.

Uncle Harold leaned across and said, "How's your soup Everard?"

"Delicious," I lied.

"Well mines damn freezing cold," he said. "Jinx, take this muck away. How are the rest of you?"

"Cold," everyone said.

"And take everyone else's away too, except for Everard here; his is delicious."

I manfully finished off my soup and the next course was served: tiny little chickens and a few mixed vegetables.

"These are small chickens," I said, "shame to kill them so young."

"Actually they are grouse," said Samantha.

"A bit high, aren't they?" I said, and she smiled as if I had said something funny.

We then had a sweet, which was strawberries and cream. At least the cook couldn't ruin that, although I did spot Jinx licking cream off his thumb after he had served me.

Cheese and biscuits came next and the port began its rounds, starting off with uncle Horace to my left, and going to everyone on the table before it reached me. I was beginning to need a meeting with Johnny Walker.

"Bit of a rum do about the old girl," said Uncle Harold. "What on earth was she doing, fooling around with trees at her age?"

"Probably a bit ga ga," said cousin Cedric, winking at me. I gave him a dirty look back.

Samantha said, "What do you think about it, Marmaduke?" giving me a fierce dig in the ribs when I failed to answer.

"Oh, er, I haven't a clue," I said, which wasn't exactly the truth, for my detective's instincts were beginning to put together some interesting pieces of the puzzle.

"Would you like a little stroll, my dear," I said to her, and Clarissa and Oscar's faces fell.

We got up and strolled out of the room, arm in arm.

"Have you solved the case yet, Mr Slade?" Samantha whispered.

"Maybe I have," I told her. "I just need to check something out."

We made our way out to the garden and down to the horse chestnut tree, and I looked around a bit, nothing at all. A few yards away there was some garden furniture, so I went and fetched a wooden garden chair and placed it at the foot of the trunk and climbed up onto it. I felt around and there was some carving on the trunk.

I lit a match and looked, and there, carved into the trunk was **'BALLS'**…..

Yes, that proved my theory ok, and now it was time for that drink.

Samantha declined to accompany me, so I retired to my room and locked and barricaded the door; Clarissa I could just about stand, but no way did I feel like sorting out young Oscar tonight.

The next morning, I struggled awake and gazed at the row of empty bottles. The entire percussion section of the London Symphony Orchestra seemed to be playing inside my skull, which quickly segued into a gentle tapping on my door.

"Mr Slade, are you awake?" said Samantha's voice from the other side of the woodwork.

I struggled to the door and opened it.

"Oh Mr Slade, are you ill?" she asked.

"No, I'm fine," I lied. "Why are you here so early?"

"Well it is 11.30am, Mr Slade," she said. "They are reading the will in half an hour, and I wanted to know if you had any conclusions."

"I certainly have," I told her, realising that I was standing there in my vest and pants. Give me fifteen minutes to wash and dress, then I will be right down.

She disappeared down the hall and I sucked on the cork of the last whiskey bottle as I washed and shaved; then, dressed in my sharpest private detective-type suit, I made my way down to the study where the family were gathered.

They were all there, and Jinx pottered around with a tray of coffee in chipped cups. Mr Scroat, the solicitor, was trying to get everybody seated so he could start reading the will. Finally it was time and he opened the envelope and cleared his scrawny throat.

A hush came over the room as he read from the sheet of paper before him.

I, Belinda Smith, Lady Toadmore, being of sound mind, do hereby bequeath and leave the following items and property as listed hereafter:

1. *I leave all of my jewellery to my dear granddaughter Saman-tha Smith.*

A few sniggers and tut tuts ran around the room, Mr Scroat cleared his throat disapprovingly, and silence descended again.

2. *I bequest the sum of £200 to my faithful butler Jinx.*

This time the buzz around the room was louder and more disapproving. Mr Scroat raised his voice and said,

146

3.   *Toadmore Hall and all its furniture, fixtures, fittings, grounds and all items pursuant, to be sold, and all monies raised by all such sales,*

Mr Scroat paused, and every person in the room leaned forward mouths open,

Is to be presented to the Toadmore Society for the Rescue and Housing of Stray Cats,

he finished, triumphantly. A babble of outraged protest filled the study, and Jinx laughed.

"Ok, Samantha. Introduce me. I have something to say," I whispered to the girl beside me. She stood up and walked to the desk where the solicitor was sitting.

"Quiet please, everybody," she called, and the noise subsided.

"May I introduce you all to Sam Slade." I stood up and joined her at the desk.

"Mr Slade is a famous private detective," she said, "and he is here to look into granny's death and the disappearance of her jewels."

They all looked at me with renewed interest, and Oscar winked. I tried to ignore him.

"This is an interesting case," I began. "The first question I had to address was, was she murdered or did she fall? The next question was, what has happened to the jewels? And lastly, who was responsible?"

I paused for dramatic effect, while the family looked at each other with suspicion.

"First I shall give the answer to the third question," I told them. "It was, of course, Jinx the butler. Why? Well, let's face it, the butler always did it."

But not only that, I found the clue carved into the fatal tree - BALLS."

"How dare you, sir," said Uncle Horace.

"That's what it says," I told him, "and it stands for 'Belinda Adams Loves Leonard Smith,' doesn't it, Jinx, or should I say Great Uncle Leonard?"

"By Gad sir, this can't be true," said Uncle Horace, "you can't be Uncle Leonard?"

"I'm afraid it is, Your Lordship," I told him. "When did you come back, Leonard? A couple of years ago, when the old Lord died: and what was the scandal that made you flee abroad? Let me guess. Were you her Ladyships secret lover? Did she have your child? Haven't any of you noticed the resemblance between Jinx and Uncle Harold, and how Harold always got the choicest portions at dinner last night."

Everyone in the room turned and stared at Harold who was turning a delicate shade of purple.

"So, the old Lord died, and great uncle Leonard seized the opportunity to return home to Lady Toadmore, who of course knew exactly who he was. But what he really wanted was the house and money, so when he found out that the property was going to the cats' home and only £200 to him, he persuaded the old girl to have a romantic walk in the garden with him, and took her to the tree where all those years ago he had carved their initials.

Of course, after all those years the initials had gown nine feet from the ground, so he fetched a garden chair for her to stand on, and while she balanced on the chair, admiring the carving, he kicked the chair from beneath her, causing her to fall to her death.

He couldn't change the will so he rushed inside to the duchess's room, and stole her jewels. After hiding them in his own room he went back out into the garden, removed the chair and phoned for an ambulance.

All he had to do was wait for the will to be read, get his money, and then go abroad again with the ducal jewels, enough to keep him in luxury for the rest of his life, with a bit left over to leave to Harold."

The door opened and two policemen entered the room.

"Leonard Smith," one of them said, "I am arresting you on suspicion of the murder of Lady Toadmore, and the theft of the ducal jewels. Anything you say will be taken down, and may be used in evidence against you."

I was hoping that he might say 'trousers', but he didn't, he just said,

"It's a fair cop," and left the room with them.

I turned back and faced the family. Uncle Harold in particular was looking extremely deflated, and flopped down into his chair.

"And that, your Lordship and ladies and gentlemen, ends my investigation," I told them. "I took the liberty of informing the constabulary before I came in here, and if you ever need the services of a private investigator, here is my card." I snatched the card back from Oscar and passed it to Lord Toadmore.

"Dashed clever stuff is all I can say," said the duke, dropping my card into the fireplace from where it was retrieved by Clarissa.

Samantha grabbed hold of my arm and said, "I knew that you would solve it Sam, so where are my jewels?"

"Right here my dear," I said. "You see, I took the further liberty of searching Jinx's room before I phoned the police, and there they were, packed in his suitcase ready for his escape," and I produced the collection of rather splendid jewels from my pockets, rather like a conjurer producing rabbits.

"Well bless my soul," said Lord Toadmore, "so there were jewels after all."

"Yes of course there are," said Samantha. "Grandmother always told me there were, and that she was going to leave them to me, but I intend to share them with Clarissa and Oscar." Both Clarissa and Oscar squealed in delight, and Samantha turned to me with that gorgeous smile of hers.

"Mr Spade," she said, "I can't thank you enough."

"Just part of the job, ma'am," I drawled.

"Well how about a lift back into town?" she asked.

I paled as memories of the previous day's ride flooded back, and said,

"Well its only twenty miles, and this rain isn't going to last forever, so perhaps I'll walk it."

"Well, ok then, Mr Slade," she said. "I'll tell the chauffer to put the Roller away," and she skipped off and hugged Clarissa and Oscar, while I went up to fetch my bag to begin the long but safe walk home.

And that, gentlemen, is the 'case of the tree-climbing duchess,' finished Sam, looking suitably tough, while finishing off his large scotch.

TWELVE
The Great Game

Like most Income Tax Inspectors, Herbert Hinchliffe was boring. He could make a passing comment on the weather last for half an hour, and no one in the club dared to mention Herbert's passion of stamp collecting, less he became buttonholed in a corner, to have the intricacies of perforations explained to him in excruciating detail.

Tonight the unthinkable had happened, he had decided to tell the members a story. Confidently they had waited for the oldest member to put him in his place and shut him up, but no, the old man seemed to be in a spiteful mood, and made no attempt to intervene. The members nursed their drinks and prepared to be bored to the point of death and beyond.

"Well I have listened to many of your stories, and enjoyed them immensely, although most of them are a bit sparse on detail" Herbert began. "So tonight I am going to tell you about the time I attended the National Accountants Annual Conference or NAAC for short." There was a stony silence, which was interrupted by a few little whimpers from some of the younger members.

I shall skip telling you about getting up and what I had for breakfast on that day; suffice to say that I was dressed in my navy blue pinstripe suit, white shirt, brown and cream striped tie, brown brogue shoes, and I was on the bus for nine am, a number forty nine I recall, and heading for the railway station.

I purchased my second class return ticket to Macclesfield, for two pounds ten shillings, which is the return ticket rate you understand, although it doesn't apply at weekends, nor Bank Holidays. And carefully placed my receipt into my wallet, so I could place a travel claim once I returned to the office.

Then I stood on the station platform waiting for the nine fifty am train's arrival. It was platform three of course, unless you are thinking of changing at Crewe, then it would have to be platform two.

As you might have expected the 9.50am train was running late and didn't even pull into the station until 9.57am, and I made a note of the fact in my diary. It was actually 10am when the train pulled out of the station; while I found a seat in a compartment in a corridor carriage. I put my brown imitation leather suitcase on to the luggage rack, amongst the four other cases which were already up there. Then I sat and relaxed and looked at my fellow passengers.

Next to me sat a slim blonde girl. She allowed her knee to press against mine and I immediately pulled my leg away, why we hadn't even been introduced. Opposite sat a vicar, who was reading a magazine called Variety. Next to him sat a dapper chap wearing a chequered suit, he had a pencil line moustache, and a beer belly. The final person who had just followed me into the carriage, was a tall thin saturnine man dressed entirely in black. He took off his black overcoat and hat, revealing his black suit, black shirt and tie, even black shoes and socks. I remember wondering what his favourite colour was.

It wasn't long before the man in the chequered suit began to chat up the blonde girl, and she was soon laughing and giggling at his jokes.

"So there was this tax inspector," he said, "who went to his doctor, and said, doctor somehow I have injured myself all over, the doctor said, why do you think that.

The tax-man said, well, wherever I touch myself it's agony, here owww, touching his leg, here aaaahhhhh touching his arm, here ouch! touching his chin.

The doctor said, you have a broken finger."

The vicar looked his disapproval over his spectacles, and the man in black ignored us all.

"What goes, black white black white black white?" he asked,

"A zebra, a small African member of the equine species, generally inhabiting the grasslands of central and southern Africa, taxonomic interpretations do vary, but most experts would place them in the genus equus. Although there are three quite distinct sub species." I informed him

"No a nun rolling down a hill," the self appointed carriage comedian told us triumphantly, and the vicar looked even more disapproving.

"I must tell you about this tax inspector who fell down a rubbish chute and broke every bone in his body," he said.

Well I couldn't let that go. "There are actually two hundred and seventy five bones in the human skeleton," I informed him, "however a fusing process does occur through maturity, leaving a total of two hundred and five different bones, in a fully developed adult Why the axial skeleton itself, comprising of skull, vertebrae, ribs and sternum consists of eighty bones alone, so to break every one of them would be an almost impossible task.

Besides how could he break the tiny anvil bones of the inner ear just by falling down a rubbish chute? Which would presumably have some sort of containerized receptacle positioned in an optimum position below it to contain and preserve any rubbish that happened to descend by way of the chute."

The chap in the chequered suit shut up, and we all settled down into a gloomy silence. Before too long had passed I began to feel tired, and started to amuse myself by mentally working out the square roots of prime numbers. Even that failed to keep me awake, and before long I had snoozed off.

Eventually I awoke and opened my bleary eyes, I was alone in the carriage, all the suitcases were up on the luggage shelf, while coats, a handbag, and a variety magazine were strewn over the seats, just no fellow passengers.

Probably in the dining car, I thought, just as well, they were a bit boring. I looked out of the window and it was pitch black, puzzled I checked my watch, it was 10.45, no way, I couldn't have slept for over twelve hours, yet it was dark outside, we must be in a tunnel. I sat and listened to the rumble of the train wheels, and ten minutes later we still appeared to be in the infernal tunnel. I gave it another ten minutes; we were still in the tunnel.

I checked my watch '10.45'. It must have stopped, and that's very unusual, you see my watch was an Ingersol, noted for their reliability and refined style. Also I had wound it the requisite fifteen turns that morning, directly after I had had my toast, lightly buttered with polyunsaturated margarine. I shook my watch and gave it a couple of winds, nothing. I waited another ten minutes or so and we were still in the blessed tunnel.

That was enough, I decided to investigate what was happening, and got up and looked down the empty corridor, it seemed very quiet.

I got a chain and padlock out of my pocket, and secured my suitcase to the luggage shelf. One can't be too careful these days. I then put on my overcoat, and left the compartment.

I walked down the corridor looking into the other empty compartments. No one anywhere, plenty of hats and coats, bags, shoes, books, but no passengers. I looked into the toilet compartment, it was as empty as the rest of the train appeared to be.

My own compartment was near the back of the train and I moved forward checking all the carriages. Not a soul anywhere, and the train still appeared to be speeding through the total darkness. Four carriages were checked and still I hadn't seen anyone.

I entered the dining car. It was as empty as the Chief Tax Inspector's heart, plenty of half eaten meals on the tables, drinks, even money lying on the table tops, but no diners or staff.

The next carriage was the bar, and I went into it. There was no one behind the bar, half empty glasses were all over the place though. I continued going forward, then at last I saw someone sitting at the end table with his back to me.

That was a relief, I was beginning to think that I was the only person on the train. As I drew closer I noticed that he was dressed all in black. Hmmm probably the quiet man from my cabin, I thought, perhaps he knows where everyone is. I walked up to him, and without looking up he gestured for me to sit opposite him.

Bit of a cheek, we haven't been introduced, I thought, but sat down across the table from him anyway.

"This seems to be an awfully long tunnel," I began, "the wheels seem to be clicking once every second, each section of rail is seventy five feet long, so that's four thousand five hundred feet a minute, which is two hundred and seventy thousand feet an hour, or fifty miles an hour."

He looked at me from beneath his arched eyebrows and said, "fifty one, point, one three six actually".

"Aha, are you going to the NAAC?" I asked him. He shook his head.

"Shame, you would have enjoyed it," I said, "Two hundred accountants, talking figures, and tax thresholds" He winced slightly.

"The strangest thing is though, that we must have been in this tunnel for at least an hour, how could any tunnel be fifty miles long?" I asked him.

"Oh, I know of some," he said.

"Do you have the time?" I asked him.

"10.45," he replied not even looking at his watch.

"What, 10.45pm, where on earth are we," I asked.

He laughed, a wicked sounding laugh, "Who said you were on earth," he chuckled.   I'd had enough of this nonsense and began to get up.

153

"Stay right there," he snapped. And the power drained from my legs.

I slumped back into the seat. "Who on earth are you?" I managed to croak.

"I have many names, and many faces," he said. "Do you wish to see some of them?"

"No thank you very much," I said hastily. "Where are we?"

"I am the dark one, the taker of men's souls, and we are heading for my world," he told me.

"Am I dead?" I asked dazedly.

"Not dead, not yet anyway, not until we have decided who has your soul."

"I d d d don't understand," I stuttered.

"I'm a sport, and I'm willing to play a game with you for your immortal soul, if I win, you will spend eternity in the flames of damnation; if you win, you don't die this time."

"And what is the game?" I asked shaking a bit.

"That's the interesting bit, you get to choose the game, it makes little difference, for I have played games for thousands of years, what is it to be? Chess, cards, dominoes, hangman, just name it."

I sat and thought, I had good mathematical skills but so obviously had he, perhaps I should ask for a game of golf, I would have liked to see how he would have managed that on a train.

"Good choice old sport," interrupted Spencer Harris, the clubs golf fanatic.

"The trouble was, I wasn't any good at golf," continued Herbert, much to Spencer's disappointment.

At last I said, "Very well, I choose a general knowledge quiz.

He laughed and said, "My favourite game," my heart sank even further.

"It will be 'Sudden Death', an apt phrase, don't you think, we shall take it in turns to ask each other questions and the first to answer wrong will lose," he explained. "You may ask the first question."

"Alright," I said, "The worlds population is just over two point six billion people, can you tell me all their names?."

"No," he said, "now it's my turn,"

"Wait, you didn't answer it," I told him.

"Yes I did, the question was, 'Can you tell me,' and the correct answer was, 'no I can't.' Now my question for you is, what is the square root of 666?"

"Twenty five point eight zero six nine seven five," I told him. "Ask me another one." He shook his head.

"No it's your turn to ask a question, stick to the rules," he said...

"Ok, what's the boiling point of water?" I asked.

"Fahrenheit or Centigrade?" he wanted to know.

"Centigrade,"

"Easy, that's One Hundred degrees Centigrade," he smirked.

"No, that's an incomplete answer," I told him, " you should have said one hundred degrees centigrade, is the ambient temperature at which distilled water will boil at sea level, however the higher one goes above sea level the lower the requisite temperature will become, thus giving an almost infinite variation in the barometric pressure against temperature to boiled distilled water.

I say almost infinite because it would be unlikely that there are actually infinite variations, although it would be an enjoyable exercise trying to work them out. Not only that but….."

"Will you shut the hell up," said the Dark One, "OK, I will give you that one."

"So I win then," I said.

"No it's the best of three," I was told.

"But that's not sudden death."

"If you don't shut up it will be," the Dark One told me. "Now here's a question for you,"

There was a racehorse
That won great fame
What do you think
Was the horse's name.

I sat and looked at him, until finally he said.

"Well are you going to answer the question?"

"What question?"

"The damned question I just asked you," he replied, his fingers tapping up and down on the table.

"Well the subject of your vaguely couched statement was not submitted to me in the form of a question, but rather as a statement to the effect that there was a racehorse called 'what do you think'," I informed him."

He groaned, and glared at me through eyes that appeared to be turning redder by the minute.

"Just get on with it, and ask me a question," he said.

"Ok, which is the heaviest, a pound of gold or a pound of feathers?"

"Ha ha, stupid trick questions will not fool me, they both weigh the same," he said, with a laugh

"Not at all," I told him, "Gold is weighed in Troy ounces at twelve to the pound while feathers are weighed at sixteen ounces to the Avoirdupois pound, so quite obviously a pound of feathers are the heaviest...

Of course Avoirdupois comes from the middle English avoir de pois, itself taken from the old French aveir de peis, literally meaning goods of weight, from property, goods from aveir, to have; which comes directly from the Latin habere, to have, or to hold or possess property. Of course pies is from the Latin pensum, which means weight, so you see..."

"Will you please just shut up," he said holding his temples.

I was beginning to enjoy this, "Go on ask me another question," I said.

"No it's your turn again," he replied

"OK what's black white black white black white?"

"Is it a nun rolling down a hill," he asked

"No it's a Zebra, a small striped member of the genus equus, shall we make it the best of a hundred?" I asked him.

He flinched and said, "No! The game is over, I can't take any more," he clicked his long pointy nailed fingers and my eyes closed. I opened them and I was back in the carriage.

The vicar was reading his magazine, and the guy in the chequered suit was winking at the blonde girl. There was no sign of the tall man dressed in black, and the train exited a tunnel into the morning light. I looked at my watch it was ten forty five and the second hand was sweeping round.

"I have just had the most extraordinary dream," I told my fellow passengers, but they all jumped up and began grabbing their bags and coats, before disappearing into the corridor and heading in the direction of the dining car.

156

"So that completes the story of the first forty five minutes, of the two hour twenty minute train journey," said Herbert, as the last of the clubs members disappeared into the corridor, heading in the direction of the bar. All except for the oldest member of course, who appeared to be asleep, although with him you could never tell.

Herbert settled himself down in the leather armchair opposite and said. "Now I am going to tell you the interesting bit, all about the conference itself...."

THIRTEEN
The Man Who Should Be King

It seems as if every place has one, no matter where it is. Yes, every workplace, regiment, university and school has one: the know it all, get on your nerves, pain in the neck, and unfortunately the Lyre Club was no exception.

The cross the members had to bear was one Percy Planter. Anything you have done, he's done it better, and he had the sort of face you just wanted to smack. If you have climbed the North Face of the Matterhorn so had he, and had read a good book on the way up. If you had swum the English Channel, he had swam it both ways without even bothering to claim the record. In fact, Percy was the very epitome of unpopularity.

Little Martin Fletcher had put him up for membership one April the first, as a joke against the oldest member, and everyone was laughing so much that they had all left it to someone else to blackball him, which of course hadn't happened, so he was a member, like it or not.

It was a quiet Friday; most of the members being away on holiday, with only a dozen or so regulars in the lounge when Percy jumped up and said,

"I bet you are all wondering about my name 'Planter'."

"Not at all," grumbled the oldest member from his chair by the fireplace. "Why should we care what you are called?"

Percy silenced the chorus of groans coming from around the room by calling for a round of drinks, and then rather spoilt the effect by telling the waiter to make sure that he got the correct amounts charged to the members' individual tabs.

"Now then," said Percy again, "I'm sure you are all wondering about my name 'Planter'."

The oldest member just bit his tongue and glared, and Percy, who wouldn't have recognised a' put down' if it came up and bit him on the butt, continued,

"Well I was wondering too, so I did a bit of research, and what do you think I discovered?" Percy ignored the stony silence and triumphantly said, "I found that it was a corruption of a very very distinguished name." This was met by a series of disbelieving groans, and even mutters of 'rubbish' could be distinguished.

"It's perfectly true," said Percy. "My research led me to the British Museum, where of course I am well known."

"How so?" asked the oldest member.

"Because of the dozens of archaeological treasures and artefacts I have discovered and presented to them," said Percy. "Why, they are even thinking of naming a gallery after me, 'The Sir Percy Planter Gallery', I should think. Anyway, armed with a few notes on my family history, such as my grandfather, 'The Saviour of India', and my great grandfather, 'The Hero of Waterloo'"…

"The Hero of Waterloo?" said the oldest member, in disbelief.

"Oh yes, said Percy. Great grandfather Herbert Planter saved Wellington's bacon many times on that day."

"How come? Was he fighting on Napoleon's side?" asked the oldest member.

"Not at all, old boy," said Percy, blind to the obvious sarcasm. "He was the man who rode off and fetched Blucher and his Germans, and got back in time to defeat the Old Guard. It is said that after the battle Wellington presented him with his boots in gratitude. Great grandfather called them his Wellington Boots, and the name stuck."

"So why was Granddad called the Saviour of India?" queried the oldest member, who had done his time out there.

"Well, it was during the Great Mutiny," said Percy. "Grandfather had just finished fighting in the Crimea. He rescued the remnants of the Light Brigade, which had just committed the most incredible feux pas. Lord Cardigan was so grateful that he gave him his knitted pullover. Grandfather put some buttons down the front and called it his cardigan. Well of course everyone else wanted one and the name stuck."

"India," said the oldest member.

"Yes, well grandfather turned down the VC, just didn't have time to go see the Queen to collect it, troubles brewing in India you see. The Sepoy Regiments had been issued with cartridges greased with pork fat, Great uncle Henry had instituted that; there is hardly any use for pork fat in India, religious thing you see, so great uncle had sold the army 500 tons of the stuff to grease the cartridges with.

Well the Hindu and Moslem regiments weren't at all happy about it, even after they had been told that there were perfectly valid business reasons for it. Threw them all away they did, and when their officers admonished them, they just killed them and mutinied.

You can bet that granddad wasn't going to stand for that sort of nonsense, so he caught the first ship over and arrived to find absolute chaos.

A desperate Governor General and his staff met granddad on the quayside, and briefed him on the situation,

"What should we do?" they asked.

Grandfather took out his pocket map of India and said,

"I'll look now."

"Of course, Lucknow, that's the key to central India." They all shouted and raced off to mount a relief expedition. Grandfather joined the expedition that relieved the besieged residency and led to the defeat of the mutineers.

"Hmmmm," said the oldest member, "so what happened in the British museum?"

"I was interested in tracing my family history," said Percy, "so I told the head curator to fetch me all the books that mentioned my family. Of course there were dozens of them, and I pored over them for days, reading about the exploits of ancestors such as Henry Planter, the first discoverer of electricity, and Captain Hadrian Planter who taught Nelson all he knew. Further and further back I went, to Ichabod Planter who persuaded the colonists in America that they shouldn't pay tax on tea, and Lady Mary Planter who was close friends with Charles II. I quickly skipped that one. Ebenezer Planter was the hero of the battles of Dunbar and Worcester, where he taught the rascally Scots a thing or two, and saved Cromwell's hide.

Big Hamish Mactavish turned a dangerous shade of red, but Percy carried on with his story.

And so it continued. Whenever great events happened, a Planter was there to help destiny and save the nation. What would Raleigh and Drake have done if Sydney Planter hadn't visited America first, and hadn't drawn them a map of how to get there?

Who snitched on Guy Fawkes and saved Parliament? A Planter of course, but then suddenly in 1550 the name completely disappeared from the history books. What could it mean? I searched and searched, but drew a complete blank.

I was about to give up when I looked at a really old book. It appeared to be from the fifteenth century, and the curator had told me that only a few special people, such as myself, had been given access to it. It was obviously a contemporary account of the events during the turbulent reign of Richard III and the events after the battle of Bosworth.

So where was the reference to Planter, I wondered, reading about Richard's coronation. And what was this? It appeared that far from murdering the Princes in the Tower, he actually made them part of his family, declaring Edward as his true heir. Upon hearing of Henry Tudor's landing in Wales, Richard had sent Edward and his young brother to York for safety while he dealt with the pretender.

Unfortunately, we know what happened then; Richard died trying to swap his kingdom for a horse.

Henry usurped the throne, and young prince Edward fled from York along with his brother, to hide until he could claim his crown. It was tucked away on this page that I found a note written in a medieval hand. It said,

'And the true kinge, to hide his identity did take the false name of Planter for Plantagenet, and married a lady of noble birth and had issue of a son'.

There then followed a family tree, which led directly to my ancestor Jasper Planter, founder of the Royal Navy.

So you see, it was there in black and white. I was the true heir to the throne of England, not these Jerries who inhabit it at the moment.

It took a while for the laughter in the club to subside before the oldest member was able to ask, "So what are you going to do about that then?"

"Well, I already did it," said Percy. "The first thing was to make copies of all the books and papers, then a visit to my solicitor, Mr Souhem, of Souhem Forral & Runne. He was intrigued, and told me that my claim to the throne was beyond question, and that he would be happy to represent me. He even suggested that I demand the hand of the young royal princess to unite the dynasties. Things were certainly looking up for yours truly.

When I got home that evening, however, I immediately sensed that something was wrong. The broken door lock, and my possessions scattered around the floor reinforced this belief. If it was burglars, why hadn't my money and valuables been stolen, not to mention the manuscript of my memoirs? Obviously, someone had been looking for something, but what? Then it struck me; it must be the evidence of my right to the throne.

Well, I wasn't going to stand for that, I can tell you, and picked up the phone to talk to an old school chum who just happened to be the head of Scotland Yard. The double click on the line told me that my phone had been bugged.

I decided to leave the Rolls in the garage and walk into town, and as I walked I realised that two men in black overcoats and derby hats were following me. Luckily I was a black belt in judo, karate, and Tai Kwando, so I had no fear at all. I carefully led them on until it was dark and quiet enough for me to turn and overpower them. I threw them over my shoulder and prepared to finish them off, when one of them managed to croak,

"Careful guv'nor, we're police."

"Police," I echoed. "What on earth are you following me for?

They clambered up and produced warrant cards. "It's a matter of state security, sir," they said in unison. "We must ask you to accompany us to the tower of London."

Well, as I theoretically owned the bally tower, I agreed to accompany them, and we walked back to their black Rover car and set off for the tower.

"Can you drive past Buckingham Palace?" I asked them. "I want to check out the colour of the curtains." We soon arrived at the tower and drove inside the grounds.

"This way, sir," said one of the special policemen, and led the way into the White tower, and I shortly found myself locked in the same room as my ancestor prince Edward had been.

A couple of hours passed and I amused myself by mentally working out some advanced mathematical theories, until the door swung open and two bowler-hatted individuals, and one of the secret policemen, entered the room.

"So this is the Young Pretender," said the older and obviously senior of the two.

"Yes sir," said the policeman.

"Oh dear, what a mess," said the junior one. "I suppose that there can be no doubt about it?"

"Of course there isn't," said the older one. "Besides, you only have to look at his regal bearing and fantastic good looks. It was only a matter of time before a Planter put two and two together and worked out the connections."

"I'm sorry, your majesty," he said to me, "but we must ask you to remain here as our guest while we consult with the prime minister."

"No, I wish to leave now," I said, but I was talking to a rapidly closing door, and then there was silence.

I went into the small toilet which had been built into the corner of my room, and sat down and read the graffiti of centuries which had been carved into the walls. One little verse caught my attention; it said,

> The ultimate nemeses never ever y leaves
> Even now the rope awaits y needs
> Can enemies here entombed repent y errors
> Preserve us saints y hide its terrors

That's a strange thing for the noble prisoners who have been locked up in here to write, I thought to myself. The rhyme didn't even scan properly. I turned my attention to little poems about sitting here broken hearted, and the little chart that said 'days to go', Anne Boleyn. Ah yes, Anne Boleyn, I mused. Hadn't she been beheaded? So why would prisoners like her fear the rope?

I reread the little verse, and almost instantly my brilliant mind worked out the code. If I just took the first letters of the words, it read: 'T U N N E L E N T R A N C E   H E R E   P U S H   I T'. Push it, I wondered. Push what, exactly? I stood up and prowled around my cell like a caged lion. It had no window, and the door was oak - hundreds of years old and hard as iron. The floor had been concreted at some time and was as smooth as a baby's bottom.

I examined the walls; nothing there offered any hope. Was it some sick sixteenth century joke? I had another look at the poem. It was carved into the wall next to what appeared to be a bricked up fire place, hmmmm. I took a look at the stones cemented into the opening; they appeared to be as solid as a rock. They had names carved on them, and one of the names was Indigo Turner - that spelt IT.

I pushed against the stone, and fraction-by-fraction of an inch it began to move back.

A bare hour later I had the stone out of its seating, and was looking into a large cavity that had once been a chimney. So there was a tunnel, and through pure genius I had rediscovered it after centuries of secrecy. Dawn wasn't far away, so I replaced the stone and waited to see how events unfolded.

At 8am a surly secret policeman brought me a bowl of gruel and a glass of water.

"What time can I leave?" I asked him, but I would have got more answers from the stones in the walls. Fifteen minutes later he returned and removed the plate and utensils. I poured some cold water from the jug into the bowl on my bedside cupboard, and had a quick wash, then sat and waited to see what would happen next. It was 2pm before the door reopened and the two bowler hats came back in.

"Mr Planter," said the older one, "we have a paper here that we wish you to sign."

IT WAS QUITE OBVIOUS THAT THESE JERRIES SQUATTING ON MY THRONE WOULD HAVE TO STAND DOWN.

"What is it?" I asked.

"It's your abdication and renunciation of the throne," he told me.

"And why on earth should I agree to that?" I asked him.

"Because no one knows that you are here, and you're not leaving until you sign it," he said.

"And if I refuse," I asked.

"Well, just look at some of the names on the walls in here. They all refused simple requests, and think of what became of them," he replied.

The young one said, "Rather".

The older one gave him a dirty look and said to me, "You have 24 hours to consider your situation. We will be back," and with that they turned and left the cell, so once again I was left looking at a locked door.

The hours passed slowly, and I rested so as to be ready for my escape attempt that night. Had anybody ever succeeded in escaping from the tower, I wondered? Probably not, but then they hadn't been Percy Planters, had they. During the afternoon I used the toilet, and found a good use for the second copy of the abdication documents.

At 6pm the secret policeman came in and set down another bowl of gruel and a cup of weak tea. I could tell immediately that they hadn't warmed the pot. I had my meagre meal, and fifteen minutes later the pots were retrieved and I was locked up for the night.

I waited until midnight, and then made my move. I prised the keystone from the fireplace, and within the hour had made a hole big enough to crawl through.

"How could you see anything?" asked the oldest member.

"Well, there was no gas or electricity in the cell, so they had left me some candles and matches. Had to, you see, as there was no window."

Anyway, I had a look around in the old fireplace. The chimney had been bricked up centuries ago, but someone had burrowed out through the side of it and into the wall which must have been six feet thick. Even so, the tunnel was small, and I had to remove my clothes to fit in, slim and athletic though I am.

Pushing my clothes and shoes in a bundle ahead of me, I inched down the narrow tunnel. Down I went, through what must have been several floors, and then the tunnel entered what appeared to be an abandoned sewer, sterilised by age and quite spacious after the tunnel. I quickly got dressed and made my way along the sewer, and after about fifty yards I saw a tiny chink of light. I went up to it, looked through the gap between two stones, and what do you think I saw?

"Your house," said the oldest member.

"No, I was looking into the room that housed the crown jewels, actually into the back of the display cabinet where they were kept at that time.

Now then Percy, I thought to myself, those crown jewels belong to you by divine right, so why don't you take them with you?

I used my house keys to remove the soft mortar from around the stone with the gap, and by 3am I was able to remove the stone and look upon my crown.

I had to be a bit selective as there was too much to carry at once, so I placed the crown on my head, a perfect fit I remember, filled my pockets with jewels and took the orb and sceptre in my arms; I must say that they felt so right in my hands.

I continued along the disused sewer tunnel, always sloping slightly downwards, until it began to fill with water. I took a deep breath and ducked below the surface and carried on for another twenty five yards underwater; luckily, I was a champion diver and swimmer.

Then I felt the remains of an iron grate, which had all but rusted away over the centuries. I swam through a gap and surfaced some way out in the river.

In spite of the weight of the crown jewels I managed to float on my back and kick my way downstream, and after about half a mile I swam ashore and crawled out amongst some warehousing.

I quickly hid the crown and emblems of royalty in a disused warehouse, and then made my way back into town. It obviously wouldn't have been safe to go home, so I made my way to the home of an old school chum, who just happened to be editor of a national newspaper. I knocked on the door and he let me in, saying, "Percy old chap, it's 5am, what on earth is going on?"

I quickly explained to him the events of the last couple of days, and he looked at me in utter disbelief; that is, until I began to empty my pockets of the jewels and the abdication documents that I still carried.

"My word, Percy, this is the scoop of the century," he said. "How do you wish me to play it?"

"Can you call a press conference?" I asked him, "and invite the government as indicated by the names in that document."

"No sooner said than done," he told me, and rushed off to make some phone calls.

So after a good meal and a bit of a rest, I was ready to face the world to claim my birthright, and 10am found a whole crowd of reporters, television crews and government officials ready for the press conference at my friend's house, including of course, my two bowler-hatted friends from the tower.

They sought me out and said, "Please sir, may we have a word in private before you begin?" and, not wanting to get off on the wrong foot with my subjects, I graciously agreed.

We retired to the study and I said, "Make it quick, because today great events are going to unfold."

"Well sir," said the older bowler hat, "we have checked out your claim and you are the Plantagenet heir."

"So you agree that I am the true king then?" I asked.

"Well, of England and Ireland, possibly. You see, the Plantagenets were never kings of Scotland."

"Well that will do for starters," I told him. "I'm sure that the rascally Scots will want me to be their king too."

"If only it was that simple, sir," said the civil servant. "You see, your claim goes back to Edward the fifth, a possibly illegitimate son of Edward the fourth."

"Never mind that, he was adopted by Richard the third which makes him legitimate," I told him, "and the true heir."

"True," he said, "and that is the real problem. You see, after Richard was killed at Bosworth his treasury was never found, but we know that it amounted to over four million pounds."

"So?" I asked.

"Well," he smirked, "in the proscription following the Tudor accession, the Plantagenets had a treasury tax levied at eighty percent on all money and possessions."

"An illegal tax levied by usurpers," I said.

"Not at all, sir," he told me. "It was voted on by parliament and made law."

"Just what are you trying to tell me?" I asked.

167

"Don't you see, sir? The tax on four million pounds at eighty percent, at compound interest of six percent since 1485 amounts to £730,448,000,000,000."

"Yes indeed," said the younger one, "and it's increasing by £84,297,945 a minute."

"And you, sir," said the older one, "as sole heir and beneficiary, are liable for the full amount. Mind you, you will be able to offset your £400 tax allowance for this year against it. How would you like to pay?"

"B b b b but what about all the palaces and jewels and things that go with the crown?" I stammered.

"Oh no, sir. Most of those things only go back to the Stuarts and Hanoverians, or they belong to the government. You, sir, have only a mountain of debt. However, it should clear the national debt for us."

I sat down and gazed at them in disbelief.

"What should I do?" I asked them.

"Well, you could announce the date of your coronation, sir," said the younger one.

"Or you could renounce your claim," said the older one.

"Do I have a choice?" I said.

"No, not really," they replied in unison.

"Where do I sign?" I weakly asked.

"Not just yet, sir," said the older one. "You must cancel the press conference, and no one must ever know what has happened these last few days."

"But my friend in the next room already knows, and so does my solicitor, Mr Souhem."

"Well, Souhem is one of our agents, as are most solicitors, and the official secrets act plus a couple of nice scoops will take care of your newspaper friend," said the older bowler hat.

"Let me sign," I said.

"Just one more thing. We'd like the crown jewels back first," said the younger one.

"There is, of course, a nice little reward for them, sir. Shall we say £100,000?" said the older bowler hat.

"And so I signed, and received a cheque, and the civil servants went off to announce some different news to the press conference, while I retired to a life of gentlemanly seclusion."

Percy rose and prepared to leave the club.

"How did you get here tonight?" asked the oldest member.

"Oh, in the Rolls of course," said Percy, leaving through the door with a regal tread.

There was a bit of a pause until the oldest member said,

"So if he was in a Rolls, why was he still wearing his bicycle clips?"

FOURTEEN
The Quiet Man

Toby Mathers had attended the Friday night sessions for as long as anyone could remember. Even the oldest member regarded him as a permanent fixture. He was a very modest man, quiet and polite, but he would never volunteer information, or start conversations. He always sat in his favourite chair near the window and listened intently to the member's stories, smiling and nodding every now and again.

As usual, Spencer Harris was trying to tell yet another golf story, and the oldest member was having none of it. "Hey, Toby," he called across the floor, "we've never heard a story from you. Well, tonight's your chance."

Toby's face turned the colour of a baboon's bottom, and he said, "No really, nothing has ever happened to me."

"Nonsense," said the oldest member. "I've seen your wife; she's the most beautiful woman I have ever seen. There must be a story there, a quiet chap like you winning the hand of a girl like that."

"Well, come to mention it, I suppose there is a bit of a story there," said Toby. "Are you really sure you want me to tell you?"

Now of course any mention of beautiful girls was enough to grab the attention of the members, so they made themselves comfortable and listened in. So Toby began.

"It was back during the years before the war. I was in the Diplomatic Corps, and had been posted to the small Grand Duchy of Ruritania. It doesn't exist now, of course. It was swallowed up by their neighbours during the war.

Anyway, it was the night of the Grand Ball, hosted by the Archduke, and the British Consul and I attended as representatives of His Majesty's Government.

I can remember it as if it was yesterday; the ballroom was crowded with elegant people, when I glanced across the floor and saw a perfect vision of loveliness. It was a girl, but what a girl. She was about twenty years old, and dressed in a simple white ball gown, her light blonde hair was brushed straight down her back to below her waist, her features were perfection, and she was slim, elegant, and full of grace.

At that moment she glanced in my direction and it was like being struck by lightning. The crowd blurred and all I could see were her enormous blue eyes, which widened as she looked at me. I edged towards her and she moved towards me, so we met near the edge of the dance floor. We stood and looked at each other, and she blushed a beautiful shade of pink.

"How do you do," she said, holding out her hand. I took it, and bolts of electricity shot up my arm. Her hand was as slim and delicate and cool as a princess's, and I was hopelessly in love. I had never believed in love at first sight, yet I would have died just to spend a few minutes with this girl.

"Would you like to dance, miss?" I asked her, and was rewarded with a gentle nod and a dazzling smile. We waltzed around the floor and I was dancing on air, she was so light and graceful. She told me that her name was Penelope, but her friends called her Penny. I begged to be numbered amongst her friends, and I received that smile again, and she rested her head on my chest and gently squeezed my hand.

As we danced I noticed that almost everyone in the ballroom was watching us. Hardly surprising, I thought, because who couldn't help but stare at a girl like this.

Gradually the dance floor emptied, until Penelope and I were the only ones still dancing. Obviously something was about to happen, but I couldn't let her go, so we continued to waltz, with her looking up in to my eyes and smiling. I felt as if my heart was going to burst. Then the music stopped, and we just stood there looking at each other, until I became aware of a pair of pretty girls hovering anxiously by our side, and we turned to face them, holding hands.

They both dropped into a curtsey, and one of them said, "We are sorry to disturb you, but your father is looking for you, your highness."

Penny smiled and said, "Toby, please come and meet daddy."

My mind was reeling by this turn of events, and I asked, "Penny, who are you?"

One of the ladies in waiting said, "Sir, this is Princess Penelope, the only daughter of the Archduke, and the heir apparent."

I let her hand drop and bowed to her in utter confusion, "I'm so sorry Ma'am," I stuttered, "I didn't realise."

"Oh Toby," she said, "Please don't go, just because of whom I am." She put her sweet lips close to my ear and whispered, "I think I love you."

Well that was enough for me. I would go and meet daddy and face whatever consequences came along.

Penny caught hold of my hand and led me through the glittering throng, men bowing and ladies curtseying as we went, until we approached the Archduke, whom I immediately recognised.

I bowed, and Penny pulled me back up and said, "Daddy, I want you to meet Toby Mathers."

"Delighted to meet you, Mr Mathers," he said, looking anything but delighted, and he turned away.

Penny whispered, "Would you like to go out on the veranda and talk, Toby?" and I led her outside.

The moon was full, and I sat for hours and chatted with the most beautiful girl in the world. She told me that her upbringing had been very strict, and that she had been destined to marry Prince Boris of Transylvania in a political match, but now she knew what love was, and wanted to be mine.

I took her in my arms and gently kissed her. I'd not noticed that all the bells were ringing, but then, they weren't; they were in my head. Yes, we were madly in love.

At midnight we were sought out by a pair of giggling ladies in waiting and my princess had to go in, but not before whispering,

"Please Toby, will you meet me here tomorrow?"

"My love," I said, "of course I will. Shall we say 8pm?" and I watched her disappear into the palace with many a backward glance.

Well, there are no secrets in a place like that, and I got a bit of a wigging from the Consul, but notwithstanding that, 7.45pm the next day found me standing at our tryst spot on the palace terrace. On the dot of eight I was startled by the tramp of boots along the terrace. I turned and was confronted by an officer of the Guard Uhlans and two troopers.

"Please to come with me," said the officer, and I had little choice but to follow him through the palace and into the throne room.

The Archduke sat on his throne wearing a grim expression, surrounded by a crowd of toadies and lickspittles.

My princess Penelope was there too, and it looked as if she had been crying.

An obese red-faced guy was talking into the Archdukes ear. He kept looking at me.

"Who's he?" I asked my escorting officer.

"That's Prince Boris," he told me, "the Princess's intended."

The Archduke beckoned me forward, and I approached and stood in front of him. Penny gave me a little wave and smiled encouragingly.

"What's this nonsense?" asked the Archduke. "My daughter tells me that she loves you and wants to be with you."

"I'm sorry, your Highness," I said, "but it's true. We do love each other."

Prince Boris glared at me and said, "Does he know what he will have to do now?"

The Archduke slumped down on his throne and looked wearily at me.

"Young man," he told me, "I couldn't refuse my daughter's wishes in this matter, but there are conditions that you must fulfil if you are to be a suitable match for her."

Penny smiled at me and nodded.

"Just tell me, your highness," I replied, "and I will fulfil any conditions that you may care to name."

"So be it," said the Archduke. "You must complete the 'Labours of Hercules'. If you are successful you may demand my daughter's hand. However, fail and you will never see the light of another day."

"There is no way I can fail," I told him, and was treated to one of Penny's dazzling smiles.

Prince Boris stepped forward and said, "Be here at 7pm tomorrow."

I waved to my princess and left the palace, my escort leaving me at the gates.

I arrived at the palace the next evening at 7pm, and was taken to the ballroom, now stripped of its furniture, and with resin spread all over the floor. There was quite a crowd there; the Archduke, Prince Boris, at least fifty toadies, and of course my sweetheart Princess Penelope and her two ladies in waiting.

Prince Boris, who had obviously made himself master of ceremonies, said,

"The 'First Labour' that you must complete is to prove yourself the strongest man in the country, and you must fight."

"Oh no," I told him, "I couldn't possibly fight you, it wouldn't be fair. I was a boxing blue at Oxford."

He laughed, and said, "It's not me you have to fight. It's the champion of the army. Meet Ivan the Terrible." The crowd parted, and a giant grenadier of the guard pushed his way through and stood sneering at me. He was around seven feet tall, and built like a brick outhouse. He began to take off his jacket and shirt, and Boris told me to strip to the waist.

I did so, taking a few sideways glances at the giant. He had muscles on his muscles, his teeth were filed to points, and he was covered in scars. I tried to appear nonchalant, and said,

"I'd rather be facing him than the men who gave him those scars."

"That's not possible," said Prince Boris, "they are all dead."

We squared up to each other on the chalk line drawn across the floor, and I put up my fists. Everyone laughed, except for my princess.

"Put your hands down," sneered Boris. "You will be using these," and an officer of the Grenadiers came up holding two sabres. Ivan snatched one off him and took a few cuts at the air; it sounded like a train whistling.

I took the other sword and felt the balance: not as good as British Steel, but I supposed that it would do.

The oldest member interrupted, "so do you know anything about swordsmanship?"

"A bit," said Toby. "You see, I would have probably captained the British fencing team if the 1940 Olympic Games had taken place, and the sabre was my preferred weapon."

"Oh, so you were good then," said the oldest member.

"OK, I suppose," said Toby modestly, "although I did beat that awful Heydrich fellow three nil when we fought." This statement was met with a ripple of applause from the assembled members of the club.

"Please continue, Toby," said the oldest member.

We faced each other and touched the points of our swords together.

"There is only one rule," said Boris, "and that is, there are no rules. The last man alive is the winner; now fight."

Ivan the Terrible launched a furious attack and drove me backwards. I had to admit to myself that he was good, very good, and I desperately defended myself from his lunges and cuts. He was not only as strong as a bear, but also deadly fast and extremely well practiced. I counter-attacked and drove him back along the ballroom, and back and forward we fought for about fifteen minutes. He had the strength but I could match him for skill.

Eventually I could sense that he was tiring, and made my move. As he charged in again, hurling meat-cleaver-type swings at me, I ducked below his guard and my sword flashed out twice. His braces were neatly cut, and as he tried to step forwards again his trousers fell down around his ankles. He tripped and fell to the floor with a crash. His sword clattered across the floor, and I hurled mine so that it stuck into the floor and quivered between Prince Boris's legs.

I heard the sound of clapping, and turned to wave and smile at Princess Penelope and her two ladies, who were standing and applauding. It was then that I was hit in the back by what felt like an express train, and I hit the floor twenty feet up the ballroom.

Boris laughed, and said, "The fight has only just begun. Let's see who is the last man surviving." I ignored him, for I could see Ivan racing up the room to take a mighty kick at my head.

At the last second I rolled out of his way, and he kicked at the empty space where my head had just been. I jumped up and we faced each other man-to-man, fist-to-fist.

His fist fighting was the same as his swordplay, violent and forceful, but he was slowing, and gradually I was getting in two punches for every one of his. I finally gave him a crashing right uppercut and he sank to his

IT WAS TO BE A FIGHT TO THE DEATH....

knees. I pulled back my right arm to deliver the coup de grace, and looked into his eyes. They were full of despair and a trace of fear.

"Kill him," I heard Prince Boris calling. I pushed my hand forward and helped him to stand up.

"A good fight, my friend," I said, "but haven't you had enough?"

He sank to one knee before me and said, "Lord, I am your servant." The crowd burst into applause, and Princess Penelope rushed down and planted a kiss on my cheek.

"My hero," she said.

"My angel," I replied.

"You swine," said Prince Boris.

I approached the Archduke, hand in hand with the Princess. "Your Highness," I said, "I wish to claim the princess's hand."

There was a burst of laughter from Prince Boris. "Do you think that's it?" he said. "You must complete the 'Labours' of Hercules, not just one task."

"How many tasks are there?" I asked him.

"Just the four," he told me. "Be here at 3pm tomorrow," and I was again escorted out of the palace.

The next day, I presented myself to the palace at 3pm, and was shown into the throne room. Prince Boris again took it upon himself to be master of ceremonies.

"Alright, so you are the strongest man in the country," he said, "but now you must prove yourself to be the fastest." I looked across at Princess Penelope, who gave me a little wave and a smile.

"I'm ready," I said. "Who do I have to race?"

"Not who, but what," said Boris. The crowd parted, and a beautiful thoroughbred horse was led into the room.

"You have to be joking," I protested. "A man racing against a horse, it's not possible."

"Are you backing out?" said the fat prince. "You have been told what the penalty for failure is, haven't you? It's death."

"I will have to race then, won't I," I told him.

"Yes, and I shall be riding Brown Bess here," said Prince Boris. "We start at the palace gate, race through the town and up the mountain, and the winner will be the man who gets the flag planted in the cairn at the top of the mountain."

Princess Penny said, "It's alright, sweetheart, the mountain is only three thousand feet high."

We moved outside and lined up, me on foot and Boris mounted on his fine horse. There was a bang from the starting pistol and I felt the wind from a passing bullet close to my ear.

Boris cantered off, and I ran lightly behind him. He wasn't going too fast: obviously saving the horse for the steep mountain paths.

I followed him through the quaint medieval town and out into the country. The route was lined with spectators, obviously my fame preceded me. After five miles, we came to the foot of the mountain and I was about a quarter of a mile behind. The horse and rider disappeared round the first bend, and I ran on until I reached the base of the mountain.

I paused for a breather before tackling the arduous run up the winding path that led to the summit. It was all hopeless. There were about six miles of path to get to the top, and most of it was very steep. You see, I had hiked to the top on several previous occasions and knew the route.

But wait a moment, I thought. It's six miles along the path, but it's only three thousand feet straight up. If I climbed up the cliff face rather than run around it, I still had a chance. I found a stout stick and began the climb upwards. The first half mile wasn't too bad, and I made good time. Then it got steeper until I was shinning up a vertical cliff face. Luckily I was an experienced climber and knew how to take advantage of every hand and foothold. Half an hour later I had the immense satisfaction of crossing the trail and ascending the next section of the climb, knowing that I was ahead in the race.

Up and up I went, in some places having to swing hand over hand, and even having to leap across a five hundred feet deep chasm in one place.

The climb became more shallow as I got nearer to the peak, until at last I was on the gentle slope that led up to the cairn. I ran on and reached the pile of stones, plucking the flag out of the top, and leaning on it for support. There were a couple of dozen spectators up there who cheered and applauded. A minute or so later, there was a clatter of horse's hooves, and a disbelieving Prince Boris reined his horse to a stop beside me.

"This is impossible," he roared. "How did you get here?"

"Oh, quite simple," I told him. "A straight line is the quickest way between two points." I put my flag over my shoulder and began the walk back to the palace; all down hill I'm glad to say. Of course I was overtaken by a furious Prince Boris mounted on his lathered horse, while I was followed by an admiring crowd. As word went ahead the crowd swelled, until

I arrived back at the palace with around four hundred followers. I went inside and placed the flag at the Archduke's feet. My princess put her hands on her heart and mouthed a little kiss towards me.

The Archduke glanced at Prince Boris, who appeared to be in a bit of a sulk.

"Young man, you have proved to be the fastest man in the country," he told me, "and have completed the second labour. Come back tomorrow for the third test."

"What's that?" I asked. "Walking across a river on the backs of crocodiles?" Prince Boris perked up at that, but the Archduke shook his head.

"No no, he said, now you must prove yourself to be the cleverest man in the country, and out think the Grand Chamberlain. Be here at 7pm." Once again I was escorted out of the palace.

I went back to the palace the next evening, and was shown into the throne room. The usual crowd of toadies and hangers-on were there, and my princess and her ladies looking very worried. Prince Boris, who I was beginning to dislike intensely, took over again as master of ceremonies.

"Allow me to introduce you to the Grand Chamberlain, who has devised a little test for you," he told me.

"Good evening, sir," said the Grand Chamberlain, who wore rimless spectacles and had a great thatch of white hair and a bushy white moustache. "Over here there are two doors."

I looked at the two iron bound oak doors. Each one had a soldier standing on guard in front of it.

"You must open one of them. Behind one is life, and the other, death. You may ask just one question of each of the two guards, but one will lie and the other will tell you the truth. The door you choose to open will give you life, or death."

I looked at the doors, and then at the guards, and pondered for several minutes, and then I said to the left hand man, "If I asked the other guard whether this left hand door is the door of life, what would he say?"

The guard said, "He would say no."

I turned to the right hand man and said, "Is he telling me the truth?"

The right hand guard said, "No he isn't."

"So," I said, "if the left hand man is telling the truth, the right hand man must be the liar, and he would say 'no' if it's the door of life. But if the left hand man is lying, the right hand man must be telling the truth, so he would say 'yes', it's the door of life. But the left hand man would lie about that, and tell me that the right hand man would say 'no'. Therefore, the right hand man must be the liar, as he proved when I asked him if the left hand man was telling me the truth.

I walked forwards and opened the left hand door. Behind it was a table with a bunch of white flowers on it. I picked up the flowers and took them across and gave them to my princess.

"Just a minute," said Prince Boris, "now he has to crawl naked through all the poisonous snakes in the other room."

"No he doesn't," said the Grand Chamberlain. "He has passed the test, the third Labour of Hercules."

The Archduke looked from me to the princess and back, and said,

"Come back here tomorrow at 10am for the final and hardest labour. You must now prove yourself to be the bravest man in the country."

And so, at 10am I presented myself to the palace, full of trepidation.

The courtiers sat out in the courtyard, sipping drinks and placing bets.

My Princess and her ladies all waved and blew kisses, and I wished that I felt as confident as they appeared.

Prince Boris wasn't there for once, and the Grand Chamberlain un-rolled a scroll and read aloud.

"The fourth labour is to go alone into the forest, and bring back the head of the 'King of the Forest' before dark."

"Now look here your highness," I said, "I can't go and cut off a king's head. It's just not British."

The crowd laughed, and my Princess stood up and waved them to silence.

"It's alright, Toby," she said. "The 'King of the Forest' is a ferocious wild boar that has terrorised the forest for the last ten years."

"Ah, I see," I said, and went to the gate and picked up the boar spear that rested against the wall. "I'll see you soon, my love," I called, and she waved, and treated me to that dazzling smile of hers.

I walked out of town and was soon at the edge of the forest. As the trees closed over me I came across a woodman's cabin, and knocked on the door. It slowly creaked open and a woodcutter said,

"Whatever it is you are selling, we already have one."

"I'm not selling anything," I told him. "I've come to hunt the king of the forest."

179

He looked at me in amazement. "Are you mad?" he said. "That beast has killed twenty hunters. They say that it is not of this world: the devil's familiar, it is."

"Nonsense," I said, "it's a beast, and I intend to have his head today. Where is its lair? If you show me I will give you a hundred Marks."

"Nay sir, not for a thousand", he answered, "but if you give me the money I will make you a map."

I handed over the money and he scrawled a crude map on a piece of paper. It just showed the trail I was on and some trees.

"What's this?" I asked him. "Where is the beast?"

"Just you walk down this track," he said, "and the king will find you."

I set off, holding my spear out in front, alert for any movement in the undergrowth. I had this feeling that I was being followed, but couldn't see anything untoward.

Half an hour later, I entered a clearing that was shaped like a natural amphitheatre, and there sat the biggest wild boar I had ever seen. It was the size of a lion, but twice as massive; shoulders like tree trunks, and tusks a feet long. It leapt up and glared at me with red eyes; I stood my ground and it charged. At the last moment I jumped up, and using my spear as a pole, I vaulted over him.

He wheeled around and charged back. I skipped aside and swapped blows with him, with me getting a cut below the knee from a razor sharp tusk, and him a cut on the shoulder from my spear.

It was like a gladiatorial contest. We circled and cut and thrust until I thought that I was going to collapse. A dozen cuts bled, and things were starting to black out.

I fell to my knees, and the King made yet another charge. I pushed my spear forwards and dug the base into the ground. The beast leapt at me and impaled himself on the spear. It wasn't enough, and he forced his way forward, driving the spear deeper and deeper into his huge body.

I smelt his rancid breath, and the tusks flashed towards my face: then it was over, and the brute collapsed on top of me, pinning me to the ground under twenty five stones of dead pig. I lay there for about five minutes, hardly able to breath, when a voice said,

"Pity the boar killed you, wasn't it, Mr Mathers." I opened my eyes, and there was Prince Boris with two evil looking henchmen. "Princess Penelope will be impressed when I tell her how the boar killed you, and

180

then I killed it with my bare hands to avenge you," he gloated. "Yes, the foolish girl will cry for a bit, and then accept that she has to marry me. I will soon tame her, and rule the Grand Duchy while she stays locked up in her quarters."

He turned to his henchmen and said, "Kill him, and make it bloody."

I gritted my teeth and was preparing to die like an Englishman, when there was a squeak, and I saw a pair of boots fly over my head.

Then, a crash and the sound of a falling body was followed by the sound of Prince Boris begging for mercy. There was another thumping sound and the pleading stopped. A giant figure came into view, and lifted the great carcass off me. It was, of course, Ivan the Terrible. He helped me stand, and then kneeled.

"Lord, I heard of the plot to follow you and kill you, so I followed these men and stopped them from hurting you," he told me.

"They aren't dead, are they?" I asked him.

"No, I haven't hurt them. I've just broken their arms and legs," he said. "They will recover in time."

So Ivan took care of the villains while I cut off the King of the Forest's head, and then carried it back to the palace. There was great rejoicing, and the Archduke granted me his daughter's hand. We married, and have lived happily ever after.

There was a stunned silence in the club, until the oldest member said, "Come on Toby you're not really married to a princess are you?"

"No, of course not," replied Toby.

"I thought so: it was all lies then," said the oldest member.

"No, it's perfectly true, but there was a socialist revolution a year later. The Archduke was overthrown and all titles were abolished. My princess became just Mrs Mather and we escaped to England, assisted by our butler."

"Your butler?" asked the oldest member.

"Yes. Ivan the butler," finished Toby, with a smile.

FIFTEEN
We March on England

"Is that a Tank Regiment tie you are wearing Smithie?" asked the oldest member. Reggie Smith admitted that it was.

"Tanks eh," said the oldest member, as always unwilling to let a subject drop, "so did you serve in tanks during the war?"

Reggie admitted that he had indeed served in tanks throughout the war.

"Dangerous beasts, what," said Jumbo Fowler scenting a story.

"They certainly were, absolutely full of hatches and moving parts, all especially designed to trap your fingers and chop them off. It was said that our tanks presented all their worst aspects to their crews, and smiled benignly on the enemy."

"So when did you first see action?" asked the oldest member.

"It was in France in 1940," said Reggie bowing to the inevitable fact that he was going to have to tell a story.

"Yes, the early hours of May 10th 1940, the squadron was bivouacked in woods somewhere in northern France covering the rear areas of the Maginot Line. I was a sergeant and our tanks were Matildas.

At around 4am we were 'Stood To' with the warning that Jerry was on the move, and to be ready to move out at a minutes notice. As one usually does at times like this we put the kettle on for a cup of tea, and awaited orders to move into action. Twelve hours later we were still waiting for the order to move, when I was called to an orders group to be briefed.

I walked down to the headquarters barn with Lieutenant Elliot my troop leader. The Squadron Leader quickly called us to order and the gin and tonic began to do the rounds, well for the officers at least.

The briefing was brief alright, it appeared that Jerry had been playing his usual foul tricks, and instead of hurling himself at the impenetrable Maginot Line, he had gone through Belgium and had just gone around the end of it.

182

The building was full of calls of cheeky blighters, and that's not playing the game. And that wasn't the worst of it; they appeared to be advancing at thirty miles an hour.

"Well what can one expect, fighting against non cricket playing nations," whispered my troop leader.

We were going to move north and quickly defeat Jerry who was allegedly fighting in cardboard boots, ate powdered acorns, and had tanks which were really motor cars with plywood tops.

Let's hope that it isn't all over before we get there, seemed to be the general feeling. We were issued with maps of Belgium and the location of the fuel depot where we would fill up with petrol before we crossed the border, and then we went back to our tanks to be ready to move out.

Actually the Matilda wasn't a bad little tank, slow of course in spite of having two engines, and it had a tiny little 2 pounder gun, but the armour was thick, probably six inches in places, and the Jerries only had little guns as well, we had been told. So we had the king of the battlefield. And it was time to kick some German ass.

We waited another twelve hours, and the crew got some sleep while I stood by waiting for the order to move. There were four of us in the crew, me the commander, I had been in the Territorial Army before the war, and had volunteered for active service on the day war was declared.

The driver was Peter Sands, who pretended that he knew all about engines, a short guy, which was just as well considering the tanks cramped driving position. The gunner was Don Brown, who made a religion out of servicing, cleaning, and shooting his gun. The last crew member was the loader, Mick Carroll, a real wide boy, with a penchant for avoiding work, Greasy Mick they called him in the Squadron, due to his ability to slide out of any onerous tasks.

I looked at them all sleeping soundly and wondered how we would do, when we went into action.

I checked the tank, it all seemed in good order, like all of our tanks it had a name, Mick had suggested Maggie, but someone had said that it would be an iron maiden, a ridiculous idea, so we had called it after that great American hero, Benedict Arnold.

Dawn was lighting up the sky and I was ready for a spot of sleep, when the order came through to mount up and start engines. The men hastily rolled up their blankets and we climbed into our tanks, the air was soon full of blue smoke as the drivers warmed up their engines.

A white flare was shot into the air and First troop trundled out of the woods and set off up the road heading north. They were followed by Second Third and Fourth troops, then the Squadron Headquarters Lorries, the Fitters section, and last of all us, Fifth troop, and of course my tank was the last one in the whole squadron.

We spread out to one hundred yard spacing, and were soon stretched out over a mile and a half, of French roads. The weather was glorious as we drove on, and the roads seemed comparatively deserted, after two hours we stopped for a halt, and the troop peeled off the road and into an empty farmyard. The crew dismounted and stretched their cramped limbs.

Sands walked around doing his vehicle checks, he paused by the front left bogey, which was wet.

"Oh no, it looks as if we have an oil leak," he informed us. He knelt down and smelt it. "Doesn't smell like oil," he said, wiping some on his fingers and tasting it.

"It's not oil," said Mick, "I've just had a wee over it. "

Ten minutes later we were on the move again, driving through the beautiful early summer sunshine, Greasy Mick crawled down into the turret and Don Brown appeared in the hatch beside me.

"Where are we Sarge?" he wanted to know.

"I don't know, somewhere near Berlin probably," I told him.

"Oh, it still looks like France," he said.

He passed me a mug of tea.

"Have you been using a solid fuel stove inside the turret, against every regulation in the book?" I asked him.

"Yes," he replied cheerfully.

"Good," I said.

We drank our tea, while I wondered where the war had gone to. This was quickly answered when somebody in the column up ahead claimed to have spotted an aircraft, and all the tanks hurried under the cover of trees.

Eventually at around eight pm we arrived at the fuel depot, which was situated in a woods, we drove in and picked up a dozen fuel cans from the hundreds of thousands which were stored there.

184

We drove on further into the woods and refuelled our tanks. Then on to a cookhouse tent where we were thrown bags of sandwiches, and dumped off our empty cans.

Greasy Mick who had been asleep all afternoon, took over the driving, changing places with Sands,

Don Brown said, "Sarge why don't you get a couple of hours sleep? I'll take over on top." I was exhausted, so I agreed to let him take command, and as we trundled back out of the woods I slipped down on to the gunners seat and closed my aching eyes. It must have been several hours later when I awoke, with the uneasy feeling that something was wrong.

The tank was silent and motionless, and I was alone in the turret. I scrambled up through the hatch and took a look around, it was dark, and in the moonlight I could see that we were in a country lane.

But where were my crew? I jumped down into the road and took a look into the driving compartment. That was empty as well. I drew my pistol from its holster, and walked slowly up the road. A minute later I saw a dark figure walking towards me, so I slid into the roadside ditch and waited. I didn't have to wait for very long as I heard the figure saying.

"Oh no, he is going to bloody kill me." In Brown's voice.

I said, "Brown it's me," and stood up, he jumped at least two feet into the air.

"Where are we?" I asked him.

"I don't know Sarge," he replied

"Let's start again," I said patiently, "where are the Squadron?"

"I don't know Sarge," he stuttered.

I took a step closer to him, "hazard a guess," I said.

"Well Sarge, you know that we were the last tank in the squadron"

"Yes."

"So we drove out of that fuel place and the tank in front was already out of sight, so we came to a crossroads and went straight across, then lots more crossroads and junctions and after two hours we still hadn't caught a glimpse of anyone.

"So what country are we in?" I asked him.

"Well we aren't in Kansas that's for sure, he said.

"And where are Mick Carroll and Pete Sands?" I asked.

"We were driving so fast trying to catch up with the squadron, that the engines overheated and boiled up, They have gone to find some cans of water for the radiator."

185

I asked the obvious question, "So while all this was going on, why didn't you wake me up?"

"Because I was afraid to Sarge, and please stop strangling me."

I released him, and walked slowly back to the tank, I took a look at the sky and found the North Star, we were facing north east, well that was the direction of the enemy alright.

"It's ok Don, make some tea, I'll sort it out," I told him, and took out my map.

If we had been travelling for two hours we were probably around thirty to forty miles to the north of the fuel depot, which would put us in Belgium. I got out my torch and examined southern Belgium, it all looked Dutch to me.

I heard the sound of Greasy Mick's loud mouth in the distance, and waited until he and Sands arrived back at the tank, Sands struggling with two drums of water, while Mick carried half a dozen beer bottles.

"Bloody hell Mick, there's a war you know; they can probably hear your big mouth in Hamburg," I said.

"Sorry Sarge," he replied, passing me a bottle of beer. I took it.

"That's twenty francs," he said, I ignored him.

"Did you find out where we are?" I asked, throwing the beer bottle over the hedgerow

"He gave an exaggerated sigh and said, "Belgium, there is a village a mile up the road called Oosternuik,"

While Sands topped up the radiator, I took a look at my map; yes it was on, and quite close to where I had estimated us to be.

"Gather round lads, I said" and they grouped around the map.

"We are here," I told them pointing to the village, "and there is a main road leading north from there to Namur, there will be plenty of our guys up there, because Jerry will never get across the River Meuse. Let's mount up and get back to our Squadron."

We climbed aboard, the engines started, and we rattled up to the village and turned left on to the main road.

We drove on for a couple of hours then pulled into a small copse, to rest the engines. It was getting light and I could see a couple of aircraft flying around several miles to our north, I decided that we had better camouflage the tank up.

186

We draped the turret and hull with nets, and wove an assortment of branches into them, clods of turf helped to break up our shape, and finally we resembled a large mobile bush. At last I was satisfied and we headed north again. We crawled on making around eight to ten miles an hour, taking time to have frequent stops to rest and service the engines; we couldn't afford a breakdown, isolated as we were.

Every now and again we passed groups of civilians walking south or east; they pushed prams and carts laden with possessions.

"I wonder where they are off to?" I said to Greasy Mick. "Let's ask them if they have seen our Squadron."

"We pulled up and I leaned over the side and called out to a group of passers by.

"Bonjour, monsieur," I called to an elderly man. He stopped and looked up at me.

"Ave ou seen tanks today?" I called, he looked at me blankly.

"What's French for tanks?" I asked Mick.

"Is it the same as German, don't they call them pansies or something?" he said.

"Ave ou seen Panzers?" I called down.

He understood that and pointed up the road, "Oui, panzers, cinq kilometres," he told us.

"Merci monsieur, I called down as he hurried off to the south.

"Well that's about three miles to the Squadron," I told the lads, "let's go home."

We set off again with lighter hearts, and fifteen minutes later, Don spotted some vehicles moving about on the edge of a wood off to our right

Cutting off the road and across some fields we found a track which led into the woods, and headed along it to rejoin our comrades. Suddenly there was a soldier wearing some sort of anti gas suit standing in the track, he held up a stick with a red circle on it and pointed us into the undergrowth, we swung in and drove further into the woods then parked up.

"Who the hell was that?" asked Greasy Mick, "he wasn't British, must be a Belgie."

I looked at the other tanks which were parked amongst the trees and all around us, they were all camouflaged up like ourselves but they didn't feel right.

"Mick," I said, "get down and ask Don to put his head out."

Two minutes later Don's head appeared over the edge of his hatch.

"Just take a look at that tank over there and tell me what you see Don," I said.

He did a sort of double take, and then looked all around us.

"Jesus H Christ Sarge," he croaked, "they are Panzer IV's, bloody Jerries!"

I slid down into the turret and looked at my map, they couldn't be Germans, what were they doing this far west? Where were the British and French armies?

I inched up and took another peek out of the turret; more and more tanks were driving into the woods. Also little scout cars and motorcycle combinations which were clearly German.

A couple of Jerries came up to the side of the tank, carrying a big wooden box. One of them shouted up, and I looked down at him, he called again,

"Wievielmal menschen?"

I held up a hand and waved, he nodded and threw up five paper bags, and then they walked off to the next tank. I looked inside a bag, it contained a bar of chocolate, an apple, and a piece of coarse bread. Gratefully I distributed the rations amongst my crew. And we sat and had dinner.

It was growing dusk when a voice from outside called, "Marschbefel."

I looked over the top and a Sergeant passed an envelope up to me; before moving off to the next tank. I slid back inside and took a look in the envelope, it had a page of German writing, which contained some times, and a map.

I took a look at the map; it was of southern Belgium and northern France, very similar to my own map in fact. But this one showed our present position, a line of arrows leading back down the road we had travelled up today, and then directly back to our Petrol Depot, which was red circled. So that was it, Jerry was after the petrol.

Midnight came and tank engines started up all over the woods, I signalled Sands to start ours up as well. Ten minutes later a dark figure stood in front of us and waved a red torch, we followed him and were fed into a column of tanks that seemed miles long.

"Panzers Angreifen," came the call along the line, and the mighty host swept on to the road and headed south.

"My God Mick," I said, "we are invading France."

The miles passed and we drove back down the road, there was no other traffic, and the houses were dark and shuttered. 5am and we were just north of the petrol dump, moving into a position overlooking the woods. As the dawn lit up the sky, German planes flew overhead and dropped dozens of paratroops on to the woods.

From my position I could see British and French Lorries fleeing from the trees and heading south.

"Shall I fire on them Sarge," Don called up from the gunners seat.

I kicked the back of his head.

"They are on our side, you moron," I reminded him.

We saw red flares shooting up into the sky and the German Panzers burst from their cover and roared down on to the woods from the north, Sands gunned our engine and Benedict Arnold rolled out of our bushes and raced down the slope, along with the hundreds of German tanks that were intent on securing the petrol dump.

We burst into the tree line and smashed our way through the undergrowth. A German paratrooper jumped up in front of us and Sands promptly run him down, squashing him into the ground.

We were soon through the woods and taking up a position covering the road to the south. It appeared that the Germans had delivered a 'coup de main' and captured enough petrol to roll on and take Paris.

We waited for an hour, as more and more columns of German tanks and lorries poured into the woods; then four German paratroopers came trotting up to us; each one of them humped up two cans of petrol onto our rear deck, they then disappeared back into the interior of the woods.

Greasy Mick joined me in peeping out over the rim of the turret.

"What are we going to do, Sarge?" he wanted to know.

I looked around for inspiration, we were fairly isolated, there was a jerry tank about fifty yards to our right, and in the sky above us about forty German Stuka dive bombers were circling around ready to pound any opposition to the German breakthrough.

I looked at them speculatively and asked Don Brown to come up and take a look

He peered around through his thick spectacles.

"See that jerry tank there to the right," I said.

He looked at it.

"Do you think that you could take him out with one round?" I asked him.

"No problem Sarge, he has his side hatch open towards us, I could put a shot straight inside his turret from here." He assured me.

I ducked down into the turret and explained my plan to the crew.

Mick loaded the two pounder gun with a High Explosive shell and checked the co-axial machine gun, while Don slid into his gunner's seat and slowly traversed the turret right. I looked over the edge of my hatch and crossed my fingers.

Our turret stopped turning and Don took very careful aim. I looked around, and couldn't see anyone.

I gave the order "FIRE!" and our high velocity cannon cracked out, the shell flew into the enemy tank turret which exploded into a fireball. Don continued traversing and elevating the tank gun which Mick reloaded.

The gun cracked out again and the shell burst in the wing root of a low flying Stuka: as the plane lurched and began to head earthwards the other Planes bunched and then peeled off and hurtled down in steep dives.

The first bombs began to land right in the middle of the Petrol dump and giant fireballs began to rise into the air. The air was full of explosions and it looked as if some of the Germans deeper in the woods were firing at their own planes.

Someone started firing green flares into the sky; I quickly loaded up my own flare pistol and began firing red ones into the sky. Talk about a red rag to a bull, down they screamed again releasing yet more bombs and straffing with their cannons. .

Sands started the engines and 'Benedict Arnold' roared out on to the road and sped south. One of those little Jerry Volkswagens tried to follow us, but a burst of machine gun fire from our rear facing turret, soon dealt with him and he plunged into the ditch.

I looked back at the dive bombers which were still attacking the woods with Hunnish ferocity, and smiled, it didn't look as if much would survive in there.

We drove on for half an hour and began to see a few British Lorries moving westwards, I told sands to pull up under some trees. The lads began to fill the tank up with petrol and check the oil, while I stood looking around; as if on cue a motorcycle came up the road towards us.

I stepped out and waved him down, he pulled in and pushed up his goggles.

"Bloody Hell! It's Sergeant Smith," he said. It was Corporal Cox, the squadron despatch rider. "We thought that you were all dead."

"Just tell me what's happening Cox," I said. "Where are the squadron?"

"Jerries broken through." He informed us, "the Squadron moved southwest and we are regrouping at Arras. I'm heading there myself, do you mind if I follow you."

I got out my map and took a look, yes, Arras was about sixty miles to the south west.

We climbed back on board and Peter Sands started the engines.

Don Brown looked at me. "You look a bit tired Sarge, why don't you get some rest I'll take aaaaaaaaah!!" The rest of his offer was lost as my large boot connected with his skinny backside.

The oldest member asked, "So did you join up with the rest of your unit?"

"In a manner of speaking we did, but I will tell you about that another time." finished Reggie.

SIXTEEN
Enter the Cricket

Mr Julius Absolam was small, unassuming, and quiet; he always seemed to exude an air of mystery. The oldest member was never one to put up with a mystery, and wanted to know about Julius's past.

"Someone said that you had been out in the Far East for many years," said the oldest member

"Yes," came the reply.

"Army then was it?"

"No."

"Navy?" continued the oldest member.

"No"

"Air Force, or civil service?" the oldest member was as remorseless as ever.

"If you are really interested, I suppose that I had better tell you," said Julian.

"It happened like this".

Far out east, near the land of the rising sun,
Your search for enlightenment is never truly done
To learn the ancient, honourable and noble art
One must show total dedication from the very start.

As a young man I had left England's fair land
To seek my fortune on some distant strand
Young and wild I washed up ashore one day
In the foreign land once known as Far Cathay

I considered myself the best there'd ever been
But my technique was as crude, as ever seen
I pushed my weight all round the China town
And was long overdue for the big put down

As I strutted my stuff on the tough waterfront
My challenge was taken up by an elderly Monk
We faced up to each other I made the first move
But he moved like lightning quickly and smooth

My skills stood no chance, he made me look small
And it wasn't too long before my back hit the wall
I sunk to my knee's and said I was through
I'd met my master in the land of Kung Fu

He smiled upon me and touched his chest
Said, would you like to learn to be the best
The road is hard and filled with pain
If the secret wisdom you wish to gain

Why yes, I said, I wished to become
England's absolute number one
I wished to learn, to stand the test
Whatever it takes to become the best

We set off towards the distant hills
I walked behind on blistered heels
The time had come for me to be a man
And to learn the secret ways if I can

The Shaolin Temple would be my home
As I studied and trained there all alone
Under the eye of the watchful master
I learned to meet each disaster

I was put to work in the lowest spot
Fetching water in leaky pots
Running up and down a hundred stair
Ten thousand times, my feet quite bare

At last my legs were made of steel
My muscles began like iron to feel
I learned not to boast or look for fame
And Cricket was my given name

The chopping board I had to pound
Day and night without a sound
Building hand and eye co-ordination
It would be years before my ordination

As I earned respect, I learned I should
Refine and use my skills for good
Never judge nor demand or bully
But to assess every situation fully

For ten long years I studied there
Out of the world, and without a care
Every move I learned from the master
And soon they knew there was no one faster

Up to twenty hours a day I'd work
Knowing my duties I could never shirk
Learning things from the ancient tradition
Never thinking of my own condition

I could pluck a fly from out of the air
Then let it go, not harming a hair
Every technique, skill and art
I knew them backwards from finish to start

I could walk without a sound
As if my feet weren't on the ground
Tread on rice paper leave no mark
Find my way about the dark

Wandering Dragon, Monkeys ball
Standing Crane, I knew them all
The ancient secrets were now all mine
Time to cross the invisible line

I took the oath, and received the mark
Put on the white suit to make a start
Back out in the world, home to the West
Time to prove that I was now the best

For at long last I was a master rare
A pastry cook beyond compare
My ten years in the Shaolin Temple Bar
Had made me a culinary superstar

Back to England my native land
The home of food forever bland
My restaurant became the absolute best
As I put my ancient arts to the test

"Would you like to hear some more?" asked Julian.

"No, that's alright, just book me a table for six on Sunday night," said the oldest member.

SEVENTEEN
The Long and Winding Road

Jonathon Hunt was a bit of a rum character. He'd been everywhere, and often entertained the members with some of his wild stories.

And on this particular Friday he was at it again. The port had done its rounds and the members were in the mood for something a bit different.

"You may be interested," said Jonnie, "in hearing of my time in Labamba."

"Where on earth is that?" asked the oldest member, who claimed to know just about everything.

"It's a little country south of the border, down Mexico way," replied Jonnie. "What you might call a Banana Republic."

"What were you doing there?" queried the oldest member.

"Looking for diamonds, a girl's best friend," said Jonnie. "Anyway, I was friends with the president, Tom Jones."

"Tom Jones?" said the oldest member. "Is that a common name there, then?"

"It's not unusual," said Jonnie.

"Anyway, I was a long way from the green green grass of home, and on my way to visit the President, who lived in a big house, with acres and acres of ground, and a big high fence all around."

"This sounds strangely familiar," said the oldest member. "Have I heard it before?"

"No, I shouldn't think so," said Jonnie.

"Anyway, my girlfriend Frankie and I arrived at the Presidential Palace at the height of the silvery moon, to find the place in a bit of an uproar.

You see, Prime Minister Chaplin had asked for an emergency meeting between the Government and the President. All the cabinet were there; Chancellor Marx, Foreign Secretary Curly, Home Secretary Larry, and, of course, the Secretary for War, Moe. I remember thinking, the gang's all here.

As we awaited the President, Larry the Home Secretary tried to chat up Frankie, who was really a little town flirt.

"Listen. Do you want to know a secret? Let me whisper in your ear," he was saying to her when the president arrived.

"Now then Charlie, what's the buzz? Tell me what's happening." he asked the Prime Minister.

"I'll let the Chancellor tell you," said the Prime Minister. "Go on Groucho, it's now or never."

"I'm afraid it's war," said Groucho.

"It's impossible," said the President, "we only have friends and neighbours."

"You'd better believe it," said Moe, the Secretary for War. "We're going to fight a savage foe, hurrah."

"Well, did you ever?" said the president. "Who are the enemy?"

Curly, the Foreign Secretary, answered, "Pasa Doble."

"Goodness gracious me," said the president. "Why would President Capone want to fight us?"

"The party's over, and we might meet our Waterloo," said Charlie.

"Just a minute," said the oldest member, "you're just reeling off a list of song titles, aren't you."

Jonnie joined in the general laughter and admitted that he was.

"If you aren't going to take it seriously," said the oldest member, "you had better sit down and give up the floor to someone else."

"I'm sorry, so sorry, please accept my apology," said Jonnie, and he received a withering look from the oldest member.

"Ok then," said Jonnie, "I'll behave. Where was I?"

"The president had just learned that his country was in an imminent state of war with their neighbours," said the oldest member.

"Ah yes," said Jonnie.

"The President immediately sent for his chiefs of staff, General Hardy and Admiral Laurel.

Frankie had succeeded in fighting off the Home Secretary.

"Can't you control your stooges?" she asked Charlie, who shrugged and did a funny walk up and down the room.

It wasn't long before Laurel and Hardy arrived, and we began to discuss the looming conflict.

"How strong is the army, Oliver?" the president asked.

The general fiddled with his tie.

"Well sir, we haven't actually got an army," he said.

"No army? Well, who are all those guys in uniform I see around the palace?" asked the President.

"They work for the Acme Removal Company," said Oliver. "It's a little sideline that I run."

"Well thank goodness we have a navy," said the President. "What's the strength of the fleet, Stanley?"

Stan looked as if he was about to burst into tears.

"Just the two boats, your Excellency," he replied.

"Surely you mean ships," corrected the President.

"No, they are rowing boats," said Stanley.

"What on earth use are they?" asked the President.

"Actually they are quite popular with the children at the boating lake," said Stanley, looking even more tearful, while Ollie tut tutted.

"And what has happened to the defence budget?" asked the President.

"What defence budget?" asked everyone in the room.

The President quickly and skilfully changed the subject.

"So, if we don't want to fight, we will have to negotiate. We'll have to send a representative to meet with President Capone. Who should it be?"

Laurel and Hardy folded their arms and stared into space. Charlie did a funny walk up and down and Groucho puffed on his cigar, while the three ministers got into a heated argument, and I could hear an odd slap coming from the corner.

Tom turned to me, "Jonnie old chap," he said, "I don't suppose I can prevail upon you can I?"

"Just say the word old man," I said, "and I'll be straight down there seeing what I can do."

"Not without me, you wont," said Frankie, grabbing hold of my arm, and we went with the President through to his private study, leaving the assembled government to fight it out amongst themselves.

Tom sat down at his desk and asked, "How can I fight a war with those clowns out there? Besides I don't even know what it's about."

"Surely sir, they must have sent you an ultimatum," I said. "Countries don't just have a war without a reason."

The president frowned, and looked through the pile of unopened mail on his desk.

"My secretary, Harold Lloyd, is on holiday," he explained, "so I am a bit behind with the mail."

He selected a plain brown envelope and said, "This one has a Pasa Doble stamp on it".

He passed the envelope to me and said, "My Spanish isn't too good, will you read it for me?"

I took the envelope and looked at the stamp. It had President Capone on it, complete with scar. It was from Pasa Doble alright.

I opened the envelope, and scanned through the contents. It was sent on behalf of President Alfonso Capone, and was signed by Chancellor Frank Nitty. It said,

> HEY!!!
> I'm a going to make you an offer you can't refuse.
> You got a nice little country.
> We think thata you need some protection.
> Or some bad guys, they might just come along,
> And someone could geta hurt.
> You know accidents can happen,
> Fires can a get started, so what you say that we protect you.
> Let's say 10,000 pesos.
> A week.
> We will be sending the third armoured division around on Thursday to collect.
>
> Signed, Frank Nitty
> On behalf the President, Al Capone.......

"Ten thousand pesos," said the President. "That's the whole gross national income for a week. We will be bankrupted."

I quickly worked it out; it was nearly five hundred pounds a week.

"But Mr President," I said, "your country has been bankrupt for years".

"Jonnie," he said, "will you go down to Pasa Doble and see if you can sort something out for me? Normally I would have sent Groucho, but he will only make things worse. The last time he met Capone he said, 'I never forget a face, but in your case I'm willing to make an exception'."

"Tom," I told him, "I'm on my way. What do you want me to tell him?"

"You'll have to lie," he said. "Tell him that we have a million men fully armed and raring for a fight."

"But that's your entire population," Frankie said.

"Well, Jonnie will have to work out the details," replied Tom.

"Right then," I told him, "can Frankie stay here?" She laughed and said, "In your dreams. I'm coming with you. It will be a lot safer."

I knew better than to argue with a woman, and we went back into the antechamber.

I'm not sure what had been happening out there, but Stanley's hat had been pulled down over his ears, while Ollie's shirt was ripped down the front. The three stooges were laid out on the floor, and Charlie and Groucho were exchanging insults.

"OK guys, lets come to order," said the President, and the cabinet went and sat down at the big table, although there was a bit of pushing and barging between Laurel and Hardy for the chair with arms.

"Gentlemen," said the President. Groucho looked round to see who he was talking to.

"I'm not sure that I want to be in a government that would have me as a member," Groucho said, and Moe smacked Larry around the back of the head.

"I am sure that you are all aware of the gravity of the situation," continued the President, ignoring Larry, who was twisting Curly's nose.

"Those hoodlums in Pas Doble are declaring war on us if we don't pay them 10,000 pesos a week protection, so first of all, does anybody have 10,000 pesos that they can lend me?"

Groucho said, "If I had 10,000 pesos I wouldn't be sat here". Premier Chaplin emptied his pockets, and inspected the 12 cents he had found there. Ollie looked as if he was about to say something then changed his mind, while Curly kicked Moe under the table.

"I thought as much," said the President, "its plan 'B' then. Jonnie and Frankie are going to meet with President Capone and call his bluff."

The next morning, Tuesday, we met on the palace steps. Tom had arranged for us to go down in his car, along with his chauffeur Danny. The car wasn't quite what I was expecting: it was a Ford, a model T, I believe. The government had a whip round to buy some petrol, and Tom was briefing the driver, Danny.

"The map is in a packet in the pocket of your jacket," Tom was saying.

"While the order for the border is in the hankie held by Frankie.

And the letter for Capone must be just for him alone.

And if it all goes right, you'll be back for Wednesday night.

Have you got that?"

"The packet for the border is in the pocket with a rocket.

But the Hankie that belongs to Frankie is in a letter at the border," said Danny.

"It's alright Tom," I interrupted, "I'll drive."

And so we set off to see President Capone, to try and stop a war.

It wasn't hard finding the border; after all, there was only the one road south and we sped along, listening to Danny saying,

"The letter's in a packet stuck in Frankie's jacket. No, the pocket with the locket's in the order for the border. No."

And a couple of hours later we reached the border. We had no trouble on the Labamba side, a couple of border guards were sat in deckchairs, wearing bowler hats and tight jackets with baggy trousers, and they cheerfully waved us through.

CAN ANYBODY LEND ME 10,000 PESOS?
ASKED THE PRESIDENT.

On the Pasa Doble side however, we were ordered from the car by four black-suited border guards.

"Give us your border tax," said their leader, a broken nosed thug who wore a badge saying 'East Coast Mob'.

Frankie fished out her hankie and passed over the order for the border.

The guard took the envelope and opened it. It was a postal order for fifty pesos; the guard quickly put it in his pocket and said,

"Do you have anything to declare?"

"No," we assured him, kicking Danny when he started on about letters and pockets.

We climbed into the car and headed south for the capital city of Speakeasy.

Four hours later, as we approached the city's northern outskirts, we passed the encampment of the third armoured division. Mean looking men stood in groups around their black tanks and armoured cars.

After La Samba, the light hearted capitol of Labamba, Speakeasy was a grim and terrible place. We drove down the strip, looking at the gambling joints and bars, until we arrived at the presidential palace. Our car was stopped at the iron gates by the guards, who all wore long overcoats with bulges at the armpits, and black homburg hats.

Danny said, "Delivery of Bootleg Gin for the President," and they opened the gates and let us in.

"That was easy," I said to Danny.

"Yes, it always is," he said. "I've been making this delivery every Tuesday for six years."

We parked beside the main entrance, grabbed a case of Gin apiece and made our way inside. Danny knew where he was going and made straight for the President's office.

As we entered the office, the guards on the door searched us. Frankie was searched twice, and then we were in the presence of President Alfonso Capone.

I looked at him: a large brutal looking man with a scarred face. He was sat at a round table, playing cards with three members of his government.

Danny whispered to us, "John Dillinger, minister for burials Bugsy Segal, minister for the collection of debts; and Legs Diamond, minister of scores to settle.

Capone looked up and said, "What you want?" and I handed over the letter from Tom Jones. He opened it, and read it aloud:

Dear Alfonso,
I was most distressed to get your latest letter, requesting 10,000 pesos a week. Please appreciate that if we had that much money we would gladly give it to you.
I have sent my good friend Jonnie Hunt to talk to you, to see if we can reach a reasonable compromise.

Warmest regards
From Labamba.

Capone laughed and said, "OK, I'll compromise. The payment has just gone up to 12,000 pesos a week."

"We can't pay," I said.

"In that case we will be paying you a visit tomorrow," said Al. "Send for Frank Nitty and tell him to have my car ready for 8am. I'm going to lead this little expedition myself."

I could see that it would be a waste of time trying to persuade this bunch that it was a bad idea to invade, so I said,

"Well, on your own head be it, but you will be sorry."

Capone laughed and said, "Get out of town, or my boys will be taking you for a ride."

Danny and Frankie grabbed my arms and pulled me from the room.

"Quick, Jonnie," Danny said, "it's not safe to hang around here; we must get out of town. There is a motel just north of town where we can stay until morning."

And so we found ourselves at the Heartbreak Motel, desperately trying to think of a way to save Labamba from the invasion.

"I could sneak into the palace and poison him," said Danny.

"How on earth could you do that?" asked Frankie.

"Well, the poison's in the chalice on the trestle in the palace, but the pestle…"

"Enough already," I said, "forget all that, you will just give us a headache. All we can do is set off before Capone, and warn the President that they are on their way," and it was agreed we would set off at 7am in the morning.

So 7am found us heading north, back towards Labamba. As we drove, we passed the lined up vehicles of the invasion force, awaiting the arrival of Capone and his ministers.

At 10am we arrived at the Northern crossroads and stopped for a breather. It was more of a T-junction really, and there was a signpost; it pointed right to 'Labamba 10 miles', and left to Bosa Nova 10 miles.

"Just a cotton picking minute," said Frankie, and she jumped out of the car and span the signpost round, so it now said left to Labamba and right to Bosa Nova.

We sat and waited, until twenty minutes later the first black armoured car pulled up and an overcoated hoodlum jumped out and looked up at the signpost. Minutes later the air was filled with the roar of engines, as the hoodlum directed the invading army left and towards Bosa Nova.

We waved cheerfully as the last of them went past, and the pathfinder hoodlum jumped into his car and followed them down the road towards the unguarded border with Bosa Nova, the most powerful country in the southern continent. Not only that, but I had heard that their allies, the Americans, had their Marine Corps and Air force there, carrying out combined battle manoeuvres.

"Well, it's a long and winding road," I said, "but if they keep right on until the end of the road, they are in for a big surprise, for President Eliot Ness and his army of government men have been looking for the chance to sort out President Capone for a long time, and he's about to have his wish come true."

EIGHTEEN
Sink The Bismarck

Everyone in the Club thought that Bernie Montgomery was looking distinctly peaky, he was pale, shrunken in size, and his eyes were sunken and red rimmed.

The oldest member, never noted for his tact, said. "What have you been up to, to make you look that bad, Monty?"

"I've just come back from holiday," he told us, trying to sip his port from the glass, which he held in a shaking hand.

"Well that must have been some holiday," remarked Harry Cummings, where did you go?"

"On a boat," Monty told us, looking even more despondent.

"So what's the problem, did it rain or something?" asked the oldest member.

Monty gave a hollow laugh, and began to tell the members about his holiday.

This year we wanted to do something a bit different, we had already decided that we were going on holiday with our best friends, the Jones's. My wife Cynthia had been best friends with Gladys Jones since school. Our sons and daughters were the same age and best friends, while Jack Jones and myself had played many a round of golf together.

Spencer Harris, the clubs golf freak jumped up and said, "come on then, tell us about the golf." Luckily for the members Spencer was shut up by the oldest member, and despatched to order a round of drinks.

We spent many an exciting evening, planning this years holiday, first of all where to? We looked at twenty brochures, Greece, Spain, America, they all had their own attractions but the boys wanted a boating holiday, and the more we examined the brochure the more attractive the idea became.

The calm quiet magic of Britain's waterways, we read, two weeks of perfect tranquillity on unspoiled canals and rivers. Friendly welcoming hostelries dotted the bank sides. Beautiful towns and cities waited to welcome us, in our modern graceful narrowboat. Time would stand still as we cruised through the elegant and historic industrial heritage of Britain. Far away from the maddening rush and bustle of today's traffic. We were sold on the dream, and posted off our deposit for the holiday of a lifetime.

The weeks passed slowly and everyday seemed to be full of planning and preparation, 'D Day' was nothing, compared to the planning that went into this holiday.

Cynthia had packed clothing for every eventuality, ranging from the Arctic Wastes to the Sahara desert. Clive my boy had packed every computer game and girly magazine from his crowded bedroom, while Daphne my daughter had a dozen suitcases, most of them full of music cassettes.

My friend and neighbour Jack Jones told me that his wife Gladys, was exactly the same, and had probably packed the refrigerator somewhere amongst all the bags and cases. While his son Brian had even more games and magazines than Clive had.

He hadn't managed to get into his Daughter Louise's room which appeared to be completely filled with suitcases.

DAY 1.   At last the great day dawned and we set off. We had planned to leave at 8.30am. But by the time we had our bags packed into the overloaded cars, and squeezed everybody in, it was ten past nine, notwithstanding that we set off in good cheer.

Five miles down the road Cynthia said, "did you lock the front door?"

"I think so," I replied, but the seed of doubt had been sown.

Ten miles further down the road, those tiny seeds had blossomed into the absolute certainty that my front door had been left wide open, and vast gangs of burglars were probably ransacking my desk at this very instant. I couldn't stand it anymore and pulled into a lay-by.

Jack pulled in behind me and I walked back to his car.

"You had better carry on Jack," I told him," it looks as if Cynthia has left the front door unlocked, I have to go back." He pulled away and left me fuming in the lay-by. We did a u-turn in the road and sped back to the house, where I found the front door locked tighter than Fort Knox. I stumped back to the car got in and drove off, refusing to even speak to the wife.

Five miles later almost exactly at the same spot where the wife had suggested that the house was unlocked, Daphne said.

"Dad, I need to go to the toilet."

"There will not be any toilets until we arrive there and that's a hundred and twenty miles, and at this rate that will be some time tomorrow," I informed her, she immediately burst in to tears.

"You just turn this car around this instant," said Cynthia, giving me one of her looks.   Wearily I obeyed, and once more we were heading homewards.

It was 10.30am, as once again we pulled up outside our house, and both Daphne and Cynthia rushed inside.   Clive and I waited for fifteen minutes and there was no sign of them; worried I got out of the car and went inside, Daphne was lying on the settee talking into the telephone, while Cynthia was sat watching TV.

"That's it, I'm not going, the holiday is cancelled!" I said.

"Now then grumpy, you need a cup of tea," said Cynthia," just let me fetch the milk from the car."

I managed to get them back out into the car, made them belt up, and set off again. Five miles later Cynthia said.

"Did you lock the door?" I ignored her and put my foot down.

We made good progress in spite of the puncture, having to stop for petrol and getting lost a couple of times, and 3pm found us driving up and down the main road of the small village where the headquarters of the luxury hire fleet, were supposedly located. As we drove back up the road for the third time, Clive spotted a tiny sign that pointed down a rough dirt track, it said 'BOATYARD'.

Relieved I prepared to turn left, when a large silver Mercedes Benz Saloon cut in front of me and took the track.   I followed him down, hardly able to see through the great cloud of dust that he was throwing up.

He swung through an open gate and took the last available parking space in a nondescript yard. I stopped in the middle of the yard and a scruffy individual came out of the shed.

"Are you a boat hirer?" he asked me, I admitted that I was.

"Well you can't park there, take your cases out, then go park it in the next field," he told me.

We unloaded the car, building a huge pile of suitcases and bags in the yard, and I looked at the Mercedes, it was German registered, and it had a humorous sticker on the back bumper, which said, 'My Other Car Is Not a Mercedes, Ha Ha.'

The Germans unloaded their matching leather suitcases while I parked my car in the next field, and walked back to the yard.

"Mr. Montgomery?" the boatyard man asked me, I confirmed my identity.

"Herr Rommil?" he asked the German, who answered "Ja!"

"Right, pick up your bags and follow me," he ordered.

"Where are we going?" I wanted to know.

"To the boats of course, they are through the next field."

We picked up the bags and cases and struggled after him through the next field, passing my car some ten minutes later. We then scrambled down the bank to the canal towpath, and there they were the holiday boats.

I got a sinking feeling as I looked at them, one was new and painted shiny grey and black, it bristled with shining brass and stainless steel fittings, and it was called, NB MARCK, the other was old and decrepit, was all black, and was called   NB HOOD, I just knew which one was going to be ours. Sure enough the Germans were being shown aboard the new boat while we stood on the bank waiting.

Cynthia was looking at the boat somewhat doubtfully. "It's made of iron," she whispered, "how can it possibly float?"

"Well so was the Titanic," stated Clive, somewhat unhelpfully.

At last the boatyard man climbed off the German's boat and approached us.

"You're late," he informed us. We simply nodded and awaited instructions. He took a bunch of keys from his pocket and jumped down on to the miniscule back deck of the boat, we all crowded down behind him.

"Get the hell back up there on the towpath," he roared as the back of the boat dipped dangerously low towards the water. We scrambled ashore again and watched as he unlocked the back doors and disappeared inside. A couple of minutes later he reappeared at the front end and ordered us aboard.

I climbed down and entered the main cabin, it was Spartan to say the least, I moved back down the boat and opened a side door and took a look inside.

"Well at least there's plenty of closet space," I remarked.

"Closet! That's the master bedroom," the boatman said, "and you can't go in there Mr. Jones and his wife have already moved into it," and sure enough there were the Jones clothes hanging everywhere.

"Where are our friends?" I asked.

208

"They were here hours ago, I think that they went to the pub for lunch," I was told.   Clive had found the boy's cabin fitted with bunk beds and disappeared, while Daphne dragged her multitude of cases into the similar 'girl's' cabin.

I looked expectantly at the boat man and said, "where's our cabin?"

"You're stood in it," I was told.

I looked around, I couldn't see any more bedrooms, he pointed to the table.

"It drops down between these two seats to make the second double bed," he informed us, as if we were imbeciles. I heard both the children's cabin doors being slammed and locked to prevent me from making a take over bid.

Cynthia began to unpack some bags, and it was time for me to undergo the full training and instruction programme, as extolled in the holiday brochure.

I followed the boatman down to the back end of the boat, walking sideways most of the way. The boat appeared to be a hundred foot long and only four foot wide. We passed a tiny kitchen, then a small toilet and shower room, and at long last we reached the engine room.

I looked doubtfully at the great oily lump of black metal that must be the engine; it was festooned with wires and pipes. Climbing past it and up onto the tiny steering rear platform, I got ready for my training.

"Turn this key and the engine will start," he told me cranking up the engine which coughed and rumbled before firing up and filling the canal with white smoke.

"This lever, push it forward and you will go forward, pull it and you will go in reverse."

"Where are the brakes?" I asked but he had already jumped ashore and was disappearing up the towpath. I left the engine running and went back inside, keeping well away from the bellowing vibrating machinery.

Cynthia had made all the bags disappear and was boiling up a kettle to make a pot of tea, so I went out on to the front deck for a look around. The Germans on the other boat were running up a German flag on the small mast, I turned and looked at our mast and saw that a raven was perched on it, looking like an omen of doom. I waved at Herr Rommil who turned his back and gazed into the distance.

I looked at my watch, it was after five pm, we wouldn't be sailing far today, better to stay here and make an early start in the morning, and where on earth were our friends, the Jones's?

I sat on the bare wooden plank that served as one of the front bench seats, and waited for my tea, looking at the German crew as they polished their gleaming brass work, and dusted the boats roof. There were five of them, Herr Rommil was directing operations, while his blonde hausfrau, two teenage sons and a five or six year old daughter cleaned and polished furiously. Whenever they spotted me looking at them they stuck their noses in the air and ignored me, obviously considering my boat to be one of the Leper Class.

I sighed and went back inside, groaning as I struck my head on the steel door lintel, and sat down on the seat that made into a bed. The seat-cushion was about two inches thick, an uncomfortable night was the forecast.

Cynthia produced mugs of tea, and the kids left off fighting for a few moments to come and join us.

"Where on earth are Gladys and Jack?" she asked me, as if it was my responsibility as captain to know everything.

"Apparently down at a pub, shall I go and find them?" I ventured hopefully.

"You must be joking, just look at the dust in this cabin, grab hold of this duster and start cleaning from that end, " I was ordered, as the offspring fled into their cabins locking their doors behind them.

By 7.30pm, the cabin was clean enough to pass Cynthia's preliminary inspection, although she wasn't too impressed with the cleanliness of the outside of the windows. She even suggested that I crawled along the two inch wide side decks to clean them.

"Let's go down the pub then, for a couple of hours," I said making sure that my wallet was to hand.

"Don't be silly, we have the keys, what if Gladys and jack come back, they won't be able to get aboard will they." She told me sounding like a matelot with a lifetime of ships under her belt.

We turned on our transistor radio and listened to the news, rain and high winds were forecast. Never mind our luxury self contained boat was immune to weather and we were sure of having a wonderful holiday, well that's what the brochure had said anyway. Cynthia prepared some sandwiches, and the offspring reappeared like magic.

"This is so boring, when are we going home?" asked Daphne, grabbing the last sandwich. My rude reply was cut short as the boat suddenly dipped to one side.

"We're sinking!!!" Cynthia yelled, and the kids began to scream.

The font door opened and a soaking wet Jack Jones entered the cabin, immediately followed by his soaking wet family.

"My goodness, you should see the rain," he told me, "the canal bank is an absolute quagmire." He sat down on the opposite bench, dripping water all over my double dinette bed.

"Did you have a nice meal?" I asked sarcastically, and was treated to half an hours description of the culinary delights of the hostelry, and the great local beers.

I looked at my watch, "don't even think about us going out in this rain," Cynthia informed me, I refrained from telling her that she hadn't figured in my plans. But never mind, it was only the first day, and after all, tomorrow would find us in beautiful towns and cities, which were just waiting to welcome us.

We all sat in the main cabin, which was also my bedroom, while the wives made yet more tea, and the windows steamed up and dripped down on to my dinette bed.

We examined the rather tattered map, which we had found in the cabin and attempted to plot the next day's journey.

"This village Winchcombe looks pretty good," I said, pointing out the signs that said, shops restaurants and pub.

Jack measured the miles, "that's only twelve miles," he told me. "We will be there in half an hour, shouldn't we try to drive for a full day?"

"I suppose we could," I agreed, "what are these little arrows across the canal?" We looked at the Key, it meant locks, we looked at each other blankly.

Jack counted them, "Well whatever they are, there are twelve of them between here and Winchcombe," he informed me.

Clive interrupted us, "It means water locks, and they make the water level go up and down, so the boat can reach the next level of canal, which is called a pound."

Jack and I laughed, and agreed that we had known that all along.

It was soon time for bed, and everyone else disappeared, leaving Cynthia and I to struggle with converting the Benches and table into a double bed

At long last we managed to get it bed shaped and rearranged the cushions. It was around five foot six long and four foot wide. It was quickly made up with duvets and pillows and we crawled in. My hand reached out and touched my wife's waist and was slapped hard, I withdrew it, turned over and tried to get some sleep on the hard bed.

DAY 2.   Sunday morning and I was suddenly awake, I was alone and it was eight o'clock. Better get up before everyone else came out into the main cabin I thought, and crawled out of the bed. I made my way down to the small bathroom at the other end of the boat, and pulled the door open and looked in. Cynthia was in the shower and I could distinguish her shapely rear end through the shower curtain.

I went in and pulled my pants down and sat on the small toilet. I couldn't resist leaning forward and giving Cynthia a quick goose, through the shower curtain.

"Jack! Behave yourself!" Gladys's voice giggled from the shower cubicle. I quickly stood up crept out of the bathroom and made my way back down to the front of the boat where I found Cynthia, who had been out on the front deck feeding the ducks.

"When you use the bathroom, watch out, because the door doesn't lock," she informed me.

Well, within an hour or so everyone was up, washed showered, breakfasted, etc, and ready for the great adventure. I unlocked the rear doors and climbed out on to the tiny rear deck. I tried to remember what the boatyard man had told me and turned the ignition key, the engine rumbled and coughed out black smoke but nothing more.

Jack came back and said, " have you used the heaters? " I looked at him blankly. He reached inside and pressed a button, thirty seconds later he said. "try it now," the key turned and the engine roared into life. With rather a smug expression, Jack made his way forward again.

I turned the tiller arm over, pushed the gear stick into forwards and waited for the boat to cruise off. Of course nothing happened, Jack made his way back again.

"Shouldn't we untie the mooring lines before we try and set sail," he said, sounding as if he had spent a lifetime before the mast, he smirked his way back along the bank, untying the mooring ropes.

Yeah, you can smile, I thought to myself, but I've felt your wife's arse.

Visibility disappeared as the German boat in front of us suddenly started its engine, and great clouds of black smoke rolled back down the canal. Five minutes later the smoke had dissipated enough for me to start off again.

I turned the tiller arm, pushed the gear-lever in to forwards, and the boat slowly began to move away from the bank, and forwards towards the holiday of a lifetime.

I increased speed and we came up to the rear end of the German boat, and that's when he pulled away from the bank and cut across our bows, there was a chorus of screams from our front end as I wrenched the tiller arm over and our boat ploughed bow first into the opposite bank. The German skipper gave me a disgusted look as his beautiful boat pulled away; leaving us stuck side ways across the canal.

We all pushed and shoved with the engine roaring away in reverse, until eventually we floated free again, all the while watched by the occupants of a tiny little plastic motor boat.

They roared past us with the old guy behind the wheel shouting to his wife, "Bloody tourists in hire boats, they shouldn't be allowed on the cut!"

I pushed the lever into forward and at last we were off.

Now I don't know if you are familiar with narrow boats, but they are about two hundred feet long on the outside, but very strangely on the inside they only seem around twenty five feet long. And they are only about four foot wide, with two inch wide side decks, for mice to walk along. At the back end there is a little tiny deck for the helmsman to balance on, while the rest of the crew sprawl around on benches on the front deck, sunbathing and drinking.

I put the front end of the boat into the canal bend half a mile ahead and prayed that there was nothing coming in the opposite direction, five minutes later the back end of the boat followed and I was heading down a long straight.

On the bank ahead I could see a lone fisherman, his fishing rod out across the canal. I had read and reread the brochure and it had said, 'Slow down when passing moored boats or fishermen.' I pulled the lever back until the engine was just ticking over, and our boat crawled past him. At the last second he had lifted his line from the water and a maggot wriggled three inches above our heads.

I waved cheerfully as I passed, and he shouted. "SLOW DOWN CAN'T YOU!"

I ignored him for the next bend was coming up, I guided the boat around it and there two hundred yards ahead was our first canal lock,

The German boat was in the lock and I pointed my bow at the gap beside him, only to see the wooden gates slammed, and the German crew begin to furiously wind up paddles flooding the lock.

I looked around for the brake, where on earth was it, Commodore Jones came up through the engine room shouting, "PUT IT INTO RE-VERSE GEAR FOR GODS SAKE!"

I threw the gear lever back and the boat began to slow down, and I brought it to a halt by hitting the front end into the mooring stage in front of the lock.

My crew jumped ashore and shouted for me to throw them the rope, I threw it and it landed in the water. I pulled it back aboard and got covered in foul smelling canal water.

I threw the rope again, it was caught and the boat was hauled in and tied up. I put the gear-stick into neutral and jumped ashore. Then to-gether with Jack and the boys I made my way up to the lock and we stood and watched the Germans work through the lock with typical Teutonic efficiency.

Paddles crashed up and down and the water in the lock slowly rose, bringing the   N.BISMARK up to the level of the next stretch of wa-ter.

"Who chalked the 'IS' in that boats name?" I asked, and the boys smiled knowingly. Eventually the Germans opened the upper gates, and drove out without a backward glance, leaving the top gates wide open.

I pushed one gate closed, and then walked the seventy feet to the bottom gates and balanced my way across them, while the others went back to the boat to find the lock key. I walked back up to the top gate and swung it closed, feeling a bit like Conan the Barbarian, in that film; and then stood watching as the first gate swung open again. Luckily my crew arrived back at that moment with the lock key, and the boys ran up and closed the other gate.

We prepared to empty the lock when we heard a boat horn blaring and looked to see another narrow boat about half a mile away with the crew waving furiously. We opened the gates again, and waited ten minutes while the boat slowed down, and crawled into the lock.

It was a real gin palace, brilliant paintwork, brass everywhere, even tubs of flowers on its roof, it was called NANCYBELL. The couple on board sat and waited for us to close the gates and lower the water level in the lock, which after much experimentation we managed to do. We opened the bottom gates and the private boat slowly crept out, while its crew looked their contempt for us hirers.

Nobody would volunteer to drive the boat into the lock, so we pulled and hauled on the ropes and dragged our boat inside. We were about to close the gates when we heard shouting and saw a two man canoe paddling up the canal towards us.

Again we waited ten minutes for the tiny vessel to catch up and join us in the lock. The occupants were a middle aged couple, the woman ignored us, but the grey haired guy, shouted instructions to us, making everyone very confused and adding yet another ten minutes to the time.

At last after opening and closing all the paddles several times, the water level slowly rose, and lifted the boat up to the next level. It was then just a simple matter of opening the gates and jumping back as the canoe shot out of the lock, and paddled off up the canal.

As we dragged the boat out of the top gates I realised that there were no females in the group.

"Where are the women?" I gasped, as we tied the boat to the mooring rings.

"I think that they walked back to the village to do some shopping," said Clive, as he disappeared into the boat. I looked at my watch, eleven am, it had taken us two hours to travel half a mile and one lock. So that meant that we should arrive at Winchcombe for eleven am tomorrow, if we maintained this speed..

Half an hour later the girls turned up, we untied the ropes and set off again, we passed a couple of fishermen and I turned my back and studied the other bank, I was learning the etiquette of the waterways fast.

We sailed on through overgrown areas where the waterway narrowed to eight foot wide, and past open fields, sprinkled with notices that said 'NO MOORING'. There are few places in the world, as lonely as the steering platform of a narrow boat, I thought, as I looked at the tops of the heads of the rest of my crew, who sat hundreds of feet away in the forward deck area, drinking and sunbathing.

Ten minutes later we espied another lock and prepared for action, I pulled the boat up with the engine screaming in reverse, and we bumped into the side of the canal tow path.

The boys jumped ashore like a couple of nautical monkeys and fastened the ropes. We then walked up and took a look at the lock; the Germans had obviously passed this way, leaving the lock full and the gates open.

We went into action like a well drilled team with four captains and no crewmen, pushing gates open and closed and spinning paddles up and down. Slowly the level of the water came down and we hauled our boat into the lock.

Another burst of furious winding and paddle bashing had the boat moving up to the level of the next stretch of canal.

I was by now getting used to the intricacies of driving and charged the boat around the next corner, a chorus of screams from the front end made me throw the gear lever into reverse and we bumped into the next set of lock gates, which our German friends had just closed, completely ignoring us they began filling the lock, while we drifted into the canal path scattering the gaggle of fishermen ensconced there.

We stood around waiting for the Germans to work their way through the lock, which they did with a commendable Germanic precision, and they quickly set off again leaving the gates open.

"Let's make an early start tomorrow and get in front of those prats," said Jack, as diplomatic as ever, while I moved forwards to close the gates.

The day progressed, with a monotonous round of short sections of the canal, and lock after lock. We did of course meet other boats and soon learned that as hirers we were the pariahs of the waterways. It didn't help very much when Clive had a go at steering and wedged us fast in a tiny little bridge-hole.

Of course the instant we ground to a halt, the canal instantly filled up with a variety of private boats, with all the crews looking at us with disbelieving detestation.

Eventually we got underway again, and worked the locks, heaving that barge and toting that bale, until 7.30pm when we limped into the village of Winchcombe. We sailed past all the houses with their no mooring signs until we arrived at the official moorings, just enough room for two boats and the Bismarck and a canoe took all of them up.

We continued on, looking for somewhere to stop. Out of the village and past some railway lines, until I nosed our boat into a bed of nettles. We jumped ashore, hammered in some mooring pins and tied up.

Everyone raced for the bathroom, but as always Cynthia got there first, and by 9pm, we were ready to go into the village. We made our way through the field and up on to the road; although it had been around half mile by canal, it was at least two miles by road.

So at ten pm we made our way into the village High Street. As we should have expected everything was closed, we went to the restaurant, there was a shop called poundsavers where it used to be.

"Mmmmm," said the girls, "we must come back here in the morning".

We finally found the pub, went inside and ordered a round, it was no sooner served when the landlord rang a bell and shouted.

"Last orders please." Quickly followed by, "Time gentlemen please," and once again we were stood in the deserted village.

Wearily we wound our way back to the boat; everyone disappeared into their cabins while I made up our dinette bed. We climbed in and I sunk into a deathlike slumber.

DAY 3.   I awoke late, it was almost 9am, so much for the early start, I thought as I struggled up and got dressed, I staggered back to the bathroom, the door was wedged shut, so that was where Cynthia was. I moved back to the front of the boat.

I was bursting; so out on to the front deck, a quick look up and down the canal which was deserted, and what the heck we were out in the country, so I had a pee over the side.

217

My reverie was interrupted by a loud scream from somewhere near the waterline, and the two person canoe came paddling past us, the middle aged woman holding her wet hair, and the guy shaking his fist at me, I hurriedly zipped up and hurried back inside. Everyone was crowding into the main cabin.

"What was all that screaming and shouting?" asked Gladys.

"Oh just some canoeists showing off," I explained.

We scraped together a quick breakfast and I started the engine. Cynthia and Gladys were demanding that we sailed back to the Poundsavers shop, I refrained from telling them how difficult that would be, to turn a hundred foot boat around in a twenty foot wide waterway. Eventually Jack came to my rescue, and told the girls that we were only a couple of miles away from the Major City of Snodbury, with its myriad of shops and smart restaurants.

Mollified they agreed to push on, and peace reigned once more. As the boys untied the front rope from the 'NO MOORING' sign, and tried to loosen the rear mooring pins, the German Bismarck swept past us without a backward glance. We set off, turning a deaf ear to the fishermen yelling at us to slow down, as we crept along at around two miles an hour.

This was a long, lock free, stretch of canal, I was much relieved to see, and we soon caught up to the Germans who slowed down even further and sat in the middle of the canal, we followed them patiently for several miles, appreciatively sniffing their diesel fumes and smoke.

And then, like the skyscrapers of New York must appear to transatlantic voyagers, the factory chimneys of Snodbury appeared on the horizon, and the girls began to get their shopping bags ready.

"Lock coming up," came the call from the front deck, and I slowed the boat down, and bumped into the gate, that the Germans had slammed shut in our faces.

We tied up and me, Jack and the boys walked up to the lock to watch the surly German crew work their way through.

As they opened the top gates I noticed their lock key, the handle for winding the paddles up and down, lying beside the bottom gate. No one was looking so I kicked it into the canal, and smiled to myself. That will slow the buggers down a bit, I thought, as Herr Rommil jackbooted his way back towards the stern of his boat, he flipped his coat open revealing a leather holster holding his lock key.

The Bismarck cruised out of the lock, and Clive said, "HEY, where's our lock key gone? I left it by the bottom gate!"

"So that's what that splash was," I said, "I think that German kicked it into the canal."

"That's it, war is declared." Jack snarled, while the boys whooped with glee.

For the consideration of five pounds, Clive was persuaded to strip off, and dive for our lock key, and within the hour we were ready to proceed through the lock. Then 2pm saw us cruising through the outskirts of the romantic city.

We looked at the derelict factories with their broken windows, and graffiti covered walls. This must be the elegant and historic industrial heritage of Britain, I thought as I attempted to steer around a half submerged supermarket trolley. The decayed ruins went on for miles, and I lost count of the objects lurking in the canal, old bicycles, mattresses, armchairs, and wasn't that a dead dog?

Eventually we came up to the City moorings, and saw the Bismarck tying up at the last available one. All the other moorings appeared to be occupied by travellers boats, with piles of rubbish beside them on the towpath, and great piles of logs and flotsam covering their roofs.

Three quarters of a mile further on we spotted a place near some railway arches and we stopped and tied up. The four women almost trampled me, as they leapt ashore and headed up towards the shopping centre. Us males, tied up the boat, battened down the hatches, and then made off back up the towpath, at a far more leisurely pace.

I wouldn't say that Snodbury exactly welcomed us, completely ignored us would be more accurate, and we mooched around the shops, which were exactly the same as the shops back home. The boys went off to the games shop, while Jack and I headed towards a rather nice looking public house. Several pints of best bitter later I was feeling happy for the first time in days.

We sat and discussed our route for the next couple of days. It was out of the city, through a couple of locks, and on to the river. Then down stream for about twenty miles to the quaint market town of Oldwick, with its welcoming restaurants and hostelries, Hmmmm. We had a couple more pints and were a bit surprised to hear the landlord call last orders please.

We jumped up with our hearts in our mouths, and prepared to go back to the boat and face the music. Sure enough the boat was in darkness, with no sign of Cynthia. We climbed into the main cabin, which was full of shopping, and jack tried his locked cabin door, while I read the note pinned above the fridge.

It said, 'I'm sleeping with Gladys in the cabin, as you like him so much you can sleep out here with Jack!. Cynthia.'

We turned in, and lay listening to the trains which ran over the arches, every half hour or so.

DAY 4. I was awoken by the sound of rain drumming on the boats metal roof. I got up and made my way back to the bathroom, it was occupied as usual. The penalty for sharing a boat with four girls, I reflected.

Soon Cynthia turned up and graciously accepted my grovelling apologies, for abandoning her, and her poor innocent little children, in this strange and dangerous city. Yes she would share my bed again, but I needn't get any ideas about any funny business for the rest of the holiday. I resisted saying, nothing new there then. I was already in enough trouble.

We waded through an ocean of tea and a mountain of toast, and decided to brave the rain and set off. The boys untied the ropes and I steered the boat away from the bank, while my gallant crew hurried back inside.

Ten minutes later they had to hurry out again as we approached the first lock, and yes the bloody Germans were in it. We stood in the rain and watched them work their way through, I noticed that it now lowered the boat to a lower stretch of canal, so we had obviously reached the summit.

"All down hill from now on," I remarked cheerfully.

"Don't forget we have to come back," Clive reminded me, spoiling the moment completely.

The Germans drove out of the lock and we waited while a couple of pensioners in a boat which looked just as old, crept in. We went back and sat in our boat, leaving them to work through on their own, we were learning. At last the lock was clear, we drove into the lock chamber, and then paddled the water level down.

I drove out and two hundred yards round the next bend we came up to the next lock. Another half hour and we were through; I steered along the narrow canal trying to avoid the half sunken black Plastic bags filled with rubbish or worse.

I waved at two cute little lads walking along the canal path, and was pelted with rubbish by them. I pretended that I hadn't noticed and sailed on. At last we came to the lock which would drop us from the canal down on to the river. The Germans had obviously been through and left the bottom gates open. Undeterred we set the lock and worked our way through it.

We all climbed back aboard and I threw the gear-lever into forwards, the boat just sat there, I put it into reverse and it still refused to move. We tied it back up to the landing stage and I switched off the engine.

"Call the AA," said Gladys, Cynthia agreed with her.

"Certainly not, I just enjoy a drink, I'm not an alcoholic," I informed her.

We got out the engine hand book, and looked for clues, as usual Jack spotted it, "we probably have something wrapped around the propeller," he informed us, sounding for all the world like an old sea dog.

"Well I'm not going in again," Clive said, and disappeared into his cabin.

We read on, and it appeared that the boat was fitted with a thing called a weed-hatch; it was situated in the engine room, behind the engine, and gave access to the propeller. The book was also very adamant about correctly fastening the cover back down after you had finished, why if you tried to drive the boat with it off, the boat would sink.

"Leave it to me," Jack said, making his way purposefully back to the engine room.

With much grunting and swearing he got the steel hatch cover off, and looked down at the propeller, or at least at the black plastic bag which was wrapped round and round it, like a giant black ball.

He began to break off pieces of plastic bag, cursing whenever he came across a tin can, or the particularly nasty slimy green things which smelt awful. At last he had cleared the prop and refitted the weed-hatch, we were ready to start off again, I climbed out into the rain, started the engine and off we went, heading downstream in pursuit of the Bismarck.

The river seemed miles wide after the narrow canal and I gunned the boats engine to a fast walking speed. We sailed past derelict factories, and decrepit boats, which seemed to be moored up at every suitable stopping

221

place. I felt quite heroic as I steered the boat through the driving rain, every now and again catching a glimpse of the fleeing Bismarck it seemed.

I amused myself by trying to work out torpedo angles and ranges.

"Lock," came the warning yell from the front deck, and I saw our first river lock looming out of the rain, and looking like the Hoover Dam.

We crept up to the waiting area and tied up behind the Germans, then looked in wonder at the gigantic gates as they began to slowly open, like two mighty steel mountains. A veritable fleet of small boats issued out of the lock, and then a waterways worker waved the Germans in.

I waited for instructions, until finally he came stamping back to our boat and said, "well are you going in on not?" his little toothbrush moustache positively bristling.

We untied and I allowed the boat to creep into the lock, which was about five hundred foot long, and fifty foot wide, but I had the immense satisfaction of hitting the Germans up their stern as we pulled up behind them. Herr Rommil turned and shook his fist and shouted something in German, I gave him a cheery wave and a smile.

We waited twenty minutes as a tiny wooden cruiser limped down the river and entered the Lock, hooking on as far away from us hire boats as possible. The mighty gates swung shut behind us and the lock began to empty, down we went for about fifty feet, with jets of water were streaming out of the lock walls and pouring all over us and our boat.

Cynthia passed me a cup of warm tea and we watched the bottom gates open, the Germans gunned their engine and sailed out, leaving us choking in their diesel smoke, a minute later we pulled through their smoke screen and set off in pursuit again. Now we were out in open country, what bit I could see of it through the driving rain, and the river meandered back and forth as we made our way downstream.

Three more of the gigantic Locks were negotiated, and as dusk began to fall we arrived at Oldwick, where a sort of canal took us through the town. There was a big castle on the bank, with moorings opposite, the last remaining one containing the Bismarck which was just finishing tying up.

We sailed on for another half mile and tied up to a thirty foot high wall. The girls looked at the tiny steel ladder set in to the wall and informed me that there was no way that they would be climbing up there.

I began to say that's ok, me and Jack would go and explore, but a Medusa like stare, made me change my mind. We dined on beans on toast and played scrabble, letting Clive and Brian win every game.   At long last we turned in, I lay looking at Cynthia's back and listening to the rain drumming on the roof.

DAY 5.   "Are you going to lay in that bed all day, we can't have break-fast until you get up," said Cynthia's voice. I opened my eyes and looked at the seven crewmembers who sat or stood around looking at me. I dressed under the covers and crawled away to the bathroom, pretending not to hear the remarks about lazy so and so's.

Well at least it had stopped raining, and there was a glimmer of sunshine out there. We put the dinette up and had breakfast, tea and toast, I tried to work out when I had last had a proper meal, but it was to far back to remember properly.

A bit of a dispute developed, the four males wanting to push on and get onto the tidal stretch of river, and the four females wanting to sail back to the castle moorings to do some shopping.

We untied and turned the boat around and headed back to the castle moorings. The Bismarck was the only boat there now and we manoeuvred and tied up in front of her.

The four girls stampeded off the boat and headed for the town centre, followed at a safe distance by the two lads, while Jack and I checked the oil levels and water tanks, as instructed by the handbook. Eventually Admiral Jack declared himself satisfied and we locked the boat up before heading Townwards, carefully stepping over the masses of equipment belonging to the anglers, who filled the bank-side.

The Town wasn't too bad, no more miserable than anywhere else really, we mooched around the shops, and our carrier bags bulged with cans of ale and magazines.

We went into a café and ordered coffees, and bacon sandwiches. The door immediately opened and in came the entire tribe, with Cynthia making loud remarks about me sneaking off for crafty meals. I ordered more food and paid up.

Eventually everyone was ready to get back to the boat and I helped Cynthia carry her numerous bags of clothes and shoes; as if she hadn't packed enough in the first place. I also noticed that she had bought some bread, and tins of beans.

223

We bustled around and made ready to cast off and set sail, when the bow of the Bismarck crashed into our stern making me bite down on my tongue. The Germans sailed past us and Herr Rommil gave me a cheery wave and a smile.

Once again we set off in pursuit and followed them down to the deep lock, which dropped us back down on to the tidal section of the river. This was the mother of all locks, big enough to take ocean liners. There could have been an aircraft carrier somewhere in there and we probably wouldn't have noticed it.

The Lock-keeper came up and looked us over, I returned the compliment, why did they all wear little toothbrush moustaches I wondered.

"The tide is falling," she told us, "make sure you keep well over to the right of the channel and you will be OK."

She did the mystery things and made the gates close, and the water level fall. Soon the bottom gates began to open and I gunned the engine, the boat leapt forward and we got in front of the German boat as we left the gigantic lock. The river was running quite fast and we made good speed as we swept down with the current.

I looked behind and saw the Bismarck trying to claw her way up to us; she was a newer boat and appeared to have more power, but there was no way she was going to get in front of us again.

I heard shouts coming from the front and looked forward to see a huge barge steaming up the river towards us. I pulled right in to the right hand bank as the great boat swept past us, her bow wave breaking over our front deck. I looked back to see the German boat rocking in the barges wake. The race was on again and the Bismarck began to creep up on us once more.

Ten minutes later his nose was up to our stern and I waved him past on our left hand side

Inch by inch he crept up on us, as I allowed our boat to drift further and further to the left forcing him into the middle of the river.

I could hear jeering coming from our front deck as the kids pulled faces at the German crew, we were now almost neck and neck and I pulled the steering tiller well over swinging our nose towards their bow. Instinctively Herr Rommil swung his bow out of the way, and headed towards the left hand bank. There was a thumping noise, and we cheered as the Bismarck ran aground on the submerged mud bank in the centre of the river.

We pulled back over to the right hand side of the channel and swept on down the river, leaving our German adversaries stranded high and dry, on a falling tide.

Jack made his way back with two cans of ale and we toasted our victory. We even sang a few choruses of 'Rule Britannia', much to the disgust of Cynthia and the girls.

It was if a great cloud had lifted, we had the river to ourselves, and sweet little children waved and blew kisses at us as we cruised past, while sheep and cows looked on approvingly.

Every half hour or so a huge aggregate barge swept up the river, dwarfing us and making our boat bob around like a cork in a colander. We stopped at a riverside pub, there was no German boat taking up the mooring for a change, and enjoyed our first proper food for days. Fully refreshed and laden with cans of ale, we set sail again and had a blissful trip down the river to the small market town of Ratford.

It was made even better by the fact that the boys took over the driving, allowing me to lounge with the crew on the front deck, supping beer and telling jokes, even Cynthia appeared to be thawing out.

We sailed on to Ratford and into the prime mooring position, near the shops and restaurants, what a day it was turning out to be. By 11pm we had shopped, eaten, and drank so much that we were ready to go straight to bed.

I lay down in our dinette bed and Cynthia climbed in beside me, a minute later her hand crept out and touched my waist, I slapped it away. And as we drifted off to sleep, no one saw the sleek grey shape of a wounded narrow boat limp into the moorings. The Bismarck had returned.

DAY 6.   It was 9am when I came back to life, and gave Cynthia a nudge, the boat was rocking up and down alarmingly.

"Those damn barges are out early today," I told her, "we had better get up before the hordes descend on the cabin." She disappeared towards the bathroom and Gladys came forward wrapping a towel around her hair, she bent down to get the tea bags out of the cupboard and I admired her dressing gown. Daphne and Louise, the two girls came out of their cabin and stood trying to keep their balance.

"The water seems to be very choppy," said Louise.

"Yes it's the big barges speeding past and setting up a wake," I informed them.

"Let's go and feed the swans," said Daphne, and the girls went out onto the front with some pieces of bread. My reverie was broken by loud screams coming from the front deck, and I rushed forwards, my heart in my mouth, had the canoeists returned?

I stood beside the girls and looked at the ocean, where on earth had the town gone? Where was the land? Water water everywhere. Oh my god we were at sea.

The rest of the crew climbed out on to the front deck, and all four girls started crying, a lot of use they were going to be in an emergency. We packed them off below and looked around for inspiration, while Clive checked the mooring ropes.

"They have been cut," he informed us, "and someone has chalked 'DEUTCHLAND UBER ALLES' on the side of the cabin."

"Look, we will start the engine and sail west," I told them.

"Ah, so you have brought a compass have you?" asked Jack.

I had to admit that I hadn't.

"The sun rises in the east so if we sail with it at our backs we will be heading west," said Clive. We looked at the overcast cloudy sky, there wouldn't be any sun today.

"Its simple, lets make a compass, like we did at school," said Brian, which were the first words that I had heard him speak, since we had started the holiday.

We went back inside, and Brian got a needle from one of the sewing kits that Gladys had brought with her. He laid it on to the step and started hitting it with the lock key. A few minutes later he got a saucer of water, pinned the needle to a piece of card, and floated it in the saucer of water. We sat and watched as the compass card slowly revolved around, and around, and around.

"So why is it going round and round?" asked Jack.

"Probably because the boat is made of steel," said Clive.

"OK, we go on deck and wave down a passing boat and ask directions," I told them, and all the men went back on to the front deck, after all this was the North Sea, one of the busiest sea lanes in the world. I suggested starting the engine and sailing on until we sighted land, but I was outvoted, seven to one.

Darkness began to fall and we kept a lookout hoping to see a light house or something, but the sea was empty. And at midnight we called it a day and went below to get some sleep.

DAY 7. The next morning we were all up at dawn, and rushed up on to deck to have a look at the empty ocean. The sea was choppier now, and Daphne started to throw up over the side, shortly followed by Louise, Gladys and Cynthia in that order.

One of the girls stood up and turned to face me. I took one look at her speckled chin, and deposited my stomach contents over the side, soon to be followed by Jacks.

The two boys thought that was very funny, and laughed as they ate the bacon sandwiches that Gladys had recently finished making. The hands on the clock had crawled round to 11am, with still no break in the clouds, when Clive yelled from the front.

"There's a boat!" We all rushed out on deck and sure enough there was a fishing boat heading off into the distance. We sprinted back and started the engine, then swung our bows in pursuit of him.

We followed him for three hours, and at last the outlines of land crept over the horizon. Gradually we got into the shore and by five pm we thankfully crept into the river estuary, ready to seek and destroy some Germans. We sailed on for over an hour.

"I didn't realise that it was so flat around this part of the country," said Jack as we stood together on the steering platform and looked at the tulip fields.

"Yes there are a lot of windmills too, aren't there," I replied.

"Yes, very pretty, and I can see a pub coming up on the left hand side," he said, getting ready to stop. The narrow boat cruised in to the landing stage and the nautical monkeys, jumped ashore and fastened up the spliced mooring lines to a sign which said 'Politie en Zeemacht Boots Enkel, while Jack and I stood and stared at the sign which said '**EETHUIS'.**

We got out our map and looked for a village of that name, but we couldn't find it

"Never mind," said the admiral, "I shouldn't think that they put every single building on the map." The girls got their shopping bags, and we prepared to move inland for a bit of relaxation.

"First a drink and a meal at the pub, I suggested, and we made our way up the jetty and went into the bar.

"Fancy having a theme pub, all the way down here," said Cynthia, as we sat down and looked at the foreign signs and labels everywhere, "I think that it supposed to be a Beerkellar." She was right of course; it did look a bit foreign, if somewhat over the top.

The landlord came up to our table and said, "Ja."

I entered into the spirit of things and said, "Zwei bier unt zwei schnapps unt feur colas bitteschon." He looked at me blankly and then went off and fetched our drinks.

We supped them, and made some plans for the evening, which mostly involved finding some shops and doing some shopping. Cynthia and Gladys were no respecters of rank, as usual.

The door suddenly opened and two chaps in uniform came in to the barroom. They made a bee line for our table and stood in front of us with their hands on their pistols.

"Waiters, in German army uniforms," Jack explained to us. "Our friends on the Bismarck would be right at home here."

"Do you do fish and chips?" Gladys asked, and the two men jumped back a few feet.

"Be you illegal immigrants?" one of them asked the table at large, in heavily accented English. We laughed and started an explanation of our previous day's adventures.

"So vere do you tink you iz then?" He said in excruciating English.

"Don't tell me that this isn't Lincolnshire," I said with a laugh.

"No, diz iz der Nederland," the policeman said. The rest of his sentence was drowned out by the girls screaming and the men shouting.

Eventually things cooled down and the police took over everything. We slept on the boat, and settled down to another exhausted sleep.

DAY 8. The next morning a Dutch Coast guard boat came alongside and tied our boat to their side. We all climbed aboard the Dutch ship, and it sailed off, taking us back across the North Sea, and towards England.

Ten hours later we transferred to our boat, cast off and headed towards the river mouth, while our Dutch friends waved us goodbye and headed for home. We cruised back up the river, realising that we were truly home by the fact that all the fields had 'NO MOORING' signs in them. And by 9pm, as dusk was falling, we arrived back in Ratford and tied up very firmly to the mooring rings.

Jack and I suggested the pub, but the girls insisted that we stopped on board, and checked the mooring ropes every fifteen minutes; so it was scrabble night again. Of course we had to let the boys win every game as usual, but I wasn't too happy about some of the words they used, like 'peroration' or 'zirconium'. Clive even tried 'xenophobia', but I wasn't letting him get away with made up words like that.

At last everyone disappeared into their cabins, and Cynthia and I made up our bed and crashed out.

DAY 9.   The next morning we made an early start, and were soon heading up river, mixing it with the other boats, making rude gestures at the anglers, and generally behaving like a gang of cut throat pirates. All the time we kept out a sharp watch for the Bismarck, there was a reckoning due.

At around 3pm in the afternoon we negotiated the great tidal lock, and cruised up to Oldwick. And there she was, tied up opposite the castle, the long sleek grey shape of the Bismarck. The boys rushed below and came back up holding Knives.

"Put those back in the cutlery drawer at once," ordered Cynthia, and the boys reluctantly obeyed.

We pulled into some moorings a dozen boats behind them and tied up, perfect for observing without being spotted. The women got their shopping bags and headed for town, they were certainly feeling shopping withdrawal symptoms.   Jack, myself and the two lads, fixed the boat up and checked all the oils, and water levels, before we headed into town and replenished the ale supplies.

We all met up in the market square, and the children headed off to MacDonald's, while the adults went into a restaurant for a meal.

"Those Jerries aren't going to get away with it," Jack informed us over the meal, the women urged caution, but let's face it we were at war.

"We can't touch them on the river, Jack," I said, "they have a little girl on board."

"You are right, we shall wait until we get back on the canal," the admiral said.

Quite a bit later we went back to the boat, where we found Clive in the girl's cabin with Louise, and Brian in the boy's cabin with Daphne, we soon put a stop to that.

DAY 10.   We were up at dawn, getting ready for the battle which was going to take place at any time. It was overcast and raining, as we watched the Bismarck slip her moorings and sail up river.

Twenty minutes later we cast off and followed, then fifteen minutes after that, as we left the outskirts of Oldwick behind, we caught a glimpse of her about a mile ahead. Mile after mile, hour after hour we trailed her, keeping well back to avoid being seen.

We held back at the locks and let them proceed, blissfully unaware that their nemesis was dogging every movement. Nine hours it took us to sail back up the river, and six pm saw us sailing through the industrial wasteland that was Snodbury.

As we left the dereliction behind us, and approached the open fields on the other side of the City, we saw them tied up against the side of the canal towpath. They were setting up a bar-b-q.

"No doubt they are going to cook some sausages," I told Jack.

We cruised on for another half mile, stopped, then tied up to the canal bank. The wives and kids got ready, and as dusk descended they headed for the Marina Club. Meanwhile Jack and I got dressed up in black sweaters and trousers, balaclava's and gloves, then stealthily made our way back to the Bismarck, like a pair of ninja's.

We hid in some bushes and observed the Germans who were busy with their bar-b-q. We could see that their back doors were open. Jack kept watch, while I crept along the path, using every bit of cover.

I got to their stern by almost crawling on my belly as I passed the bar-b-q site, and slid on to their steering platform. I ducked down and entered their engine room. Very impressive too, I thought, looking at the gleaming engine, and brass dials. I worked quickly and removed their weed hatch cover, sliding it under the engine.

Quiet as a ships rat, I climbed back out and rejoined Jack up the canal bank. We walked quickly back up to the club and joined the girls. An hour later the Germans walked in and sat as far away from us as they possibly could.

It was almost midnight when we staggered out of the club and weaved our way back to our boat.

"Hey you left the back doors open," said Jack.

"I thought you were locking up," I told him.

"Never mind, no harm done," he said, "I locked the internal engine room door, so no one can get in."

Reassured we climbed back onboard and turned in for the night.

230

DAY 11. We were up early again, and had just finished our breakfast of tea and toast, when the familiar shape of the Bismarck swept past. We hurriedly started the engine and cast off in pursuit.

Ten minutes later we were up to them, and they immediately slowed down to two miles per hour. We observed their stern closely and it was obvious that it was lower in the water than usual.

Twenty minutes later and their steering platform was level with the waterline, and Herr Rimmel suddenly steered for the towpath. All too late though, and we watched with glee as the sleek grey shape slid below the waves. Or at least she settled on the bottom of the canal in three feet of water, her decks awash and her roof literally covered in Germans.

We swept past them and I shouted, "WELL, THAT'S YOUR DE-POSIT LOST!" And we cruised round the next bend leaving the furious Rimmels behind, and well and truly sunk.

Five minutes later Clive went below, and rushed back up shouting "WE ARE FULL OF WATER!" I looked down and the steering platform was awash. I steered for the towpath, but all too late though, and our gallant ship, the Hood, slid below the surface, gently settling herself on the bottom of the canal.

"THOSE BLOODY KRAUTS HAVE TAKEN OUR WEEDHATCH OFF," roared Jack as we all scrambled up onto the roof.

Well that was the end of the holiday, and of our deposit, but we were actually all quite happy about it. It had been the most stressful eleven days of our lives, and we all needed a holiday to get over it.

"So what are you going to do next year, invade Normandy?" asked the oldest member.

"No, something nice and peaceful, like white water rafting down the Colorado River," said Bernie with a gloomy finality.

NINETEEN
The Fishing Trip

Young Billy Norman said, "I've never been in the Legion, nor won a fair princess, but perhaps I can tell you about a little fishing trip I went on a few weeks back."

As no one else seemed to be ready to tell a story, the oldest member said, "OK, we are listening."

So Billy began.

It was the annual fishing trip
All the lads were there
Heading up to Whitby
And all that North Sea air

We'd all met up at 5am
We didn't make much fuss
Even though Dangerous Brian
Had booked the minibus

All the wives had packed our lunch
I had jam and cheese and bread
Even though the lazy sod
Had not got out of bed

Paddy Fitzmaurice had taken charge
Each one had his place
And as he passed round cans of ale
A frown lit up his face

Bloody hell our leader roared
Am I going nuts
Or is it true that I can smell
Someone has dropped his guts

I sat there all quiet and calm
As if it wasn't me
And then I said to Alan Brookes
You should try the lavatory

It wasn't me young Alan squawked
He who smelt it dealt it
You cheeky sod Paddy roared
My sandwich box has melted

And at long last the bus set off
Heading out of town
While the lads opened up a few more cans
And swigged the contents down

Ten miles north the greasy spoon
Beckoned us all in to
Fill our guts with and chips and beans
And a quick trip to the loo

Little Andy had double everything
Including bacon and fried bread
He ate it all then had some more
Was his stomach as big as his head

And then once more we headed north
After the North Sea cod
While Andy tried to hold it down
The greedy little sod

Half hour later Paddy awoke
And said where the hell are we
We should be on the motorway
This looks like backcountry

For the road had all but disappeared
Down to a dirt track
Dangerous said we took a turn
Almost half hour back

You stupid fool Paddy roared
Your directions are all crossed
Can't I rest for just one sec
Without us getting lost

The bus reversed back up the track
And Dangerous turned it round
Back down to the greasy Spoon
Where the motorway we found

Paddy now watched like a hawk
As Dangerous made up time
Overtaking all the cars
For the boat set off at nine

Bob Hilsely told a story
About a naughty nun
Locked inside a candle works
She was having fun

Then all at once we were there
Driving through the town
Dangerous knew that we were late
And kept his foot pressed down

Until a police car pulled us in
Sorry sir said Brian this bus it is on hire
To the traffic policeman who answered him
So where's the bloody fire

Three points and sixty quid it cost
And Brian was having a moan
It's all your fault he told the lads
Paddy can drive it home

And then at ten past nine
We pulled up on the dock
And went to meet the old sea dog
Who was scratching at his nose

So you have all turned up at last
You've made me miss the tide
It's now an extra £10 a man
That's if you still want the ride

We all paid up and took our seats
Inside the leaking boat
Don't worry lads the skipper said
I'm sure that it will float

The boat set off out to sea
And was several miles from the shore
If you want some rods the captain said
You have to pay some more

We all forked up £10 more
And the skipper produced sticks and string
Its £10 more if you want some bait
That's if you want to catch anything

We all paid up and tried to smile
Though Paddy was looking grim
If the swine tries this just one more time
The bugger's going in.

The boat was swooping up and down
Over the mountainous sea
Andy was leaning over the side
His breakfast was history

The captain turned the boat around
And now the engine stopped
We all baited up our hooks
And into the sea they dropped

The skipper looked down at his watch
And said the sea is getting rough
I'm ready to take the boat back in
As soon as you've had enough

That sounds good little Andy said
I really need to get ashore
Paddy was having none of that
We've paid for six hours more

And so we sat with baited hooks
Awaiting our first bite
Paddy and Ian tangled their lines
And nearly had a fight

I opened my box of sandwiches
Jam into the cheese had run
So then I made a special point
Of offering Andy one

ARE YOU READY TO
GO BACK IN YET? ASKED THE SKIPPER.....

We all looked in appreciation
As he heaved up over the side
7 out of 10 for content
We heard Paddy decide

What's that brown hairy thing
Floating over there
Andy has spewed up his ring
We heard Dobbo declare

And so we continued fishing
Although it seemed in vain
And well before half past one
We were sat in the driving rain

Ready yet the skipper asked
For me to go back to port
Not until I've got a fish said Paddy
That I can tell my wife I caught

Half-hour later I got a bite
And hauled up on the rod
All the lads gave out a cheer
As the line broke what a sod

Let's go in lads our leader said
This is lousy sport
Quick as a flash the skipper was up
And heading back to port

Fifteen minutes later
We tied up at the quay
There's a broken rod the captain said
That's twenty quid you owe me

Paddy said no bloody way
You don't get another pound
But the arrival of ten tough sailors
Made us have a quick whip round

And so we left the dock behind
And the rotten leaky tub
Where to first our leader asked
The Fishmongers or the Pub.........

TWENTY
It Never Rains

The major was in the club, and a couple of members were asking him about his days in the French Foreign Legion.

"So did you do all of your service in North Africa?" asked the oldest member.

"No, I spent a considerable amount of time in French Indo China," said the major.

"Were you involved in any fighting over there?" asked Jumbo Fowler?

"I'll say," said the major, "do you want to hear about the 'Battle of Loc Dien Phut?'"

"Do tell," said the oldest member, quickly asserting his prominence over Jumbo.

And so the major began.

"It was back in '54'. Word had gone round the first battalion that volunteers were required for service with the third regiment in Vietnam. Well, I was about ready for a little holiday in the exotic Far East, so I went to find Sergeant Schulz and the boys to discuss going.

They didn't take to much finding; the unconscious military policemen piled up outside Black Mikes saloon told me that they would be in there.

I pushed through the swinging doors, deftly ducking the empty bottle that flew in my direction.

"Sorry L'enforcer," said Legionnaire Chunderer the crazy Australian, not really sounding sorry at all. "I thought it was those chain dogs coming back in.

"Are you talking about the military policemen?" I asked, "What did they want?"

"Cheeky schweins vanted to know vy ve vas in here at this time," said Sergeant Schultz, the tough Dutch sergeant.

I changed the subject and said, "Mes amis, I have just come from the colonel." They pretended to ignore me and dealt out their cards.

"And we have a once in a lifetime opportunity to visit French Indo China. It will be the holiday of a lifetime; sun, sand, surf and girls."

Corporal Crowell the giant Texan looked out of the window at the sun and sand, then said,

"Tell us about the girls and surf."

"It's a paradise," I began, "great cities like Hanoi and Saigon, cheap booze, pretty girls, lots of time off."

"I'm in," said Corporal Crowell. "Me too, Pom," said Legionnaire Chunderer. Legionnaire Carlos, who they called 'le mercer', also looked a bit interested.

Sergeant Schultz, however, was having none of it.

"Nein, nein," he snarled, "I haf never heard of anything good coming from volunteering, besides der Third Regiment are out there, and they haf a price on my head."

"But Sarge," said Legionnaire Chunderer, "things are getting pretty damned hot for us here. Wouldn't a change of scenery benefit us a bit?"

"Aw, come on Sarge," said Corporal Crowell, "just think of all those little ladies over there just waiting to meet us."

Le mercer said nothing; he just sat and sharpened his stiletto.

Black Mike the barkeeper chose that moment to approach the table.

"Hey Schultz, your bar bill is over two thousand francs. When are you going to settle up?" he demanded.

Schultz whispered to me, "When are you going?"

"Wednesday. In two days time we leave for Siddi-Bel-Abbes and legion HQ," I told him.

He turned to Black Mike, and said,

"My friend, I vill settle my bill in full on Thursday."

"Just make sure that you do, or some of my men will pay you a visit," said the bar owner, stumping off.

"Not in Vietnam, they wont," chuckled the sergeant to the lads.

"Hey Mike," shouted Corporal Crowell, "bring out a couple of bottles of brandy and put them on sergeant Schultz's bar bill."

I sat with my men for a couple of hours and spoke to them about Vietnam.

"It will be French for another hundred years," I told them. "True, there is a little trouble with some people called the Viet Minh, but we are the Legion, and will soon make them behave themselves, eh!"

I eventually left the party and staggered back to my quarters. I had my men, and all I had to do now was pack my uniforms and bathing costume. The next two days were spent doing a ton of paperwork, then Wednesday arrived and we paraded at the guardroom at 6am; well I did, but there wasn't a sign of my men.

At 7.28, just before our transport was due to leave, a sour-faced Schultz turned up, followed by Corporal Crowell, and Carlos carrying Legionnaire Chunderer, who appeared to be unconscious.

"Ach, so you meant this guardroom," he snarled at me.

I said, "Yes sergeant. Isn't this the only guardroom?" He shrugged his shoulders and turned to supervise the throwing of Chunderer into the back of the lorry.

And so, right on the dot of 7.30, the lorry set off on the 100km trip to legion HQ at Siddi-Bel-Abbes. We sat in the back of the lorry and I launched into the Marseilles, but they already had the cards out and were dealing hands.

"How about a game, L'enforcer?" asked Corporal Crowell, expertly shuffling the cards with one hand.

"Non, non, I think that I will sit this one out," I said, checking that my wallet was still in my shirt pocket.

At 9am our lorry pulled into the Legion Barracks at Siddi-Bel-Abbes and ground to a halt in front of the main headquarters block.

We all piled out and stood looking around.

"This just looks like all the other Legion Barracks," said Corporal Crowell, "where's the Kasbah?"

"Vait," said Sergeant Schultz, "time for dat later." They slapped Legionnaire Chunderer back into consciousness, and we picked up our kit and entered the building.

The corporal on desk duty shot to his feet and saluted me

"Major L'enforcer," he said, "what an honour. How can I help you sir?"

"We are the men for Indo China," I told him.

He paled visibly, and said, "I shall inform the colonel that you are here."

We were quickly ushered into the presence of an elderly Frenchman, the colonel.

"So, you are my volunteers for Vietnam," he said, looking us over, and frowning as he caught sight of a dishevelled Chunderer.

"What's wrong with him?" the colonel asked.

Before any of the men could make a cutting reply I jumped in and said, "He has been travel sick mon colonel."

"Let's hope he can survive the sea trip to Indo China," the colonel said.

"He will be alright, he is just very excited about going," I lied.

The colonel pushed a bell on his desk. The door opened, and two more soldiers came in to the office; a large corporal about six foot two, and about the same across the shoulders, with great hairy arms, a granite chin and small close set eyes, also a slim elegant legionnaire of average height and build. Their shoulder flashes proclaimed them to be men of the second battalion.

"May I introduce you to Corporal Pierkowsky and Legionnaire Hastings," said the colonel. "They will be going with you as part of your specialist team."

Sgt Schultz and the Polish corporal exchanged sour looks, while I shook hands with Hastings, another Englishman.

"Tomorrow," said the colonel, "you will be going to Paris for a week's leave, and then you will catch the transport leaving from Bordeaux."

And so, as we left the colonel's office my team was complete, or, as we became known throughout the Legion, 'Le Sept Magnifique'.

"The Magnificent Seven," interrupted the oldest member. "Next you will be telling us that they based a film on you."

"Wait and see," said the major.

The next morning we met at 10am to catch the train for Algiers. The lads had obviously been celebrating, and Corporal Pierkowsky was sporting an enormous black eye.

"What happened to you?" I asked. He shrugged. I turned to the others, "What's going on?" I asked them.

Hastings laughed and said, "Jan had a dispute with Sergeant Schultz about whether the second battalion has to take orders from the first battalion."

"And?" I asked.

"It appears that they do," Hastings said with a laugh, which was echoed by the rest of the squad.

We had handed our North African uniforms in, and were now dressed in new dress uniforms ready for our leave in Paris. We boarded the train, and it began its four-hour journey to Algiers. The men got out the cards and began a game of poker, except for Legionnaire Hastings who sat beside me and said,

"So you are the famous enforcer of the Legion."

"I have been called that," I admitted, "but you are obviously a gentleman, what on earth are you doing here?"

"I joined the Legion to forget," he told me.

"Forget what?" I asked.

"Actually I've forgotten," he said.

"I've been told that you are a top man with explosives," I told him, "in fact you can blow up a skyscraper with two boxes of matches."

"Yes, and half a ton of TNT," he answered.

"And what does Corporal Pierkowsky do," I asked him.

"Well Jan's pretty good at killing people," he said.

"Hmmm he should fit in well then," I said, "not that I am expecting anyone to do any fighting."

Hastings looked at me and raised an eyebrow.

"Really," he said, and smiled that casual English smile of his.

Eventually we reached Algiers, the principal port of Algeria, and found our way to our ship, a rusty tub of a tramp steamer on route for Marseilles. The Legion certainly had no intention of us travelling first class. The boat was crowded with passengers, and Corporal Crowell, or Texas Rouge as the men called him, was soon off pursuing a French girl on her way back home to France, while the remainder of the squad produced some bottles of brandy and settled down for the crossing.

The crossing was uneventful, except for Corporal Pierkowsky having a fight with two French sailors, Legionnaire Chunderer throwing up over the side for several hours, and Sergeant Schultz threatening to take over the ship. Hastings just polished his already immaculate shoes, and Carlos sharpened his knife, while I pretended that I wasn't with them.

The ship reached port, and the squad were escorted off the ship by the Gendarmes, who put them on the Paris train and told them not to show their faces in Marseilles again, or else.

By nightfall we were in the magic city of Paris, and were settling into our cheap hotel. I unpacked my bag and went to see if the men were going to come out for a meal, but they had already gone, forgetting to tell me.

I dined alone as an officer should, and retired early to bed. I awoke late and had a leisurely breakfast, then headed up to Sergeant Schultz's room. I was sure that the men would want to come with me to visit the wonders of Paris; the Louvre, the museum of the army, the Eiffel tower, there was so much to see.

I quietly opened the door of Schultz's room. All the men were gathered around a map, and Sergeant Schultz was saying.

"So ven der ambush is sprung, der armoured car vill come to a halt here. Hastings runs out and places der explosive charge on the rear door, unt boom, ven der crew bail out they vill be taken out by me unt Texas Rouge."

My heart swelled with pride. My men were discussing tactics and training, even on leave.

I stepped forward and said, "Sergeant, may I join in?"

Schultz jumped, and said, "You join in? Are you sure, L'enforcer?"

"Of course I am," I replied, "we are a team and comrades of war, and I am your leader."

"OK," said the sergeant, "so Le mercer unt Jan vill seal off the end of the road and fight off any intervention from der gendarmes, and Chunderer vill grab der cash bags unt load dem into der escape car, vitch vill now be driven by L'enforcer."

"Just a minute," I said, and moved forwards to look at the map. It was a street map of Paris, and there was a red circle drawn around the National Bank.

"What exactly are you planning here?" I asked, somewhat confused.

"Don't you know?" asked the Sergeant.

"I'm not sure that I do," I told him.

"Ah vell, ve is just discussing how we would fight in der jungle," he said.

"What, on a street-map of Paris?" I replied.

"Ja, dat's all ve have," he said.

"Get your kitbags packed. We are going to Bordeaux today," I ordered, "and you will all be confined to the naval barracks until we leave for Vietnam."

And so it came to pass that we spent most of our leave in the barracks in Bordeaux waiting for the ship to take us to Saigon.

At last the great day dawned and we were off to sunny Vietnam for a well-deserved spot of rest and recreation.

Things settled into their normal pattern; Corporal Crowell was soon off in pursuit of a Vietnamese girl on her way home to Vietnam, Sergeant Schultz and the rest of the men ensconced themselves in the bar and tried to drink it dry, while I attempted to learn Vietnamese, a hopeless task, all their words sound like metal pans being bashed together; well, French or English would have to do.

We sailed across the Mediterranean and through the Suez Canal, down the Red Sea and around India and Malaya, until at long last we were off the coast of Vietnam.

We lined the side of the ship and looked at the land as we approached.

"There seems to be a lot of smoke rising everywhere," said Hastings, and this was true, one could smell the smoke in the very air.

The ship made its way into port and docked against the main Quay.

"How come the customs buildings are on fire?" asked Legionnaire Chunderer, and I had to confess that for once I didn't know.

Everyone was running around at a frantic pace, and in the distance I could hear fireworks exploding.

"Listen, they sound just like mortars," I remarked to the sergeant, and was treated to a cold Dutch stare.

We carried our kitbags up the quayside, and I looked in vain for some sort of transport to take us to the Legion HQ in Saigon City.

"Excuse me," I said to a scurrying uniformed figure, "where is our transport?"

"How should I know?" he replied, "I'm a general in the Army of the Republic of Vietnam."

I saluted, but he was already running into one of the buildings.

Sergeant Schulz turned to Carlos and said, "Le Mercer, go and find our transport."

Carlos disappeared, and five minutes later drove back onto the quay in a Jeep.

"Where did this vehicle come from?" I asked suspiciously.

Sergeant Schultz said, "It must have been left for us," as he reached down and prised off the plate that said 'General of the Army of the Republic of Vietnam'.

We piled on our kit and crowded aboard. It was a bit tight trying to fit seven men into four seats, especially when two of them were giants. Hastings and Chunderer had to stand on the rear fender and hang on for dear life as Carlos drove at high speed through the burning streets.

Half an hour later we were driving through the streets of Saigon, looking for the Legion Headquarters, eventually finding it hidden behind an army of heavily armed soldiers.

"Are you sure that this is going to be a holiday?" asked Corporal Crowell from the rear seat.

"Trust me, mes amis," I said, "the Legion will soon settle things down, and who are the finest soldiers in the Legion?"

"Who?" they asked.

"Why it is us," I told them, "le Sept Magnifique." We pulled up with the sound of happy laughter filling the Jeep.

I headed up to the Commandants office and reported to the hard looking Legion colonel.

"L'enforcer," he said, "I have heard about you, and you are just the fellow to lead a special team that I wish to set up," and we sat and discussed our role in Vietnam.

An hour or so later I left the colonels office and sought out my men, it didn't take me long to find them in the soldiers canteen, polishing off bottles of brandy, and playing cards.

"Mes enfants," I said, "I have come from the colonel and he has a special job for us." I received six suspicious looks.

"We are going to form a special unit called the Tactical Weapons And Tactics Squad."

"What's that, we are going to be called the TWATS?" said Corporal Crowell. "No darn way."

"It could have been worse," I told them, "first of all, the colonel wanted to call us the Area Reserve Special Elite Squad."

"Shut up, Texas Rouge," said Sergeant Schultz. He turned to me, "Just vat haf you agreed to do?" he asked me.

"Er, not much; we are just going up jungle, to help out at an outpost called Loc Dien Phut," I informed them.

"I thought as much," said the sergeant, "dat place is under siege - two hundred French soldiers surrounded by twenty thousand Viet Minh fighters - unt I haf heard dat those little guys are one hell of a fighter."

"Ah yes," I answered, "but we are the Legion Etranger." He looked at me in utter despair.

Hastings laughed and said, "It's OK, the outpost is completely cut off. It would take a division a week to fight its way in."

"Ah ha," I said triumphantly, "that is why we are going to parachute in."

"You what?" said six disbelieving voices, except one of course, which said. "You vat?"

"It's quite alright men," I said. "We start our parachute training course tomorrow."

"How long does that last?" asked Corporal Crowell.

"Not too long, because we drop on Loc Dien Phut, the following day," I told him.

The next morning I was at the airfield at dawn, awaiting the arrival of my men who seemed a bit late. I was sure that I had said 6am, and at 7.20am their jeep drove onto the airfield and pulled up beside me.

"Ach, so you meant dis airfield," said Sergeant Schultz. I refrained from reminding him that this was the only military airfield in the command.

The training was tough, but the men waltzed through it, except for me and Legionnaire Chunderer. No matter how hard we tried, we always fell out of the back of the moving truck like sacks of potatoes.

Sgt Schultz and the others landed gently on their feet and executed elegant graceful sideways rolls, always finishing up on their feet, while Chunderer and myself either landed head first in the mud or hard on our bottoms. I glared at Hastings, who was saying that they amounted to the same thing anyway.

Eventually the dour instructor corporal said that we were ready, and we went and fitted our parachutes on, being very careful not to let the others touch or fool around with our own chutes. We all climbed into the Cessna light aircraft, the engine revved and I closed my eyes. After a while I opened them and looked out of the open door.

"My word, look at those people down there," I said, "they look just like ants."

"They are ants," said Corporal Crowell, "we haven't taken off yet."

The men laughed happily as the plane taxied down the runway and staggered up into the air. The happy laughter increased as Legionnaire Chunderer leaned across me and threw up through the open door, literally pebble dashing me at the same time.

The plane circled, climbing all the time, and we seemed to be above the clouds.

"How high are we going?" I asked the instructor.

"Three thousand feet," he replied.

"Merde," I said, which the men seemed to find funny.

The plane levelled off and throttled back. The instructor pointed at me and said,

"Get into the doorway."

I obeyed, and stood there, desperately clinging on, while the ninety-mile-an-hour slipstream threatened to pluck me out.

"Look down there," said the instructor. "Make sure that you land to the left of the tower, or you may finish up amongst the trees."

"Where's the airfield?" I croaked, for all I could see was trees.

Sergeant Schultz pushed up behind me; a large boot planted itself onto my backside and I hurtled out of the door.

I plummeted towards the earth and began to say my prayers. Then there was a jerk, and I was suddenly floating under a beautiful white silk circle. I looked around and I could see my six men drifting down behind me in a straight line. I waved to them and was rewarded with six 'V' for victory signs.

I enjoyed the descent for a couple of minutes, and then decided that I had better prepare for landing, because the ground appeared to be coming up awfully fast, and where on earth was the airfield? All I could see was trees. Down I fell, faster and faster. A tall tree lunged up at me and I opened my legs, allowing it to pass between them. I crashed through a network of branches and came to a halt six feet above the ground.

I swung there and groped for my combat knife to cut the cords, when CRASH, a pair of size eleven boots thudded into the top of my head, and Chunderer and I hit the ground in a tangled mass of equipment and parachutes.

I quickly struggled out from underneath him, before he thought of throwing up again.

We gathered up our parachutes, and looked at the dense jungle, then back at each other.

"I think that the airfield must be that way," I said, pointing around in a semi circle.

"Well, on the way down, Pom," he said, "I noticed a gang of little fellows wearing black pyjamas. They are just up that way a couple of hundred feet. Why don't we go and ask them?"

"Well, if it makes you happy, we could do that," I told him. "You just lead the way."

He pushed his way through the undergrowth and I hurried to keep up with him.

We burst into a small jungle clearing and stood looking at a dozen or so small men wearing straw hats and black pyjamas. Not only that, but they were all carrying Kalashnikovs.

They did a double take at us and one of them yelled, "Frogs!" Chunderer and I dived to the ground and rolled away, as an absolute fusillade of bullets whistled over our heads.

"Jesus, Pom," Chunderer croaked, "they must be ruddy Viet Minh."

"And we are the Legion," I said. "Circle around them and cut them off."

Chunderer crawled behind a large tree, and said, "Wouldn't it be better if we had some guns?" as I crawled up to him.

"Hey, go and find your own tree," he yelped, as a hail of shots followed me and tore the undergrowth apart.

"It's OK," I told him, "they are far more frightened of us than we are of them."

Chunderer caught a hand grenade which had come sailing through the air towards us, and threw it back in the best Australian tradition.

"Well, they must be pretty damned frightened, then," he said, as the grenade exploded, sending a straw hat high into the air.

"I shall think of a plan to defeat these insurgents," I told him, as we tried to burrow into the ground.

Minutes passed, and Chunderer said, "So what's the ruddy plan?"

"We are a bit outnumbered, so you should go for help, while I hold their attention here," I ordered.

"In your dreams, Pom," said Chunderer, "the air's so full of bullets that there's not enough room left for me out there."

At that moment I heard a familiar Dutch voice shouting, "Achtung, achtung," and my men burst through the jungle and laid into the enemy fighters. Within a minute it was all over and the Viet Minh fled back up the trail, dragging their walking wounded with them.

"I wondered when you were going to show up, Sergeant Schultz," I said, as the men crowded around Legionnaire Chunderer, shaking his hand and asking for the money he owed them.

I was treated to a cold Dutch stare, and we followed the sergeant back through the jungle and onto the perimeter of the airfield.

"Who's up for another jump?" shouted Chunderer.

"Nein, no more jumping today," said the sergeant, "you haf used up too many of your nine lives today already."

And so we returned to barracks. I went to my room to write up my diary, and the men went to the soldiers' canteen for cards and drinks.

The next morning, bright and early, I was back at the airfield, looking for my men, and sure enough an hour later they turned up. We were laden with a veritable armoury; guns, grenades, knives, rocket launchers, bottles of brandy. And we were shoehorned into the little Cessna plane.

"Don't we have a bigger plane?" I asked plaintively.

"Oui monsieur L'enforcer," said the pilot, "but it is running a cargo of liquor to Cambodia for Sergeant Schultz."

The tiny plane rattled down the runway and clawed its way into the air, slowly climbing up until it was at three thousand feet. It then headed northwest over the dense jungle.

I ducked back as Legionnaire Chunderer crawled to the door and chucked his breakfast over the fuselage.

We flew on for over an hour, and the jungle was like a green carpet, all perfect peace.

"Mes Amis, we are going to enjoy this," I told them. "Where else in the world could you get a little holiday in a tropical paradise, and get paid for it as well?"

"Vat is dat column of smoke ahead?" said Sergeant Schultz. We all looked, and sure enough, there appeared to be a volcano burning away in the middle of the jungle about five miles ahead. As we flew closer we could see that over an area of a square kilometre or so, the jungle floor seemed to be on fire.

"Don't tell me, that's Loc Dien Phut," said Hastings.

"Loc Dien Phut immediately ahead," said the pilot. "Get ready to jump."

"What, into that maelstrom?" said Hastings.

"Yep. It's still a bit quiet at the moment, but it's sure to hot up later," said the pilot.

I stood up, and a large boot propelled me out of the door. I wish that they would let me have time to hook on my chute cord, I thought as I spun through the air trying to release my parachute. Eventually it opened, and I drifted downwards, followed by my six men.

As the ground approached I could hear the guns firing and see trees toppling beneath explosions. I guided my chute into a clear space between some burning trucks and the ruins of a house, and quickly gathered up my chute as my men landed around me.

"Quickly men," I ordered, "follow me to the commandant's office," and we set off up the remains of the road.

"Vy don't ve go dis way?" said Sergeant Schulz, pointing in the opposite direction.

"Any particular reason?" I asked patiently.

"Because that sign, saying 'Commandant's Office', is pointing up in that direction," said Hastings, just as patiently.

"Then what are we waiting for, let's go," I ordered.

Ducking and weaving, we made our way through the beleaguered base, until at last we arrived at the headquarters ruins. I pushed my way inside, followed by the men. The door had been blown off the Commandant's office, and inside it, seated on a sandbag, was a colonel of the legion.

He looked at us and jumped up, "Thank god," he said, "its Sergeant Schultz and he has brought Crowell, Pierkowsky, Hastings and Carlos; pity about Chunderer though."

A giant sergeant major looked round and said, "Mein Gott, its Schultz. I haven't seen you since Stalingrad." Schulz frowned, looked at me and shook his head.

I AM QUITE SURE THAT THE AIRFIELD
IS IN THIS DIRECTION.

"So, you are the TWATS that HQ has sent out to reinforce us," said the colonel.

"Ah yes, mon Colonel," I said, "your worries are over. The men of the first battalion of the first regiment are here."

"Don't mind him," said Schulz, "he liffs in zum sort of dream vorld."

"I see," said the colonel, "well it's still very good to see you, Major L'enforcer."

"Come over here and look at this map," said the colonel, and we gazed down upon a map showing the perimeter and buildings of the base. "Now, we are protected on three sides by swamp and minefields, but here on the Eastern side we have been pushed back to the line between the soldiers' canteen here, and the Nurses Quarters over here."

"The Nurses quarters look as if they need defending," said Corporal Crowell adjusting his Raybans.

"No," said all the others, "we must fortify the soldiers' canteen."

"Actually," said the colonel, "I was thinking of sending you TWATS a hundred metres forward to dig in, and blunt any enemy attacks before they reach the main buildings."

"Perfect," I said. "We shall be in the thick of the action."

"Oh, Jesus Christ," said Hastings, "do you mean this place that says, Suicide Point?"

"That's it, Point de Suicide" said the colonel, "drop your kit here and off you go." We made for the door.

"Just one more thing," said the colonel, "be careful out there."

We made our way back down the shell-cratered road, heading east and ducking the incoming shells and bombs. The men found the soldiers canteen with unerring accuracy.

"Let's check it out," said Sergeant Schultz, and we headed towards the bullet-holed door.

Just before we could open it, a legionnaire stuck his head through a hole in the wall and shouted,

"Bloody hell, its Sergeant Schultz from the First Regiment!" More faces appeared at various holes and windows, and bullets began to whistle around our ears.

We quickly retreated out of range and took cover.

"Hell! Sergeant Schulz," I shouted, "what's all that about?"

"It's der Third Regiment," said Schultz, "ve owe dem rather a lot of money in gambling debts."

"Don't forget the incident in Algiers as well," said Corporal Crowell. Schultz hissed at him, and he shut up.

"Come, mes enfants," I said, "we have a job to do, and a battle to win," and we crawled off accompanied by a chorus of exaggerated sighs from the men. What jokers they were.

We crawled forwards a hundred metres, "Now where is the strong point?" I asked.

"Can you see all the churned up ground around that hole over there?" said Hastings, "well that's it."

"How can you tell that?" I asked him.

"Just looking by at the couple of dozen sticks stuck into the ground with helmets on top of them," he replied.

I decided that he was right, and followed Sergeant Schultz across the open ground and into the bunker.

It was the bunker from hell alright. The roof had been blown in, and everywhere was covered in bullet scars. Schultz got the men to work digging out rubble and reinforcing the walls. Pierkowsky dug enough for two men while Hastings cooked up a meal of bacon on French sticks.

It all seemed quiet to our front, and I decided to recce into the edge of the jungle, to see what the enemy were up to.

"I need a volunteer to come with me," I told the men, and was met with a stony silence.

"Now I know that you all want to come," I told them, "so let's go, Corporal Crowell."

I pretended not to hear his colourful cowboy curses as we slid out of the bunker and crawled to the edge of the jungle seventy metres away.

At last we reached the jungles edge and slid into the undergrowth. It all seemed very quiet. Was there any enemy, I wondered, standing up. Perhaps the news of our arrival had reached them and they had retreated.

"Follow me, corporal," I ordered, and carefully pushed into the undergrowth.

We moved through the dense jungle for maybe a quarter of a mile, and then there they were, thousands of them, little guys dressed in black pyjamas and armed to the teeth. They were sat in an enormous semi circle, being addressed by some officers wearing khaki uniforms and sun helmets.

We carefully backed off until we were a hundred yards into the jungle, then turned and ran like the wind back to the bunker. We scrambled in and sat gasping for breath.

"Did you see anyting?" enquired Sergeant Schultz, looking up from the newspaper he was reading.

"Hell Sarge," said Corporal Crowell, "there was about ten thousand of the little buggers having a meeting."

"Ach so, it looks as if ve are a bit outnumbered den," snarled the tough Dutchman.

"Huh, we are the Legion Etranger, men of the Kepi Blanc, they wont dare to attack us," I said, diving for the ground as the first salvo of mortar shells fell onto our position.

"Have you seen those pictures of the Somme?" asked the major, "Well, that's what it seemed like as we suffered the barrage of bombs and shells for several hours."

Then suddenly all was quiet.

"Get ready," snapped the sergeant, pulling me back down into the bunker as I tried to climb out. And then there they were again, the jungle's edge became alive with black pyjama'd figures, all of whom seemed to be shooting at me.

Hastings was talking into the radio he was carrying, and seemed to be giving some map co-ordinates, and then the air was alive with French artillery shells as the jungle edge was pounded. The Viet Minh disappeared back into the jungle, dragging their casualties along with them. Hastings spoke into the radio again and the shelling ceased.

"How on earth did you organise that?" I asked him.

"I had to do something, while you were out exploring the jungle," he replied.

"Yes, I wondered who would be the first to think of it," I told him.

"Don't vorry, dey vill kom back tonight," said Sergeant Schultz, and so we waited; Schultz reading the newspaper, Crowell topping up his sun tan cream, Carlos sharpening his knife, while Pierkowsky and Hastings played cards with Chunderer, winning enormous IOU's off him.

Night in the tropics falls quickly, and well before 7pm it was dark. Sergeant Schultz got everyone into position, and we prepared to take on the entire Viet Minh army.

"You TWATS had better fight like heroes," he snarled, my heart swelled with pride, "because tomorrow, I am going back and blowing up those TWATS from the third Regiment," he said.

It was certainly a beautiful evening. I could hear the crickets croaking away and the gentle rustle of the breeze through the trees. Sergeant Schultz suddenly stood up and fired off a flare. It shot up like a big firework and burst into light, and there they were, hundreds of small black figures moving towards us at the run. Corporal Pierkowsky opened up with his machine gun, while Legionnaire Chunderer began to throw hand grenades with unerring accuracy.

"That's a four," he said as a particularly well-timed grenade went off, blowing four straw hats into the air.

"How's that?" yelled Chunderer, as another grenade went off beside a khaki clad officer, knocking him down.

"Not out," said Hastings, as the officer got back up.

"Will you two stop playing baseball for a minute," shouted Corporal Crowell, shooting his colt 45 and sending the officer toppling back over.

"Huh, bloody yanks have no appreciation of the finer arts, have they," said Hastings.

"Well, us yanks wouldn't be stupid enough to get involved in a place like Vietnam either," snarled corporal Crowell, picking off another black clad figure.

Schultz shouted to Hastings, "Now, give the signal now." Hastings spoke into his radio, and the whole section jumped up out of the strongpoint and hared back towards the camp.

I couldn't believe my eyes. Now, right in the middle of a battle, my men were running away.

Well, L'enforcer didn't run from the enemy, and I prepared to die fighting. I stood up, and a giant hand grasped my collar and dragged me out of the trench.

"You god dam stupid limey," shouted Corporal Crowell. "Get your ass back to the nurses' quarters like now!" Pierkowsky and Crowell grabbed my arms and I was rushed back towards the nurses quarters, reaching them as the first wave of Viet Minh poured into our previous position. The French artillery opened up at precisely that moment, and rained fire down onto our abandoned strongpoint. Bodies were flying everywhere.

"Hey, it's just like the fourth of July," said Corporal Crowell, leaning out of the window. Sergeant Schultz joined us and looked over towards the inferno to our front.

"Get ready," he shouted, and the men hefted their guns. The shellfire went on for another two minutes. "Let's go," shouted the sergeant, and the men charged out of the ruined building at the exact moment that the shelling stopped. I followed them in the charge back across the open ground, desperately trying to get to the front, but the men were very fast, and I arrived at Suicide Point some seconds after them. Pierkowsky already had his machine gun going, and Chunderer was happily throwing grenades with quite a good bowling action. The rest of the men were firing at anything that moved, except for Sergeant Schulz, who was in the trench furiously punching the head of someone in the bottom of the hole.

Eventually the firing petered out, and nothing was moving to our front anymore. The sergeant stood up and hauled up a khaki-uniformed figure that was semi-conscious.

"What's that, Sergeant?" I asked.

"I'd say a Viet Minh colonel," said my Dutch sergeant. "Here Carlos, kill him," he said.

Legionnaire Carlos already had his knife moving towards our prisoner as I jumped between them, receiving a bit of a nick off the razor sharp knife.

"Just hold it right there," I said, "we do not kill unarmed prisoners." Hastings jumped forward and kicked a knife out of the prisoner's hand.

"Now he is unarmed," he said.

"So vat iz you going to do mitt him," snarled the sergeant, "I am not going to guard him for effer."

"It's OK Sergeant," I said, "I'll look after him. Let's try to get some rest before they come back again."

Carlos took watch as we settled down in the churned up strongpoint, and the enemy started calling from the jungle. It went on and on, until suddenly our prisoner started shouting out in Vietnamese.

A great fist shot out from Corporal Crowell knocking him out cold.

"Would you mind awfully shutting the hell up," he said, somewhat unnecessarily.

The long night went on and on, interrupted only by the sergeant changing the sentries and the odd shouts coming from the jungle. Our prisoner had come round and was lying in the bottom of the hole, bound and gagged.

Then, at 6am it was getting light. "Stand to, men," said the sergeant, "dey could come now."

"Sell your lives dearly men," I said, "we are the Legion, and we shall fight to the last bullet and then use that on ourselves. How many rounds do we have left, sergeant?"

256

"One each," said the sergeant.

In the event, they never came, and at 8am I considered it safe enough to send some men to fetch food and ammunition. Corporal Crowell and Hastings slid out of the strongpoint and sprinted across the open ground before disappearing behind the nurses' quarters.

Then, an hour or so later they reappeared, staggering under huge loads of ammunition and food. They slid into the trench and gratefully dropped their burdens. Sergeant Schulz cocked an eyebrow at them, and they nodded. At that very moment a loud explosion sounded from the direction of the soldiers' canteen.

"What on earth was that?" I asked. Sergeant Schulz just smiled knowingly.

Legionnaire Carlos knelt down and began to cook some breakfast, a nice pottage of frogs legs I recall, while Corporal Pierkowsky shared out the ammunition. Chunderer took watch and we were soon tucking into breakfast and drinking black coffee.

"How about feeding the prisoner?" I asked, and Hastings untied him and removed his gag.

As the prisoner ate I looked him over. He actually looked quite distinguished, in a smart khaki uniform with three stars on the collar, standing around five foot five with iron grey hair and a smartly clipped moustache, highly polished brown boots, belt and empty holster. Obviously he was no ordinary soldier.

He noticed me staring at him and he nodded to me, and I wished that I spoke his language so I could question him.

"Bonjour Major," he suddenly said.

"Ah, you speak Français," I answered.

"Oh, you are English", he said in a perfect Oxford accent. "There are so many strange chaps in the legion nowadays. What on earth are you doing in it?"

"Now look here," I said, "I'll ask the questions if you don't mind. Who are you?"

"General Li Huen," he said, "commanding the Fifth Division of the Peoples Liberation Army."

"You don't command anybody now," said Hastings.

"Good lord, another Englishman," said our prisoner. "It is the French army we are fighting, isn't it?"

"No, no, we are the TWATS from North Africa," I said.

"You certainly are," the general said with a smile.

"L'enforcer, don't give him any more information," said Hastings, "I've heard of him. He commands the army which is besieging us."

Sergeant Schultz pushed forwards and looked down on him.

"He has to be valuable," Schultz said.

The general laughed and said, "Sergeant, I am worth nothing. My life belongs to my country."

Schulz looked at me and said, "Huh, you two make ein gutt pair."

The general looked at me and said, "Major, you have no chance. Why not surrender honourably to me?"

"Surrender? I do not understand the meaning of that word," I replied, striking a heroic pose. He sadly shook his head.

Time marched on, and the men settled down to a game of cards. I could see that our prisoner was interested, sitting closer and closer and making remarks about the game and the playing abilities of the men. It wasn't long before the general was dealt in and they were going at it hammer and tongs.

Chunderer relieved Corporal Pierkowsky on watch, and I settled down for a nap. Having been up all night, I can tell you that I was pretty tired.

I woke up at around 4pm and it seemed very quiet. All the men were lying asleep in the bottom of the trench, and there was no sign of our prisoner.

"Sergeant Schultz," I shouted, and he jumped up, pointing his rifle at me.

"Vat on earth iz der matter?" he shouted, glaring at me.

"Everyone was asleep and the prisoner has escaped," I told him.

He relaxed and put the gun down. "Ach so," he said, "he hasn't escaped at all. I sent him back to his army".

"What on earth for?" I asked.

"Vell, while you vas sleeping like ein baby, ve played cards to decide the outcome of der battle. De general happens to be a gambling fanatic."

"Playing cards to decide a battle? I've never heard of anything like that before. It's outrageous," I told him. "Anyway, who won?"

"Corporal Crowell, of course," said the sergeant. "It was his pack of cards."

"And where the hell is Corporal Crowell?" I asked, realising that the giant Texan wasn't there either.

"Gone to collect his money," said Schultz. "He won three thousand francs from him as well."

"As if he will honour that little gambling debt," I said.

The sergeant said, "Don't you haff any understanding of honour? Off course he vill pay. He iz an officer and a 'true' gentleman."

At that moment, Corporal Crowell's head appeared over the parapet, swiftly followed by his body as he slid into the trench. He passed a couple of bottles of rice wine over to the sergeant and sat down.

"Any problems?" asked Hastings, who had now woken up along with the rest of the men.

"Nope. They've all done and gone," drawled the Texan.

"What do you mean, gone?" I asked.

"Packed their bags and cleared off, the siege is over," said the blonde cowboy.

"Come with me. I want to check this out," I said, climbing up on to the parapet. We walked to the edge of the jungle, me moving from cover to cover and Corporal Crowell as if he was out for a Sunday stroll.

Further and further into the jungle I pushed, and - nothing - no enemy, no equipment, not even rubbish.

"Very strange," I said.

"Not at all," he replied. "Sergeant Schultz won the hand that decided who should clean the mess up before they left."

The jungle was absolutely deserted, and we made our way back to Suicide Point, where the men were just finishing packing their kit. Bemused, I followed them back into the camp and reported to the colonel.

"It's over, mon colonel," I told him. "The enemy have lifted the siege. We have won."

"Yes. Well done, Sergeant Schulz," said the colonel. "I knew I could depend on you, and you too of course, major," he said hurriedly, as I opened my mouth again.

"So now it's back to Legion HQ in Saigon for you TWATS," said the colonel. "We shall radio the good news immediately, and a relief column will soon be here."

And just one week later we were back in Saigon, where I had a short meeting with the commandant. Leaving the colonel's office I made my way to the wet canteen where the men were playing cards and having a drink.

"Guess what, mes amis," I told them, "the colonel is sending us for a spot of rest and recreation."

"Oh really, and where is that going to be at?" enquired Hastings.

"Apparently some place out in the country called Dien Bien Phu," I said.........

"C'est la vie," said Hastings. "It never rains but it pours."

TWENTY ONE
The English Uncivil War

The Reverend Grenville Turner, vicar of Saint Bartholomew's, parish church of the village of Soddingbury, had made a rare appearance in the club, and the members could not help noticing that he was sporting an enormous black eye.

The oldest member, never noted for his tact said, "Grenny, how did you come by that shiner? What have you been up to now?"

The vicar blushed and said, "Well actually I was involved in a battle."

"A battle? You? That's impossible," chorused the members.

"I only wish that it was," said the vicar.

"Well come on man, tell us all about it," demanded the oldest member.

"It all started two months ago at the monthly meeting of the parish council," said the vicar. We rattled through most of the agenda and finally came to the main item for discussion, the Soddingbury Annual Fete and carnival."

"One of those awful village fetes, I suppose," said the oldest member, "fancy dress and raffles."

Well not quite," said Grenville, "you see, every year we try to have a different theme, such as the Farmers Union, or cricket. The normal discussion was taking place with 'The Women's Institute' emerging as a favourite theme, that is until Charlie Stewart, landlord of the Kings Head public house said, 'Why don't we do a battle re-enactment?'

The room fell into silence as the council members tried to get their heads around his suggestion.

"What sort of battle re-enactment are you talking about, Charles?" I asked.

"Well, reverend," he said, "it's all there in the history books. In the year 1643, when England was split by Civil War, a small party of royalist foragers were confronted by a Parliamentary patrol from the town. They met up near the crossroads."

"My goodness," I said, "then what happened?"

261

"There was some shouting back and forth, stuff like 'Roundheads' and 'Frilly Knickers', 'Gadzooks', you know the sort of stuff, then they turned round and retreated to where they had come from," Charlie informed me.

"Hey, that sounds just the ticket," said Alan Cranwell, the member for the coal miners' housing estate.

And so it was decided. This year's carnival theme would be Soddingbury's part in the English Civil War, culminating in a mock battle on the school playing field.

The royalist general had to be Charlie Stewart of course, and the roundhead cause was quickly taken up by Alan Cranwell.

Now as some of you are aware, the village of Soddingbury is in effect two villages in one. The older and original village dates back to the seventeenth century and earlier, and then the new pit estate was built to house the coalminers in the 1950s.

The two halves of the village hadn't really got on for years; the miners calling the villagers snobs, and drinking and socialising at the Miners Welfare Club, while the villagers called them those new people, and stuck to the King's Head and the church hall.

I was hoping that the fete would draw the two sides closer together, but the exact opposite seemed to be happening, polarising the two factions even further, and councils of war were being held both in the welfare and the village hall.

As the village hall was actually the church hall, I attended one of Charlie's meetings. The atmosphere was a bit tense and got even tenser when Melvyn Mawer came into the room.

"Guess what I just heard," he said. Everyone looked at him. "Those roundheads are bussing in fifty skinheads from south London." Everyone groaned.

"That does it," said Charlie. "Give me the phone." The phone was found and passed around to him.

He dialled a number and said, "Hello Captain Robinson, I wonder if your huntsmen would like a bit of sport on Sunday week; yes that's right, the village carnival. I would like to field a royalist cavalry unit; yes, about twenty horses. You will? Oh that's grand. Nip into the King's Head tomorrow and we will discuss tactics."

He turned triumphantly to the meeting, "OK, so those roundheads are not the only ones with a secret weapon," he gloated. The room burst into a bedlam of patriotic cheering.

"Now look here," I said, "I hope that nobody is going to do anything silly at the fete."

"Absolutely not, reverend," agreed Charlie, "in fact we would like you to be umpire and control the event."

Reassured, I agreed, and the rest of the meeting was spent designing and discussing uniforms for the event.

I should have been forewarned by the insults that were beginning to be bandied around the village streets, but in my innocence I thought that it was just to add atmosphere to the big event, and indeed it was threatening to be the most successful village Fete ever, with tickets selling like hot cakes.

Then, last Sunday the big day dawned, and at twelve o'clock, after morning service, dressed in my tabard and tights, I made my way to the school sports field.

As you probably remember, Sunday was indeed a fine day, bright and sunny, and as I arrived the two armies were marching onto the field from opposite ends, and were lining up facing each other, all the while being applauded by a capacity crowd of around five hundred people.

Charlie Stewart lined his troops up at the village end of the field, and very impressive they looked too.

On his right was the block of battleaxes from the Women's Institute, dressed in lavender coloured uniforms, white stockings and lots of lace. In the centre was the pike block of pub regulars, dressed in blue velvet tops and black trousers tied in at the knee. They were wearing cardboard hats, and carried an assortment of clothes props.

The left hand block consisted of the combined local Boy Scout and Sea Cadet troops, dressed in a variety of fantasy uniforms including bits of armour, and armed to the teeth with sticks.

In front of his army stood Charlie Stewart and his staff; Melvyn Mawer the village postmaster holding a wooden sword, and Colin Harris the plumber, holding up a flag, plus a couple of self-conscious boy scout drummers dressed in pink lace uniforms.

Charlie fingered his collar a little nervously and looked at the enemy forming up on the other side of the playing field. On their left, and facing the Women's Institute, were the south London skinheads.

"I don't believe it," said Charlie, "just look at their uniforms." We looked, and they were wearing red football shirts, blue denim jeans and Doc Martens. They had a variety of saucepans on their heads and were carrying dustbin lids and clubs.

In their centre was a pike block made up of the biggest members of the miners' welfare club.

"Bloody typical," muttered Melvyn, "their pikes are at least three feet longer than ours." We looked at their right hand block. It was formed by pupils from the local comprehensive school, dressed in their grey school uniforms with the odd bit of ribbon tied here and there. They were jeering and shaking their sticks at the scouts who were facing them. Out in front stood Alan Cranwell, backed by a couple of bodyguards dressed in black leather motorcycle suits and crash helmets.

"I'm not having this," said Charlie. "Come on, let's have a parley." The drummers beat out a tattoo, and the command party and I moved out into the centre of the field. A minute later the roundhead drums sounded and Alan and his guards moved into the field's centre.

"Just listen to that," said Charlie. "They are playing a ruddy steel band."

The generals stood and glared at each other.

"Now what is it?" demanded Alan. "Are you surrendering already?"

"That'll be the day," said Charlie, "but I'm not happy about those skinheads."

We all turned and looked at them.

"So what's wrong with them," asked Alan.

"They're not authentic," said Charlie.

"What do you mean?" asked Alan.

"Well, how about the saucepans, football shirts, dustbin lids and the fact that they are all smoking," said Charlie.

"Authentic eh," said Alan, "well, what's the time?"

"The time," echoed Charlie.

"Yes, the time. I see that you are wearing your wristwatch; and how about your flag, the one that says, 'Watneys Red Barrel'?" said Alan.

"That does it," said Charlie, "get ready to fight."

"Now hold on a minute chaps," I said, "this is just a friendly village fete," but I was talking to myself as the generals went stumping their way back to their armies.

I hurried after Charlie and began to tell him to cool down, but he ignored me and said "Now," to Colin Harris.

Colin began to wave his flag back and forth and the crowd burst into applause, well at least the royalist section of the crowd did, as twenty horses carrying smart royalist soldiers dressed in white uniforms trotted onto the field and formed up in front of the Royalist Army.

"Ha ha ha," said Charlie, "now watch those roundheads start to run back to their estate." Captain Robinson, the master of the hunt, was very good. He pulled his sword from its scabbard and raised it aloft. Instantly nineteen more swords snicked out and were pointed at the enemy. "Forward," shouted Captain Robinson, and the line of royalist cavalry moved towards the waiting roundheads.

Suddenly the roundhead steel band burst into life, and the roundheads centre block began to move backwards, a step at a time.

Charlie was beside himself with glee.

"Look they are leaving," he shouted, but his laughter suddenly petered out as the enemy line moved back behind a line of huge black cannon, at least ten of them, with large gaping mouths pointing straight at the royalist cavalry.

"Oh my god," said Melvyn, "I thought they were working on something in the colliery workshop."

Captain Robinson had also seen the cannon. "CHARGE," we heard him shout, and his sword came down.

KABOOOOOOOM....... Went the cannon as they fired off in unison, and the playing field disappeared under a pall of dense black smoke.

We stood and waited until the smoke began to disperse, and as the last of it cleared we saw the last couple of riderless horses leaving the field, while twenty or so blackened scarecrows crawled towards the sidelines.

We then became aware of a loud chanting coming from the direction of the skinheads block as they began to move forward.

"What are they shouting?" asked Charlie, nervously feeling his neck.

"It sounds like,   'Red is the colour
                     Fighting is the game
                     We are all together
                     Roundheads is our name,' said Colin Harris.

265

"Right. Give them some back," said Charlie, and Colin dipped his flag.

'We are rough
We are tough
Alan Cranwell is a puff,' roared the royalist pike block.

"Come on gentlemen, cool it down," I protested, but nobody was listening to me.

"Stand fast men," said Charlie, "and women," he said, looking over at the Women's Institute who were preparing to receive the skinheads charge.

With a clattering of dustbin lids, the skinheads crashed into the village matrons, and a series of high pitched squeals filled the air as the ladies ineffectively swung their handbags.

We heard an angry shouting, and looked in amazement as about fifty husbands and elder sons left the crowd and rushed to the defence of their women, and a great melee developed, interspersed with red football shirts and lavender petticoats.

"Let's go," said Charlie, and the pub regulars launched themselves towards the Miners Welfare Pike block which had also began to advance. I looked over towards the scouts and comprehensive school blocks and saw that the sky was full of stones and bricks, with catapults engaging furiously on both sides.

With a thunderous crash the two main pike blocks smashed into each other, and the air was full of shouts and screams. Higher pitched yells from the left told me that the scouts and school detachments had got stuck into each other, assisted by parents, brothers and sisters.

I clawed my way out of the melee going on around Charlie Stewart and made my way to the edge of the field. This was terrible; over a thousand people were knocking seven shades out of each other and bodies were piling up everywhere.

I looked for the St Johns Ambulance detachment and spotted them fighting with the local drama group.

I had to do something. I was the umpire, and it was up to me to stop this. I pushed my way back into the middle of the main scrum, ducking the swinging fists and waving clothes props, until at last I was back beside Alan Cranwell. I tapped his shoulder and he spun around and planted his fist right in my eye. I saw red and punched him hard on the nose, and I was then clouted by the royalist flagpole. Back and forward the battle raged, but it was obvious that the royalists were now losing and had been pushed back to the edge of the playing field.

"Reform across the main road," roared Charlie, and the bloodied and weary army fell back and formed a ten-deep line across the main road. Moments later the seemingly unstoppable roundhead pike block crunched into them, and the fighting moved towards the centre of the village.

Parked cars were overturned, and the main street was a sea of broken glass as we retreated onto the village green and prepared for a last stand by the War Memorial.

There was a sudden pause as a waft of smoke blew over the village, and we looked back to see flames and smoke rising from the direction of the miners welfare. At the same time flames began to sprout from the church hall and the Kings Head public house. It looked as if the younger contingents had been busy.

As we stood there weary and confused, we heard the rising crescendo of police sirens heading for the village. The crowd began to break up and disappear, and only Charlie Stewart, Alan Cranwell and I were left standing in the main street as the first police car pulled up.

THIS WAS TERRIBLE, 1000 VILLAGERS WERE GOING AT IT HAMMER AND TONGS!....

And that, gentlemen, describes the battle of Soddingbury," finished the vicar.

"Well, I bet you won't be doing that again," said the oldest member.

"No of course not," said Grenville, "next year they want to re-fight the great Viking raid that took place in the year 995ad, and I have the part of Olaf the Saxonslayer !!!....

TWENTY TWO
The Ballad of Hamish Mactavish

Hamish Mactavish, the big Scot sat and savoured his whisky. He cleared his throat and the club fell silent.

"Tomorrow is the anniversary of the day I met my dear wife, let me tell you about it."

"It's not one of your ghastly poems is it?" queried the oldest member, "the last time you came out with one, it emptied the club."

Hamish smiled and carried on regardless.

Now I'm a Scot and proud as hell, and a tale to you I'll tell
Of how I met the girl of my dreams, and got rich as well
Like all young men from our highland isle, a wife I had to find
And there are no girls who weren't my kin, on the isle of Locherahind.

I went off to see our Highland chief, the rules to me he said
Any race or colour was fine, just as long as her hair wasn't red.
For well we remember the evil witch, who was called Red Susanne
Her name on the Isle is still abhorred, three hundred years on, ye ken

A Scottish name would be very nice, or Irish would do as well
Singh or Chandra were O K too, just as long as it wasn't Campbell.
Now we are not ones to hold a grudge, for a very long time,
But it's only two hundred and fifty years, since their terrible crime.

And the last of all, but most important rule, that I must understand.
Was that any girl who joined our clan, must not come from England.
It would not do at all he said, to bring the auld enemy in
And to taint our stock with English blood would be a mortal sin.

So putting on my best kilt, and the nice thick tartan plaid
I took passage to the mainland, and five shillings fare I paid
That's a lot of money I thought, for a measly ten mile ride
Not to mention the cost of the meal I threw up, over the side.

Three o'clock in the afternoon, we tied up in the mainland port
I picked up my bag and staggered ashore, to find a girl I thought
The traffic was horrendous, there were a dozen cars it seems
But they weren't going to stop me, from finding the girl of my dreams.

I walked along the busy main street, staring wide eyed at all the cars.
There was even a Double Decker bus, it was almost like being on Mars
The buildings were so enormous, however were they built
And all the while as I walked around, the wind blew up my kilt.

I could see that it was getting dark, it was time to find a bed
What could I get for one and six, was the thought that filled my head.
Finally I went into the Albermarle, the only hotel in sight
And nearly had a fit when I saw that they wanted ten bob a night

But needs must is a powerful thing, when you are in a strange town
And managing to suppress a groan, I laid my money down
I took a look at the woman, who showed me to my door
And decided not to chance my luck, she looked about sixty four.

Will you be taking dinner sir, the ancient harpy said
Of course I will, I've paid for it, so just take it as read.
I see you are a MacTavish, from the isle of Locherahind
If you've come here to find a bride, you'd better change your mind.

And why is that, are there no girls? I said clutching at my head
Oh yes there's girls, but they're not daft, they'd rather wind up dead
Then go and live on that grim isle, working fingers to the bones
When they can stay here all their lives, in the comfort of their homes

I went in my room and sat and thought, what on earth was I to do
I'd set my heart on getting wed, and to a nice girl too
If no one here wanted a man, the best they have ever seen
I would just get myself onto the bus, and go to Aberdeen.

Dinner was a gloomy affair, with not a single haggis in sight
And if I was going to the city next day, I needed an early night
I was up at dawn the following morn, having my breakfast
I had to get to the big city fast, if these oats weren't to be my last.

270

The bus left town at ten am, and yet another ten and six I paid
I had never dreamt that it would cost so much, just to go get laid
The ride it was interesting, there were houses were everywhere
But where were all the nice young girls, of them it was quite bare.

At two o'clock the bus pulled in, to Aberdeen's civic square
We all got out and it pulled away, leaving me standing there.
I carried my bag around the town, and a blush lit up my face
Because I was the only one wearing a kilt, in the whole darn place

I could see everybody was looking, at my hairy knees and head
It's a wild man from the outer isles, they might as well have said.
Time to find a cheap hotel, so I would have a base
To find the girl of all my dreams, complete with an angel face.

The Gaelic Arms was where I chose, to set up my first base
And the poond a night I had to pay took the smile right off my face
I began to yearn for my island home, and the cheap and simple life
I never thought that it would cost this much, to find myself a wife.

I took my bag into my room, and sat and count the cost
Two poond five and six so far, was how much I'd lost
And I'd not even seen a girl, fit to be my wife
Maybe being married wasn't the best thing in this life

I tipped my sporran on the bed, and counted all my change
It seemed a shame that this hotel was the cheapest I could arrange.
Three poond twelve and nine pence, was all that was on the bed
I'd better quickly find that girl, before my cash was dead

I made my way down to the bar, I needed a strong drink.
And as I sat and sipped my scotch, I had a good long think
There had to be a girl somewhere, that needed a good man
And marriage and a family, should be her long term plan

For I was the island champion of fighting with my fists
My muscles hard as iron from running through the mists
I'd never met a man nowhere, that I couldn't beat
And if there is one anywhere, well him I'd like to meet

271

Time to go and find a bride, somewhere in this city
I didn't mind if she was short or tall, as long as she was pretty
So around the town I searched away, avoiding all red hair
Until at last I came upon, a travelling Showman's fair.

I looked amongst the sideshows, and the big electric ride
But what I was really looking for was a girl to be my bride
But then the fairground boxing show came into my line of sight
Which offered twenty five poond, to whoever could win a fight

And twenty five poond is a gladsome sight, to a man with hardly a bean
It shouldn't be hard to beat the champ who was probably an old has been
I paid my one poond to the man, who put me on the lists
To stand and fight with Iron Mike, an expert with his fists.

I stood there in the icy tent, awaiting my turn to fight
And I quickly lost count of all the men, who fell to Iron Mike.
For Iron Mike was a fearsome man, with dynamite in his glove
But I was willing to take him on, for the money to search for love.

And all to soon my turn had come, to enter the square ring
To touch my gloves to Iron Mikes, who wouldn't feel a thing.
The bell it rang to start the fight, the crowd let out a roar
A left and a right started the fight, and I quickly hit the floor

I got straight back up on to my feet, quicker than a flash
This couldn't be right, I would have to fight, if I wanted to earn my cash
We both stood there in the centre of ring and traded blow for blow
And Iron Mike, sneered out of his beard, and stamped down on my toe

To the worst of my fears he bit both my ears, and hit me low and high
And as I tried to hold down my kilt, he gouged me in the eye
I turned away and held my face, and brushed away my hair
It almost felt like the end of the world, as he hit me with a chair.

Lucky for me, I have a thick skull, and he was making me mad
I gave him a kick that made him feel sick, for I could be just as bad
As he bent over holding his groin, I got ready to give him some hell
When his seconds jumped in and dragged me away, so he was saved by
the bell

The next round began, with a frenzied attack, as he tried to finish the
fight
But now I was enjoying myself, and I could have done this all night
I punched his head all round the ring, he really hadn't got a hope
And before they could ring the bell again, I knocked him over the rope

Iron Mike measured his six foot six, on the boxing booth floor
While I looked over the edge of the ring, and invited him up for some
more
But that was the end of the fight for tonight, and I got my winnings
When I asked if I could fight next night, they said you've had your in-
nings.

I took my fortune away with me, and walked back to the Gaelic Arms
Now that I had some me money, as well as my other charms
I would very quickly find a girl to love and to marry as well
Just as long as she wasn't red haired, English, nor a Campbell.

I went into the hotel bar, and looked at the girl sitting there
She was pretty and slim but not to thin, though a smart hat covered her
hair
I ordered a scotch and sat down to watch, and my smile at her was
returned
I swallowed my drink before I could blink, and in my stomach it
churned

I turned bright red as I stammered and said, please can I buy you a drink
She smiled and said no, I'm alright with this, my heart began to sink
You are kind to ask I can see you are shy, I am a stranger here too
It's seven o'clock, I'm about to have dinner would you like to come
through

I was up like a shot, escorting her in, to a dining booth set for up for two
We sat down, introductions were made, and I found out her name was
Sue
And what was this pain I felt in my chest, whenever I looked in her eyes
Which were green and wide and beautiful and ever such a size

She took off her hat and revealed a head, of wonderful long red curls
Well two out of three wasn't so bad, when it came to choosing girls.
We talked and talked for several hours, until it was time to close
And it was about this time, I discovered that, she was an English rose

That really should have put me off, but I was well past caring
For if I could get her to marry me, the island wasn't sharing.
I escorted Sue up to her door, my heart was filled with bliss
And I almost floated to my room, the result of a goodnight kiss.

Early next morning I hurried downstairs, I had never felt so well
I asked at the desk, have you seen Sue, they said do you mean Miss
Campbell
She checked out half an hour ago, she couldn't even manage her bill
Perhaps she thought we would need all these penny's, cluttering up our
till

In fact she was so hard up, her reckoning was threepence short
She'll not be stopping here again, we can do without her sort
I thought my heart would break in two, could she have got too far
I would find her wherever she was, I threw threepence on to the bar.

I rushed outside where would she hide, my angel with red hair
If she was hard up, I had twenty five poonds that I had won at the fair
I ran down the street with wings on my feet, my heart was in my mouth
For if I'd heard right as we talked last night, she would be heading south

In to the bus station I ran, and there I saw my sweet lovely rose
Sat on a seat with her bag by her feet, staring down at her toes
I joined her there on the hard seat, and grabbed and held her hand
I'm not letting you go until I know, just what it is you've planned

Oh Hamish, I am so sorry she sobbed, as tears ran down her cheek
But I have lost my job you see, and my future now looks so bleak
I came up north to do this job, and all the money home I sent
And the firm went bust and turned me out, without a single cent

I haven't even got the fare, to take the bus back home
And I really don't know what I'm to do, just sat here all alone
Is that all the trouble is, I pushed twenty-five poond into her hand
But if I have my way I hope you'll stay, and let me be your man

Those big green eyes swallowed me up, a little sigh she gave
You are the nicest man in the world, so generous and brave
But I can't take money from a strange man, it's not done you see
So if you want me too, take money off you, you will have to marry me

I plighted my troth right there on the spot, and swore to love her true
We sat and held hands and made our plans, which included a baby or two
And as we sat there with both our knees bare, a new thought entered my head
Sue Campbell was English and wouldn't be welcome, she was even a redhead.

We couldn't go back to my island home, my croft was lost as a life
How on earth once I married my girl, would I support my young wife
We sat there on the wooden bench as I tried to think it through
When a dapper little gentleman said. At last I have found you.

Please let me introduce myself, my name is Alfie Hyde,
And it is to find a man like you, I've scoured the countryside
I stood and watched you fight last night, I never have seen better
I'm a wrestling impresario you see, and I need a Tartan Terror

If you will come and fight for me, ten pounds a night I'll pay
One day, you may become the champ, come on what do you say
And so we hit the wrestling trail, and I never lost a fight
Truly a Tartan Terror, my fists packed with Dynamite

I fought my way from town to town, and beat them one and all
And even got to fight top of the bill, at the Albert Hall
We sailed over to America, across the ocean wide
And every time I had a fight, my bride was by my side

And my lovely wife supported me, until World Champion I became
A man of wealth with businesses, registered in both our name
And my Sue is very popular now, home on our Scottish Isle
Because I bought her the whole darn place, she's owned it for a while.

The moral of this story is, Search and you shall find
There is a girl for every man as long as he is kind
And if you really want a girl who is beyond compare
Go and find an English girl, with beautiful red hair.

"Well I agree with the English girl bit, not sure about the red hair though,"
said the oldest member.
        "But at least it wasn't a poem......."

TWENTY THREE
The Last Man Standing

It was many years since Frank Cass had told the members a story, and the oldest member had decided that now it was his turn. Frank 'ummed' and 'ahhed' a bit and then said,

"Perhaps you would like to hear about an episode from the last war." The members enjoyed war stories, so there was no dissent from any of the members, not even the oldest one.

"It was late 1944," began Frank, "and as most of you will know, I was a pilot with the Fleet Air Arm. On this particular occasion I was flying a long range reconnaissance mission in the south west Pacific. I had taken off from my carrier, and had flown north-west before taking a dogleg to the north. The first problem I had was that the radio chose to pack in, and I wasn't really sure where the carrier group was, except that it was around one hundred and twenty miles south east, and I would only just have enough fuel to get back - that's if I could find them at all.

Then it happened. From out of nowhere, it seemed, a Jap plane appeared on my right hand side. I rolled the Seafire over and closed in on him. There then followed a classic dogfight, first me gaining the advantage and then him. He was flying some sort of modified Zero, and while I had the speed, he could turn tighter.

The fight lasted for about ten minutes, until I shot a long burst of machine gun fire into his engine, and black smoke began to pour from his plane. And do you know what he did? The beggar spun his plane and rammed me, his propeller chewing a great chunk off my tail fin. I was a goner. My plane began to go down, and it was too low to allow me to use my parachute.

Then, about a mile ahead I saw a small island, and I estimated that I would just have enough height to make it there. I cut the engine and released the canopy, and the plane glided down towards the beach. I braced myself, and the battered plane bounced and skidded a quarter of a mile along the sand before coming to a stop just short of the tree line.

Gratefully I climbed from the wrecked remnants of my plane and staggered to the trees. This island hadn't appeared on my flight map and it had looked quite small as I had glided in, so it was possibly uninhabited, also I didn't think that the Japs had reached this far east. So I just had to make myself comfortable and see about rescue.

It seemed that the plane wasn't going to catch fire, so at least I had a starting point to work from.

I spent the next couple of hours recovering anything from the wreckage that could be of any use. It was around 4.30pm by the time I had stripped the plane of everything recoverable, I considered dismounting one of the machine guns and setting it up on a mounting, but I had used just about all of my ammo in the dogfight, so I didn't bother.

I used my parachute silk and lines to make a tent, and got a small fire started with my Zippo. I checked my supplies: ten cigarettes, half a bar of chocolate, and a bottle of water.

Not much to win the war with, I thought. Luckily it was autumn and some of the trees bore fruit, so I dined on coconut and banana, and then had a cigarette. As I went to sleep I felt very confident about the future.

The next morning I was up at dawn, making plans. The first thing was to claim this island for Britain. I cut a square of silk from the parachute, and using soot from the engine and blue and red berries, I made a smart union flag affixed to a bamboo pole. Then, taking it to the highest point of the island, a hill around half a mile inland, I planted my flag and formally annexed the island.

"I name this island 'Frankland'," I said.

I needed a bath and decided to go for a dip in my lagoon. I spent half an hour swimming and scrubbing with sand, and then went back to the beach to get my clothes, but they were gone. I searched the tree line but they just weren't there, and I knew that I had left them folded on top of the flat rock.

I frowned. There was no wind to speak of, so where were they? Had an animal, perhaps a monkey, moved them, or was the island inhabited after all? I moved back along the beach, looking all the time, but there was not a shred of clothing anywhere to be seen.

I arrived back at my camp, naked and angry, and set about making myself a pair of pants out of parachute silk; after all I was British, and one has to maintain standards. I went to my banana plant and it was also bare, not a single banana left. I dined on chocolate and coconut, quite tasty actually. Time to explore further now, I thought, and tying my pocket knife onto the end of a bamboo pole, I made a spear. Perhaps there were wild pigs on the island.

I made my way back into the island's interior, climbed back up the hill to my flag pole, and then froze in horror. My flag had gone, and in its place flew the rising sun flag of Japan. I ducked down and took a long look around. Nothing untoward appeared, so eventually I made my way to the flag, and hauled it down. It was obviously home made, and on looking closer it was actually made from my flag. Some cheeky blighter had washed it out and had repainted it with the rising sun.

I carefully made my way forward using all the available cover. The island was no more than a mile wide by two miles long, so it didn't take me long to reach the other side, and there on the beach was a crashed Japanese plane. So that was it. The nip had also landed on the island.

I crept further forwards and looked at the neat campsite that had been made on the edge of the beach, and what was that on the small table made from an aircraft wheel? A great stack of bananas, that's what.

"That's it, this is war," I muttered, and then remembered we actually were at war. I looked around for the Jap, and there he was, in the water, holding a wooden spear and using it to spear fish. I crept further forward until I was at the edge of his camp.

"Aha," I said to myself as I spotted his uniform neatly folded and laying on top of some empty ammo boxes. I ran into the camp and snatched it up and then sprinted back to my own campsite.

He was obviously a small guy, as none of his clothes came any where near me. I managed to get into his shirt as long as it was unbuttoned, and cut the legs off his trousers so they sufficed as shorts. The seat of the pants split though. And his little baseball cap with the star on the front fitted me quite well.

Now I was clothed and ready to take the war to the enemy.

First I had to see to my defences. I didn't want him attacking my camp. Perhaps I should dismount a machine gun after all. My planning was cut short as smoke drifted over my campsite and I stood up to look at my blazing wrecked aircraft.

Four hundred yards up the beach I could see the rapidly disappearing Jap. I jumped up and sprinted back across the island to his camp site. I lit my Zippo and threw it into his cockpit; seconds later his wrecked plane was also a mass of flames. I then rushed into his camp and began wrecking everything in sight.

I heard a shouting, and saw him come running into the camp. I pointed my spear at him and charged. He turned and ran, with me in hot pursuit. As he ran past his bed he ducked down and came up holding a samurai sword.

Now it was my turn to run, back across the island and to my own camp. He was right behind me, and he ran round my camp slashing at everything in sight. My tent was shredded, as well as the bits and pieces I had recovered. Well, I wasn't having that vandalism going on in my camp, and as he hacked at my bed I jumped onto his back and we went down fighting.

He lost his sword and fought like a wildcat, but I was bigger and stronger and eventually finished up on top, throttling him. He began to turn blue and his eyes rolled up, so I eased the pressure on his windpipe and said,

"Have you had enough?" He nodded, and I released him. I stood up and grabbed the sword, and waited to see if he tried again, but he stood up and made a little bow.

"Now then old chap," I said, "we can't carry on like this, we just won't survive. Shall we call a truce?"

He narrowed his eyes and said, "Truce? You started it."

"No I didn't," I replied, "you started it. You bombed Pearl Harbour!"

We looked each other over. He was wearing an oversized Fleet Air Arm shirt, cut down trousers and a British side cap with the flaps hanging down. In other words, my clothes.

We looked like members of a defeated Afrika Korps at the gates of Moscow.

"OK. Shall we swap our clothes back?" I asked him. He didn't seem to understand so I started to undress. I passed him his shirt, and he said "Ah so," and also began to undress.

Five minutes later we were back in our own clothes, although he had cut a foot off each of my trouser legs, making me look silly, and he wasn't too pleased when he saw the split in the seat of his pants. But at least we were officers in our own air forces again.

"So shall we have a combined camp?" I asked.

"Ah yes, we camp," he said. His English was atrocious, but I had no Japanese at all, so it would have to do.

"This island is called Frankland," I told him, and he looked at me blankly.

We decided to use my campsite as it was on the lagoon.

"In there plenty fish," he told me and set off to fetch his things.

As darkness fell we sat in front of the fire and ate some fish and coconut.

"My name is Frank Cass," I informed him.

"Ah Hai, Wank Ass," he said.

"No no," I squawked "it's Frank!!!"

"Fwank," he said, "what Fwank?"

"Never mind," I said, "what's your name?"

"Ah name, me Sensei," he told me.

"Well I'm very pleased to meet you Sensei," I told him.

"Thank you Wank," he said. I bit down on my tongue.

We settled down for the night, after I had thrown the sword way out into the sea.

I was up at dawn the next morning, and saw that Sensei was already standing in the lagoon, spear fishing. I fetched some spring water and set it to boil over the fire, using the propeller boss from the remains of my aircraft as a kettle. I baked some nettle tips over the fire and dropped them into the boiling water. This, I had been told in jungle survival school, made very passable tea. A moment later, Sensei came up and dropped a couple of small fish into my tea which was just brewing nicely. I sighed, and went to sort out two plates which Sensei had made from some aluminium wing fabric. We had a passable breakfast - tea flavoured fish isn't too bad at all. I then lit up a cigarette, and when it was half smoked, I passed it to Sensei.

"Ah so, a thousand blessings Wank Ass," he said.

"NO! it's Fwank, no I mean Frank," I shouted.

"Ah so," he said with an inscrutable expression on his face.

We divided up the work and soon had a spick and span campsite. I went and rustled up some bananas while he climbed a palm tree and got down some coconuts, and by the time I got back he had made up a sign board. It had two flags; the ring sun over the union flag I noticed, and also the fact that it said 'Wankland'. I got a charred stick from the fire and wrote an 'F' in front of it. Sensei smiled and nodded.

I decided that the best way for us to get rescued was to keep a large fire going, and we worked together to build up reserves of wood and vegetation for fuel.

That night we sat side by side in front of the roaring fire. "You know what, Sensei," I said, "this reminds me of Guy Fawkes Night, bonfires and fireworks."

"Guy Fawkes?" he asked me, "what is this?"

"Oh he was a British traitor who tried to blow up the king," I said. "We burn his effigy every November the fifth. We build big bonfires and put a guy on top. The wife and I love bonfire night."

"Ah so," he said, "so your wife always likes to have a big guy on top."

"Erm yes, that's right," I said, taking her photograph from my wallet, and passing it to him. He took it and studied it.

"She looks fit," he said.

"Well she actually has acute angina," I told him.

"Yes, her breasts are quite nice as well," he told me.

I snatched the photograph back off him and replaced it in my wallet.

"And where do you build these bonfires?" he asked.

"Oh usually out on the back lawn, so the neighbours can see it," I told him.

"So you have a substantial erection on the back lawn once a year in full view of the neighbours," he said.

"Er yes, but it's the fireworks that we really like," I told him.

"What kind of fireworks?" he wanted to know.

"Well sparklers are very popular," I said.

"Ah yes, I know of sparklers," he said, "so you go around the garden holding it and waving it in the neighbour's faces."

I looked at him but he was perfectly serious.

"What other fireworks?" he said.

"Well bangers are popular," I said, "but you have to be careful with the animals. They get very frightened. One year I accidentally left the cat flaps open and my wife's ginger cat got frightened and ran off; we didn't see her for ages."

"Ah I see," he said, "you didn't check whether her flaps were open before a bout of prolonged banging, and as a result you didn't see your wife's ginger pussy for weeks afterwards."

"Ahem yes," I told him hurrying on, "of course size isn't everything. One year I spent ten bob on a big rocket and it was a dud."

"I see," he said, "you mean that it stood up for a few seconds with its end glowing, and then it just collapsed."

"Hmmmmm, well I never have any trouble lighting my bonfires," I told him, "a bundle of oily rags pushed into the middle usually does the trick."

"Yes I see, you push your wad into the mound as far as it will go, and use plenty oil," he said. "Don't you ever have any accidents?"

"Well one year we had a rocket which fell over and went down the passageway instead of into the sky," I told him. "It was shooting white sparks everywhere."

"You mean you let it go up your wife's back passage and it shot white stuff everywhere," he said.

"No, I don't mean that at all, Sensei," I said. "I'm turning in."

The next morning, Sensei made breakfast; fish and banana. He was singing his favourite song which seemed to go.

"Titty bum bum, a titty bum bum.

"Ah Sensei," I said, "I do miss being at home. My wife used to make toast for me every morning. I used to like a few slices before work."

"Ah yes, so she spreads them on the table for you every morning before work," he said.

"I suppose so," I said. "At least we didn't have to manage with an open fire. We had a good old fashioned solid fuel range. It was my job to stoke it up last thing every night."

"So your wife made sure you gave hers a good poking every night or you got no breakfast," he said.

"Erm, I'm just going to have a look around the island," I said, "and see if there are any materials to build a boat with."

Well this went on for months. He misunderstood everything that I said, or even worse, completely turned it around. One day he was teaching me how to spear fish.

"Can you not swim?" he asked me.

"Oh yes," I told him, "me and the wife often used to go swimming before the war."

"Yes," he said, "the deeper you go in the warmer it feels."

"Well, when we are swimming, I like to get a couple of lengths in on my back," I told him, "while she prefers doggy style."

"Ah yes, I understand," he said, "and it is very important that you finish together."

"I'm not sure that you do understand," I told him despairingly.

Another time, when we were eating bananas, "My wife likes a banana with her breakfast," I told him, "I peel the skin off and put it into a little cool box, until she is ready for it."

"So when you have peeled the skin back you pop it straight into her box," he said. I beat a hasty retreat.

If I mentioned fruit he spoke about my big purple plums, or my wife's big melons, and so it continued, and soon it was Christmas Eve.

As we sat in front of our fire, toasting bananas, I tried to explain Christmas to him. He listened with a puzzled frown.

"So what you are telling me," he said at last, "is that tonight, some fat old man with a white beard will be coming down your wife's chimney. Surely he would be better coming up her back passage."

"No, that wouldn't be traditional," I said. I was beginning to make allowances for his poor grasp of the English language.

"We always have a tree," I told him.

"Hai," he said, "I bet you have a big one."

"Yes," I replied, "we always get ours from a friend who has a farm. Sometimes it is so big it won't go through the front door."

"I see," he replied, "so your wife will have to take it up the back passage again."

I ignored him and carried on. "We decorate the tree with rolls of crepe paper. I cut it up and my wife drapes it around the tree."

"OK," he said, "so you just stand there slipping her a length."

"We always try to visit our families on Boxing Day," I told him. "Mine live in Lancashire, in Oldham, and hers live in North Wales at Bangor."

"Ah so," he said, "so first of all you get her to Oldham, then Bangor as fast as you can eh?"

"Goodnight Sensei," I said...

January came and we were in 1945, with no sign of any rescue. It was as if we were the last men in the world. Sometimes we talked about after the war.

"Hai, I would like to visit you in England, after Japan has won the war," he said. That made me laugh.

"You would be welcome Sensei," I told him. "The wife and I are both very keen members of the local drama society."

"Ah so, so you are an actor," he said.

"In a small way," I modestly told him. "Why, just before the war my Dick Whittington was played in front of the Mayor and Lady Mayoress, and it was really well received."

"So your Dick was well received in the Lady Mayoress's box then", he said.

"Well my wife is the real thespian," I told him. "I bet that when the war ends she will soon be back on the boards. She likes to get her teeth into a large part." He seemed to find that remark very funny.

"If I come to England I would love to see her 'Little Nell'," he said. "She could certainly count on me for a warm hand on her openings."

"Ok, that's quite enough about the theatre," I replied. "Perhaps we should start to build a boat or raft."

So after some argument about whether the boat was going to be called the 'Hirohito', or the 'King George VI', we made a start on the boat that would sail us back to civilisation.

It was a slow business, and it took us weeks to salvage materials from the two wrecked aircraft. We needed a break, and I decided to teach Sensei the game of cricket.

I explained the rules, and he looked at me blankly.

"It's really quite simple," I told him. "There are two teams. One of the teams is in, and the other one is out. So the team that is in goes out, and the team that is out goes out into the field. The batter goes to the crease, and usually takes middle stump, and the bowler bowls at him."

"So what are the rest of the team doing?" he wanted to know.

"Well they are trying to get him out, of course," I said.

"So how many in a team?" he asked.

"Eleven," I told him.

"That sounds very noble," he replied.

"What does that mean?" I asked him.

"One man against eleven, that is very brave," he said.

"No, there are two batters," I told him, floundering a bit, "and every member of the team gets to bat."

"Ah, until all eleven are out," he said.

"Well no, until ten are out," I informed him.

"Hai, I thought that it would turn out to be something like that," he said.

"Yes, well the bowler bowls down the wicket at the batsman, and sometimes his balls are a bit short, they are called bouncers," I explained.

He smiled and nodded.

"The weather has to be dry though," I said "or they put the covers on."

"So what are you, a bowler or a batter?" he asked.

"Well, I was quite a good fast bowler in my day," I told him, and nothing gave me greater pleasure than bowling a maiden over." He smiled.

"Hai, I bet your bouncers were the talk of the dressing room," he said.

"Hmmm, well I even bowled against some county players," I told him.

"Ha, how often did they tickle one of your balls under the covers?" he said.

"Not that often," I told him. "Are you ready for a game?"

"Hai, lets have a knock up," he said. "Get your equipment out."

I set up the three stumps and some bails that I had fashioned from bamboo, and gave him the bat carved out of a piece of wood.

"Keep your arm straight and give me a good long toss," he said.

I ran up and bowled the ball made out of a small coconut filled with rubber sap.

WHACK. He hit it way up the beach. I ran and fetched it, getting back as he completed six runs.

"You have good a length," he said, "you're just not getting it up though. Try holding it a bit tighter."

"I don't need you telling me how to bowl," I said, starting another run up.

WHACK. Again I chased the ball up the beach while he ran six more.

"That was a hard one," he shouted. "Have you noticed, the quicker the stroke the further it goes."

Ten balls later and he was on seventy-two not out. "I declare," he said. "I want to bowl."

"Very well," I told him, "watch and learn." I took my guard in front of the wicket, and he began a very long run up.

The ball came screaming in at full toss and bounced off my shoulder.

"YEEEEEEEOOOWWWWWW!!!!!" I shrieked as he ran forward and scooped up the ball.

I took guard again. He ran up and the ball hurtled down, smashing into my thigh.

"JEEZE!!!," I yelled, as he danced up and down.

Six balls later I had been hit in the shins, both of them, the elbow, the backside, the shoulder again, and the last ball had smashed into the half coconut shell that I had tucked into my trousers as a protective box.

"Ok Sensei," I croaked, "it's tea time. Let's break for tea."

We sat in front of the fire and brewed up some nettle leaves.

"What a wonderful game," he said. "This will play very well in Japan."

"Why so?" I asked him.

"The rules fit in with our code of Bushido," he said.

"Really, why is that then?" I asked.

"Oh yes, having to stand in front of your little castle the bally wicket, while the bowler tries to hit you with the missile, and defending yourself with the wooden sword," he said.

THIS GAME WOULD PLAY VERY WELL IN
JAPAN, SAID SENSAI....

During the evenings we spoke of many things. We had a common interest in train spotting, and he was intrigued to hear that all of our engines had names, such as famous people or places.

"Hai," he said, "I would have liked to come down your sidings and watched the Duke of Argyll coupling with the old Duchess of Windsor."

"Have you served in India?" he asked me once. "Well I did some training up on the Afghan border," I told him.

"Ah so, you have been up the Khyber Pass a few times then," he said.

"I suppose so," I answered.

"Did you ever get to Calcutta?" he wanted to know.

"Yes of course," I told him, "I spent a leave there."

"Hai, I bet you was straight into the black hole then," he said.

I admitted that I had seen it a few times.

"And have you read that Indian training manual for young British Officers?" he wanted to know.

"Which one?" I said.

"The Karma Sutra," he told me.

"I've never heard of that," I told him.

"You must try it," he said. "You will probably need your wife to help you with it. You have to be very hard to complete it."

"Thanks for the tip, Sensei," I said, "I will certainly look into it."

"Hai, you most certainly will," he replied.

As spring turned into summer, we completed our boat and began to stock it up. We had salvaged several containers from the wrecked Jap plane, and Sensei had the good idea of converting the inner tubes from his plane's wheels into drinking water holders that would float behind our boat. And best of all we recovered his compass and flight maps.

"Very good," he said. "If we sail South West we will reach Malaya or Indo China."

"Oh no," I told him, "that's Jap territory. We sail South East into the allied areas."

"Don't make me kill you, Wank," he said.

"No, it's you who will have to die," I replied, "for tomorrow morning at first light I sail South Eastwards."

We had a restless night, neither of us daring to sleep in case the other made off with the boat, or worse. As soon as it was light I grabbed my spear and made my way over to where he had been lying. He stood up, grasping the cricket bat. I winced, for I knew how handy he was with it.

"This is it then, Sensei," I told him. "We must fight each other for the boat. The last man standing takes it, OK?"

"Hai Wank," he said, "but isn't that a destroyer moored out by the lagoon entrance?"

I turned and looked, and yes, there it was, a sleek grey warship, which was lowering a boat over the side.

"What is it, British or Japanese?" I asked him.

"I don't know, it could be either," he said.

We stood on the beach and watched as the ship's boat was rowed towards us. Suddenly I realised that they were Americans. I jumped up and down, waving excitedly, but Sensei slumped and sat down on the sand.

"We are rescued, old friend," I said.

"No, Wank," he said, "I can not be a prisoner. I will have to kill myself."

"Kill yourself," I echoed, "what ever for?"

"It's the code of the Samurai," he told me.

The boat landed and a dozen American sailors jumped ashore. Their officer approached us and asked,

"What do have we here?"

I must say that we didn't look like naval officers or pilots. We both had beards and our uniforms were in rags.

I said, "I am Flying Officer Cass of the Royal Navy, Fleet Air Arm, and this Japanese officer, Sensei, is my prisoner."

"Your prisoner eh," said the American officer, "so why do you call him 'master'?"

"Master?" I said, "Is this true, Sensei?"

"Yes Frank," he said, in a very cultured English accent.

"And how come you can say 'Frank' all of a sudden?" I asked him.

"And what about your misunderstanding everything, and why aren't your eyes so slitted?" I said.

"Ah, the double entendres," he said with a smile.

"So it was all a wind-up then," I said.

"I'm afraid so, Frank," he answered. "I was just carrying on the war verbally, but now you are the last man standing, can I borrow your knife please?"

"Hold it right there," said the American. "The war is over. Japan surrendered ten days ago. We dropped some kind of big bomb and it's all over."

"I don't believe you," said the Jap, who I suppose was my friend even if I didn't know his true name.

"Here is a written order from your High Command, ordering you to surrender in the name of the Emperor," said our rescuer. "We are stopping at all the islands, trying to communicate with any out of touch garrisons, and there is a senior Japanese officer on our ship, just in case they don't believe us. You are going home to Japan."

"And you, sir," he said to me, "will be going home as well."

"Ah so," said Sensei, "well Wank when you see your wife, tell her that I will be coming over one day to see her 'Fanny by Gaslight'."

TWENTY FOUR
Jerry Has A Gun

The oldest member had been forced into a literal corner. All the members of the club had got together, and were insisting that it was his turn to tell a story.

"What about? Having to sit here every Friday night listening to you lot telling stories?" he complained.

"Not at all," said Phil Porter, "You won the MC during the First World War, didn't you? Tell us about that."

"Stuff and nonsense," said the old man.

"Well what was it for?" demanded several members.

"Having the cleanest boots in the battalion," said the oldest member.

"No it wasn't," said Jumbo. "You might have got your MBE for that, but not the Military Cross."

"Oh, alright then," moaned the oldest member, "but don't say that I didn't warn you!"

"It was 1916, and I was a young subaltern in the County Regiment, commanding a Platoon in the front line trenches in Flanders. It had been a bit quiet for the last few days, with only the morning and evening barrages from the Boche, plus the usual sniper fire, trench raids, fighting patrols and bombing raids; well, you know how it was.

I sat in the trench bottom listening to the men chatting.

"I heard a cuckoo this morning," said one of them, "I bet it's the first one of spring."

"No, I heard one the day before yesterday," said another, "but what about those noisy buggers over there," he said, gesturing towards the German trenches. They were letting off bloody fireworks all night; whiz bangs, crackers, rockets, you name it, I hardly got a wink of sleep.

"Yes, it's a bloody disgrace," said another. "Someone should really do something about it. I've a good mind to write to the Times."

"Yes," said Corporal Kennedy, "they are the neighbours from hell, right enough."

Sergeant Woolcut, my platoon sergeant, came up and saluted.

291

"It's a message from Company HQ sir," he said. "You are needed at a meeting at 1900 hours tonight."

I sighed. That meant a five-mile walk in each direction. It was already 5pm so I thought I had better make a start.

I went down into my dugout, which had been carved into the side of the trench. It was just a muddy hole in the ground, but it was home to me. Barnes, my batman, was in there cutting up some stale bread.

"We won't be needing that, Barnes," I told him. "We are off to HQ. There's some sort of flap on."

We set off, walking crouched down, back along the communication trenches to the second line, a mile or so to our rear. This was held by the Australians, a rough crowd.

"Hey Pom," one of them shouted, "Got any booze on yer?"

"Who the devil are you?" I demanded.

"Colonel Foster, the commanding officer," he said.

I handed over my hip flask and he took a swig of the contents.

"Off to Company HQ then are you?" he asked, helping himself to another swig.

"Yes sir," I replied. "There must be some sort of flap on to let me out of the front line for a couple of minutes."

"Flap? I'll say there's a flap, Jerry's got a gun," he told me.

"That's the whole problem," I answered. "Jerry has lots of guns."

"Yeah, but this one's a whopper," he informed me. "They say it has the longest range on the Western Front."

"Well that must be some gun, because apparently there's one on the French sector with a range of fifty miles," I said.

"Fifty miles? That's nothing. This one can reach your Battalion HQ," he informed me.

"Wow, that is a hell of a long way," I said.

"Well, good luck mate," he said, handing me back my empty flask.

Barnes and I set off again, taking the churned up road that led back to company HQ. The road was full of men carrying supplies up to the lines, and wounded men being helped or carried back to the Aid post. An hour later we arrived at the châteaux that served as the area headquarters.

We entered the main hall and it was like being transported back two years, to happier times. The place had an air of elegance and peace. Even the hammering that the front line was receiving from the Boche guns sounded like a gentle murmuring.

I was taking a look at the oil paintings on the walls when a sour voice said,

"It's about time you turned up Walter, the meeting is about to start."

It was Major Brown, the company commander.

I saluted and said, "Good evening sir, I haven't seen you for a long time."

"I should hope not," he retorted. "Some of us have a war to win, you know. We can't all be fooling around in the trenches."

"No of course not, sir," I replied. "I spent this morning just sat listening to a cuckoo. Very boring stuff."

"Exactly," he said, "now let's go in. The general will be wanting this to be over quickly; he is already late for his dinner."

We walked into a small office, and there sat the general - a short, round bellied balding caricature of an English WW I general.

All the members looked at the oldest member. "It wasn't you, was it?" asked Spencer. The oldest member ignored him and carried on with his story.

"Lieutenant Walter Edwards," Major Brown announced. "He commands at the point we were talking about."

The general didn't ask me to sit; there wasn't a chair anyway. "We have a problem, young Edwards," he told me.

"We, sir?" I asked in astonishment.

"Yes. Jerry has a gun," he told me.

"Yes, I had heard rumours to that effect," I said.

"Well, I expect you to do something about it," he said. "I've got the Commander in Chief visiting Battalion HQ at the weekend, and it wouldn't look good on you if Jerry lobs a few shells into the gardens while he's there, would it."

"What's it got to do with me, sir?" I asked him.

"You, sir? Well, Jerry's long-range gun is somewhere in front of your position. That's what it has to do with you, sir!" he roared.

"And what must I do about that, sir?" I asked, with a sinking feeling.

"It must be destroyed before the weekend," he said.

"Oh, is that all sir? How do you want me to handle it?"

"You could try the usual way," he said. "Just line your men up and have them walk slowly across no mans land into the rising sun, fight your way through the Boche lines, find the gun and destroy it."

"Yes, I suppose that we could try that again, sir," I said, "but it didn't work the last dozen or so times."

"Confound it, Brown," roared the general, "is he a bloody socialist or something? Just get him to destroy that damned gun, or else!"

He turned away, and I saluted and marched out of the room.

Major Brown followed me out. "You want to be careful with that mouth of yours, Edwards," he said. "It could get you into a lot of trouble."

"Oh dear! What will happen to me? Will I get sent to the front line on a suicide mission?" I asked.

"Have a look at this map," he said. I looked. It was a large-scale map of our sector.

"Our artillery experts have worked out that the gun must be somewhere in this area, to the south of the village of Beaucoop," he informed me.

I took a closer look. The village was about three miles behind the German second line, similar to this place.

"So why don't we just flatten everything in the whole area?" I asked.

"We are talking about an area of ten square miles," he said. "Don't you realise how much that would cost in ammunition?"

"Well you have flattened the rest of this country, why not that bit?" I said.

"Edwards, you are a bloody socialist," he said. "Get back to your unit. I want that gun silenced within four days. In fact, I am ordering it."

I collected Barnes from the kitchen, and we began the walk back to our unit. He handed me a large bully beef sandwich and I chewed on it gratefully. We reached the Australian position an hour or so later, and sat down for a breather before making a run for the front line trenches.

Colonel Foster came and sat down beside me.

"Hiya mate, how's it hanging?" he asked.

I sadly explained my orders to him. He whistled and handed me a bottle of beer, explaining that the rations had at last arrived..

"You're not seriously thinking of taking your boys over the top, are you?" he asked me.

"Well, it's either that or a firing squad for disobeying orders," I told him.

"Yeah, I know what yer mean mate," he said, "but how about trying something like this."

I listened to his idea and had to admit that it was a hundred times better than that of the general.

"Thank you so much, colonel," I said, "I'll try it. Will you make the arrangements with your artillery?"

"Yeah, of course I will, mate," he said. "Best of luck to yer."

We set off again for our trench, and I walked with a lighter heart.

By 10pm we were back in my dug out, and I called in the non-commissioned officers for a conference.

There was Sergeant Woolcut, my platoon sergeant, Corporals Brittain, Brown and Kennedy, and Lance Corporals Madden and Smith. Poor old Lance Corporal Stevens had been shot while I was away, and was waiting for evacuation to the field hospital.

I drew a sketch map of the area, showing the positions of the trenches, the village and the area where the gun should be.

Woolcut asked the obvious question. "How the hell are we going to get through a mile of German trenches?"

"OK, sergeant," I said, "this is the plan. Tomorrow night I take a dozen men out into no mans land. We know that the Jerries are sending out wiring parties every night to repair their wire. We find a nice break in the wire and set up an ambush. They always work in pairs, so when two of them come along and start working, we silently take them out, repair the wire, and then I and another man will follow the rest of the wiring party back into the German lines."

"Surely you will look a bit conspicuous when you get there," said Corporal Kennedy.

"Not at all, because we shall be wearing captured German uniforms over our own," I told him.

"If you get caught you will be shot as spies," said the sergeant.

"Do you mean shot like Lance Corporal Stevens, and half the rest of the platoon has been shot?" I asked him.

"OK sir, I suppose it's the same thing, isn't it," said the sergeant. "Can I come with you?"

"I'm sorry sergeant, but I need a fluent German speaker with me, so we can have him dressed as a senior officer. Then we can bluff our way through to their rear area. Who do we have who can speak German?"

"The very man," he said. "Private Goldstein. His parents were German, and he is fluent in the lousy language. In fact, he wants to be an interpreter back at HQ, questioning prisoners, but he has the wrong name."

"OK, fetch him in," I said. Corporal Kennedy disappeared, and reappeared two minutes later with Private Goldstein; a medium sized, wiry, dark haired man; he should pass in the dark, I decided.

After bringing Goldie, as the men called him, up to date, I continued.

"We have to bluff our way back through their lines, and then join the traffic which is sure to be heading for this village. As we approach the village we cut off to the south and search for the big gun's position. Once we have found it we have to set off some green smoke bombs two hundred yards south of that position, at 12 noon. The artillery will have a spotter up in a balloon, and when he sees the smoke he will call down heavy artillery fire on them, and 'voila' the gun will be destroyed."

"That sounds straightforward enough," said Woolcut. "And how are you going to get back?"

"That's where you come in, sergeant," I said. "On Wednesday night at midnight I want you to lead the men in a trench raid on the Jerry trench directly opposite here. If Goldstein and I have made it, we shall be there, join up with you, and make our way back here.

The men trooped out, and Barnes produced a cup of tea.

"Get some rest sir," he advised. I lay down and went over the plan again in my mind. It might just work.

The next day we spent some time on preparation. Corporal Kennedy's section was to provide the patrol, and got blacked up. They weren't to carry any equipment, just rifles, bayonets and clubs.

Goldstein and I went back to the Australian line, where Colonel Foster produced some captured German uniforms and equipment. Goldstein's was that of a colonel of the 42nd Infantry Regiment, and mine was a sergeant's. We carried them back to our own trenches - no point in getting shot before we even started.

As darkness fell, we put on the uniforms, and Goldstein entertained the men with some German comic opera stuff. He quite looked the part, with his little black waxed moustache with pointed ends.

On the dot of 10pm we slid over the top of the trench and crawled out into no mans land, freezing whenever a flare went up. We had long known that at night time the only thing that was visible to the enemy was movement. By 10.20pm we had taken up positions in shell holes around a likely looking break in the German wire.

We lay there for over two hours. Then at 12.30am we spotted movement. Two Germans crawled up to the break in the wire and began to repair it with some big things like pliers, wrapping the broken ends around each other and twisting them together.

Corporal Kennedy and big Private Jowett crawled forwards. There were two muffled thumps, and they crawled back dragging a pair of unconscious Jerries behind them.

We quickly dragged them down into a large shell crater, and I examined their uniforms. They appeared to be the 33rd Infantry Regiment, just our luck. Well, there was no turning back, we would just have to hoof it.

The patrol crawled away, back towards our lines, dragging the prisoners and leaving Goldstein and I behind, as if in exchange. We gave it fifteen minutes and then began crawling in the direction the Germans had arrived from, and ten minutes later we saw shadowy figures moving slowly and quietly back towards the German front line. We allowed a couple of them to pass us, then stood up and followed them in. The pair in front of us suddenly halted and whistled.

"Password?" came the demand from the trench ahead.

"Valkerie," said the figure ahead, and they were invited into the trench.

We gave it five minutes and then moved forwards. We reached the same spot and Goldstein whistled.

"Password?" demanded a guttural voice.

"Valkerie," said Goldstein, sounding even more German than the German had.

"Wilkommen," said the guard. We moved forward and entered the German trench.

"Keep moving," said the guard, gesturing to a communication trench leading back. We moved quickly into it, walking past several Germans standing around. At last we reached a clear sap, and removed our overcoats, revealing our uniforms. I kept my steel helmet but Goldstein ditched his, and taking a peaked cap from his coat he placed it jauntily on his head. I watched in disbelief as he screwed a monocle into his eye.

"Are you ready, sergeant?" he said with a smile, and led the way along the trench.

A minute later my heart sank as we rounded a corner and were confronted by a captain and two private soldiers.

"Halt right there," he said, shining a torch on us. "Who the hell are you, and what are you doing here?" He reached for his pistol.

Goldstein was like ice. "How dare you speak to a senior officer like that, you pig," he hissed. "I will have you shot."

The German shrank and took a closer look, "Hauptman, I apologise sincerely," he stammered, "but you are not of our regiment."

"And I'm very glad about that, if they are all like you," said Goldstein, playing a blinder.

"Sir, can I help you in any way?" said the captain.

"Yes you can," said the resourceful Goldstein. "I command the 42nd Infantry Regiment, and we are shortly going to relieve you in this part of the line. I have just come up to have a look at what we are going to move in to."

"Ah, now I understand sir," said the German, saluting.

"Well, now you and your men can guide me back to Beaucoop," said Goldstein.

The German clicked his heels, "Captain Franz Fastabend at your service, sir," he said.

Goldstein nodded and said, "Give me a cigarette." The Germans hurried to obey, and Goldstein puffed away with a casual nonchalance.

I must say that having the Germans guide us back through their lines was a master stroke, and for the first time I began to believe that there was a chance of success.

3am found us on the outskirts of the village. Goldstein turned to the German and said, "Far enough, get back to your post."

The German officer saluted and said, "I thank you, Hauptman," and he and his two men disappeared back towards the front.

We cut off the road and made our way through the fields towards the south of the village, and two hours later it began to get light.

"Needles and haystacks come to mind, Goldstein," I told him. "It appears that they are hiding from us, and as it's getting light I think that we will soon have to hide from them."

We sat down on the top of a low hill and I produced my cigarette case. "Here, have a smoke, Goldstein," I said,

He took one and said "Can I have one for Ron?"

"Ron who?" I asked.

"Later on," he told me.

As we sat puffing away there was an almighty 'BANG' about one hundred yards to our front. The ground shook and we put our hands to our ringing ears.

"What the hell was that, sir?" he asked as our senses came back.

"I've got a pretty shrewd idea," I told him, and began to crawl through the bushes towards the spot where the noise had come from.

My suspicions were right. We soon found ourselves looking over the entrance of a railway tunnel, and fifty yards down the track was probably the biggest railway gun in existence, and the German gunners were winching up a shell as big as a motor car to reload it with.

"So that's it," I whispered. "Our aircraft can't find it because they whip it back into the tunnel as soon as our planes take off."

We backed off and took cover in the woods, flinching every hour or so as the big gun fired, and at 11.30am we moved two hundred yards south and waited for twelve o'clock.

On the dot, according to my army wristwatch, we set off the half dozen green smoke bombs that I had been carrying in my pack, along with half a dozen hand grenades, and a great pillar of green smoke rose into the sky as Goldstein and I sprinted back through the woods. We were three quarters of a mile away as the first shells fell onto the enemy gun.

SO THERE WAS THE BIG GUN.

299

I will say one thing for the Aussies, they can certainly arrange a good artillery barrage. About two hundred heavy shells landed directly onto the German gun position.

One particularly loud explosion and a mushroom cloud told me that their ammunition had gone up. The blast knocked us over almost a mile away. At last I decided that we were far enough away, and we hid in some ruined farm buildings close to the road back towards the German front line. Around 8pm it began to rain, coming down in vast sheets and turning the countryside into mud, we were glad that we were under at least a bit of cover.

Suddenly we froze. Someone was coming into the building. Two German soldiers appeared, carrying large boxes. They saw Goldstein sitting there in his colonel's uniform and snapped to attention.

"We are very sorry, Hauptman," one of them said, "we are a ration party from the 33rd Infantry Regiment, and we are just trying to shelter from this rain."

"Well that is very good," said Goldstein producing a pistol, "so why don't you just take your wet uniforms off."

I moved around behind them and levelled my rifle, and they quickly began to undress.

"We just want the coats and helmets," said Goldstein. "You can have ours. Who wants to be a colonel?"

Ten minutes later, we were dressed as privates of the 33rd Regiment, and our prisoners were tightly bound and gagged. We took a look in the boxes. They were full of Belgian chocolate. We sat and ate a bar each, and finished off my water bottle. I looked out of the doorway - it was 10pm and the rain was easing.

"Let's go Goldstein," I said.

We picked up the ration boxes, and walked up onto the road, joining the line of men carrying rations and ammunition up to the front line.

By 11.30pm we were actually in the German front line trench, handing out bars of chocolate, and stuffing quite a few into our own pockets. By 11.45pm we had found a couple of rifles and were pretending to be standing guard right where we expected our trench raid to hit.

A German corporal and two privates approached us.

"What are you two doing here?" he demanded.

Goldstein was up to the occasion, "Punishment duty, Corporal. Captain Fastabend ordered us to stand sentry here all night," he said.

The German laughed, "Do you hear that? We have the night off," he told his men, and they quickly disappeared.

I looked at my watch. It was midnight, and I heard a quiet 'cuckooing' out to our front. It was the signal. We took the hand grenades from out of my pack and threw them both ways down the trench. Germans went down all the way along, and a moment later smoke grenades flew into the trench from our front.

As the trench filled with smoke we gave our signal, blowing furiously on our whistles. A head appeared over the edge of the trench.

"Is that you sir?" shouted Sergeant Woolcut.

We threw off our German helmets and coats, revealing our British uniforms, then climbed up the parapet ladder blowing our whistles, and rejoined our men.

"Let's go home," I said, as we faded back into no man's land.

The next morning, Goldstein and I headed back down the line to Company HQ to report our success, stopping off to shake hands and share a drink with the Australian colonel.

"Good on yer, mate," he said. "They will give you a gong for this."

We arrived at the châteaux and went inside.

"And what are you doing here, Edwards?" asked Major Brown.

"Reporting the results of my mission to the general," I told him.

He smirked and said, "Let's go in then."

"This is Private Goldstein from the platoon," I said. The major ignored him.

We entered the office. The general was sat drinking tea and reading the 'Times'.

"Well, speak up man. What do you want?" he asked. "Can't you see how busy I am?"

"The Jerries don't have a gun anymore, sir," I informed him.

"Is that all?" he roared. "I know that, the artillery got it yesterday dinner time. We heard it go up from here."

"But sir," I said.

"Brown!" he roared. "Get this blithering cowardly idiot out of my sight."

We marched out of the room, and as we left, the matron from the field hospital arrived and went in, closing the door behind her.

"You two wait out here," snapped Major Brown. "I'm going to find you a really nasty dangerous job," and he disappeared down the corridor.

"I'm sorry sir," said Private Goldstein, "but I've dropped my cap in the general's office, we came out so fast."

"That's OK Goldie," I said, "I'll see if I can get it for you." I went back to the general's door and tapped it lightly. I heard a voice saying "yes."

I pushed open the door and walked in, and was treated to the sight of the general's bare buttocks as he pumped away at the matron who was reclining on his desk.

He spun around and faced me.

I smiled and said, "I see we are both standing to attention, General."

"Now then, Walter," he said as he pulled his pants up, "this isn't what it looks like."

"Oh, she isn't the Commander in Chief's wife then sir, because that's exactly who she looks like," I replied, as the nurse, blushing furiously, jumped up and rushed past me.

"Now look here, Walter," the general said, "there must be something that I can do for you. Please let me."

"Well sir, Private Goldstein would like to be a sergeant interpreter at HQ," I said.

"Damned good idea," said the general.

"And Major Brown would really love to move his office to the front line trench," I told him.

"Absolutely!" said the general. "And what about you? What would you like? Just name it."

And that, gentlemen, concluded the oldest member, is how I got my Military Cross.

THE END

I doubt it.

Printed in the United Kingdom
by Lightning Source UK Ltd.
110950UKS00001B/256-276